PRAISE FOR *THE VIBRANT YEARS*

"Bursting with humor, banter, and cringeworthy first dates, Sonali Dev's *The Vibrant Years* is a joyful and fun read, but it's also very much a timely tale about a group of underestimated women demanding respect and embracing their most authentic selves."
—Mindy Kaling

"These Indian American women and their struggles will appeal to readers from every age and culture."
—*Washington Post*

"An intergenerational tale of self-discovery and the relationships that matter most . . . A cozy cup of chai for the soul."
—*Kirkus Reviews*

"Dev easily gets the reader to root for her well-rounded characters, and the intertwined story lines wrap up with a delightful ending. This effervescent tale is sure to please the author's fans and win her new ones."
—*Publishers Weekly*

"Three generations of Indian American women strive to find what makes them happy in this heartwarming rom-com about the compromises that held them back and how they finally reclaimed their freedom."
—*Booklist* (starred review)

"Dev weaves humor and romance through her tale of three generations of women."
—Audible

"A super-fun, bingeable story about three generations of vibrant women navigating relationships, friendships, mishaps, and ambitions."
—*Ms.* magazine

"I would give this book five stars for the concept alone, but it's Sonali Dev's trademark character depth and beautiful writing that really make *The Vibrant Years* shine. A gorgeous story of evolving female relationships and how love, hilarity, and the bonds between three generations of women help them thrive in even the fiercest winds of change."
—Christina Lauren, *New York Times* bestselling author of *The Soulmate Equation*

"Oh, what a glorious tangle of love, career, the past, and family is *The Vibrant Years*! Sonali Dev writes beautiful prose and complex, delightful characters in this story of rediscovery and girl power for three generations of the Desai women. A delicious treat."
—Kristan Higgins, *New York Times* bestselling author

"A vivid and touching story of the relationships between three women who love each other and their quest to find each other's soulmates. Funny, fast paced, and insightful, *The Vibrant Years* gracefully explores questions of meaning and hope and regret and most of all the love between women. A beautiful book!"
—Barbara O'Neal, bestselling author of *This Place of Wonder*

"I loved this story of three generations of women navigating life, love, and the patriarchy. Sonali Dev's writing is lush and evocative, her characters vibrant with rage, humor, and wisdom."
—Virginia Kantra, *New York Times* bestselling author of *Meg & Jo* and *Beth & Amy*

LIES and OTHER LOVE LANGUAGES

ALSO BY SONALI DEV

LIES and OTHER LOVE LANGUAGES

A Novel

Sonali Dev

LAKE UNION
PUBLISHING

Published by Lake Union Publishing, Seattle

www.apub.com

Amazon, the Amazon logo, and Lake Union Publishing are trademarks of Amazon.com, Inc., or its affiliates.

ISBN-13: 9781662513978 (hardcover)
ISBN-13: 9781662509513 (paperback)
ISBN-13: 9781662509506 (digital)

Cover design and illustration by Kimberly Glyder
Cover image: © Kodochigov / Getty

Printed in the United States of America
First edition

Friends who feel like family are my special gift. Smitha, Smita, Vibha, Divya, Teertha, and Kavi, you are the sisters around whom I need no filters, no plans, no reason. Thank you for always making me feel right and whole and enough. Without you there would be no story, only backstory.

VANDY GURU'S RULES FOR LIFE:

1. Identify what you want
2. Take action to get it
3. Embrace the consequences

CHAPTER ONE

VANDY

Saturday, 2:00 p.m. . . .

Ever since her daughter was born twenty-seven years ago, Vandy Guru's greatest fear had been losing her. As she read her brother's text, the full impact of that terror hit her in one fell swoop.

> Any idea why Mallika didn't show up for dance practice today? Pinky is livid.

Vandy had built a thriving career as an advice columnist on helping people transcend their fears. How many times had she explained how worry stifled the joy out of relationships and crushed your chance at happiness? And yet reading those words made Vandy forget every wise and equanimous word she'd ever fed to her millions of readers around the world.

Her heart raced as she dialed Mallika's number.

Scenarios of doom flooded her mind: A white van into which a serial killer had shoved her child. A lone hungry shark making its way into the crowded waters of one of LA's beaches, where Mallika loved to swim, and seeking her strong dancer's legs from among hundreds of others. A stray bullet, an undetected aneurysm, a scaffolding dropping on her as she walked along the pavement animatedly talking on her phone. Which she always, always answered when her mother called. Except she hadn't since yesterday.

Vandy left her daughter a voice mail in her calmest tone. "Trying to reach you. Call when you get this. Love you."

Mallika hadn't shown up at the airport last evening to pick up Vandy as promised either. The last time they talked was yesterday afternoon before Vandy boarded the flight to come home from the last stop on her speaking tour. Vandy had told herself that Mallika had probably just forgotten. She'd simply texted her to say she was taking a cab home and was looking forward to catching up soon.

Mallika had been far too busy recently. Since Vir's death, she'd thrown herself into her work with heartbreaking desperation. Vandy had done the same thing. The mix of distraction and exhaustion was a potent drug for numbing grief. Vandy got it. Even though her daughter had recently accused her of not understanding.

This couldn't possibly have anything to do with that argument she'd had with Mallika two days ago, could it? It had completely blindsided Vandy. Unlike Vandy and her own mother, Mallika and she rarely disagreed. They'd certainly never before said the kind of hurtful things they had that day. But when they talked after the argument, Mallika seemed to have moved on from it.

Before Vandy's mind could hurtle into examining every word they'd said, Sonja, her assistant, stuck her head into the greenroom.

"Ten minutes to stage time." Sonja's voice pulled Vandy out of the spiraling whirlpool of her thoughts.

She couldn't go onstage feeling this way.

The only way to stop the spiral was to stop resisting it. Dropping the fight is stopping the fight. One of Vandy's most popular memes. One that had been set to hundreds of sunset and sunrise pictures on social media. There were some seventeen hundred videos set to Vandy's voice explaining how to drop the fight.

She nodded to Sonja and turned back to her phone as her assistant left the room with a soft click of the door. Vandy's finger hovered over the screen.

Where are you, Mika?

She had to calm herself. Closing her eyes, she embraced the sensation of not knowing where Mallika was. Her heart rate spiked, but then it slowed, because walking through the fear was the key part. The resistance was what gave the imagination oxygen and made it impossible to focus on a solution. Only when you dropped the resistance could you focus on the truth, on the facts, and figure out what was going on.

Mallika was not answering her phone. Mallika and she had argued. Mallika had missed two commitments. Every one of those things was completely out of character for her daughter.

Vandy opened her eyes, let out a shaky breath, and scrolled through Mallika's text messages. A reluctant smile escaped her when she found the video Mallika had sent just a couple of days ago. Her two aunts, Vandy's twin brothers' wives, in a dance-off. Mallika and Vandy had exchanged some laugh-until-you-cry emoji.

One of the things Mallika was so busy with was those absurd weddings. Vandy could not wait for them to be over. But they were two months away, which in Mehta-Family Time was going to feel equivalent to twenty years. The incessant and petty competitions between Vandy's two sisters-in-law, Pinky and Tinku, were just something the rest of them navigated, like land mines in the family's landscape. But now that it was a matter of their sons' weddings, the gloves had come off in unprecedented ways. Every fashion designer and jeweler in the greater LA area had been engaged; the most impossible-to-book venues and wedding planners had been nabbed.

Why were her nephews not eloping?

Because they were neither that brave nor that stupid. No one went up against Pinky and Tinku.

Mallika certainly didn't mess with their dance practice schedules.

Mallika was the only person in the family who had at least some power over her aunts right now. For one, Pinky and Tinku believed there was a chance that Mallika was going to be famous someday, and that would add pounds of weight to each woman's social capital. For another, each was determined to host the Best Wedding Sangeet Party of All Time, and Mallika was a choreographer.

Vandy sat up. Today was the day Mika was supposed to hear back from Netflix. She'd sent in her audition tape for an international musical project (*the kind streaming platforms have never seen before, Mom!*), and today she was supposed to find out if she got a callback. Suddenly Mika's silence made sense. This could not be happening. Not again.

For years her daughter had switched from dream to dream, project to project with her usual breeziness. But after they lost Vir, something seemed to have shifted inside Mallika. She'd become obsessed with her dance. Vandy pressed a hand to her chest, where grief and worry tightened painfully.

The past months had seen nothing but rejections from the ruthless and inexplicable jungle that was Hollywood. Vandy had fully expected Mallika to give up by now. Instead she'd become more and more invested, and last month she'd sent in that tape.

Sonja stuck her head into the greenroom again, demeanor efficient as ever, eyes serious.

"They're ready for you, AA."

Vandy's staff called her AA. Short for Agony Auntie, the stupid name Vir had come up with when Vandy had decided to start her blog on a whim, twenty years ago. Neither her husband nor she could have imagined that Dear Agony Auntie, her holistic riff on a Dear Abby–style blog, would turn into this: a syndicated column in the *LA Times*, three bestselling books, and a social media following of four million. To say nothing of the seminars, which Vandy had to admit were her favorite part of her work.

Six thousand people waited for her in the Microsoft Theater. Each one of them filled with the hope that the next two hours were going to change their life. What would they think if they saw the mess inside Vandy right now?

Vandy patted her gray bob into place and adjusted the string of pearls that sat on her cream silk button-up. She threw another glance at her phone, then typed out a response to her brother. In a seminar. Let me know if you hear from Mika.

There was still nothing from Mallika. Not even a check mark to show that she'd seen Vandy's messages.

How would you understand me, Mom, when I'm nothing like you? You've never had to fight for anything. Papa would have understood.

How could Mallika have said that? For one moment, Vandy wished she could correct her. For one brutal moment, everything she'd gone through to have Mallika came rushing back. But dwelling on the past was not the solution. The solution was in the here and now.

Sonja cleared her throat. Concern tightened her lips into a flat line.

From the direction of the stage, a cheer rose up. The member of Vandy's staff who was hosting today was obviously doing a good job of introducing Vandy. It was time to be present for the people waiting for her.

She turned to follow Sonja out of the room, then stopped. There was one person who might know what was going on with Mallika. Usually Vandy would do anything to avoid talking to her mother before a seminar. The one thing she did not need before she went up onstage was her mother making her feel like she had to prove her competence. But she had to know if her daughter was okay.

"Mummy," Vandy said when her mother answered. "I'm about to start a seminar, but I wanted to check if you'd heard from Mika." For all her effort to keep the worry from her voice, the words sounded like *Mummy, I've misplaced my child.*

"Vandy? Oh, are you back in LA?" Naturally Usha Mehta would start the conversation exactly the way she wanted to, with letting Vandy know she hadn't called her after getting back.

"Do you know where Mallika is? She didn't show up for dance practice at Raj and Pinky's house this morning."

"Do you blame her?" her mother said with all the caustic humor of a mother-in-law who had spent three decades refereeing her competitive daughters-in-law.

"She hasn't been answering my calls. Have you spoken to her?"

"Not about why she didn't show up for practice, no." Which wasn't an answer. Great, Mummy was in one of her moods.

Vandy tried a different tack. "Do you know if Mallika heard back about her audition?"

"Since when did you start indulging in this parental-spy-network business? I thought Vandy Guru was above all that."

Her mother always talked about "Vandy Guru" and Vandy's work as though they were separate from Vandy. A part she was playing.

"I'm not spying. I'm . . ." *Worried.* "Just making sure Mallika is okay."

"How can she be okay when you don't want her to dance and she loves it?"

"What are you talking about? I've never stopped her from dancing."

Her mother laughed, and something hot and ugly moved inside Vandy. "Sure. But you hate that she loves it. You don't think she can feel that?"

Why was Mummy saying these things now? Why bring this up when it had nothing to do with anything?

"Did she say something to you?"

"If you hold on so tight, your arms go with them when they leave." Another nonanswer.

Vandy didn't have time for her mother's gory aphorisms right now. She rubbed her arms. The agony of holding Vir as the breath left his body rolled through her. It had been eleven months since her husband died, and here she was, still struggling to not feel limbless.

"Please just tell me if you know where Mallika is." She needed to get on that stage and focus.

Her mother's silence was the harshest, most endless thing. It probably lasted three seconds, but every significant and insignificant choice Vandy had ever made in her life was wrapped up in it.

"Maybe," Mummy said finally, letting all the rest of it get swallowed up in that word, "Mallika just needs some space to breathe."

Vandy couldn't remember when the temptation to pick up the gauntlets thrown by her mother had disappeared, but she wasn't going back there and touching that.

"Caring for people is different from stifling them, Mummy." Fine, she could touch it a little bit. "And it's not the same as trying to control them."

"Or maybe children always think of their parents' caring as control?" Her mother let the words hang on the line.

Vandy's original instinct to not pick up her mother's gauntlets was definitely the wiser choice. This was obviously a dead end.

Behind Vandy, Sonja cleared her throat.

"I have to go," Vandy said.

Mummy took another ruthless swipe. "Of course. Go be Vandy Guru and switch compartments."

No, Vandy wasn't touching this one either. Since Vir's death, it was her work that had helped her get out of bed every morning. She wasn't going to apologize for it.

She disconnected the phone. In one thing Mummy was right: it was time to be Vandy Guru. To take her own advice and find a solution without getting lost in the problem.

She turned to Sonja. "I can't find Mallika. Send someone to her apartment to check if she's there." Vandy scrawled instructions on the notepad imprinted with a watermark of her face and the words *The Solution Is Inside You* emblazoned in gold at the bottom. "This is the code for Mallika's apartment. These are the names of her closest friends. Call them and find out if they've heard from her."

Sonja stared at Vandy in the way one stared at a doctor who might be about to save one's life. A devotee.

Devotees. That's what Mallika and Vir had called Vandy's followers. They'd found it funny. Because to them Vandy was just Vandy. Not someone who had harnessed some sort of Universal Wisdom and held the power to help them do it too.

Vandy handed over the notepad. "If you make contact with Mallika, bring me a fresh bottle of water onstage and place it on the table. That will tell me she's fine."

Sonja nodded. "I'm on it. But if you need a moment, we can ask for a delay until we figure out where Mallika is."

Vandy swallowed. She'd never been late for a single event in ten years.

There was nothing she could do that she hadn't already asked Sonja to do. Mika was responsible, sometimes a little too responsible, something she'd inherited from Vandy. Maybe Mika did need some time to catch her breath if it was the rejection.

"There's no need to let so many people down," Vandy said, and Sonja held the door open for her. "But I'd really appreciate it if we knew where Mallika is before I'm done." With that she made her way through the wings to the stage.

When she marched to the podium, hands folded in a namaste, every fiber of her being was present in that moment. Except for the one glance she threw at the table where Sonja would bring her water to let her know Mika was okay.

CHAPTER TWO

MALLIKA

Seven days ago . . .

I'm really good at what I do.

That might sound conceited, but it's simply an affirmation. Which translates roughly to a crutch for those of us not blessed with natural confidence.

If such things ran in families, I'd be bursting with confidence. Instead, I'm standing in the living room of my uncle's McMansion, struggling to navigate my aunt's disapproval.

Taj Maama and Tinku Maami live in Palos Verdes Estates, which is the epitome of LA desi aspiration. My uncle and aunt specifically chose it instead of Beverly Hills because competing with other desis is vastly more satisfying than competing with people who have a hard enough time seeing you as equal, let alone as socially superior. To my aunts and their friends, translating the finer details of flashing their success across cultural boundaries is more trouble than it's worth.

My mother's other brother, Raj Maama, lives in the neighboring house. My grandmother considers bearing twin sons who are both physicians like their father her second-greatest achievement. Naani's crowning achievement, undoubtedly, is marrying one herself. Which is absurd when you consider the fact that her only daughter, my mother, is a bestselling advice columnist and author with a social media following of millions.

My mother is the most badass person I know. She's built an empire helping people. It's a really high bar. I've never seen her experience a moment of doubt. I, on the other hand, have a body composition that is 50 percent doubt. But I am her daughter and I do have a solution for dealing with it: I just don't dwell on it.

I channel that exact energy as I face my aunt. Tinku Maami is raising her overtweezed right brow at me. Which brings me back to my affirmation: *I am really good at what I do.* But I can't say this to her without sounding pathetic.

Instead I paste a smile on my face as I listen to her telling me, in her very intimidating voice, "You have to decide what you're made of, Mika."

She makes this declaration with enough gravitas that I wish I'd heard her say it before I shot my audition tape. Her voice is filled with just the off-to-storm-a-castle energy I'd needed then.

Thinking about the audition tape makes me break into a sweat, leaving stains on my silk kurti that won't come off without professional dry cleaning, which I cannot afford.

Behind my scowling aunt is a roomful of aunties and uncles all dressed in Indian clothes befitting a wedding, despite the fact that the wedding is two months away. They're here to practice the dances for the sangeet cocktail party, which will take place the evening before the wedding. I'm tasked with bringing that spectacle together.

I'm a choreographer. Mom is always advising people to divide their goals into short-term and long-term goals. My short-term goal is to survive my aunts trying to outdo each other. My long-term goal is to choreograph for the theater and the screen.

I've been helping family and friends with choreography since I was twelve. I've done anniversaries, birthdays, engagements, and even a few retirement parties for my grandparents' friends, but mostly it's weddings. Wedding dances might be an even more important part of Indian weddings than the vows. Our community really loves dance, and they're obsessed with broadcasting this love on social media, in the style of an over-the-top Bollywood film.

Almost all my clients are people I have known my entire life, so calling myself a choreographer feels disingenuous. But stepping out of that circle has been hard. With a celebrity mother and a father with twenty published novels, doing anything without the guarantee of succeeding has always felt impossible.

After college—a dual major in business and performing arts—I've worked for big tech and my uncles' medical practices and tried my hand at assisting my father's literary agent. I've also tried working on the various parts of Mom's business. If Mom had her way, that's where I'd stay, where she could protect me.

Until I lost Papa last year, I didn't mind the safety of working for her. But ever since he left us, I've felt buried under a mountain that I need to dig myself out of. I've just never grown the claws it takes.

For years, embracing dance as my profession felt like stepping off a cliff without knowing if I had the wings to fly. Now inching closer to the cliff's edge feels inevitable. I wish I'd made Papa proud when he was alive.

Pain I've been trying to breathe around for the eleven months he's been gone squeezes in my chest.

Truth is, I love choreography. Not just the part where I get to fit steps perfectly to music but the part where I actually make the way the dancers move tell a story. Every dancer is as unique as a musical note, a building block; each movement is a piece in a larger composition. What I do with each dancer and each move, which voice I give which note:

that isn't random; it's an artistic choice. And the sheer power of what that can create fills me every time the music turns on.

These fifteen aunties and uncles who are attacking the snacks and chai in the sprawling dining room are my instruments, and I'm excited to play them until the entire ballroom of drunk wedding guests goes wild.

Tinku Maami clears her throat aggressively. "These steps feel a little . . ." She pauses with the air of someone who wants you to think they're being sensitive. "Childish."

I swallow. Tinku Maami doesn't just have two left feet, she has two left feet that belong on infant goats. So "childish" is essentially something I've perfectly tailored for her.

"I'm going for grace. So we can showcase your talent for emoting, Maami," I say with all the sincerity of someone who's honed their ability to lie over years of teaching dances to nondancers.

Tinku presses a solitaire-laden, perfectly manicured hand to her ample silk-draped bosom and bats her eyelids at varying speeds, no doubt to display her talent for emoting—a declaration I can now see I'm going to regret making.

"But see, all this emoting-shimoting is for the big screen, no? Onstage, one needs more . . . how does one say . . . athleticism?" She throws a glance around the room and lowers her voice to a whisper. "I overheard Reva telling Tanya that the steps for Pinky's sangeet are somewhat more . . ." She pins me with that accusatory glare. "Energetic."

It's hard to resist the urge to go up to Tanya Auntie and Reva Auntie and shake them as they make their way through the tray of Tinku Maami's homemade onion pakoras.

The wedding season in desi LA is serious business. Anyone who hopes to ride in on a horse for their baraat had better be armed with two years of foresight. The moment someone meets the One, they're best off booking the wedding mare before setting up a second date.

It's proof of my aunts' substantial social clout that they're managing to pull off the weddings of their firstborn sons—my cousins Arney and Aarav—on the same weekend.

My aunts, Pinky (her birth name) and Tungabhadra (whom everyone calls Tinku because her birth name is basically a human rights violation), have never passed up an opportunity to make the other one look bad.

The only fortuitous thing about being stuck in the middle of their wedding-dance face-off is that they are both equally bad dancers, but in completely opposite ways. Where Tinku only moves two beats after the music has hit a chord, Pinky moves in anticipation of it.

"Mika beta, you're not listening to me. Did Pinky put you up to this? Has she recruited you to sabotage me?"

"What? How can you accuse me of such a thing?"

"I'm not accusing you. I'm accusing *that woman.*" She snarls those last two words. "I've seen the dances you gave to the Bhosales and the Kashyaps last year, and they were so very"—another "sensitive" pause—"beautiful!"

The surprise in her voice *hurts.*

"And ours are just . . . just . . ." Tinku Maami struggles to find words for her own dancing skills.

I mirror her sensitive tone when what I want is to laugh. Or maybe cry with frustration. The Bhosales and the Kashyaps—and every living creature on the planet, for that matter—can move to music better than my aunts.

"I don't think they meant athletic as a good thing," I say as kindly as I can.

Tinku's eyes widen thoughtfully, but I don't let the minor victory fool me. It's going to be a long two months.

I've tried to pick the slowest possible songs for Tinku, hoping she couldn't possibly just stand there waiting to move until after a beat happened. Turns out she can, and she does. And she makes faces while she waits. Most of which look like she's having an orgasm (I'm going to need therapy once these weddings are over). It's like there is a lag that only she hears. There's just a different music playing in Tinku Maami's head.

On the other hand, when I run dance practice in the house next door, it's like Olympic training. Three seconds before the music starts, Pinky takes off and spins through the entire routine before half the song is done. I had, naively, believed that the fastest songs would make it impossible for Pinky Maami to flail past the beat. Another miscalculation, because now the rest of the aunties and uncles in the group are considering dropping out for fear of injury. Most of them are doctors, so it's a medically informed choice. One that I have to find a way to prevent from being made.

"Mika!" My aunt snaps her fingers in my face with some exasperation. "If you learned to *focus* instead of going off into la-la land when I'm trying to help you improve your craft, maybe you'd be in a different situation."

A *different situation* sounds like a dream right now.

I'd give anything for it. I've been putting dances and dance tutorials out on social media, I've gotten myself an agent, and I recently sent out an audition tape for a project that makes goose bumps rise up my arms. M. Night Shyamalan is collaborating with Karan Johar to create a musical based on the *Mahabharata*. India's greatest epic is going to be brought to the screen by two entirely disparate but huge South Asian talents. An unprecedented amalgamation of Bollywood and Hollywood. A phrase I've always used to describe my dance.

This project is my spirit brought to life. My identity given form. If this isn't the universe giving me a sign, I don't know what is. As soon as that thought touches my mind, another one swallows it up. I'm being entirely unrealistic in thinking I'll get it. Karan Johar and Shyamalan would never pick a no-namer like me who has nothing to her credit but a few choruses in commercials.

As my aunt stares at me like I'm a lost cause, I try not to think about the fact that today is the day my fate will be sealed, the very last day of the four weeks the producers said it would take them to announce the callbacks.

"Has Pinky *offered* you something?" Tinku Maami interrupts my spiral of despair. Her eyes are bright with more-than-usual suspicion.

"I can't believe you'd say that!" I say with as much outrage as I can muster. Not easy, given that Pinky did, in fact, offer to introduce me to Kelly Clarkson's production assistant so I might be able to pitch a piece where I teach Kelly some Bollywood steps on her show.

In response, my aunt narrows her kohl-lined eyes at me. The fact that I don't immediately deny the accusation tells her everything she needs to know. It's a well-known fact in my family how "unworldly" I am. This, of course, includes the inability to lie with any kind of skill.

"Whatever she's promised you, I can do better. Everyone knows that!"

My family has always been endlessly baffled by my lack of street smarts. It's the most dominant of the Mehta genes, after their aquiline noses, which you could spot from five hundred feet away. Mom and her brothers and all four of my Mehta cousins have both in spades. I have neither. But while I lack street smarts, I inherited Papa's smaller nose. I also inherited his dreaded love of "art-shart," as my family calls it.

The only person who ever really got my love for dance was my father. And he's gone. Never again will he hold my hand and tell me that I'm going to find my passion. That all the searching I've been doing is fuel for when my jets explode, even though in this moment it feels like they never will. All his life he struggled to tell his stories but never wavered from his path. Then eleven months ago, a rare and rabidly fast form of cancer took him from us within six months of the first blow of diagnosis.

Mom acts like she understands me. She probably does. Mom understands everyone. Four million people on the internet will attest to this. But how can she understand how much I struggle with going after what I want, with not knowing how to get past all the fear and doubt?

Unlike Papa and me, Mom opens her palms and the universe places things she wants into them. Struggle and Vandy Guru have never had a chance to get properly acquainted. To be fair, struggle and I haven't had much of a relationship, either, thanks to my parents. Until Papa's death, I had struggle avoidance down to an art. I was completely comfortable not reaching for anything the universe didn't want to give me. It's already given me too much.

I am aware that my mother is right in believing that a project of this magnitude is probably too much of a reach. When she found out I was going to audition, the company that manages her events magically created a position for me. A year ago, I would have taken the job.

This time I couldn't. That doesn't change the fact that sending in that tape was the scariest thing I've ever done.

Being a South Asian choreographer in LA, in America, is like trying to bang a hole in a brick wall with my head so people might see me through it.

As I stare open mouthed at my aunt, an image of Papa winking at me across the room as we navigated Mehta-land slashes ruthlessly through my heart, his thick brows rising up into his mop of salt-and-pepper hair, his kind eyes crinkling at the edges.

"Do you truly believe I'd give anything but my best to either you or Pinky Maami?" I ask, and my stupid voice cracks.

Tinku looks horrified. For all the heightened emotions that constantly explode out of my aunts, the slightest show of real feelings totally throws them.

Tinku places an awkward hand on my shoulder. "Maybe it's too soon after Vir. Maybe I was insensitive in thinking you could handle this."

She genuinely believes that choreographing wedding dances for my family is a task too big for me. And here I am thinking I have a shot at an international project.

A laugh escapes me.

Untimely laughter as a way to deal with the Mehta side of the family is another thing I inherited from Papa. Mom always knows exactly how to deal with her family.

I shouldn't have laughed, because it makes the discomfort on Tinku Maami's face multiply. She lets out another super-awkward throat-clearing. "I'm sorry . . . I should not have been so cruel. You know what? You don't have to go through this. I will find someone else. You relax and enjoy the wedding."

Wait? What? Is my aunt firing me? From a job I'm not even being paid for?

She hurries off, sequined purple silk swishing around her.

Before I can follow, my phone buzzes, and a text from my agent lights up the screen. Call me . . .

Every other thought flies out of my head. There's an ellipsis at the end of her text.

Jane Drake is not the kind of person who uses ellipses without cause.

The phone feels heavy and hot in my hand. The reality of how much getting this gig could change my life flashes through me, and moisture gathers under my arms. I hold them out to keep my kurti from staining.

Around me pakoras, chai, and gossip mingle freely in the cavernous room. I know I'm procrastinating, looking for something to do instead of calling my agent, extending this time when there's still hope.

Jane's words seem to glow and vibrate on my phone. There's also a text from Mom, casually checking in. I should never have told her that I sent in the audition tape, because she seems to know exactly how badly I want this. I'm suddenly glad that I lied to her.

I told her I won't hear back from them for another week. Enough time to manage my disappointment and figure out how to handle hers.

Across the noisy room, Tinku Maami and Taj Maama are having an animated discussion. I would bet my life she's broken it to him that I'm not up for the job of winning the Battle of the Sangeets. Taj Maama is without doubt trying to talk her out of firing me. He throws me his signature smile. The one he's always saved especially for me. I think about him grabbing me when I ran at him as a little girl and throwing me up in the air, my belly flying into my chest as he twirled me around until I laughed so hard I turned into my own laughter.

The knowledge that my uncle is going to take care of this fills my chest like heavy concrete. My family is always there catching me as I stumble through life.

My phone vibrates in my hand. If I get this gig it will be the first thing I've done for myself in my twenty-seven years. It will change everything. My aunt will be the one begging me to stay. Breathless hope fills my heart.

I tap my phone. A picture of us—Mom, Papa, and me—lights up the screen. The last birthday Papa spent on this earth. How vital he looked, how strong his arms as he squeezed the two of us close. How easy it is for a moment to lie to you. I don't want that to be my last thought before I call my agent to learn my fate. But it is.

CHAPTER THREE

RANI

1979
Forty-four years ago . . .

This was not the first time Rani Parekh had run away, but it was the first time she had no idea where she was going. Los Angeles was scarier than Bombay. Orange County was definitely scarier than Bandra, the part of Bombay where Rani had lived for the first twelve years of her life. She'd only been in LA for a few days.

Still, she hadn't expected there to be so few hiding places. Bandra was filled with places to hide when you ran away. Alcoves behind the tightly packed tenement buildings where residents shoved garbage out of their kitchen windows, making it the last place anyone would look. The blistering windowless maze that was Elco Market, lined with clothes and shoes and plastic jewelry painted to look like metal. The alleys in the slums bracketing the railway tracks. The lanes cobwebbed between the sprawling bungalows on Turner Road. The bazaar around the masjid. The courtyards tucked into temple compounds. The pews inside Mount Mary church.

She'd been born in Bandra. She hated it just like she hated every place on earth that she'd seen in her twelve years, but at least she knew it. If there was any safety in this world, it was knowing your surroundings.

The only way to protect yourself from the things you hated was to know them. The voice inside that identified the things you should hate and whispered that hurt was coming, that voice was the only friend you had. That voice had saved Rani from many a beating from her mother. It had also not been enough to save her from many.

Which was fine. Beatings weren't the worst thing someone could do to you.

She turned a corner and found herself faced with an endless squat brick building with painted store signs and the biggest parking lot she'd ever seen. Big enough to swallow up Bandra's entire Hill Road market a few times over. Everything here was too big. There were no crowded corners to disappear into. She felt exposed by the wide openness, like she was running across a cricket field with no clothes on.

Exhaustion tightened her skin over her muscles. She'd been walking since seven that morning. She'd slipped out as soon as her aunt left for work in her blue pajamas. She called them scrubs, which sounded like a fitting name. Rani was pretty sure her aunt was lying about going to work. What kind of work could you do wearing blue pajamas? If Rani were clothing, she'd be scrubs. That's how ridiculous it was for scrubs to be a nurse's uniform. In India, nurses wore starched white dresses with white stockings.

Work clothes. Yeah, right. Just the way all those men who came to see her mother were Rani's uncles. Just the way the clear liquid that filled her mother's bottles and smelled like the doctor's dispensary were medicine her mother needed to save her life.

I'm not stupid, Mama. She'd wanted to scream it every time Pushpa Parekh lied to her.

You're a stupid girl, Rani. Your soul is stupid. Why else would it choose me to birth you? Who asked you to get inside me? Who asked you to choose me and ruin my life?

Whether someone screamed in your face or whispered into it, the whoosh of alcohol was just as overpowering.

Obviously Rani knew she wasn't actually stupid.

Just like she knew that the medicine was what had killed her mother. That had to be the truth. Because what she'd heard the nurses say at the hospital where Mama died was something she couldn't believe. If what they said were true, Rani would be dead too.

It was all those men.

Rani pushed away the nurses' whispers. Whatever Rani felt about Mama, her aunt was worse. At least Rani had known Mama. Tina Maasi kept trying to be nice, and it was nauseating. Like flat, cold drinks, without fizz.

A huge yellow **M** sign loomed above her, and the smell of frying food punched her in the nose. Around the corner from their tenement building in Bandra was a shanty tea stall where a bare-bellied man fried batata vadas and jalebis in a giant iron kadhai all day long. This smell was exactly like that one, yet also completely different.

There was nothing on earth worse than the smell of frying food when you were hungry. That felt exactly the same here as it had back home.

Maybe Mama had been right about Rani being stupid. She had run away without stealing any money. Basically, she hadn't planned this very well. If she got caught, she was just going to be accused of attention seeking again and beaten for it. What could be more stupid?

Last year, Ashwini, a girl who lived in her building in Bandra, had tried to kill herself. Something about a boy she was in love with marrying another girl. Ashwini had swallowed something called sleeping pills. Rani couldn't understand why anyone would take pills to sleep. Sleeping that deeply felt dangerous. You couldn't hide when you were knocked out. But Rani was losing her thought train again. Something she tended to do when she had gone without food too long. Point was,

Ashwini had not taken enough of those pills. They had taken her to the hospital and washed out her stomach.

Mama had called Ashwini a stupid bitch. Which she wasn't. She was studying to be a teacher, and she was always kind to Rani. When Mama wasn't home, she'd brought Rani food. Several of the neighbors had done that, slipped Rani leftovers as though they knew there was never any food in their home.

The stupid bitch knew those many pills wouldn't kill her, she was just seeking attention. Like you, Rani, when you pretend to run away. As if sympathy can make people love you any more than it can fill your stomach.

Rani pressed her nose to the McDonald's window. The glass was cold on her skin. The smell reached down into her gullet and twisted her belly, making her head swim. Inside, people waited in line to place their orders. A man in a faded black suit. Another one in jeans with splashes of paint. Another with hair down to his shoulders and a thick black mustache that made Rani's heart start to race with fear.

She pulled away from the window and broke into a run and crashed right into someone. A girl a head shorter than Rani fell back and landed on her bum with a squeal. The big box of fries she was holding flew from her hands and scattered on the concrete.

"I'm sorry," Rani said before she could think the better of it. Apologizing meant asking for punishment.

"No, I'm sorry," the girl said. She had the roundest face, as though she spent all her life munching on fries. Her hair was in two pigtails, and her dress was a cloud of pink frills. She looked like a doll one of the uncles who visited Mama had given Rani. Except this girl had the biggest nose Rani had ever seen on a face.

Rani squatted next to her and started picking up the still-hot fries off the dusty concrete.

"Leave it. They'll clean up," a woman with exactly the same nose as the girl said. Fortunately her nose didn't look quite as big on her face. Lucky for the girl, because she really needed to grow into it.

Instead of waiting for Rani to respond, the woman helped the girl up and started dusting her dress.

Rani's tummy chose that moment to let out the loudest growl. The mother and daughter turned to her in alarm. Rani put the last bright-yellow stick of potato back in the box and straightened up.

The strangest recognition lit the woman's eyes, and for the first time Rani realized that the girl and her mother looked Indian. Since arriving in LA last week, Rani had seen only American people with skin the color of a peeled potato, and a few with very brown skin. But no one looked like Rani except her aunt.

"Are you Indian?" the woman asked in English that sounded the way it did when people spoke it in India. The familiarity of the sound made something strange move in Rani's chest.

"Mommy, please," the girl said. Unlike her mother, she sounded like the people here, like the people in Hollywood movies. American. Her round cheeks turned pink with embarrassment.

"Oh, look, Mummy's found an Indian person," a voice said behind Rani, and she turned to find two boys who looked exactly like each other. "We're going to be here for an hour now." They were both chomping on the biggest round sandwiches Rani had ever seen.

The other boy groaned even louder than Rani's tummy had. His giant nose had picked up a spot of ketchup from his sandwich.

"Come on, Mummy, we cannot be late for this party too," he said. "Kenny's parents are not on Indian Standard Time."

"What's your name, beta?" the woman asked Rani, ignoring her sons. "Where are your parents?" She looked around, searching with such earnestness that even Rani imagined two people, dressed all rich like this woman, in bell-bottoms and collared shirts, standing behind Rani.

The girl gave another embarrassed smile and took her mother's hand. "Let's go, Mommy."

Why couldn't she just say "Mummy" like a normal person? It annoyed Rani so much she wanted to shove the girl again, this time on purpose.

Her *mommy* continued to search the surroundings for Rani's imaginary parents.

"They're inside." Rani pointed at the restaurant with her chin. Her hands were still filled with the box of warm potatoes she'd picked up. "Bathroom." The buttery smell was making her light-headedness worse.

The woman looked ready to ask Rani to take her to them, but her sons made loud protesting sounds, and the girl tugged her arm in earnest. Fortunately, they were three against one, and the woman gave Rani a kind smile and turned and walked away.

The boys made a jubilant sound and raced each other to the car. The girl's shoulders dropped in relief. She held out her hand. "I can throw those away. Thanks for picking them up."

Rani pulled the food out of her reach. "No, I'll do it. No problem." She turned quickly and started walking toward the garbage bin, which fortunately was all the way at the other end of the pavement. By the time she got to it, the three children and their mother had gotten into their huge car. Rani had never seen a wood-paneled car like this in India.

The woman reversed out of the parking spot and drove away.

So distracted was Rani with staring at them that she didn't realize that she'd started shoving the fries into her mouth. As the car turned out of the parking lot onto the street, the doll-faced girl stared at Rani through the window. Her mouth fell open when she realized that Rani was eating the fries.

Her eyes went round with disgust, or shock, or something.

Rani couldn't care less. She would never see the girl again. The fries were delicious, and the bits of dirt that crunched between her teeth weren't the worst thing Rani had ever tasted in her food.

CHAPTER FOUR

VANDY

Saturday, 6:00 p.m. . . .

Vandy's hand shook as she punched in the code to unlock her daughter's studio apartment. As always, a finely orchestrated chaos reigned. An explosion of texture and color. Roughly folded silk ghagras covered in gold and silver threadwork hung from portable wardrobe rods that lined the exposed brick walls. Clothes Mika wore when she shot her choreography videos.

Why dance? Vandy remembered the pain from when Mallika had insisted on lessons after returning from a trip to India with Vir when she was seven. *How could the universe be so cruel?*

But she had gotten over it and supported her daughter. Her mother was wrong. Vandy had never stood in the way of Mallika's love for dance, no matter how many painful memories it dug up.

Vandy's seminar had lasted two hours. Usually she went over her time and stayed for as long as people had questions, but when Sonja failed to bring her water to signal that she'd figured out where Mallika was, the minutes had stretched until the two-hour timer on her watch went off, signaling that her committed time was at an end.

There had been the usual endless questions about relationships. How did you know if your partner was taking you for granted? How did you put your own needs before those of the people you loved?

The answer to almost every question was to listen to yourself. To get to know yourself better. Who were you, and what did the real you want? Not what your ego wanted, not what the world said you should want, but what you needed to do to feel like *you*. The *you* you liked being and wanted to be.

A young woman with a soft voice and an even softer demeanor had taken the mic and asked the question that always hit Vandy in the most defenseless corner of her heart. *Should I forgive my cheating husband?* Her voice had been filled with shame. A common emotion when this particular question was verbalized.

It was the most complicated of questions, but no one ever asked it without already having the answer. What they really wanted was to either have their answer reinforced or to be talked out of it. Both were futile endeavors. People rarely left a spouse because someone told them to, or stayed with one because someone told them to. In that one thing, in that one decision, people finally became the masters of their own choices.

Vir loved to say that the answers were always in the questions themselves. It was astounding that people didn't see it when they wrote the words. But it was truest in the case of this particular issue. Vandy got some two thousand emails for her advice column every month. Easily half of those were related to infidelity.

The woman's husband had slept with her sister. A double stabbing. Vandy would bet good money that she was going to leave the man within the month, no matter what advice Vandy offered. People who stayed with cheating spouses rarely shared the details of their betrayal with the world. Who knew that better than her?

Vandy had walked the woman through her feelings, helped her see past the knot of hurt to the facts until she found her own answer. It didn't matter what Vandy's opinions on the subject were. Her job was to make people weigh things from their individual perspectives instead of the world's.

Vandy needed to do the same thing: find a way around her own feelings. She'd texted Mallika, letting her know she was going to her apartment to check on her. But there was still no response.

Vandy walked through the cluttered room. Mallika's scent, as singular as she was, soaked in vanilla and roses, flooded Vandy, and her legs almost gave out. When Mika was a baby, her scent had been like a drug. Vandy had needed to fill her lungs over and over to make sure something so beautiful really existed.

Every single person Vandy knew had called her certifiably insane when she'd been obsessed with having Mallika. They hadn't used the term lightly either. They'd actually believed Vandy had become mentally ill with her need to be a mother. Vir, his mother, Vandy's own parents, her brothers, every relative and friend: they had all at one time or another along that seemingly endless path tried to talk Vandy out of it, even shame and threaten her out of it. Seven years of refusing to accept her inability to become a mother had been too much for all of them.

Only one person had stood by her as Vandy dug in her heels. Only she had understood. Only she had never questioned.

Why was Vandy thinking about this today when the only piece of her heart that meant anything at all was nowhere to be found?

Another question that is its own answer, Vir's voice whispered in her ear.

She had to stop this. She could not think about loss today. She couldn't put that energy into the universe.

How could you leave me?

How could so much pain fill her every time she thought of Vir almost a year after he was gone? She felt carved out. Nothing inside her where he'd been. A checkerboard. Vir's pieces gone. All that was left was the pieces that were Mallika.

Where are you, Mika?

Should she call the cops?

I talked to you yesterday, Mom. Stop being Pinky Tinku-level dramatic, she imagined her baby girl's laughter-filled voice teasing her and released the longest breath.

Breathe out the worry so hope can fill its place.

Vandy always asked her readers to tune in to their inner voice. Instinct, the lizard brain, conscience: no matter the name used to describe it, it always led you to where the problem lay. Vandy's kept getting louder and louder in its insistence that something was wrong.

Vandy was not a paranoid person. Doom rarely ever gripped her, but when it did, it had never been wrong. When Vir had suffered those stomachaches, she'd known, known at the very base of her spine, that something was terribly wrong.

She swept a glance around the apartment. A purple palazzo-and-choli set draped the back of an armchair. It was what Mika had worn to shoot that darned audition tape.

The excitement that had glowed in Mallika's eyes when she talked about it squeezed painfully in Vandy's heart. She'd tried to get Mallika to manage her hope. It was the first time her daughter had looked happy since Vir's death, and the thought of having that happiness crushed had made Vandy forget all her own advice and push her daughter away from what she wanted. For the first time in her life, her daughter had accused Vandy of not understanding her.

Thanks, Mom, for your faith in me.

Well, obviously it wasn't a matter of faith. The audition was too much of a leap. And now here they were, Mallika unable to handle the result. She imagined Mika holed up somewhere, sobbing into a pillow.

Vandy had to find out what had happened with the audition.

Jane Drake!

That was it. That was who would know. Mika's agent.

Sonja had called Mika's friends, and they'd all said she hadn't spoken to them within the last two days. Vandy appeared to be the last person Mika had called, more than twenty-four hours ago.

Vandy dropped into the daybed that doubled as the couch, and apparently also as an overflow closet. The mess of clothes was pushed to the side to make a place to sit. Two cups sat on the nightstand. Someone had been here with her.

The sense that something was off sharpened inside her. Before giving it another thought, Vandy tapped her phone and hunted down her daughter's agent's number. It took her only two receptionists and an assistant before she had Jane on the phone.

"Ms. Guru!" Jane said. "What a pleasure. I'm a huge fan."

Vandy thanked her, then cleared her throat. "Ms. Drake, I'm . . . I can't seem to find . . . to find . . ." Dear lord, she sounded like a teenager's helicopter parent. She sounded like Pinky and Tinku. "I'm looking for Mallika. She's not returning texts or answering her phone."

Surprised silence greeted her from the other side.

What were the ethics on this? Jane was Mika's agent, not her babysitter. But also not her doctor or her lawyer. Were there confidentiality laws between agents and clients about things other than contracts and projects?

"I was just wondering when the last time you spoke to her was." Vandy tried to keep her voice casual. *Just tell me if she got the callback!*

This time Jane cleared her throat. The woman couldn't seem to decide between her loyalty to her client and placating someone she saw as a person of considerable clout. Then again, she might just be judging Vandy for being a too-intense parent with no boundaries. Which, of course, Vandy was being by any definition.

"I don't mean to put you in an uncomfortable position," Vandy said, "but you probably know how close Mallika and I are. I know she was waiting for news on the *Mahabharata* casting." Even as she said the words, she realized how inappropriate they sounded. "I can probably find a way for my people to call the producers. So, please, could you help me out? Did she hear back from them?"

Jane's breathing turned confused. "She heard back from them a week ago."

Vandy felt her hands go cold. The cold spread up her arms. "I beg your pardon?" That could not possibly be true. "Are you sure?"

Jane made an alarmed sound, unless that was Vandy projecting. "She was spectacular in her audition tape. They loved her. They truly did. But . . ." She trailed off. She seemed to realize that she was saying too much.

"Did she get it?" Vandy asked, but her brain was frozen on the fact that it had been a week since Mallika had found out and she hadn't told Vandy.

Jane seemed to realize something was amiss. "I'm sure Mallika will tell you the details herself soon," she said. "She's so good," she added. "One of my most talented clients."

"She found this out last week?"

Jane made a reluctant affirmative sound. She was obviously regretting letting that slip.

Mallika had talked to Vandy almost every day until yesterday and said nothing, letting Vandy try to get her to temper her hope while she waited for the call. No wonder Mallika had been so angry. In the wake of her rejection, Vandy's words had to have sounded brutal.

Jane cleared her throat again. "Ms. Guru, I have another call. I really have to go."

"Of course. Thank you so much for talking to me." Vandy felt like her chest was being crushed. She hadn't let her emotions run amok like this for years.

Mallika lying to her. Mallika fighting with her and shutting her out. All of it felt surreal. It felt too much like losing her. Like something unraveling.

She fell back on the bed that smelled so much like her child. She pulled the tangle of roughly folded clothes and scarves and sheets around herself and burrowed into it.

How many times had she wrapped herself around Vir like this? Trying to soak up his heartbreak. Every time a book was rejected by a publisher, or a book failed to make the splash he'd expected it to make, or a proposal failed to find takers. She'd felt his pain like it was her own. Now Mika had chosen that same path, heartbreak over and over and over.

Mallika wasn't built for this. She was sensitive. Vandy and Vir had worked hard to protect her from hurt. Up until now she'd seemed to understand her own vulnerability, bouncing up and away before the heartbreak took root, sometimes even before the rejection came. Like Tigger.

The memory of the animated tiger bouncing away on his tail sliced through Vandy. Just like that, she was sprawled on the couch with another body stretched out next to hers, the comforting sound of the cartoon playing on the TV.

You're Pooh and I'm Tigger.

The voice she hadn't heard in twenty-seven years was too clear in her ears. A splash of hot oil, opening old wounds, snapping dead nerves back to life. Vandy would not allow that memory here now. It had no place here.

This was about her child. She brought her mind back to the scent soaked into the fibers of the fabric she was hugging. When Mika was little, anytime she disappointed herself, she'd let Vandy hold her, squeeze the stinger out of her. *You make it all better, Mama.* Those words had made Vandy feel headier, more filled up than the praise of millions of fans put together.

Now her child didn't even feel like she could tell her mother that something had hurt her.

With another hungry inhale of the sheets, Vandy unwrapped herself and sat up. Tears weren't going to help her. They never had.

Take your ego out of the equation and look for a solution.

Her hurt at being lied to wasn't what was important here. This wasn't about her. Everything had always been about Mallika. About making sure she was okay. Vandy had to find her. Then she had to make sure Mallika knew that nothing was more important to Vandy than being there to squeeze the stinger out of her.

CHAPTER FIVE

MALLIKA

Seven days ago . . .

I'm not surprised that I didn't get it. What I am surprised by is how much I wanted it and how much it hurts. The fact that I was stupid enough to think I had a shot adds insult to the pain.

How do people do this? Deal with failure?

Rejection is part of making it in the arts. It's what my agent repeated over and over when I waited until the last minute to send the audition tape in, when I almost didn't. Turns out I never should have.

When I was ten, I missed the annual recital at my dance school because I got a raging case of the flu. I had practiced every minute of every day for three months. I remember the sheer force of my disappointment. I remember Mom holding me tight as I cried for hours. When I got better, Mom and Papa built a stage in our living room and invited all the family over for a private recital. I got to wear my costume, get pictures, and perform. I remember dancing my heart out. That was the part that I had been saddest about missing.

"I don't think I can do this," I say to Jane, whose patient silence on the phone is just adding to my shame.

"Mallika, please think about it," she says. "This is a great opportunity. All they want is to see you perform the same piece in classical kathak." She sounds so logical, but after she told me they aren't calling me in to audition with the other selected candidates, I had to tune her out to keep from making a fool of myself by breaking into sobs.

I'm just not made for this. To carve out pieces of my heart and hand them over to be turned away.

If they wanted me, they'd have called me for an audition. My style is what it is: a contemporary interpretation of classical. I can't change it to some version of what they believe Indian dance should be.

"I appreciate your support, but maybe this isn't the right project for me." My voice sounds so final.

She sighs. "Please at least just think about it," she says before letting me go.

I look at my phone, and my finger hovers over Papa's number. How is it possible to miss someone so much? All I want is one more moment with him so I can place my head on his shoulder and have him tell a terrible dad joke.

You and I are of the same ilk, he'd say, using an accent to drag "ilk" to sound like "ill-luck" in the most Papa way.

How could you do this to me? I want to scream at the universe, but I don't know if it's for taking Papa from me or because I lost the project I'd pinned so much hope on. Right now, both losses coalesce into one monstrous wave of grief.

I scroll through my contacts. So many people who love me, whom I love, and there's no one I can say the words I want to say to: *Make it stop! Soothe my feelings. I'm sad and angry and afraid I'll never amount to anything.*

The entirety of how inconsequential I am settles into my bones. The casting directors who hold my career in their hands don't want what I have to offer. My worst fears are true after all. The voice telling me I knew this already is louder than it's ever been. It screams inside me.

I do matter, I want to scream back at it. I just need someone to tell me that I do.

I want to call my mother. But the idea of disappointing her makes everything else I'm feeling become ten times larger. What's worse is that I know she'll make me feel better. She'll fix things. She'll identify a solution and then manifest it into the ether.

The only thing I've ever manifested is this, this *Mahabharata* gig, and getting to do what I love at that scale. It had felt like screaming my wanting from mountaintops and chanting it into oceans.

After losing Papa, I thought something changed inside me. I thought I'd be able to aim for something out of my reach because he'd be watching out for me.

Papa spent his life stuck in the dreaded midlist in publishing, but at least he published books. Consistently from the year of my birth until he passed. Twenty books in twenty-seven years. Books that sold a modest number of copies and received steady but not stupendous critical acclaim.

No one's shitting themselves over my books, but I love them, and they let me pay at least part of our mortgage, he'd said. As Mom had become more and more successful, it had been a smaller and smaller part. Nonetheless, he'd at least launched and stayed airborne, not a jet but a hang glider. And here I was, a dud rocket.

I can't make myself go back inside my uncle's home and face the band of aunties and uncles who are waiting for me to lead them to wedding-dance glory. Then I remember that my aunt fired me.

Just as I think of her, Tinku Maami sticks her head out of the huge carved front door she rescued from a palace in India and had restored. Some people rescue dogs; my family rescues remnants of the feudal system.

I quickly press the phone to my ear and pretend to still be on it and stick up a finger in the universal gesture to ask for a moment. Pretending to be a busy person on my important call is easier than facing the fact that my own aunt doesn't want me on a job no one else will take.

She smiles and waves her hands about to let me know I should come inside when I'm done. Apparently, I'm back on the job.

As the door shuts behind her, I burst into tears.

I don't know how long I've been crying when a hand tugs my ponytail. "All okay, squirt?" a deep voice says behind me.

Great! Greatgreatgreat! My cousin, all six foot two inches of legendary Mehta success, looks down at me as I lift my head from my elbow, where I've been weeping in great big pathetic waves.

He's in scrubs. Somehow he manages to make them look as suave as a business suit.

As though that isn't mortifying enough—because yes, tears are streaming down my face and I'm not wearing waterproof mascara—Rex, my cousin Amey's best friend, is also looking down at me.

Great

Big

Bags

Of

Shit.

I don't even have the words for what *his* scrubs make *him* look like. Suffice to say, I called him "Sex" instead of "Rex" at Amey's engagement party six months ago. After one—yes, one—measly glass of cabernet. In front of his (need I add: absurdly hot and also a physician?) fiancée.

I consider diving behind one of the two gigantic concrete lions guarding my uncle's front door, from what exactly, I couldn't say.

"Mika?" Amey says gently.

Rex, who I swear looks like Idris Elba's younger, hotter brother (I know that sounds impossible, but only if you haven't seen this guy), pulls out a packet of tissues from his pocket and holds one out to me.

I'm in pain, but I might have just had an orgasm. Face flaming, I accept the offering and scrub it across my cheeks, turning the soft white into the charcoal gray of my mascara.

Amey leans past the other lion, because apparently one lion isn't enough to fight off whatever dangers lurk in the wild streets of Palos Verdes Estates, and studies the scene inside his parents' living room through the window. "Did Mom make you cry? Honestly, Mika, I don't know why you put up with her and Pinky."

His kindness makes the tissue useless against the fresh deluge of tears. Sex hands me the entire packet, a bright spot in the pain of failure that's lancing my broken heart.

"It's not your mom or Pinky." I start sobbing in earnest, and my cousin sits down on the travertine steps and pulls me close.

My uncles' sons, four between the two of them, are like my brothers. They're the best men I know. They're probably also the reason why I've never found anyone to be in a meaningful relationship with in my twenty-seven years. To say nothing of the fact that Rex is engaged to another woman, after making me fall in love with him five years ago. But I most certainly cannot go there right now.

"I didn't get the *Mahabharata*." I finally force the words out past the choking humiliation.

"To be fair, the *Mahabharata* is a complex epic," Rex says as Amey strokes my back.

I laugh. Which makes me spray snot into my cousin's scrubs on top of the sooty tears I've already soaked him in.

How is it fair that a man who looks like this is also funny? I consider challenging his fiancée to a duel. But much as I love old westerns, I hate guns. And the sight of blood makes me faint. Also, he already chose her over me, so she already won the duel.

"They're idiots if they didn't choose you," Amey says, trying to sound both sensitive and breezy in an attempt to keep me from breaking into fresh tears.

It doesn't work. I'm a goner today. Everything is going to make me cry. "I don't want to go back in there. But we're not done with practice," I say in the tone I used to use to get him to steal extra cookies for me from our grandmother.

"Say no more." Amey hops up and makes his way into the house where he has the power to literally make anything happen. Especially now, when he's the groom-to-be.

Rex throws a look at me, in all my smudgy-mascara, snotty-face, sweat-stains-in-armpits glory. At least my hair is spilling from my high ponytail and catching the light in the cutest way. I know this because I quickly checked myself out in the lead glass windows when Amey left and Rex looked away for a moment. But also because his gaze just did the quickest skim of my hair draped around my shoulders. *And* the same shower of light from the lamppost is catching his beautiful curls. How is it fair for someone to be a doctor and look like a supermodel? To make everything even more unfair, he sings in a band. Which makes this feeling of inadequacy that has taken hold of me turn so big I know I'm going to throw up.

There's a term for this. The way I'm feeling. But it dances out of my reach.

He clears his throat and sounds as though he's in pain.

Well, then don't look at my hair like that, buster! Especially since you're engaged!

"Dude?" Amey sticks his head back out of the door and snaps, "You coming?"

"Of course," he says and then follows Amey in.

My heart, along with my dignity, drags on a string behind him. I try not to think of how much in love with him I used to be. I was twenty-two, and Amey had brought him home from med school one Thanksgiving.

It was the best Thanksgiving of my life. He spent the entire time looking at me as though I'd stepped out of his dreams and if he looked away, I might disappear. We flirted on the phone for months after. Then he'd gone and fallen for someone else.

"Mallika?" This time it's my grandmother who catches me with my pride pooled around my ankles. "What are you hiding from now?" She makes her way up the cobbled path to the front porch. The car that dropped her off circles the sweeping driveway and zooms away.

She's carrying a cane. This is new, but it suits her.

Her eyes flash something at me that tells me I am not to mention the cane.

I push off the giant concrete lion I'm leaning on and wonder if I should help her up the stairs. She is not someone who takes help without making you regret offering it.

"I'm not hiding, Naani," I say with a giant sniff and sink down on the step next to the lion.

"That's good," my eighty-year-old grandmother says in a bored tone that would put a teenager to shame. "Because if you were, you'd be doing a terrible job of it."

When I was little, my grandmother used to be the sweetest person. Always cooking for everyone and letting me fall asleep cuddled into her with her lavender–talcum powder smell soaking my senses. Over the years she's turned progressively meaner. Like someone who's had it with the world's nonsense. Even her daughters-in-law, who terrify all humanity, seem afraid of her now.

"Is it that tamasha they're planning to turn the *Mahabharata* into?" Naani says, staring down the gigantic nose she's bestowed on all her progeny except me. A fact I'm inordinately grateful for. Although, right about now, if I were offered the Mehta nose but also got the Mehta ability to get everything they desired with it, I'd take the honker without a single thought.

My own pert nose drips as my tears return and decide that my eyes are not enough of an outlet. "It's not a big deal. It wasn't like I was ever actually going to get it." I regret the day Pinky Maami found out about the audition. Because gossip turns viral the instant it reaches my aunts' ears.

Naani emits the angriest grunt and lowers herself onto the step next to me, nimble despite the cane. I notice the slight wince that she almost succeeds in hiding, but I know better than to ask her if she's okay because I'm quite fond of my head and don't want it bitten off.

"Of course you didn't think you were going to get it. Because having faith would actually take some balls."

Instead of being hurt, I laugh. "Actually, it would take delusion. It was Karan Johar and Shyamalan. Not quite my league."

Her sharp brown eyes, with the golden star spikes, are only slightly duller with age than my mother's, but they soften as she seems to pick something up in my face.

"You remind me so much of her," she says with unexpected gentleness.

"How could I? Mom's never messed up at anything."

Confusion clouds Naani's face, and her deeply lined lids lower and then take their time to open wide again.

Then her eyes go back to being angry. "You don't think your mother has ever messed up?" The sheer magnitude of her outrage surprises me. She opens her mouth, then shuts it. Emotions gallop across her face, and she starts coughing.

"Naani?" I rub her back. "You okay?"

She pushes me away. "Don't ask stupid questions. Go get me water. Make yourself useful."

As I jump up to follow her orders, Amey comes out of the palace-rescue front door, followed closely by Rex.

"Hi, Naani," both men say and drop kisses on her head. She's suddenly perfectly composed again. Her eyes regain their glitter at the sight of them, every sign of her cough gone.

"Well, if this isn't a sign, I don't know what is," she says randomly and throws me a look that makes me wonder if I just imagined the past few minutes. "Where are you going? Come sit next to me."

It's easiest to comply, so I do.

She turns to Rex and pats his cheek and asks him about his parents and his grandparents in Jamaica. Amey is her firstborn grandson and probably her favorite person in the whole world, and Rex has been his best friend since college, so by association, she loves Rex like one of her own.

My heart does a god-awful squeeze for no reason at all.

"How's work?" Naani says to Rex and throws a look I can't interpret my way. I don't dare ask for clarification because I don't need her calling me stupid in front of him. "You ready to go public yet?" Her voice is loaded with all sorts of meaning as her gaze skewers me, then slides to him.

"We're getting there," Rex says and laughs, and I lose my train of thought.

"Mika failed at another audition," she declares with the full force of her meanness, and I have a sense that she wants to shake me. "I guess we should all be applauding because at least she didn't run before even trying with this one." She gives Rex her hand and lets him help her up.

"Everything okay, Naani?" Rex asks kindly. He's talking to her, but his eyes do a quick scan of my face. A physician studying me for symptoms.

I smile my breeziest smile.

"Everything is okay with me. But this one might be a good case for you." Naani points her cane at me.

Rex swallows.

Is she trying to matchmake? She knows perfectly well that the man is engaged. Engaged to be married.

Rex and Amey exchange unreadable looks.

"Do you know Rex studies genetic oddities? You should ask him about his work," she says to me, stressing the word "oddities" as though she's presenting me as an exhibit. Then she points her cane from Amey to me. "These two are a perfect fit for your project, don't you think? Can two cousins be any more different?" This last part she throws at Rex, but it's my heart that takes the stab of her words.

Before Rex can answer, she turns to Amey. "Your cousin is upset. Take her with you when you go out gallivanting tonight." Then before his frown gets a chance to turn gargantuan, she takes his arm. "Walk me inside." She exaggerates her limp without a whit of shame.

The door clicks shut behind them, and the silence of the evening tightens around Rex and me in an awkward cinch.

"That wasn't weird at all," I say.

Rex grins, then speaks quickly. "Listen." For some reason, he never says my name anymore. I've never heard him say it in the five years since he broke my heart. Suddenly, I have the most intense urge to hear the particular way it sounded in his voice. "It's been a long week, and Amey and I were going to head to Hogshead for some beers. Want to join us?"

Don't think the word "fiancée" . . . Don't think the word "fiancée" . . .

The word "fiancée" does a triple spin inside my head.

I know it's not like that. He isn't asking me out. My grandmother practically ordered him to take me along.

His eyes are pools of kindness, and my entire being takes a dive and does a languorous lap in them. *Stop it.* He isn't going to smooth my hair with his big hands and say my name and tell me I matter the way I'm imagining in my head. He's just trying to help his best friend's pathetic cousin because his best friend's grandmother ordered him to.

The rest is ancient history. He's moved on. I've moved on. There's no harm in drowning my sorrows in some beer and the heady euphoria of his presence. At this point, it's like fantasizing about a celebrity: harmless.

Before I can respond, Amey rushes out of his parents' house and grabs my hand. "Let's go. I told Mom you're about to throw up and I'm driving you home. You know how Mom is about anyone throwing up in her bathrooms. We have to get out of here before she tells Dad and he comes out to check on you."

I start running with him. In this moment I will do anything to not go back inside the house and make Tinku Maami dance.

The idea of ever dancing again makes me want to bring up my insides. The thought that I might be done with dancing forever hits me with the force of a battering ram.

"I don't want to go home." The words fly out of my mouth. "I want to go gallivanting with you."

I mean to say it to Amey, but my eyes land on Rex, who is laughing like I've said the funniest thing he's ever heard.

Rex breaks into a run and joins us as we race down the street and away from the house. His eyes shine like he's never had so much fun.

Good to know I am entertaining, at least off camera.

CHAPTER SIX

RANI

1979
Forty-four years ago . . .

As if being shipped off to a different country because your mother died wasn't bad enough, it had to be a country where everything was upside down. The fries Rani had scarfed down too fast made her stomach churn in that way it always did when she waited too long to put food in it. Luckily she had enough practice with this to know how to give her body a few moments to adjust. After everything settled, she started walking again, following the gray concrete footpaths.

Clusters of brick buildings surrounded by black metal fences gave way to houses that looked like the bungalows in Bandra blown up to twice their size. Some even five times their size.

All day Rani had walked and walked, but as the sun started to go down, she had a sense that she was going round and round in circles. The streets that lined these picture-postcard houses were like fishermen's nets. They connected back to one another.

When she found herself under the huge yellow **M** sign again, the smell of fries back in her nose, she knew she'd been tracing the same streets over and over.

It was also suddenly cold. How had she let herself forget that in this stupid city the afternoons were scorching, where the sun burned her skin and made it peel, and the evenings turned chilly and made her teeth chatter? On the day when they first got to LA, Rani had sat on the balcony in her aunt's apartment all day. But when the sun disappeared from the sky, she'd had to go inside. Before she got on that plane, Rani had never experienced feeling cold.

The plane had been freezing. She hadn't told anyone because what could they do? It wasn't like she could step outside and onto the fluffy clouds.

She had no escape from the cold now, either, and the inside of her chest started to tremble. Her mouth felt parched. How had she forgotten to drink water before she ran away from her aunt's house that morning?

She pressed her hands against her ears because she didn't want to hear her mother's voice calling her stupid again. But she also wanted to hear her mother's voice so badly it made the trembling ten times worse. At least with her mother she'd had water. Even if she'd had to fill buckets of it herself and carry it to their block from the tenement building's courtyard when the municipal water turned on for an hour every morning. She'd done it since she was five years old.

A mother should at least make sure her child has water to drink, Rani had heard the neighborhood women say as they watched her dragging the bucket in her skinny arms.

Something that made the cold worse filled Rani's chest. It tightened around her, making it impossible to separate herself from it. *At least water.* The voices of all the women in her building started a chorus in her ear.

At least water!

"I deserve at least water!" she whispered into her hands as she rubbed them together to warm them. Then she said it again, louder, into the sky.

Leaning her head back made it spin. Thirst dried out her tongue. She had to keep moving. There was an alley behind the McDonald's. Rani stumbled through it, chasing the smell of food, even if it was laced with rot.

There were two huge green tanks in the back. Dumpsters, that's what her aunt had called the ones in her apartment complex, where she took bags of garbage from the house when they filled up.

Rani ran toward them. One of them was open. She stretched up on her toes and peered inside. Sitting at the very top was a huge plastic cup filled with orange liquid. Rani reached in and grabbed it and emptied it down her throat. It tasted like Gold Spot, the orange soda that one of her mother's men had brought her once. The memory of his face as he handed it to her made her want to bring up the sweet liquid, but it felt too good going down, and she knew her stomach needed it because it was doing that burning thing again.

Anger. Her stomach was angry with her.

Her entire being seemed to catch the anger and dissolve into it.

She sat down on the pavement. Then scooted between the two dumpsters so no one would see her. The cold seemed to be angry too, chewing through her thin T-shirt and pants and attacking her skin. She wrapped her arms around herself.

She just needed to rest for a moment. To feel strong again. She had barely closed her eyes and caught her breath when she heard sounds above her.

Men's voices. That sound could startle Rani awake from death. She jumped, but her body collapsed back into itself, too tired to move.

"Hello?" the man's voice said, and Rani grabbed the dumpster and forced herself to stand.

There were two of them. Her legs buckled. There were dumpsters on either side of her and a brick wall behind her.

Something on Rani's face might have given away her terror because they stepped back and away from her and raised their hands.

"We're police," one said. "We're not going to hurt you."

Did they think she was stupid? They were dressed in blue and not in khaki, like policemen.

"Did you run away?" Then, instead of slapping her and feeling her up to check for what she'd stolen, one of them opened up a blanket and wrapped it around her.

"We're LAPD," one of the men said when Rani tried to throw off the blanket.

She racked her brains to think of what that meant: *elaypeedee*. She'd never heard the word before. All she knew was that no policemen helped you unless they wanted something from you. If these men were even that. If her mother had taught her anything, she'd taught her that much.

"We're going to take you to the station," the taller one said, and there it was. Rani immediately knew their plan.

Shoving him aside with all the strength she had left, she broke into a run. She knew that stations were places where men took you when they were going to put you on a train and abduct you. She'd heard enough stories about what happened to girls when strangers put them on trains to take them away.

It's what had happened to Mama, even though the man had never had to force her on that train. She'd gotten on it herself.

Just because the man had given Rani that warm blanket, did he think she'd just go with him? Before she'd made it to the end of the alley, he grabbed her from behind.

She started screaming and scratching, fighting him with everything she had. No one was putting her on a train and shipping her off, not while she still had breath in her.

He didn't hit her, but his arms tightened around her, restraining her. He made shushing sounds behind her, as the other one squatted down in front of her. "We're not going to hurt you," he said. "No one's going to hurt you. Calm down."

Rani knew what that meant too, when men shushed you and said you wouldn't get hurt if you just stayed quiet.

That was when she knew it was the end. She was trapped, she wasn't going to be able to get away from these men who were taller and bigger than any of the men her mother had brought home. The cold drink gushed up her gullet and projected from her mouth as she threw up all over the man squatting in front of her.

The fries she'd stuffed in her mouth too fast spurted out of her, mixed with the orange liquid, so much force in it that it almost tore her nose open.

The man reared back, and the other one let her go. She braced herself, but they still didn't hit her. Her eyes started to water—not tears, because Rani never cried, but from the force of the vomit.

"Dear God, what have you been through, child?" the older man who hadn't touched her but was covered in her throw up said, wiping himself down with a towel he pulled from the car at the mouth of the alley. The letters **LAPD** were painted across it, LOS ANGELES POLICE DEPARTMENT.

Before she could process that, another car pulled up next to them. A wooden car with the round doll-faced girl in the window.

The moment the car stopped, the girl jumped out, and her mother followed quickly. The boys with the giant sandwiches were nowhere to be seen.

"Everything okay here, Officer?" the woman asked as she walked toward Rani, a concerned look tightening her face.

The girl ran back to the car and brought Rani a towel. She was no longer wearing her frilly dress but a jean skirt and bright-yellow sweater, and her hair was wet. The towel she held smelled acrid, like chemicals, and was damp. "I'm sorry. My brothers pushed me in the pool, and I had to use the towel." She still talked funny. Like the white police officers.

Rani's head was swimming, so she had to focus to understand what the girl was saying. Rani had always been top of her class in English, and she'd read through almost all the English books in the library at her school, but these people stretched and widened their words in the strangest way. The accent made Rani feel like she'd come to a place where she'd never fit.

"Do you know this girl, ma'am?" the policeman who had restrained Rani said. There was vomit on his shoes, and the other one poured a bottle of water on them.

"We're the ones who called you," the girl's mother said. "My daughter wouldn't rest until I called." She turned to Rani. Rani hadn't noticed before, but the woman had the kindest eyes. Like Mother Superior at Rani's school in Bombay. "Are you lost?" she asked, her accent switching to the way Rani spoke English. Like home. Then she repeated it in Hindi. "Tum ghum ho gayi ho kya?" After she'd already spoken to Rani in Hindi, she asked if Rani understood Hindi. "Hindi? Marathi? Gujarati?" she asked.

Rani nodded, hypnotized by the way the familiar words fell on her ears. "Tino," she said. She spoke all three languages just like everyone she knew in Bombay did. But her English had been better than everyone else's.

The woman took the towel from her and wiped her arms. Rani was suddenly embarrassed by how skinny they were.

"She was acting like she's scared," the older policeman said. His head was so bald it shone under the lamppost.

"That's because I didn't want them to put me on a train," Rani said before she could think about it. The woman truly had hypnotized her.

All four of them looked at Rani like she'd suddenly spoken gibberish.

"Don't act like you didn't say you were taking me to the station," she threw at the policemen and moved to hide behind the woman.

The adults looked confused, but the girl pressed a hand to her mouth. Then she leaned over and whispered into Rani's ear. "They meant the police station, not the train station."

She didn't laugh. When the adults figured it out and looked like they would laugh, she glared at them in a way that made Rani think of what she'd be like when she was as old as them.

Rani stepped away from her. "I knew that."

"I know," the girl said. "She was just kidding," she told the others. Then she laughed. And Rani laughed. And the adults laughed.

No one laughed too much, just enough that Rani no longer felt like the idiot.

"Is there anyone we can call?" one of the policemen asked.

That's when the girl's mother took the cops aside and had a conversation in hushed tones.

"I'm Vandana, but everyone calls me Vandy," the girl said in the accent that was becoming easier to understand the more she spoke. She still said her name funny, like "bandanna" with a *V*, and not "One-Dunna," like Rani had heard it said in India.

"I'm Rani. And everyone calls me Rani," Rani said. Because the nicknames she'd been called weren't something this girl looked like she'd even understand.

"Hi, Rani!" the girl said excitedly, as though they hadn't just shared the most awkward of meetings. Despite her American accent, she said Rani's name perfectly: *Raw-knee.*

Finally, her mother managed to convince the policemen that she knew Rani, and one of the cops turned out to be her doctor husband's patient. The woman filled out some forms. Then the cops made Rani write her aunt's address down and assured her that they'd visit her the next day to make sure she was okay.

For one moment Rani considered putting her real address down. But her mother had taught her well. Never tell the police where you live.

"We'll drive you home," the mother said when the policemen were gone.

"No, thank you. I'll walk home," Rani said, trying to reflect the lady's tone. Going back to her aunt's starkly spotless and empty apartment filled her with dread, but running away without knowing where to go was worse.

Maybe the police here didn't run their hands all over you and touch you in places that made you want to cry, and ask for money. But who knew what they would do to you when they took you to their police station? Rani needed a better plan if she didn't want to stay with her aunt.

"I promised the cop that I'd get you home safely," the girl's mother said. She looked completely different now than when Rani had first seen her. In the past few minutes she'd taken on a familiarity, like the women in Rani's building in Bandra. "But first Vandy wants to grab a bite. Her brothers ate all her food." She started walking to the McDonald's where this whole saga had started in the first place.

"I'm not hungry," Rani said just as her stomach, newly empty even though it hadn't actually ever been full, growled so loudly she felt her cheeks warm with shame. "And I'm not smelling very good." She smelled of vomit and sweat and grime and the dumpster. Suddenly she was too tired to be around these shiny people, and her head swam.

The girl moved quickly for a girl who looked that soft and boneless, and wrapped a surprisingly strong arm around Rani before Rani sank to the pavement.

"Can we go home first, Mommy?" she said. "I think I need to get all this chlorine out of my hair. Rani probably needs to wash up too." She started walking Rani to the wooden car, and Rani couldn't muster the strength to do much more than lean on her and fall in step. "We don't live that far from here."

They really didn't. Before Rani could let her mind make up images of all the horrible places these strangers could take her, and all the things they could do to her, the car turned into a house that looked like a castle made of cake and iced with buttercream flowers. A powder-white garage door opened magically, and they drove into it.

The girl—had she said people called her Vanny? Vinny?—helped her out of the car. Rani stumbled, and it brought back the sharpest memory of her mother coming home on shaky feet, her hair in disarray, her lipstick smeared off her beautiful mouth, her kajal smudged around her beautiful eyes.

Vinny led her into the house, and Rani told herself that she could shove her and outrun her if she tried anything funny. But all she did was help Rani up some steps and into a house filled with carpet and wood and brightly painted walls with clusters of pictures. It even smelled like a cake, vanilla and chocolate. Vinny handed her a towel and took her to a bathroom through the pinkest room Rani had ever seen.

When Rani was done, she found a baby-pink jogging suit sitting by the sink. It was loose around the waist and short at the ankles, but it was the softest, most glittery thing Rani had ever worn, and it had that vanilla-and-chocolate smell everything around here seemed to be soaked in. Vinny was waiting for her, her own shoulder-length hair washed and wet, wearing an almost identical baby-pink jogging suit.

Rani felt too floaty and light headed to talk. But Vinny didn't seem to need words. She led Rani through corridors and down a staircase into the biggest, whitest kitchen Rani had ever seen. They sat down at a giant counter covered in food. Rotis and dal and rice and a few bowls of vegetable shaak and a giant bowl of dahi. Rani loved yogurt and roti. It was the thing she had grown up eating. At home, the neighbors had always brought her their leftover rotis, and Rani had known how to make yogurt since one of her mother's men had taught her when she was six.

Vinny's mother filled plates for them, and Rani felt her eyelids get warm. Rani never cried. Never. *People who cry never stop crying,* her mother always said.

She hadn't cried when she found her mother motionless in her bed, green foam dried around her mouth. She hadn't cried when the neighbors who'd fed her and given her their children's old clothes had sobbed while saying bye to her. She hadn't cried when her aunt had put her on a freezing plane.

Now, as she sat next to this girl who suddenly felt like the only person on this planet who was not a stranger, and ate the dahi and rotis, Rani's eyes started to leak.

No one said anything about the tears. Vinny chattered on as they ate. Her voice fell like soothing music on Rani's ears. Nobody had ever talked to Rani when she ate. The girl's mother kept filling Rani's bowl with dahi. Rani kept spooning it into her mouth. She couldn't get enough.

The dahi was sweet. Vinny kept putting sugar in it. It was the best thing Rani had ever tasted. For as long as she lived, she would remember it as the thing that brought her back to life on the day that she learned what there was to live for in this world.

Later, when Rani had eaten so much she could barely move, Usha Auntie—that's what Vinny's mother told Rani to call her—drove her to her aunt's apartment complex. When Rani got out of the car, Vinny jumped out too and wrapped her arms around her.

What are you doing? Rani wanted to ask her, but it seemed like the girl was hugging her. Before things could get properly awkward, Rani heard her name being called behind her. "Rani! Oh God, beta, are you all right?"

Rani freed herself from the girl's hug and ran into her aunt's arms, surprising herself as much as her aunt.

Ever since her aunt had come to get her, Rani hadn't been able to figure out what her game was. Tina had picked her up from the neighbor's house because when they brought Rani home from the cremation grounds, there was a lock on the block of rooms she'd shared with her mother. The landlord had been waiting to take the rooms back, and he had.

Her aunt looked nothing like her mother, but she had the same stubborn silence, as though the world didn't deserve her words. Also, just like Mama, not only did she not say much, but she didn't eat much either. All she had in the house was bread, milk, and apples. She worked at the hospital all day. Then she spent the rest of the time listening to self-help tapes on the boom box. On the weekends she spent all day at the temple, singing bhajans and listening to more lectures from people who sounded like they knew everything.

Usha Auntie explained to her aunt that they had found Rani outside McDonald's being questioned by the cops and somehow managed to make it sound like Rani had lost her way.

"My daughter loved having her over." She slipped a yellow note to Tina Maasi with her number on it. "I think our girls would love to get together for a playdate again."

Playdate.

The word made something spread inside Rani. It made the lights in her aunt's dingy living room brighten. It made the memory of the warm kitchen she'd just left vibrate to life around her.

As the adults talked, Vinny leaned over and whispered in Rani's ear. "Next time, instead of running away, just call that number. Please."

Rani nodded. She'd simply have to wait and see what her aunt had in store for her and deal with it. Maybe if she stayed, Vinny and her mother would find a way to get her inside the cake-and-icing house again.

CHAPTER SEVEN

VANDY

Saturday, 7:00 p.m. . . .

As Vandy left Mallika's apartment building, she checked again to see if she could track her phone. The words "Location Not Available" flashed on her screen.

Panic skittered up her sternum. She shoved it down and called her mother again. It went straight to voice mail. Why was Mummy not answering her phone now? Mummy rarely went anywhere. The older she got, the less she seemed to like the people she'd worked so hard to surround herself with. These days the only people she had any interest in hanging around were her grandchildren.

Vandy knew how useless it was, but she texted Mallika again.

I'm worried, can you check in please.

The words sat there undelivered.

Her call went straight to voice mail.

Usually Mallika and she spoke several times a day. Since Vir's death, Mallika checked in on Vandy all the time. There was no way she would disappear like this, knowing how much Vandy would worry. Mallika put everyone else's feelings before her own. Mallika also never lied. And she'd lied about the audition.

Vandy got into her car and started driving to her mother's condo. Much as she wanted to ignore whatever manipulation her mother was up to by tapping at the past, Mummy knew something. If she didn't, she would be just as worried as Vandy. That gave Vandy a moment of relief. But her mother was also getting more and more erratic in her behavior, so the relief didn't last.

You have to learn to give her space. It was something Vir often said too.

I will give her space when she asks for it, Vandy always responded.

She's yours, Vandy. No one is going to take her away from you.

How Vandy had hated when he said that to her. Hated it.

She's ours, she'd snapped.

I know. And we shouldn't feel the need to prove it.

That part he'd only ever said after his two daily scotches. Then apologized for saying it, of course.

Every time he apologized, Vandy felt him waiting, waiting for her to say something in return, to acknowledge something, causing a dark gaping hole to open up between them. As soon as it did, they'd each worked hard to close it up.

Sometimes Vandy had felt him getting ready to say something, the words forming on his tongue like the butterfly wings of premonition. She'd stopped him. Cut him off. Done whatever it took to seal the void that could swallow up their family in one gulp.

There were things that were best left unsaid.

But your daughter doesn't get that choice? To leave things she doesn't want to say unsaid? Vir's voice whispered in her ear.

He didn't get to be reasonable. Not when he'd left her. Not when she had no idea how to live without him. She'd never known how.

Maybe that's what had happened. Her own grief had caused her to let Mika's grief go unaddressed, and now it had festered and blown up inside her.

Vandy always advised people to heed their own opinions first: no one else needed to believe you deserved what you wanted but you. No matter what Vir's voice said, her daughter was not well within her rights to disappear without telling her mother where she was. It also wasn't who Mallika was.

What if it wasn't Mallika at all? What if someone had hurt her?

Before Vandy could talk herself out of it, she called Billu, Pinky's brother. He was a detective in the LAPD.

"You know you can call me anytime," Billu said in his big voice when she apologized for calling so late. "You're family, and you know the wife is a fan. I'll get a special treat at dinner when I tell her I spoke to you. Oh, and thank you for the aloo parathas you sent over last week." Every time Vandy's cook made aloo parathas, Billu's favorite food, Vandy sent some over.

She filled him in on how Mallika hadn't shown up at the airport or dance practice and how she wasn't at her apartment or answering her phone.

There was a long beat of silence. Vandy wasn't sure if it was professional concern or him judging her parenting.

Finally he spoke. "Has she been in touch with anyone? Told anyone if she's going somewhere?"

Vandy hesitated. "I spoke to her around noon yesterday. No one has heard from her since."

He made another thoughtful sound. "Anything else I should know?"

"She just got a rejection from an audition."

"The *Mahabharata*?" He tut-tutted. "Poor child." Naturally Pinky would tell everyone about the audition.

"Mummy thinks she needs a moment to deal with it privately."

"When did Usha Auntie talk to her last?"

"I'm not sure. I'm going over to find out. But it's been a week since Mika found out."

"Oh," Billu said with some surprise. "She seemed her usual happy self at dance practice three days ago. And, well." He coughed out a laugh. "Anyone who is happy while teaching my sister to dance has to be a-okay." He gave another chuckle. "I'll make some calls. Send me a recent picture, and I'll circulate it to see if anyone's seen anything. I'll also run a trace on her phone number. Go ahead and talk to your mother, but . . ." He cleared his throat.

"But?"

"Well, she has been spending a lot of time with Pinky and Tinku. And you know how much they always know."

Of course! Pinky and Tinku with their spymaster skills had to know something. They always knew something.

Vandy thanked him again, promised to send parathas this week and a signed copy of her new book for his wife. Then she changed course and hit the gas.

～

When Vandy arrived at her brother's house, it was unusually quiet, with just Pinky and Tinku there. Both of them were impeccably dressed as always. Matching highlights and blowouts. Linen shirts over designer jeans. Vandy was still in her silk blouse and skirt from the seminar. She'd removed her pearls in the car.

Vandy couldn't remember the last time she'd visited either Taj's or Raj's home without at least fifteen more people present. Her brothers had never had a quiet or somber bone in their bodies. Medical school and the pressure of jobs where they saw life and death on a daily basis had turned them serious there for a few years. Or maybe those were just Vandy's memories of those years when sadness and a deep sense of injustice had defined her existence.

Then both her brothers had found love in the form of Pinky and Tinku. The gorgeous and gregarious cousins had been visiting LA from Delhi for a wedding, where they'd met the twins. Chaos had returned to the Mehta family, the kind of chaos Taj and Raj had loved to cause during their childhood.

The smell of sweat and soccer gear layered under the smell of food cooking had constantly permeated their parents' home. Vandy was just three years younger than Taj and Raj, but she remembered feeling entirely alone despite their constant presence until she'd turned twelve.

Pinky placed a steaming cup of coffee in front of Vandy. South Indian filter coffee, half milk and half decoction with a teaspoon of sugar, exactly the way Vandy liked it. Pinky and Tinku were impeccable hostesses. Even more so when the other was present.

Pinky handed Tinku a cup of ginger chai. "Just the way you like it. With too much ginger and too little tea," she said with the sweetest smile.

Tinku returned her sweeter-than-sweet smile. "You know my tastes aren't common. It's so sweet that you always keep that in mind."

"As your older sister-in-law, it's my job to pamper you," Pinky said.

"You mean as my younger sister-in-law," Tinku countered.

Raj was all of two minutes older than Taj, which made Pinky the older sister-in-law, according to the outdated Indian patriarchal norms. Tinku was two months older than Pinky, which made her the older sister-in-law, because she was older. Before they could turn to Vandy and drag her into their bickering, she quickly turned to the matter at hand.

"Mummy thinks Mallika needs space."

"Space?" Tinku said as though it were a foreign word. "Children don't need space! What are they, rockets?"

Pinky nodded in agreement: parenting philosophy was the one thing that always united them. "That does not sound like our Mika at all. Mika is so attached to you. All the time, Mom, Mom, Mom."

"Exactly," Vandy said, sifting past the jibe to the part that mattered. "It's not like her at all. No matter how upset she is about the audition."

Pinky looked confused. "Upset? I wouldn't call how she was acting at practice the last two times *upset*." Her eyes glittered with meaning.

"In fact, she really stepped up her game," Tinku added. "It was like she was all reenergized after that day."

"Which day?" Vandy asked.

"The day she wasn't feeling well and Amey took her home," Tinku said.

"That's not what I heard." Pinky took a sip of her chai.

"I can't believe you have spies at my practice!" Tinku put down her cup with some force.

"As if I have nothing better to do than plant spies. I just overheard Amey talking to Aarav. I pay attention to our children."

Vandy looked from one to the other. "What were Amey and Aarav saying? I need to know exactly what happened."

Pinky raised a smug brow. "Well, maybe Tinku can tell you why she made Mika cry."

"I did not!" Tinku said, then swallowed guiltily. "It wasn't my fault." She pointed a chin at Pinky. "If *someone* hadn't bribed her for all the good choreography and songs, I wouldn't have been upset."

Pinky gasped. "If that's not the thief scolding the cop! You're the one she gave all the good songs and steps to. Everyone knows Amey is Mika's favorite. Especially now."

Vandy let out a bewildered breath. Mallika was a master at managing her maamis. She was the only one who could make them partner up for family board game night. But what had she gotten herself into with this?

"What do you mean *especially now*?" she asked.

The two sisters-in-law exchanged commiserating glances. Suddenly they were on the same side. The side where they didn't want to upset Vandy.

"I need to find her. Please. Just tell me."

"Fine." Tinku took a long, meaningful pause and another sip of chai. "Rex's fiancée cheated on him."

"Who is Rex?" Vandy said, exasperated.

They ignored her. "She cheated on him? I didn't know that. Aarav never tells me anything," Pinky said.

That made Tinku look more than a little gleeful.

"Rex Henderson? Amey's best man? What does this have to do with Mika?" Except Mika had been carrying a torch for that boy since college.

"That's the million-dollar question," Tinku said, voice dripping with intrigue.

"I heard Amey did not take Mika home that day," Pinky said, mirroring Tinku's tone.

Tinku narrowed her eyes. "Mika would never leave my practice if she wasn't actually feeling sick. Amey told me she was going to throw up."

"And, what, our sons never lie to us?" Pinky said with some relish.

"What does all this have to do with Rex Henderson?" Vandy said, trying not to snap. "Or Mika?"

"Have you forgotten the scandal from Amey's engagement party?" Pinky asked.

"There was a scandal?" Vandy couldn't even pretend to follow the conversation. Vir had been the one to keep her up to speed on family gossip.

"Our Mika had wine," Pinky whispered in her hot-gossip voice.

"You know how our girl gets when she drinks wine." This time Tinku matched her tone. "So you can't really blame her."

"Blame her for what?" Vandy said.

Both her sisters-in-law gawked at her like she was the worst mother on earth. "She called him *Sex!*" they said together.

"In front of his fiancée," Pinky said.

"She said it really loudly too. Just as the music turned down. But that's our Mika's luck," Tinku said. "Then she ran out of the party, making everything worse. How can you not remember this?"

Vandy had made a brief appearance at Amey's engagement party and then gone home because she was traveling for a seminar early the next morning.

Her poor Mika had to have been mortified. Now that Vandy thought about it, she remembered Mika telling her the story. Mika was always full of anecdotes like this. Now that it was coming back to her, a lot of people had made fools of themselves at that particular party. Pinky had climbed on the coffee table and danced the bhangra, and one of the table legs had broken.

"I still don't know what any of this has to do with Rex Henderson?"

Pinky sighed as though Vandy were a lost cause. "I overheard our boys say that Mika went with Amey and Rex to the bars that night." She slid Tinku a side-eye. "After Tinku made her cry."

Tinku glared at Pinky, then gave Vandy an apologetic look.

"Okay. But that was a week ago. Do you think Amey knows where Mika is now?" This would explain why Tinku, who was unabashedly neurotic when it came to the whereabouts of all the kids in the family and not just her own, was so calm about Mallika going missing.

"All I'll say is that rebounds are not a good thing," Pinky threw in randomly, and Vandy had the sense that she was causing a distraction to help Tinku out.

This was another reason Vandy never got involved in Pinky and Tinku's cross fire. You never knew when the tide would turn and you'd be the one taking bullets. The two women were first cousins, and they'd been at this long before Vandy's brothers had met them.

"Are you trying to tell me that something is happening between Rex and Mika?"

There was silence. Silence that spoke a million words.

"Has she gone somewhere with Rex?" Why would Mika not tell Vandy that? She never kept any of the guy stuff to herself. In fact sometimes Vandy got so much detail from her daughter that she wished for some discretion.

Vandy hadn't been able to tell her mother about Vir until after they eloped, so she loved that her daughter told her everything. It was wonderful how much the world had changed since she was young.

"They were certainly acting like they were keen on going somewhere with each other last week, if you get my meaning." Pinky wiggled her brows.

"She was here with him?" Vandy asked, losing control of the conversation yet again.

"Word on the street is that she's been with him pretty much every minute since that evening they went to the bars," Tinku said, jubilant at being able to deliver the final punch.

"What does 'word on the street' even mean?" Vandy asked. "Did Amey tell you this?"

There was no way her daughter would hide something like this from her over an entire week. Sure, Vandy had been on tour, and their conversations had been mostly check-ins, but Mika had to know Vandy would make time for anything she needed.

Vandy scrolled through her calendar on her phone. The past eleven months were a solid block of seminars and events. It was the only way Vandy had known how to keep going after Vir.

Had she not been there for Mallika? Their calls last week had lasted a few minutes, except when they'd argued. Was their argument more than it seemed? A new kind of panic tightened her chest. This couldn't be happening again. She couldn't lose Mallika.

When Pinky and Tinku shared another commiserating look, Vandy stood. "Is Amey home? Can I speak with him?"

Her nephew, it would seem, was the key to finding Mika.

CHAPTER EIGHT

MALLIKA

Seven days ago . . .

It's hard to explain what it's like to be at a bar with two men in scrubs. Especially two men who look like the two I'm with. The attention of every single woman here seems to be entirely focused on our corner, and it is *not* a small bar.

"Have you ever wondered why only women wear engagement rings?" I ask, taking a bottle of Sculpin IPA from Amey.

"Because the bloodshed involved in doubling the diamond supply to all the Western nations might be more than the world needs to bear?" Rex says, raising his beer at me.

"Oh God, are you making a reference to blood diamonds? Now, when the two of you have already slid those humongous rocks on your fiancées' fingers? Hypocritical much?"

"Grace wanted a ruby. And I used our naani's ring. So, no blood diamonds here." My cousin throws what looks suspiciously like a warning look at his friend, who is currently standing close enough to me where I'm afraid he can smell my arousal at the nearness of his body, which has a way of radiating waves of heat more intoxicating than the beer in my hand.

This is probably why I brought up the engagement status, to remind myself that he had passed on the offer of my heart several years ago.

That's one reason, anyway. The other reason I brought it up is because we're under attack from every woman in the room, and it seems absurdly unfair that they have no idea that they're wasting their lusting glances. As I know only too well.

A woman wearing only the front half of a blouse (that's actually seriously gorgeous) sidles close to where we are standing and pretends to peer at the label of Rex's (with an *R*, I firmly remind myself) beer. "I was wondering what you were drinking," she says in the breathiest voice. I want to immediately try out that voice, but I'm not drunk enough yet to not know how terribly rude that would be.

"He's engaged," I blurt out. Turns out, I *am* drunk enough for that. Because it's a myth that wine hits me fast. Beer hits me just as fast. "So you're wasting your time."

The woman looks extremely confused by this very simple declaration. She turns away from me and tries to catch Amey's gaze, but I'm two steps ahead of her. "He's getting married in two months." I point at myself, still in my dance practice ghagra. "Why do you think I'm dressed like this?"

The confused look she throws me this time is justified. This last bit of information is entirely out of context for anyone who has never been to an Indian wedding. With a shrug, she walks away, and I feel like a horrid person. This isn't who I am. "That's a lovely top!" I call after her. "Where is it from?"

She ignores my pathetic attempts at belated friendliness. When I look back at Rex, he's grinning at me as though I've done something hilarious and adorable. One of those looks that romantic heroes throw at the heroines in romantic comedies when they're being obnoxious and it's making the heroes fall helplessly in love with them.

I point my bottle at him. "You should wear a ring."

That makes him exchange another cryptic look with my cousin, who's been acting awfully strange.

I remind myself that they've only brought me with them because I embarrassed myself by being the one person in my family who can't seem to succeed at anything but failure. Is there anything more humiliating than being twenty-seven and needing to have your naani set up playdates for you? This is obviously a charitable mission to keep me from feeling like a loser.

My bottle is still in Rex's face. "And you should not wear scrubs in public places."

A smooth, glossy sliver of his chest is visible under his absurdly beautiful collarbones. Bulgy biceps push against the shapelessly cut sleeves.

He looks at me like he wants to touch my hand, if only to get the bottle out of his face. Which seems like a fair thing to be able to do. But he does not touch me.

Maybe he can smell failure and finds it disgusting.

I'm fully and painfully aware of just how much I'm wallowing in self-pity right now. I blame it on the feeling that's gripped me ever since my call with Jane. The one that's making me feel like I somehow hit all the wrong genetic branches on our family tree when I tumbled into this world. My naani's words haven't stopped playing in my head.

Oddity.

Oddity.

Can two cousins be any more different?

I'll get over it soon enough. It's not like I didn't know what a long shot it was.

I'm also fully aware that I'm not actually disgusting.

I'm objectively attractive. Sometimes my mother looks at my face and weeps. I don't know if that's something all mothers do, but it makes it difficult to not have a high opinion of your own face.

In this moment, though, that seems insignificant. I realize my beer is still in Rex's face, and I pull my hand away and take a giant swig. "I'm sorry," I say pathetically. I might as well play to my audience.

"What are you sorry about?" he asks, studiedly avoiding Amey's glare and sneaking a touch of my bottle with one absurdly sexy forefinger. Which isn't exactly like his skin touching mine, but blood roars in my ears. His dark, dark eyes change as though he feels it too.

How was his fiancée not dead from overdosing on carnal hormones? The man has cut short my life in just one evening. She's obviously a stronger woman than I am. Given that she brings babies into the world with preternatural skill (I know this because she works at Taj Maama's practice, and he can't stop raving about her) and I herd aunties through dances.

"What are you sorry about?" he asks again, and Amey's glare takes on mythical proportions. Mind you, Amey is usually the least glarey of men, so he's being super weird right now.

"Well, as a doctor, you should be able to wear scrubs anywhere you want. I shouldn't have said anything. I mean, I guess you could just revive anyone who . . ." I trail off.

Our gazes are locked, and I don't know what the hell is going on. For all my enjoying his hotness, I'm not even a little interested in men who are with other women. He is about to stroke my bottle with his finger again, but my suddenly growly cousin takes the bottle out of my hand.

"I don't think this was a good idea," Amey says just as Rex says, "There's something you should know."

Amey's glare gets downright accusatory, and Rex adds, "I'm not that kind of doctor."

My naani is back inside my head. *You should ask him what he does.* I yank the bottle back from Amey. "What do you mean you're not that kind of doctor?"

I have the sense that he's trying to tell me something. Something that doesn't have anything to do with the kind of doctor he is.

"I'm not—"

"He doesn't work as a physician," Amey cuts him off. With uncharacteristic rudeness, I might add.

Rex's shoulders, which are as wide and beautiful as the rest of him, droop infinitesimally.

"What were you going to say before?" I ask, sounding far too desperate.

He fills his lungs with breath and throws another unreadable look at Amey. "I'm not the kind of doctor who revives people when they faint from my scrubs." His half smile returns, hitching his lush lips up on one side in such an incredibly potent way that it's a miracle I don't faint and let him prove his words by letting me die.

This time Rex removes the bottle gently from my hands and hands me a glass of water.

Neither of us look at Amey when he says, "I think we should head home. I'm on call early tomorrow."

The very last thing I care about right now is Amey's work schedule. "What kind of doctor are you, then? What do you do?" I ask Rex. I know for a fact that he graduated medical school with Amey. After he walked away from me, I stopped obsessing over the details of his life, but that doesn't mean a corner of my heart hasn't been keeping track.

"He does research," Amey answers for him.

I open my mouth to say something about how he must have a line of people waiting to be researched by him. But Amey snaps, "Don't."

So I don't. "I'm working on gene sequencing research." This time the glance Rex throws Amey is placating, and it confuses me even more than everything else that's been going on between these two this evening.

"Gene sequencing," I repeat, and my heart races in a whole different way.

"We work on the piece that identifies dominant genes in families and study why and how recessive genes slip through in some cases."

Suddenly everything in the room seems to brighten and come into focus. "You mean like why some people in families are different. Like why Amey is so boring, and I'm so . . . not?"

He grins his ovary-melting grin. "Exactly like that."

My brain starts racing to match my heart. "Holy shit!" This cannot actually be happening.

"What?" both Amey and Rex say together.

I press a hand to my mouth.

"You had one beer, Mika. Please tell me you are not going to throw up." Amey looks concerned. His concern is not unfounded. My stomach wobbles, because the man I once harbored the most massive, painful, and graphic crush on, a man who obviously found me lacking, studies black sheep!

"How the hell did I not know that you study black sheep!"

That's the phrase that's been swirling at the edge of my consciousness ever since that phone call with my agent. Even my own grandmother knows I'm an oddity compared to her other grandchildren.

"That's actually exactly what it's called. The Black Sheep Project." Rex looks impressed, though I haven't done anything remotely impressive.

I drop into a barstool and cross one leg over the other. Suddenly I don't feel quite as woozy from the beer. Something furious rushes through my bloodstream. We're not going anywhere until I get to the bottom of this.

"The Black Sheep Project," I repeat, tasting the oddly satisfying words on my tongue. "So you're looking for a way to explain why I'm nothing like my cousins?"

"What are you talking about? You're exactly like us," Amey says with such force that for the first time this evening I remember why I love him so much. I lean over and hug him.

Sonali Dev

"Why do you feel like you're not like the others in your family?" Rex asks gently. Either he can see through to the storm inside me or he's slid into researcher mode.

"Because she's not a physician and she's the only girl?" Amey says.

"That's not why. For one, we look different." I pull away and tap his nose fondly.

Rex spurts his beer, splattering some on me. "Shit, I'm so sorry." His thumb brushes the liquid off my arm, and the most ridiculous electric sensation sizzles across my skin.

Both of us pull away too quickly, and Amey frowns.

"It's not just the nose. It's the fact that I'm literally the only screwup in this family." Like right now, I'm having all these feelings for someone who is soon to be married to someone else. And everyone can see it.

"You're not a screwup," they both say together.

My stupid eyes start to water again. "I just want to go home."

Rex slaps a few bills on the bar.

Amey hands me a napkin. "It's one audition, Mika," he says gently.

"No, it's not. It's everything. I don't have your confidence, your height, your science-and-math brain." A small smile slips through my tears. "And I actually have rhythm. Good hair. Did I mention a cute nose?"

"You really feel this way?" Rex says as we step out into the chilly LA night.

Leaving the noise of the bar makes everything I'm feeling louder.

I nod and blow my nose into the napkin emblazoned with the bar's name under the picture of a dismembered boar's head.

Rex's eyes have taken on a new light. "This is exactly the kind of sense we're looking for in subjects. People who feel different from others in their family."

"Seriously?" Amey veritably growls.

Rex turns to him. "What the hell are you accusing me of right now?"

"Let's not do this," Amey says.

"I get all the other shit." Rex swirls a hand around Amey's face. "But you know my work is sacrosanct. She can actually help me."

"This was a mistake. We should never have brought her with us," Amey says.

"I'm standing right here!" I snap as they discuss me like I'm not. "And I didn't ask to come here with you."

"Actually you did. You told me you didn't want to go home," Amey says.

"Quit being a jerk, man!" Rex says, getting between my cousin and me. "If you're pissed with me, be pissed with me. Don't take it out on her."

"What the hell are you two talking about?" I look from one livid face to the other.

"I'm going to tell her," Rex says to Amey.

"Tell me what?" Now I want to growl too.

"If you want her to be part of your study, let her be part of your study. Just don't—"

"Amey, what is going on?" I rarely ever raise my voice, but I raise my voice now.

Rex squeezes his temples and takes another deep breath that stretches his scrubs tightly across his chest. "If you really want to be a part of my study." He meets my gaze with an intensity that makes me feel off kilter. A memory from long ago flashes in my head, but I can't put a finger on it. "Just come to the lab tomorrow, and we'll draw your blood and Amey's, and we can run the tests, and then you can fill out the psych evaluations and get into the personality studies. Sound good?"

"Yes! But also, no!"

His thick arched brows rise into the springy curls dancing across his forehead.

"I don't want to wait until tomorrow. I want to do it now. Amey is on call tomorrow. He's here now, we're both here now." The word "now" spins in my head like a kathak dancer gone wild on chakkars. I want to say it over and over again.

Now.

Now.

Now.

"It's ten p.m.," Amey says as though I don't have a cell phone in my hand.

"I can get into the lab anytime," Rex snaps at Amey. Then he turns to me. He seems to see exactly how important this is to me, and I fathom for the first time in my life what the word "kryptonite" means. "Do you really want to do it right now?"

"Yes," I whisper, looking into his eyes as though he's asked me for my soul. Maybe this was the purpose of having him come into my life. To figure this out. To make how I'm feeling right now make sense. "Let's go."

"We're not going anywhere but straight home," Amey says.

I don't want to go home and think about the dances I spent weeks practicing for the audition. I don't want to call everyone I know and tell them that I failed again and pretend like it doesn't matter.

"I don't want to go home," I whisper, deeply ashamed of how distraught I sound. "I want to know why I'm so messed up."

The determination on Amey's face collapses.

"Let's do it. It won't take long," Rex says, before Amey verbalizes more platitudes. "Come on." He starts walking. Then he stops and takes my hand and tugs me along. "The lab is a block from here."

Amey makes another grumbling sound behind us. But he follows.

My hand comes alive in Rex's, and I try to pull it away. Instead of letting it go, Rex tightens his hold. "You're the least messed-up person I've ever met," he says. "Also, I broke up with Lydia three months ago."

CHAPTER NINE

RANI

1984
Thirty-nine years ago . . .

Rani had always wanted to ask Vinny why she made Usha Auntie come back to the McDonald's parking lot that day five years ago. They had already called the cops. They'd already done what they needed to do as good citizens. There had been no good reason to come back to check up on Rani just because she had eaten fries that fell on the ground.

At the start of their friendship, Rani had felt weird asking. Because bringing up how they met had filled her with shame. Rani had been a beggar girl that day and Vinny a princess handing out alms. Asking the question felt like putting that on a contract and signing it. Making it the definition of their entire friendship.

And their friendship was not that.

In the years that followed, the question had become moot. Rani knew why Vinny had done it, and the need to ask simply went away. Vinny had done it because she didn't know how not to stick that "aquiline" Mehta nose she was so self-conscious about into other people's business and help. The good news was that over the past five years, Vinny had grown into that nose beautifully. Although she still didn't see that. She had a hard time seeing anything about herself as beautiful.

Since they'd first met, Rani and Vinny had spent most waking moments with each other. So much so that Usha Auntie often called them by each other's name. Raj and Taj had come up with the nickname Randy—of course they had—and everyone used it as though Vinny and Rani were one unit.

They were.

Rani was no longer a beggar girl. She was in fact flush with cash today. She'd used it to get her hair freshly feathered and blond highlights put in. It was Rani's seventeenth birthday, and she knew Vinny was going to find a totally embarrassing way to throw her a surprise celebration. No matter how many times Rani told her how unnecessary her surprises were.

The first surprise party Vinny threw for her had been Rani's thirteenth birthday, exactly ten months after they first met. Until that day Rani had never celebrated her birthday. The few times her mother had remembered her birthday, she'd slipped five rupees into Rani's hand to buy a chocobar ice cream from the handcart in Bandra station market.

Rani had never been to a birthday party. The girls in her school in Bombay had thrown them, but even when Rani was invited, it had been absurd to think she'd be able to go without a present or the money to get there or a dress to wear. The only thing Rani knew about birthday parties was what she'd read in books: that they were an annual occurrence in some people's lives.

On Rani's thirteenth birthday, which came eleven months after Vinny's own thirteenth birthday, Vinny had faked a stomachache and asked Rani to come over to watch some TV. When Rani got to the Mehta house, she'd found that Vinny had invited their girlfriends from school over. She'd made everyone wear pink pajamas with Rani's face custom printed on them. Even Raj and Taj. It was the first time Rani had blown out a candle on a cake as everyone sang "Happy Birthday." Rani, who prided herself on never crying, had naturally cried for the second time since meeting Vinny.

She'd blamed it on the trauma of seeing Raj and Taj in pink pajamas. Since then Vinny had taken it upon herself to make Rani cry on her birthday every year.

She was four for four.

For Rani's fourteenth, Vinny had organized a bake sale and raised $1,000 because Nathan, the cop Rani had thrown up on after he found her hiding between the dumpsters, had been shot on the job and was in the hospital. They'd taken the check to the hospital and thrown Nathan a party there with cake and pizza for the medical staff and Nathan's officer friends. Rani never said this out loud, but Nathan was the closest thing she'd ever had to a dad. Dharam Uncle, Vinny's dad, was a close second.

For her fifteenth, Vinny had bought tickets to a concert Madonna was opening for. This might have seemed like a simple gift from a girl who could afford most things. It wasn't. First, no one understood what dance meant to Rani, because she acted like it meant nothing. But of course Vinny knew. Rani had been dancing since she was three years old. It was the one thing other than her face and her cynicism that she'd inherited from her mother. It was also how Rani had supported herself since moving to LA.

Rani might have been a classical kathak dancer, but dance had no boundaries, and the first time she'd watched Madonna dancing on Vinny's TV, her jaw had fallen open. *She's blessed by Nataraja himself,* her mother had always said about Ginger Rogers. But that's because she hadn't seen Madonna. When Rani watched Madonna dancing, every cell in her body sat up and merged with her. She became the story Madonna was telling. The only time Rani felt like she really owned her own body was when she danced. Madonna danced as though she understood this, her movements taking ownership of the air around her,

her entire being becoming one with the universe. She'd made Rani fall into her own dance in a more powerful way.

Vinny had somehow saved up enough money to get them both tickets. Then she'd made up a complicated lie for Usha Auntie and Dharam Uncle, because they would never let the girls go to a music concert. Just as Vinny and Rani were sneaking out with Taj's car (something Vinny had paid for by doing his chores for a year), Usha Auntie had caught them red handed.

She'd wished Rani a happy birthday. Then she'd driven the girls to the concert herself, even though she thought Western music was the root of "everything that was wrong with young people these days." So yes, Rani had thrown her hands around Usha Auntie and sobbed like a baby. It was the best day of her entire life. Vinny had been grounded for three months after they'd come home. For those three months, the two of them had seen each other only in school. It had been tough punishment, Madonna notwithstanding.

For Rani's sixteenth, Vinny had spent close to a year contacting every person from Tina Maasi's childhood to track down pictures of Rani's mother. Because in a moment of weakness, Rani had let slip that she didn't have a single picture of her mother. Vinny had even managed to find some pictures from Virju Maharaj's studio, the place her mother had danced at before she'd lost her ability to do anything but drink.

From never hoping to see her mother's face ever again, Rani had gone to owning a leather-bound album with seven pictures of her mother starting from when she was a toddler to her performing onstage as the most beautiful woman Rani had ever seen. Rani had lost all dignity that day and sobbed until her body hurt.

Not this year, though. Vinny had already made her way through all the things Rani had ever wanted. So Rani's crying days were over. At seventeen, Rani was a suave woman of the world. They both were. Albeit in very different ways. They were headed off to college in a few months.

In return for Vinny's gift-giving talent, Rani had never been able to do anything interesting for Vinny's birthday. Her family always threw one of their big parties with relatives and friends. Then they took Vinny's friends to Disneyland. The only thing Rani could do was help Usha Auntie decorate the house and bake the cake, and of course pick out Vinny's clothes and help her look like a million bucks. If not for Rani, Vinny would still be dressing like a twelve-year-old.

Rani had literally had to drag Vinny to the salon to get her hair layered and get some respectable bangs that Rani could tease out for her. Rani's own hair was teased out to a good six inches away from her scalp in all directions like the cool chick she was. Not everyone was as blessed with their hair as Rani, but Vinny's waves were actually better for the current style, especially with the use of the right mousse and gel. The frustrating thing was that Vinny refused to even try on her own.

That would be a waste of time, wouldn't it? You'd make me change anything I wore anyway. That was Vinny's excuse.

She was right. *Well, aren't you a lucky girl to get the Rani Parekh styling for free.*

I am. And Vandy Mehta does not look a gift horse in the mouth.

That's why they were best friends. They were good at entirely different things. Vinny was too lazy to try anything fun, and Rani was too jaded to do anything unless it was fun.

She'd decided this at fifteen. The day she'd figured out how to stop cleaning houses with her aunt. Pulling hair plugs out of drains from the age of twelve to fifteen was enough to get doing not-fun stuff out of her system.

Soon after Rani had moved in, Tina Maasi's hours at the hospital as a nurse aide had been reduced. They'd asked her to get some new certification, and she'd had neither the money nor the inclination. So, Tina had decided to start cleaning some of the big houses that were being built in Orange County.

Sonali Dev

Not only had running away brought Vinny and the Mehtas into Rani's life, but she'd also found Nathan. Every Sunday after church he took her to lunch at Taco Bell. It was the only fast-food place where Rani could get anything vegetarian that wasn't lettuce, fries, or bread.

Nathan and his partner had come by to check up on Rani the day after the dumpster incident. The fake address Rani had given the cops hadn't worked because Usha Auntie had given them the right address after she'd driven Rani home.

Nathan had made it clear to Tina Maasi that he was going to check in regularly to make sure Rani was being treated well enough to not attempt running away again. This had made Tina insist on taking Rani with her when she cleaned to make sure no more running-away incidents happened.

As spotless as her aunt's own apartment was, she was so bad at cleaning for other people that Rani had started to help, afraid that Tina would lose the work and they'd no longer be able to afford even what little food Tina bought. Rani was fully aware of how little one needed to eat to survive. But she wasn't in the mood for giving starvation another whirl, so she'd helped. The more she helped, the less her aunt did.

Basically Tina played her bhajans and her Osho lectures on her Walkman, putting on headphones and sitting in a corner meditating with her rosary japamala while Rani went down on her hands and knees and scrubbed.

This would have been a bad thing if it hadn't resulted in Rani being able to get Tina to give her pocket money like a rich girl. Rani also kept the tips for doing a good job.

Truth was Rani didn't hate cleaning, but she didn't like it either. After three years of doing it, she'd needed to move on. And thanks to dance, she could.

That first summer in LA, anytime she wasn't hanging out at the Mehta house—which turned out to be just about a mile from Tina's apartment—Rani had found herself stuck at the Hindu temple, where her aunt got her in-person satsang fix (because the continuous lectures on tape weren't enough). At the temple, Rani had met Reshma Auntie, who taught kathak to all the Indian girls in Orange County.

The only time Rani had ever seen her mother happy was when she was dancing. At fifteen, Pushpa Parekh had run away from her home in Dakor in Gujarat to become a dancer in Bombay. At least that's what the man who'd sold her the dream had convinced her of. When Rani was very young and before alcohol became Pushpa's medicine and escape, she had taught at a kathak school. Which was how Rani had learned to dance before she learned to walk. Or that's what her mother told people back when she still considered talking to people a worthwhile exercise.

It had been years since Rani had danced. Then at the temple with Tina, she'd heard the taranas playing on the tabla. She'd been on her way to the restroom to escape the sermons that put her to sleep. The music had gripped her body, and she had moved toward it automatically, her feet tingling with the rhythm and craving the beat.

Dhal tin tin na
Ta dhin dhin dha
Dha tin tin na
Ta dhin dhin dha

Over and over and round and round.

Some thirty little girls in glittery churidar kurtas filled the large hall. Each one of them was doing her own thing as the teacher struggled to herd them like kittens and get them to tap their feet and hold their hands in mudras.

Without thinking about it, Rani slipped into the class and started helping some of the girls get it right.

When Reshma finally noticed her, she hurried toward her through the rows of girls. She'd obviously meant to yell at Rani, the way she'd been yelling at the girls. But when she saw them follow Rani and lift their chins and elongate their spines, she stopped in her tracks.

Good, because it so happened that Rani had just decided that she would no longer stand for people yelling at her. Vinny's mother had demonstrated it for her just the day before. *If someone is rude to you, first you tell them, politely, that they're being rude. If they don't stop, you walk away and let them yell at themselves.*

"Who's your guru?" Reshma Auntie asked in the tone one used on adults, when Rani was in fact all of twelve.

Rani had not been inside Virju Maharaj's dance school for years, but she said his name, "Virju Maharaj," with all the confidence that her mother embodied when she danced.

Reshma touched both ears, the worshipful gesture artists in India used to express reverence for the masters.

"How old are you?" she asked.

"Fourteen," Rani lied. Because people here tended to talk to you like an imbecile if you said twelve.

"Are you visiting from India for the summer?"

"I just moved here."

"Are you looking for a new guru?" Reshma's eyes lit up.

"I can't afford it. I live with my aunt. I'm an orphan." She used abhinaya—the art of facial expressions in dance—to express the full extent of the pathos that went with being an orphan.

The poor woman took the information the way it was intended, like a punch to the heart.

Rani danced right into the hole it opened up. "I'm looking for a job for the summer. I can learn from you but also assist you when you teach." She threw a glance around the unruly bunch of girls.

And that's how Rani had managed to have two streams of income from the age of twelve to fifteen. At fifteen she'd been able to drop the cleaning and switch only to dance. Between teaching and performing at local weddings and festivals with Reshma and their troupe of students, there was enough money to be made.

Rani had saved enough to pay for expenses at community college. Her tuition was being covered by her academic scholarship.

She'd also bought herself a car for her seventeenth birthday. A used Volkswagen Beetle that was now bright orange, her favorite color. When she bought the car, it was white, but Raj's girlfriend Eva's brother owned a body shop, and Raj had gotten him to paint it for Rani. In return Rani had done Eva's hair and makeup for some fancy soiree.

Rani pulled into the Mehtas' driveway. Since today was Rani's birthday, it wasn't a surprise that Vinny had an emergency. Even though Vinny's birthday emergencies were invariably some sort of life-altering surprise for Rani, she still worried that this time it would be something bad. That this time it might really be an emergency.

Before Rani could get out of the car, Vinny and the entire Mehta clan ran out of the house toward her. Raj and Taj, Dharam Uncle, Usha Auntie, even Tina Maasi and Nathan. Rani groaned. *Here it comes.*

What the hell did Vinny have planned this year?

"I can't believe you're late," Vinny said, bouncing on her feet. "At least you look great."

"I was getting my hair done because, well . . ." Rani waved a hand at the gathered crowd. Raj and Taj were dragging bags behind them.

"Why do RT have bags with them?" Rani asked. "Are they going somewhere?"

Vinny laughed because the bags were bright pink. "No. But we are. Or we were, if you haven't caused us to miss our flight."

"Flight?" Rani said as she jumped out of the car and let everyone shower her with hugs. She hated planes. They were too cold for her.

Usha Auntie brought out a cake with a seven-shaped candle and a one-shaped candle. The cake had a red apple iced on it with the words "Happy Birthday, Dancing Queen!"

"What's going on?"

"Just hurry up and blow out the candles," Vinny said as Dharam Uncle lit them with his cigarette lighter. Vinny was in a full-blown excited panic that sometimes triggered her asthma. "We're for real going to miss our flight."

Rani did as she was told. Then let everyone feed her cake. Vinny nibbled a tiny bite when Rani fed some into her mouth. She was on another one of her diets. Usha Auntie had taken her to some new dietitian to "restructure her metabolism."

Vinny hated talking about it, and Rani wasn't about to poke at something everyone already poked at her too much about.

As Usha Auntie pushed another piece of cake into Rani's mouth, Tina Maasi and Nathan wished her luck.

Rani didn't think she'd ever seen them this excited about anything before.

"Okay, you're all scaring me. Where are we going?"

"I'll tell you in the car. We can't miss our flight."

"Okay, I'm in the car," Rani said, getting in the back next to Vinny. "Are you abducting me?"

"Yes, she's taking you to the police station to put you on a train," Taj said, pulling out of the driveway, and Raj laughed.

"Not funny," Rani said, although it was pretty funny. "Why was an apple on the cake?" she asked Vinny.

"Dear Lord, we're going to play twenty questions until you can figure out where we're going, aren't we?" Vinny made an exaggeratedly put-upon face.

Rani sat up. "New York? You're taking me to New York?"

Vinny's smile exploded with excitement.

"Why?"

"Because you've always wanted to see it."

"No, I haven't."

"No? Bummer." She slapped the side of her head. "Saroj Khan must not have known that when she decided to hold her workshop auditions there."

Rani jumped so hard she hit her head on the roof of Taj's car. She pushed a hand to her mouth. "You are flipping kidding me! How could you possibly have found that out when even I did not know?"

Saroj Khan was Rani's favorite Bollywood choreographer of all time. Rani had performed every dance Ms. Khan had ever choreographed. She was single-handedly changing Bollywood dance. It used to be either pure classical bharata natyam or kathak, or then slow awkward movements that mimed the emotions of the songs. Saroj Khan had fused classical dance and folk dance and Western dance and turned them into a new dance form all its own, the kind of dance that turned music into an invitation, made people want to jump up and join in.

"Because I wrote to her," Vinny said.

"You what?"

"I wrote to her to ask if she was ever going to do workshops in the USA."

"She did not write back!"

"She did. Because I also sent her a videotape of you dancing."

"Vinny!"

"Rani!"

"She's going to audition you first, but you know you'll ace it. Then it's a monthlong workshop. A handpicked class of twenty and Saroj."

Rani was crying. Of course she was. She didn't even care. "I can't go away for a month. I'm teaching Reshma Auntie's summer classes."

Even as she said it, she knew Vinny had taken care of it.

Vinny gave her one of her smug looks. She had cleared everything. She had even packed Rani's bag with her dancing clothes.

"Are you going with me?" She sniffled as Raj and Taj ruffled her hair.

"Are there not two bags in the car?"

Rani wasn't a hugger. Touching someone's entire body with yours was weird. Vinny was the one who initiated hugs. Rani gave Vinny's shoulder a squeeze and then leaned over and gave her a hug. "What will you do in New York for a month?"

"I'm taking a class in creative nonfiction."

"Really?"

"I've been planning it . . ."

"All year," they both said together.

"You have to stop doing this," Rani said, blowing her nose on the tissue Taj handed her.

Vinny pulled her close again. "Not on your life."

CHAPTER TEN

VANDY

Saturday, 9:00 p.m. . . .

Vandy wasn't going to be able to talk to Amey for at least a few more hours. Her nephew was performing emergency surgery. Her other nephew, Aarav, had just flown to India for last-minute wedding shopping and alterations with his bride-to-be. Vandy tried to call him, but Aarav was not reachable either.

Vandy was not one for conspiracy theories, but she had to wonder if her nephews had been instructed not to take her calls. Would Mallika do that? Could she really be angry with Vandy?

Vandy tried to remember the tone of that last fight. Had Mallika actually sounded that heartbroken? Or was Vandy bringing what she now knew to her memories?

I thought Vandy Guru never lied, her daughter had said when Vandy tried to tell her that she had faith in her. Mallika never spoke to her like that. There had been so much rawness in the accusation.

Vandy tried to explain that she didn't want Mallika to get hurt. Then she'd offered to help with Netflix, and Mallika became even more upset and accused Vandy of not understanding what it was like to truly want something.

Those were the words that rang in Vandy's ears now.

I wanted to be your mom so badly that nothing else mattered. How did she even need to say the words? It was all Vandy had ever wanted. *I know what it is to pay too high a price for wanting something that much.*

Mallika had gone oddly silent at that. She'd backed away. Apologized. They'd decided to finish the conversation after she got back from her tour. Why had Vandy ignored the feeling that something might be wrong, that Mika might have misunderstood her words?

Vandy couldn't go home. Not until she knew where Mallika was.

She pulled her car into a parking spot outside her office. But she couldn't go inside just yet. Like every other space, her office was steeped in Vir and Mallika, in their life together.

How had Vir always known exactly how to handle Mika, when he hadn't understood why Vandy wanted her so badly? Fatherhood had been optional to him.

Why isn't this enough? You and me, why aren't we enough? he'd asked over and over.

For the first thirty years of Vandy's life, it had been a live thing inside her: the faith that she was put on this earth to nurture someone else, to be a mother. The day she first held Mallika in her arms, she'd known she was right. It wasn't that motherhood completed her in the way of clichés. Instead motherhood had lit a new fire inside her, intensified her search for making her time on this earth amount to something. It didn't matter that no one understood. It didn't matter what she had to give up.

Was it worth it?

There it was again. The voice she'd avoided for twenty-seven years.

Before the memories paralyzed her, she let herself out of the car. It was hard enough to put one foot in front of the other with Vir gone. She made her way into her office, a converted old Victorian on a quiet Manhattan Beach street.

Just like with their home, Vir was the one who'd found the place and decorated it. He'd handpicked the white shabby-chic furniture, the yellow and lime accessories and accents. He'd always made spaces beautiful for her, knowing she loved the result but had no talent for the doing. Ignoring the spasm in her heart, she traced a finger over the carved desk with the glass top and signed in to her computer.

Vandy always read every single letter she got for her Dear Agony Auntie column. Almost all of them came in as emails now, with the number of paper letters having been reduced almost to nothing.

When Vandy had first started her blog, Vir had loved to send her made-up letters.

Dear Agony Auntie,

Can your wife be too perfect for you?

Sincerely,
Smitten Mutton

He'd hide the letters around the place for her to find. She'd leave him her responses the same way.

Dear Smitten Mutton,

I'm sure your wife has some flaws. Like maybe she loves the mutton curry you make more than she loves you. Get to the bottom of the cause of her love and you'll have your answer.

Mindfully,
Agony Auntie

When Mallika was old enough, Vir had pulled her into their game.

> Dear Agony Auntie,
>
> My child thinks her mother might be hugging her too hard. I've told her she does the same thing to me and I'm just fine. Is it okay to tell your young child that you have to roll with the lot life gives you, and that a mother who stifles you with the strength of her love is actually not a bad problem to have?
>
> Sincerely,
> Smitten Dad

> Dear Smitten Dad,
>
> Your wife and your daughter are both lucky to have you. I hope your wife is doing you special favors for understanding her so well.
>
> Mindfully,
> Agony Auntie

Vandy stared at her computer screen, eyes dry. How she craved the relief of tears. How easily they'd once come. How ruthlessly she'd cut them off. Now they refused to help her wash even a drop of the pain away.

She opened the new emails that had come in today. Ever since she started the column over two decades ago, Vir and she had always read the letters together. It was no surprise that she hadn't been able to answer a single letter for close to a year now.

Vir and she had continued the routine of reading the letters and answering them together through his treatment, even on the worst days.

They'd needed this normal thing from their life before the diagnosis, when the doctor had made no bones about how little time he had left.

Vir had insisted on keeping their routines. He'd insisted on not changing their life any more than was absolutely necessary. He'd kept the cancer from everyone but Vandy for as long as he could. She'd had to force him to tell Mika.

She'll never forgive you, Vir, if you take away the chance to store up her memories.

But I don't want her to have memories tainted with pain.

When they'd weighed the pain of the memories with the importance of actually having them, telling Mika had been the only answer.

They'd been good at that, at dissecting problems, dismantling them and letting solutions appear from the pieces. Together. They'd done it with the letters. They'd done it with the plots of his books.

They solved problems, didn't create them.

At least that's what they'd done in this iteration of their marriage. This second phase. After they'd lost too much and gained everything. What they had left had been too precious to risk on conflict.

Was she glad for having done what she'd done to keep him and Mallika? How could she answer that?

Vandy let her fingers tap the keys on her keyboard. Thousands of emails had collected over the year. Usually she sorted the ones that seemed like good fits for the column as they came in. Subjects she hadn't addressed recently. Universal challenges that were relevant to the broadest audience. Issues that spoke to her personally. Things with hard yet obvious answers the sender refused to see.

Every problem came with a solution built into it.

The letters sat in an unsorted mountain in her inbox, waiting for her to point out those solutions. But she couldn't touch them. Today marked 330 days since Vir had left her.

All the way inside her heart, she felt alone. The kind of alone she didn't remember feeling since she was a little girl. Through most of her childhood, the start of a new school year had caused a giant ball of terror in her belly. The terror of being seen. The terror of being unseen. A deep sense of being unwanted frozen hard inside her.

You smell.

Why is your nose so big?

Your arms are like tree trunks.

Your hair is like a bird's nest.

Your food smells like dog farts.

Her mother's secret ingredient in parathas was chaat masala, her special recipe heavy on rock salt. Vandy had loved those parathas. Then she'd hated that she loved them.

It was easier to not even try to make friends. To eat quickly and then volunteer to help the special ed teachers during lunch period. To shut everything else out—the voices of the other kids, their mocking, their discomfort at her presence. Being called painfully shy was easier.

Until she was twelve and she'd finally been seen. *Seen.*

Someone had seen her life for what it was, and just like that she'd been able to see her own life for what it was too: blessed. It had helped her see herself, helped her know she could do something with her life, even though for the longest time she'd had no idea what that was.

It had been a few years after Mallika's birth that she'd started Dear Agony Auntie as a personal blog to share answers to common parenting questions. Then the types of questions had turned toward family and relationships, and it had turned into a comprehensive advice column.

Together Vir and she had always kept a bank of answered letters drafted and ready to go. It had helped Vandy during her seminar tours and book deadlines. Dear Agony Auntie had been Vir and her joint project, but he'd never taken credit. He'd insisted that he was just a sounding board.

Sometimes I just watch you talk out the problem and I'm filled with wonder. You know you were born to do this, Vandy.

It had filled her with purpose: having answers. Seeing clearly what people didn't seem to see about their own lives. Sometimes she wondered if it was because of the lack of stakes for herself, but the clarity had been stunning. She'd helped people address everything from gaslighting parents to sabotaging in-laws to predatory friends. But even more crucially, she'd tried to help them see that we, as humans, did all this to ourselves too. That was the real bridge to cross, to know who you were and embrace that. Over and over and over again, she showed her readers that it was okay to want things and to choose them.

That was the soul of *Vandy Guru's Rules for Life.*

People thought identifying what they wanted was hard. They thought knowing what to do to get it was even harder. As for the consequences, the price, no one gave that a thought until after it was too late. But that was the part that decided the quality of your life. That was also the part that only worked out if you came at identifying what you wanted from a place of absolute honesty. Because consequences were the most brutal truth of life, and you could handle them only if your desires rose from the truest version of yourself.

Vandy's life with Mallika and Vir defined everything she was. So, yes, she'd make every one of the same choices again. And whatever her daughter was upset about, she'd make it right.

She opened one of the emails.

Dear Agony Aunty,

My wife and I have been married for ten years. I am very much in love with her. But before we married she'd told me that she needs to go away for one weekend every year and I couldn't ask her questions about it. She assured me it wasn't another man, so I promised. Outside of that weekend every year we have a near-perfect marriage. Last year, I hired a private investigator to find out where she goes and found out she has been meeting the same woman every year. I suspect they are having a lesbian affair.

I don't want to leave her, but I don't want to go on being married to a woman who might be in love with someone else.

—Hate being lied to

The words on the screen swam before her. The contents of the letters had always separated themselves into facts and solutions for her. Now she looked at the words, but she couldn't do it. She couldn't break them into pieces that made sense.

It was the last thing she'd done with Vir before she had to let him go. She'd read a letter to him, and they'd dissected it until there was an answer.

When she signed "Mindfully, Agony Auntie," Vir had been smiling. That had been his final breath.

Dear Hate being lied to . . .

The words formed in her head, her fingers hovered over the keyboard, but she could not type them.

When Vir died, he'd left Vandy with fifty responses ready to go. She was on her last two letters in the bank. He'd made sure she didn't have to get back to the letters by herself for close to a year. He'd given her a year to heal.

How did you ever think it would be enough, Vir?

The grief had gotten worse, not better.

She felt limbless. Unable to move. Just the way Mummy had said.

Go be Vandy Guru and switch compartments.

But she couldn't. She couldn't do anything until she knew where Mika was.

She called her mother again. "Please answer," she chanted under her breath. "Please."

"I can't remember the last time I had so many missed calls from you," Mummy started with a swipe. But at least she answered.

"Mallika is missing, Mummy. And you know something."

"I know many things. When was the last time you cared?"

"Why are you not worried that she can't be found?"

"Because I know she doesn't want to be found right now."

A wave of relief swept through Vandy. "So she's safe?"

"Inasmuch as we can ever be safe in the presence of lies."

"What are you talking about? What lies?"

Her mother laughed. "When we bury truths, that's a lie. Isn't that what you told me once? Anyway, it's poker night, and I can't be late. They don't deal anyone in once they've started."

"Where is she, Mummy?"

"You'll find out soon enough. Stop calling the cops and wasting their time. No one has kidnapped her. The answer is closer to home." With that she was gone.

CHAPTER ELEVEN

MALLIKA

Six days ago . . .

I just woke up in his bed. In his bed!
It's the most beautiful bed I've ever been in. Bright white with the fluffiest pillows and comforter: it's like being swallowed up by clouds.

I pinch myself so hard that a yelp escapes me. A deep chuckle reaches me from the other end of the room. My cheeks warm. Fine. My entire body heats, and I push myself off the magical mattress and sit up, clutching the white comforter to my breasts like the heroine in a very artsy, very sexy film. The kind that makes sex out to be like a slo-mo rendition of *Swan Lake.*

There is no real reason to be clutching the comforter thusly, because I'm wearing a T-shirt. *His* T-shirt.

If there is an inch of my skin that isn't already heated, it heats up now. My full-bodied blush is complete.

"You always wake up smiling?" Why is it so sexy the way he always turns statements into questions?

"You always make like Edward Cullen and watch strange women sleeping?"

"Old Eddie always left before Bella saw him. Also, you're not half as strange as you think you are."

There it is. Proof that he is trying to get me to fall in love with him again. I know it for sure now. First, he just admitted to reading *Twilight*, and second: "You think I'm less strange than I think I am! Are you trying to seduce me with that tongue?"

A blush heightens his color. Which makes me blush even more. God, why can't I be one of those smooth women who can do banter without saying something mortifying?

You fell in love with him once, I remind myself, *and he chose someone else.*

"I wasn't watching you. If you notice, I'm sitting at my desk all the way over here, and it faces away from you." He twists his body to demonstrate his meaning. "I only turned because you yelped."

"I pinched myself."

He looks confused, and I kick myself again for practically admitting that waking up in his room is too good to be true.

My mortification must be obvious, because he looks at me in that gentle way again. The look that made me jump him last night. I think.

"How are you feeling this morning?"

I would feel much better if I remembered what had happened between us last night. So I ask him instead of answering his question.

"You don't remember?" He presses a hurt hand into his chest, but his eyes sparkle with humor. Just like mine, they're so dark they're almost jet black. But unlike mine, they're lined with the thickest lashes, and there's a bottomless quality to them that has always made me feel like I'm about to drown. To lose myself.

"I remember some things." I wish I could sound coquettish, but I just end up sounding nervous, and fidgeting with the sheet doesn't help. How much did I have to drink last night? How far had my debauchery gone?

My eyes have to be filled with questions. Instead of answering, he jumps out of his chair. "Let me get you some coffee," he says quickly and leaves.

I lift the comforter and look down at myself. Yup, just the T-shirt. Am I sexy enough to get up and cavort around a man's home in just a shirt?

You're twenty-seven years old. You should be ashamed of how much of an idiot you are, I tell myself. Then I attempt to turn into a rolled-up crepe in his flat sheet. Yes, he's the kind of guy who uses a flat sheet under his comforter. Never in my seven-year-long sexually active life (although the activity has been neither extensive nor exceptional) have I ever been with a man who uses a flat sheet.

His face when he told me he broke up with his fiancée flashes in my head. Why had no one told me? Why had Amey not told me?

Because everyone and their cousin knew how smitten you were.

Had my grandmother known about his breakup too? Is that why she forced Amey and Rex to take me out last night?

I'm never speaking to Amey again.

I hadn't spoken to him the entire time we were at the lab.

Rex had let us into the ridiculously chichi space that housed the lab and the headquarters of the company he is partial owner of. Something he'd been remarkably cool about when he took us there. He'd told me he was part owner only after I outright asked what he did there. I only asked because he talked about his business and his work the way I feel about dancing.

Or the way I used to feel, because I still can't think about my call with Jane without pain lancing through my chest.

Sounds filter in from all the way across his (also absurdly chichi) apartment. It sounds like he's grinding coffee beans, and I have the sense that I've wandered inside the *Fifty Shades* movie, where I'm the ingenue held captive by a billionaire, and I'm too dumb to know it just because he has a penthouse and a body that could be in *Penthouse.* If

Penthouse were made for women, that is. This is all pure conjecture, because I've never seen an issue of *Penthouse* in my life. Also, I'm pretty certain I've never seen Rex's actual body, uncovered by clothes, outside of my imagination.

Thankfully, Rex's apartment is more Pottery Barn than the billionaire version of minimalist spaceship. As if on cue I step on the softest, deepest shag rug. For the first time in my life, I figure out where that name might have come from.

Just as the thought forms in my head, I hear his footsteps approaching and realize that I'm sausage-rolled in his sheets and standing in the middle of the room on a rug I just imagined having sex on. Unwrapping myself as quickly as I can, I struggle to tug off the sheet and try to fling it back on the bed. But, of course, the supple cotton snags in my feet, and I trip and fall facedown on the rug, just as Rex enters the room.

I moan. And I think I taste my own blood.

"Mallika!"

Now, *NOW*? He has to choose this moment to say my name? And holy shit on sweet french toast, it's every single thing I remember it being.

He falls to his knees beside me. Naturally he's in the trendiest joggers, with a henley that's hugging his body like it's in love. I must have split my lip because he makes a "sssss" sound as he raises a hand to touch my cheek, then withdraws it and reaches for the box of tissues on his nightstand.

I'm in enough pain to want to scream, but I'm not dead, so as he stretches across me and his shirt lifts, I notice the fact that there are actual cuts on his abdomen, sectioning it into a real-life six-pack.

With the kind of gentleness that one might use to thread the most delicate of flowers into a garland, he presses the tissue into my bleeding lip and lets out another of those sounds where his tongue presses into the back of his teeth as he clenches them from my pain.

"I'm fine," I say even though I know I'm not. What kind of clumsy oaf hurts herself because she doesn't want a man to see her wrapped in a sheet? What kind of uncool oaf wraps herself in a sheet when she's wearing a T-shirt in the first place?

Well, I'm no longer wrapped in a sheet. Instead I'm sitting on the sex rug in said T-shirt, and it has ridden all the way up my hip, exposing my very elegant Garfield thong. Which Rex is studiedly not looking at, after dropping one impressively discreet glance down at them and setting every cell within every cell in my body on fire.

He dabs my lip some more, then removes the tissue. "Do you mind if I touch it? I want to make sure your teeth are okay."

I'm not that kind of physician, he'd said last night. But he wears scrubs, and he's been to med school, and it shows in the careful confidence with which he lifts my upper lip and examines my teeth. "It's a surface cut, but it's going to be swollen for a few hours. Your teeth are fine. That's usually the worst part with this type of fall."

Oh God, I had actually made a joke about women falling to the floor from his hotness. Just like that, I'm laughing, and it makes my lip sting something fierce.

He pushes a clean tissue into my lip, which has started bleeding again, but he's smiling as though he knows why I'm laughing. "Hold this and let me get some ice. Try not to laugh until the cut closes."

I purse my lips and make a serious face.

He's shaking his head when he leaves the room.

I get up and spread the sheet, which is the root of all this drama, over the bed and then straighten Rex's T-shirt around myself. Now that I'm giving it a thought, the shirt seems too small to actually be his. It's also obviously a women's shirt.

A sharp spike of something stabs at my insides.

He was engaged to another woman three months ago. Had they decorated this apartment together? Had they bought the bed together?

He comes back with coffee and ice in a baggie. His eyes take another quick trip to my bare legs. I know I have good legs. They've even been called spectacular. A dancer's gift. When I show leg, I rarely walk past a person who doesn't give them a double take. It's never made me feel like this before. Trembly.

"Can you drink coffee?" He hands me the bag of ice, and I press it against my lip and take the coffee.

"Obviously I need coffee. I can't be trusted to walk while uncaffeinated."

"How's the pain?" He points his own cup at my lip.

I shrug. "I'm not usually this clumsy, you know."

"I know," he says in a rush before I finish my sentence. "I've seen you dance."

The way he says it is quick and fierce. Almost harsh with the effort to not say it. It reminds me of last night at the bar, then spins me back to the rejection call that caused me to need rescuing. Restlessness churns in the pit of my stomach again.

"Amey is not wrong," he says with the kindness that has made it impossible to let him go years after he rejected me too. The kindness and those eyes, and that mouth, and those pecs—well, fine, all of it. I'd blocked it out when he was with someone else. Now it's back, full force. "It was one audition."

I shake my head and smile as though I don't care. "You're right. And I was never going to get it anyway."

Something shifts in his eyes, and I realize there's something different about them now, all these years later. Maybe not different, but more pronounced. Wisdom. He looks at me like he sees things, and it's at once thrilling and terrifying.

"Why?" he asks.

"Why what?" The instinct to avoid this conversation pushes to the surface, and I try to stand, but he's right in front of me, and that would bring me too close to him. I sit back down.

"Why did you think you weren't going to get it?" The V between his brows deepens. "And why did you audition if you believed that?"

"Because there's always hope, right?" And because my father's death made me reckless with faith.

He looks at me in that intense way. "But is there really hope if you don't believe in the outcome in the first place?"

Suddenly I don't know what he's talking about, and the discomfort inside me grows. Maybe I know what he's talking about. I know for sure I don't like it.

He takes a step away.

Jane's words come back to me. *This is a good thing. Them wanting to see a more traditional tape is a good thing.*

It isn't, though. It's asking me to compromise.

"I don't want to give them a version of me that's not me," I say.

He looks confused.

So I explain. "Their brief asked us to come up with choreography for a piece of music. I sent them my interpretation in my classical-Western fusion style, but they want me to do another tape that leans more into my kathak training."

His face brightens like Fourth of July fireworks. "Mallika! That's not a rejection! That's them telling you they're interested."

That's exactly what Jane said. They don't understand. "Of course it's a rejection. At least a rejection of my style."

His mouth opens and closes soundlessly. "Do you know how many presentations we did when we were trying to get funding for Black Sheep?"

"How many?"

"Sixty-seven," he says. "And do you know how many times we tweaked our pitch for that?"

I don't answer.

"Ten times that. The important thing is that we didn't compromise on the work we want to do. Just found a way for it to speak to people so they'd fund it." He picks up the ice pack I put down and presses it against my lip again. "How can you give up on something so easily?" The way he says it makes me think he isn't talking about this at all, but then he swallows and goes on. "What if you don't think of it as a compromise but as a way of understanding the work better? If anything, the feedback grew our vision."

"That's great that it worked out for you," I say with some force. "It's wonderful that you get to do what you want." He's obviously obsessed with his work, but I'm done with this conversation. My work is completely different. "I'm sorry I was such a sore loser yesterday. I shouldn't have dragged you and Amey to have our blood drawn."

"You were sad about losing something you wanted. But maybe you haven't lost it." He studies me, and I can feel him wanting to push me and holding back, which I'm grateful for. They've already made up their minds, and they're going to give it to someone who fits their vision better.

Truth is, I don't care anymore. They can take whoever they want. "It's fine, honestly. I wasn't even that sure if dance is what I want to pursue. Thanks for humoring me last night."

"I wasn't humoring you. I wasn't lying when I said we're always looking for subjects. We need them."

"So you're saying you would have taken anyone at that bar to your lab if they'd fit the bill. I'm not that special."

He takes the melted bag of ice from my hand, then touches my chin with his finger. I think about his stroking my beer bottle last night, as though if he touched me once he might never be able to stop. Now his finger lingers on my chin. "Do you also think I bring everyone who becomes a subject in my program to my home and let them have my bed?"

Goose bumps dance up the side of my neck to where his fingers are touching my skin. I must be blushing again, because he has a way of getting totally thrown when I do. He swallows, and the sharp angle of his Adam's apple moves in the long column of his throat.

"What happened last night?" Why did I wake up in his bed? "Did we?" A faint memory of throwing myself at him flashes in my head.

He pulls away and takes a step back. "Do you think I'm the kind of guy who would let something happen with a girl who was too drunk to remember it?"

The force with which he says the words makes something melt inside me. "I had one drink." What a hypocrite I am, because my mind is a blank.

He smiles again. "Well, that's like other women having about five. You also had another beer when we got here. So, ten."

That explains so much.

Why did you let me? I want to ask him, but he isn't my keeper.

A memory of him making me drink a bottle of water comes back to me. It's followed by other memories from last night. They come back, slow and fuzzy at first, then take on sharp focus. Rex helping me into the lab chair, snapping on blue gloves, then wrapping the bright-pink latex band around my arm. *A little prick.*

I had exploded into laughter at that, making Amey roll his eyes.

Rex had laughed. He always laughs at every funny thing I say. Men often do that when they want you to know they're into you, but last night I sensed relief in Rex's laughter, like someone who hasn't been able to laugh for a very long time and really misses it.

I've had to force my own laughter since Papa, and I recognized the relief, and I let the feel of his real laughter ease me all the way to my bones.

He drew blood from my arm and then Amey's. Handling the vials with practiced ease, rolling them deftly between his fingers. *We'll have the first set of results tomorrow. Then we'll know which part of the study you fit into.*

I still couldn't believe the trouble I put Amey and him through.

"Seriously, thank you," I say, genuinely regretful of my behavior. "For everything."

There's the strangest look in his eyes as he takes that in. He's studying me, gauging something. "I already told you I'm always looking for subjects."

"Will it be terrible if I said that I was having a moment. That I don't actually feel like I don't fit in my family." Damn Naani for her oddity comment. "Will you hate me if I don't want to be in the study anymore?"

You have to learn to stick with things, beta. Papa's voice does a rumble in my head. *You have to learn to stay your path. No matter how easy it is to step off it.* Why had he waited until the very end to say it? My stomach churns.

Rex swallows and steps back as though I've said something terrible. "It's a study, not bondage. You should absolutely never do anything that makes you feel like you're stuck in it."

Again, the hurt that seems to have taken up permanent residence under the surface flashes in his eyes again. It yanks me back to this moment. This moment is all I can handle right now. I want to ask him about his engagement and why it ended. I want to ask why he chose her over me in the first place.

"Also, when something happens between us, I'd like to think that you'll remember it the next morning."

He just said "when" and not "if." The word hangs in the air between us like a suspended star. His obsidian eyes glitter with it.

I remember, suddenly and starkly, sobbing in his arms as I waited for my rideshare. Amey's car had arrived first, and when Amey left, something about watching him drive away filled me with a sense of loss and made me cry. I said something that made Rex bring me up to his apartment. Fine, not something: I straight-out begged him not to leave me alone. It had felt impossible to be alone. Even more impossible to be with people who knew me.

To tell them I'd failed.

Then I forced a beer out of his fridge. He tried to stop me, but I was belligerent. I'm never belligerent. Even with the multiplying factor of the one-times-five drink. I'm always easygoing. Easygoing Mallika. Shaking things off and moving to the next thing is my superpower.

You have to learn to stick with things, beta.

"Thank you," I say again, my voice barely a whisper. "For understanding about the study," I add quickly, lest he think I'm thanking him for practically promising to have sex with me someday.

Bad move because a reluctant smile slips from him. One that says "I know what you were thanking me for."

Before I die of embarrassment yet again, he speaks. "While we are reneging on promises—" The playfulness in his eyes is back. "And since you owe me a favor, can you find a way to get me out of Amey's wedding dance?"

I throw my head back and laugh. "You're Amey's best man. Would you like me to get you out of that too?"

He looks so offended I might as well have asked him to provide proof of his love for my cousin. I can tell that he's hamming it up, and it's unbearably charming.

"It's a package deal, buddy. The best man has to dance in the first row. You're lucky you're not having to do a solo."

He looks horrified. "Fine, then, another concession, perhaps?" God, did those eyes know how to sparkle. "Do I get to pick my partner?"

The aunties and uncles need a little longer to practice, so their choreography started last week. The rest of the wedding dances won't start for a few more weeks. The reminder that he'll be at dance practice soon makes my panic at going back and choreographing the wedding dances ease a little.

His eyes are watching me in the most intent way. It feels like I might get used to it. I might, actually, be too used to it already. "Was there anyone in particular you had in mind?" I say in the neediest way. "I might be able to put in a good word."

Finally he does it. He cups my cheek. Not just the touch of a finger or a stroke of the thumb. A full hand fitted against my cheek. My heart starts to thud in my chest. "I'm really hoping you might."

"I'm really hoping it's who I think it is, or I'm going to feel like a complete idiot."

A laugh huffs out of him. That laugh, the one that makes me feel like he's been waiting to laugh again, the one that's filled with relief that he hasn't forgotten how. I touch his lips with a finger. They are plump and softer than I expected. He closes his eyes. And his phone buzzes.

With a frustrated sound, he opens his eyes and looks down at it. I don't mean to, but my eyes fall involuntarily to his screen. He moves it away quickly.

"Is that Amey?"

He slips the phone into his pocket without answering it. "It's not important." His eyes search mine, something intense and hungry stirring in them. Or maybe I'm projecting.

"I can't make any promises," I say.

Confusion intensifies his eyes, before he realizes I'm talking about Amey's wedding dance again. Another labored swallow moves his throat. Just like the rest of him, his neck is beautiful. Long and strong. It tugs at me like a magnet but also terrifies me. He walked away from me once.

"I'm the groom's sister and the choreographer. So, I'm kinda a big deal."

"Oh, I know," he says with far too much sincerity. "What will it take? I'm not above bribery."

"What you got?"

"Do you like omelets? I'm kind of an omelet god." He holds out his hand.

He couldn't possibly not know how much I love eggs. Growing up, Papa and I ate omelets every morning for breakfast. I haven't touched them since he died. Now my stomach releases a hungry groan.

Taking his hand, I let him pull me up. His scent envelops me like a spell, a spell that comes with the promise of eggs. That sounds so weird in my head, I smile.

The smile he gives me in return soaks up my very essence. He squeezes my hand into the center of his very hard chest. It's decided: the man is definitely trying to get me to fall in love with him. I'm not stupid enough to forget we've been here before. It's just that right now I don't care.

CHAPTER TWELVE

RANI

1988
Thirty-five years ago . . .

The first time Rani saw Vir Guru, he was arguing with a professor about Rudyard Kipling not being an important voice in stories about India.

"Have you not heard of Naipaul, Rushdie, Narayan, Singh, Malgonkar?" he said. "Kipling is an outsider's gaze. India seen through the lens of a colonizer. It's like a zookeeper telling tales about the captive tiger in his cage. No matter how much he loves the tiger, it's a false narrative."

It had been years since Rani had read anything that wasn't specifically assigned for school, but suddenly she wanted to read again. Just for pleasure.

"A brown face. How refreshing," he said when she caught his eye after class and he walked over to her in the auditorium-style classroom. "I wouldn't have known there was another South Asian person in class, given the silence when I was arguing my case." Those words, the first he ever said to her, instantly snuffed out whatever warmth had bubbled inside her when she'd heard him talk.

Since dignifying that with an answer felt like a waste of Rani's time, she wordlessly gathered her books and walked away. Exactly how Usha Auntie had taught her to do. Let them yell at themselves.

He ran after her. "I'm sorry. I should not have said that. It's just frustrating how little anyone in the English department cares about actual opinions."

"So when people don't agree with you, your take on it is that they don't care for any opinions at all?"

As soon as the words left her, he got that expression. The one that said, *Ah! Something intelligent from that face. Who would have thought?*

People did that a lot: discounted her for the way she looked, with her big hair, big boobs, and pretty face. Rani Parton had been her nickname in high school. Rani had been proud of it. Dolly Parton had written some of the most beautiful songs in the English language. Ballads that had the raw honesty and romanticism of old Bollywood lyrics.

As though writing her off because of her face weren't enough, the man chased Rani across the hallways of Sherman Oaks Community College as she hurried off.

"You're an ABCD," he said, providing yet another preposterous explanation for dismissing her when she hadn't asked for one.

When she continued to ignore him and kept walking, he continued to explain himself. "American-born confused desi." He had one of those polished Indian accents, the kind the nuns at Rani's convent school in Bandra had insisted upon. It didn't prove you were fancy, just that you were trying to be.

"Really?" she said, making her most shocked face. "I've never heard that highly offensive acronym from a FOB before." Then she did a head nod and spoke in the ridiculous Indian accent people in America tended to do when they were imitating Indian people. "One thousand thank-yous for enlightening me, kind sir."

"Wow, and that's not highly offensive?"

"Don't you think offense begets offense?" With that she walked away again.

What a scumbag.

Rani was not the kind of girl who was attracted to scumbags. She also made it a rule to stay away from Indian guys. Even ones with intense, infuriating eyes. Nonetheless, she needed to get her heart rate to slow down because a raised heart rate made her sweat. She didn't have the time to stop and change before she met Vinny to get shakes after class. Vinny and she had a lot to discuss, and it wasn't just about planning Usha Auntie and Dharam Uncle's twenty-fifth wedding anniversary surprise party. Usha Auntie was pushing Rani to help her friend "get her life together." Again.

Her mother wanted Vinny to take the GMAT. She wanted Rani to "help" Vinny make the "right decision." Recently, Vinny and her mom had stopped being able to talk to each other.

Rani had been managing Usha Auntie while trying to get Vinny to relax so she could actually make the right decision for herself. No one was going to push Vinny. Not on Rani's watch. But Usha Auntie's worry wasn't hard to understand because sometimes Vinny was so all over the place. It came from the inability to do anything that didn't engage her heart.

Rani didn't understand it. Her own heart stayed out of her way. Survival was her guiding light. And without Vinny, or Usha Auntie, Rani wouldn't have survived quite so well.

"Why are you looking like that?" Vinny asked as soon as she saw Rani.

Rani simply tilted her head to indicate she had no idea what Vinny was on about.

"You look like you want to commit murder. What happened?"

"Just some annoying guy."

Vinny stopped in her tracks. "A guy annoyed *you*?"

"Well, honestly, I think he annoyed everybody. Except himself, of course. He seemed to find himself rather interesting."

Vinny's humongous bottle-brown eyes widened. "Wow, I've never seen you riled up about a guy."

"And you're not seeing it right now either."

"Right. Was he at least handsome along with being *annoying*?"

"How does it matter if an annoying guy is handsome? But technically, yes, he could be called handsome."

Vinny squealed as though Rani had made some grand declaration. "So it's time to move on from Mike?"

"Mark. And I moved on from him weeks ago. Keep up. As my best friend, you're supposed to be on top of this stuff."

Vinny linked hands with Rani. "When you find the One, or at least someone who'll last more than a week, I'll remember his name. I promise."

"Well then, you're just going to have to call them all Mike because that's never happening. Rani Parekh only has time for Rani Parekh. And for Vinny Mehta, of course."

"Vinny Mehta is honored and eternally grateful, of course," Vinny said as they walked the four blocks to the diner. "Although maybe what you need is someone who annoys you instead of someone who trips over themselves at the sight of you."

"It might be time to stop believing those romantic movies, Vinny. A man who annoys you annoys you. A man who treats you well treats you well. Pigtail pulling is not a satisfactory substitute for a boy knowing how to show you that he has feelings for you."

"You really internalize my mom's lectures, don't you?"

Rani threw a loaded look at her friend. It was time to turn the conversation to the issue at hand: Vinny's future. "Usha Auntie is often right."

Vinny let out the deepest, most forlorn sigh. "She is. I can't just keep running from one thing to another. Maybe an MBA makes sense."

"It makes sense if you can see yourself working in business."

Vinny shuddered. "Not without wanting to stab myself." She let out another deep sigh. "Why did I even mention an MBA? Now Mom won't get off my back."

"You know I'll support you in whatever you decide to do, right?" Rani said. "But Usha Auntie just wants the best for you."

Vinny's mom wanted her to either find a way to support herself or get married after graduation. It wasn't an unfair expectation.

"What Mom really wants is for me to be more like you."

Rani laughed. "She does not. She just wants both of us to stand on our own feet."

"Or then find a man to depend on." Vinny narrowed her eyes, but the hurt in them was a potent thing. "Which makes sense because being dependent on a man hasn't worked out all that badly for her, has it?" Vinny was being really strange about her parents recently. When they'd first met, she had hero-worshipped them. But somewhere along the way that had changed, and Vinny didn't seem to want to talk about it. She would eventually because she was horrible at not addressing things that bothered her.

"Maybe Mom is right. Hell, even I wish I was more like you. I wish I had your focus. You do so much, and you do all of it well. I've got nothing about which I feel the way you feel about dance, or numbers, or fashion and makeup."

Oh dear, not this again.

"Vinny, you're good at a lot of things. Not everyone can dance." Rani winked because she knew Vinny had a sense of humor when it came to her dancing skills, or lack thereof. "Honestly, though, you're not bad at it. You just can't stop thinking about what everyone else thinks and dance for yourself. It's self-consciousness, nothing else."

Rani herself was blessed with the Trance, as her mother called it. *The Trance of your art is a gift, Rani, but it's also the disease that will consume you if you don't learn to contain it.*

They got to the diner, and Vinny rolled her eyes and leaned into the door to push it open. At least she didn't look quite so despondent anymore. She stumbled forward as someone yanked the door open at the exact same time.

"Watch where you're going!" a man snapped.

Great! It was the douche from class frowning with all the charm he'd displayed earlier.

Vinny caught her balance. "I'm so sorry," she said with all the kindness he did not deserve. "Did I hurt you?"

"Are you following me?" Rani said before she could stop herself.

All three of them went silent following that absurd orchestra of discordant questions.

Vinny blinked, eyes taking in his lean form as though he were Tom Cruise in *Top Gun*. He was even wearing aviators. Which he removed to sneer at Rani as though he'd stepped in a turd.

Rani strode through the door Vinny and the jerk were holding open as though she were indeed a queen, as her name indicated. When she realized that Vinny hadn't followed her, she grabbed her arm and dragged her in.

"Can you stop staring at the guy like that?" Rani snapped as they made their way to the counter to place their order. A chocolate shake for Rani and an unsweetened iced tea for Vinny.

Vinny blushed. "I'm just making sure he's fine." Her eyes did a quick slide in the direction of the door, but the jerk was gone. A flaming blush covered Vinny's face. Evidently she'd already decided that he was fine. "You know him?" Her eyes continued to search the diner even as they headed to their favorite table.

"He's in my writing workshop." Rani didn't want to talk about him. "Speaking of writing. Writing is something you're really good at." She slid into her side of their booth.

Vinny gave the room one final scan. "Hardly." Her face fell as she said the words.

Raj and Taj had aced the MCAT and gotten into the medical schools of their dreams, and Rani had gotten into grad school on a full scholarship. Vinny had just changed her major for the third time without falling in love with it, and she wouldn't stop being disappointed in herself.

"I loved reading the letters you wrote to me when you visited your grandparents in India over the summers."

This time Vinny gave Rani an almost annoyed look. "Writing letters whining about the heat and boredom and how much I missed you is hardly being good at writing."

"You were funny and observant. You noticed things about people that I'd never seen. They were insightful and smart. You made me see the country I was born in with whole different eyes."

Vinny's face softened, her focus shifting from whatever was darkening her thoughts to the permanent darkness wedged inside Rani. "You were twelve when you moved here." She didn't add that there had been hardly anything funny about Rani's life when she'd been in India.

"You love to help people," Rani said without letting herself get sidetracked.

"You help people too. You help me. I can't even dress myself without you. Every girl in your dance troupe worships you, because they'd feel ugly and blimpy without you showing them how to feel good about themselves. No one cares that I help people. They only care that I'm not in med school. Do you know what Mummy said to me the other day?"

Rani braced herself. No one could slice through Vinny's confidence like Usha Auntie. "She said, 'If you can't be a doctor, you could at least try to be an engineer or an architect.' What is wrong with her?"

"She's only doing it to get a reaction out of you. She hates when you shut her out. And you . . . never mind."

"And I what?"

Rani patted her hand, which was balled in a fist on the table. "I get that you're upset with her, Vinny. And she's not being fair right now. I think she misses how close you were."

That didn't calm Vinny at all. "She'd be much happier if you were her daughter. I heard her bragging to Neela Auntie yesterday about how you were going to be an accountant on top of pursuing dance. And here I am a failure."

Actually, Rani had put aside dancing in favor of economic independence, something Vinny didn't need. It wasn't like Vinny to sidestep that fact. So she must really be hurting.

"That's not true. You're not a failure. You're figuring out what you want."

"Also, I'm not academically brilliant like Raj and Taj, and you."

"You know the only reason Raj and Taj excel academically is because they can't let the other one be better."

"I can't understand that. Doing things because it makes you better than others."

Rani took both Vinny's hands in hers and squeezed. "Sweetheart, don't you see. That's the skill no one else has. You care about why you do things. You think about why things matter. You don't use the rat race to find happiness. I don't know anyone else who knows how to do that. One of these days you're going to find the thing that brings all that together, and you're going to change the lives of millions of people."

Vinny smiled for the first time. "I don't need the rat race to be happy because I have you."

Before Rani could respond, the douche materialized at their table like an angry genie. He was wearing an apron over the white server uniform and the odd little nautical cap the waiters here wore.

He was carrying their order on a tray. "I guess this answers the question of whether I was following you," he said with enough self-importance that irritation spiked in Rani's gut. He placed the drinks on their table. The shake in front of Vinny and the iced tea in front of Rani. Bad at his job and arrogant. Fantastic.

"Thank you," Vinny said so sweetly that Rani wanted to shake her. "Rani said you're in her writers' workshop."

"I was," he said. "I dropped. I'll take it with a more open-minded professor next semester."

"Wow, you're dropping the class because Professor Smith referenced Rudyard Kipling?" Rani said.

"As an important voice in stories about India," he said.

"Your professor called Kipling an important voice about India?" Vinny said, getting all fired up. "That's nonsense."

The man's head snapped in Vinny's direction for the first time. "Right? He's obviously never heard of Naipaul and Rushdie—"

"And Malgonkar," Vinny finished.

"You've read *A Bend in the Ganges?*" he said.

"One of my favorites," Vinny said.

"There's a definitively important Indian voice. Even if it's upper caste."

"And male. Every one of those names is an elitist man. But at least Indian, not colonizer."

"I should have mentioned Amrita Pritam." His voice was entirely different now, soft, urgent. "Even though that's—"

"A translation."

Okay, great, this finishing-each-other's-sentences thing was disturbing. Rani cleared her throat.

They both seemed to startle. Oh jeez.

"I'm Vir," he said, gaze locked with Vinny's. "Vir Guru." Much the same way Roger Moore said "The name's Bond, James Bond," moving only one side of his mouth.

A flaming blush painted itself back across Vinny's cheeks. Her eyes had gone enormous and unabashedly sparkly. This guy's ego did not need more oxygen. "I'm," she stuttered, "Vandana, but everyone calls me Vandy."

For a beat, another moment overlaid this one, and Rani was catapulted into the past. To a day her ears had rung so loud, she hadn't been able to hear Vinny's name. Vinny hadn't corrected her through their first few playdates. Then it had become their nickname.

"It's a pleasure meeting you, Vandy," he said, stretching her name out like a benediction.

"Aren't you supposed to be working?" Rani asked.

Vinny turned to Rani like she had kicked her shins.

Fortunately someone called his name, and he hurried off with an "excuse me." Then ran back again and slid to a stop next to their booth. "Please don't leave. I'll be back."

Vinny looked dazed. *He called me an ABCD,* Rani wanted to say, but it felt too mean to say it, given how Vinny was looking. So Rani pulled her shake from under Vinny's nose and slid the tea he'd placed in front of her to Vinny.

Vinny took a sip of the tea and started to cough. Violently.

Rani patted her back. "Jeez, Vinny, he's just a guy." *Get a grip.*

Vinny swallowed and threw a look behind the counter to where the manager was having a conversation with Vir. It didn't seem to be a pleasant conversation.

Suddenly Vinny's head snapped back in Rani's direction. She narrowed her eyes. "Was he the annoying guy?"

"Sorry?"

"Rani! Was Vir the guy you were riled up about earlier? From school."

How could she possibly know that? Rani nodded.

"What did you guys fight about?"

"We didn't fight. You heard him. He was pissed off that I wasn't pissed off with Professor Smith for *calling a colonizer an important voice about India.*" Yes, she overenunciated that last part.

For a second Vinny looked at her like she couldn't believe how Rani could let such sacrilege pass. Then she looked at her tea. "He had to have said something more to you."

"How on earth would you know that?"

And he was back. Big sappy smile on his face. "Can I get you anything else?" he said, eyes fixed on Vinny. Then he extracted a piece of paper from his pocket with a number scrawled on it and slid it at her. "I have a signed copy of Malgonkar's *A Bend in the Ganges*. I'd love to show it to you."

For a moment Vinny's face brightened, and her cheeks reddened again. Then her face went cold. She slid a look at her tea. "What did you say to Rani?"

He slid a glance at Rani. She'd expected anger, but he seemed to have forgotten that she was even there. And that he had called her that rude name. His gaze bounced between the two of them. Rani was pretty sure he was going to feign ignorance.

"I should never have called her an ABCD. I'm sorry," he said quietly.

"You called her what?" Vinny stood.

"I'm sorry." He looked ashamed. It was delicious.

"She's not." Vinny grabbed Rani's arm and pulled her out of the chair. "But I am."

He looked like he obviously didn't follow her meaning.

"An ABCD," Vinny explained. "But you know what I'm not confused about? Who my friends are. And that list starts and ends with Rani."

"I shouldn't have said that. I really am sorry." He turned to Rani, the genuine remorse on his face not quite so gratifying anymore. "Can we start over?" His eyes returned to Vinny. They couldn't seem to stop returning to her.

Vinny scratched her head. "I'm sorry, we're too *confused* to know how to do that." With that she started walking, dragging Rani in her wake. Suddenly she stopped and turned to him again. "Oh, and the iced tea was for me, not for her."

His jaw dropped open as he took in the full glass she'd left behind.

"Everything okay here?" The manager swooped in, surveying the three of them. There was an odd distaste on his face. It struck Rani that they were the only three brown faces there.

Vir's eyes were locked on Vinny's.

"Everything's perfect," Vinny said to the manager without looking away from Vir, the tone of her voice reminding Rani of Usha Auntie. "The service was fabulous. Thank you."

Rani had no idea what had just happened here, but before she could ask, Vinny dragged her out of the diner.

CHAPTER THIRTEEN

VANDY

Saturday, 11:00 p.m. . . .

A framed picture of Vir, Mallika, and her greeted Vandy from the console as she entered the home they'd raised Mallika in. Mallika was in the center, and Vir and Vandy were kissing her cheeks. *A kiss sandwich,* Mika had called it when she was little. They had a hundred versions of this picture over the years.

Where are you, Mika?

Vandy picked up the picture. They'd taken this one exactly a year and a half ago. Mere weeks before Vir's diagnosis. At LAX, just before Vir left for India. He hadn't been back for seven years, since his mother had passed away. When his mother was still alive, he used to go back every year and take Mika with him every three to four years.

Vandy had tried to go with him only once, when Mallika was six months old. As soon as the aircraft started taxiing, Vandy had had such a massive panic attack that she'd passed out. They'd had to evacuate her off the plane on a stretcher.

She remembered it like it was yesterday, the feeling of her heart exploding in her chest. It had started with her thinking that Mika was not with her. That she'd somehow been left behind at the terminal. Vir had slipped their baby into Vandy's arms in an attempt to calm her.

It hadn't worked. Vandy pressed Mika to her chest, but she couldn't feel her. She kept imagining her disappearing from her arms and almost dropped her. Then when Vir took Mika from her, the explosion had come, ripping her insides, stealing her breath.

At the hospital, they'd pumped Vandy full of calming drugs. When they came home, baby Mallika peacefully asleep in her stroller, unaware of the drama inside her mother, Vandy knew with absolute certainty that she was never going to India again.

They'd been trying to take Mika to Mumbai to meet Vir's grandmother, Mika's only living great-grandparent. Ever since they'd started making plans, Vandy had been uncomfortable, terrified that Mallika would get sick.

After everything they'd been through to have her, the Mehtas were also against the idea of Mika traveling when she was so young. But India was where Vir had grown up. It was his home.

Mallika is a perfectly healthy baby. We'll be cautious. And even if she does get sick, there's a reason there are so many Indian doctors here in the United States. Your father studied medicine in India. Some of the best medical care you can find in the world is there. It is not a different planet.

But that's exactly what it felt like to Vandy sometimes. As a child, she'd gone once every few years to see her grandparents until they passed away. The last time had been when she was eighteen—the last summer before starting college.

Long before she met Vir.

After they met, they had planned to go together, but between school and their elopement and Vir's green card, years had passed. Then they'd started to try to have children, and the nightmare years had begun.

The first miscarriage had hit like a bomb going off in the middle of the night, blowing their blessedly routine existence to pieces. Up until that moment, Vandy had prepared for their life to turn out one way.

Then suddenly, she'd found herself empty handed, empty wombed, everything she believed about herself in shreds.

Her logical brain understood the politics of female identity and how it was tied to having children because society taught women to believe that they were complete only when they became mothers. Her own mother had treated motherhood as a calling she had to excel at, as her purpose for existing. The belief system had been coded into Vandy deeper than she could have ever predicted. Despite the counseling, despite being lectured to death by every person who knew her, being childless had felt unfathomable to her.

When Vir assured her that she was all that mattered to him, that they were enough, it felt like a betrayal. Unbearable.

All her life she'd had this sense that solidified only when she was connected to someone else. A connection that left no distance between someone else's wants and needs and her. Others saw it as a need to be useful, but it wasn't that simple. It was about being essential to someone else and having someone else be essential to her, like breath.

The first time she became pregnant, that obscure sense she'd chased all her life had become tangible. Like the sun coming out from behind clouds. A brightness, an aliveness she'd only ever felt in spurts before. Finally she could touch it, taste it. She was born to be a mother. She knew that with the kind of certainty she couldn't explain.

When they told her she would never bear children, it had just felt like being told she had to try harder. Give more. Give everything.

Every day Vandy watched people butting up against the cruelty of life. Little pieces of it, mountainous cliffs of it. Small cruelty that stuck in your windpipe like a crumb gone rogue. Unthinkable cruelty that buried you whole like a roof caving in. In the end the impact was the same. It cut off your breath, killed you. Took the person you were and turned you into someone else as you struggled for existence. A rebirth in this very life.

You'll never understand because you've never wanted something so much that nothing else mattered.

There was a whole chunk of her life that her daughter knew nothing about. What was the point of sharing something that caused so much pain? Vandy had found a solution, and she'd borne the consequences.

That didn't mean Mallika didn't know her. Their connection was the foundation of Vandy's life. Mallika knew this. Mallika felt the same way.

Her argument with Mallika had been playing in an endless loop inside Vandy. Other than those few moments of conflict, Mallika had sounded happy, which was her default setting. Sure, she'd had the requisite moodiness as an adolescent, but for the most part her daughter was irrepressibly happy.

You sound happy, Vandy loved to say.

I'm always happy, Mom. You raised me to be able to be happy. Thank you.

It was an incredibly lovely thing to have your child say that to you. Mika said stuff like that all the time. Having a child who verbalized the love in her heart so freely was a gift. Vandy didn't take it for granted even for a minute. Except these last eleven months, when Vandy had forgotten everything but holding herself up.

Vandy pressed a hand to her mouth. She'd let Mallika down. She stared at herself in the giant marble-framed mirror. Her cheeks were high against the angles age had given her face. Her arms and legs were lean and ripped from hours of yoga. A body that proclaimed a healthfully lived life. Also a body that hid a heart filled with sadness.

Everyone saw only the strength and grace with which she'd handled losing Vir, but her grief wasn't sangfroid. It was an inferno. There was no walking through it, so she'd skirted around it. But it hadn't budged, and now she was stuck circling it. Around and around, where she couldn't even enter her own home without having to steel herself.

And she'd left her child to fend for herself for the first time in her life.

Making her way through the cavernous entrance foyer into the living area felt like struggling to escape your own body when it was in pain. She forced herself to look around, to take in the details. The floor-to-ceiling windows that looked out at darkness now but would flood with light when daybreak came. Vir had designed their placement to capture the sunrise. How very much he'd loved every little thing about their life. And she'd let it fall into neglect.

Her bottle of water and a half-eaten bowl of yogurt sat on the coffee table. After coming home from the airport last evening, she'd sat here and talked to her editor as he reminded her that they only had two more weeks of Dear Agony Auntie covered. Then instead of answering letters she'd fallen asleep right in the chair.

She pulled her laptop from her handbag and put it on the table. It was time to figure out how to do this. People took solace from her column. She took solace from their solace. But she couldn't flip her laptop open. Couldn't look at words that sought a way out when she was so very lost herself.

The answer is closer to home.

Was her mother right? Was the answer to where Mallika was right here?

The climb up the sweeping stairs that led up to their bedroom had felt mountainous this past year. Vandy had avoided the bedroom she'd shared with Vir as much as she could. She'd lived out of a suitcase in her own home to avoid going up.

Time felt like sludge. Sticky.

One summer in middle school, there had been a rodent issue in her parents' house. Vandy had seen the pest control guy pull a trapped mouse off a sticky pad. The gluey gunk on the pad had webbed and pulled at the little squirming body, refusing to let it go. That's how time felt since Vir.

She stopped at the bottom of the staircase now, the curved metal railing cold in her grip. How could she go up there when she didn't know where her child was?

I've lost our child.

She'd lost six of their children before Mallika came. Six.

Stop it! Vir's voice said in her ear.

She forced her feet to do what they had to. As she emerged at the top of the stairs, her bad knee shot a jolt of pain through her.

This aging thing was a bitch. She'd fallen on her knee a few years ago while getting off a stage, and it had just never been the same since. She gave in to her limp and made her way to their room.

The door was open. She never left her bedroom door open. It was a problem she had. She wasn't the tidiest person, but open drawers and doors made her restless. It was one of her mother's rules that had stuck with her into adulthood. Mallika and Vir always left doors open, no matter how many times Vandy told them it bothered her.

"Hello?" she said, stepping inside the wide-open door, her heart beating in the strangest way.

Mallika was the only one with the code to enter the house. "Mika?" The sound of her daughter's name wobbled and cracked on her tongue.

Every fiber in her being willed Mallika to run into her arms. Or to be sprawled on her bed. Mika sometimes hugged her father's pillow and slept on his side of the bed. Vandy found it harder to gouge up the memories his smell came wrapped in.

The bed was made. Vandy's gaze swept her room, the carved, distressed, whitewashed four-poster that Vir had waited six months to have custom built, the Kashmiri carpet he'd brought home from one of his trips to India. It had cost an entire book advance. It had been one of those things he'd done to prove that he was comfortable with how much more money than him she'd started to make.

The nightstands were copper handis from Vandy's grandparents' kothi in Baroda. After her grandparents died, the pair of high copper pots in which her grandmother stored water were the only things Vandy wanted from their house. For years they had sat in a corner of her parents' garage. Then Vir had repurposed them into nightstands. He'd used a blowtorch to create turquoise flame patterns on them. It had been one of his projects driven by the frenzy he felt when words eluded him, when his stories fought him.

Losing himself to working with his hands helped the stories untangle inside him. Creating one thing helped him create another. He'd given those handis new life by putting round glass tops on them and filling them with river rocks from Tahoe, where they'd spent the few weeks before Mallika was born. Their breaths held. Waiting for something to go wrong the way it had in the six pregnancies before.

Five embryos had slipped from her, her helpless uterus cramping to hold on. She pressed her hand into her belly, into the phantom pain.

Then the sixth one. The piece of her she'd handed over, slid into a borrowed cocoon. That one hadn't made it either.

Her eyes scanned the nightstand and sought out the silver-framed picture of Vir that had sat there for years. It was her favorite picture of him. She'd taken it at one of his first book signings, back when he still did them, before his disillusionment with publishing had made him stop.

There was nothing on the nightstand.

No Vir smiling at her as he scrawled a signature across the page.

Someone had moved the picture.

Vandy broke into a run. "Mika!" She was shouting now.

She ran into her daughter's room, into her bathroom, her walk-in closet, the balcony outside her room. But nothing.

Vandy ran back into her own room, then into her bathroom. And there it was. Vir's picture. His soulful eyes searched her face as he looked up from his book. His eyes were the one thing that had stayed unchanged from the day she had met him to the day she'd had to close them with her hand.

Someone had moved Vir's picture. Someone had been inside her home, inside her bedroom, inside their life.

CHAPTER FOURTEEN

MALLIKA

Four days ago . . .

I've heard people say things like "those were the two best days of my life." I've always laughed at those grand declarations. As though life were poetry and all of us poets who took ourselves too seriously. But these past two days have in fact been the best days of my life.

I feel lit up on the inside. Like I've swallowed the sun.

This is a minor miracle, given that two days ago I felt like all my dreams had been tossed to the curb. I'm still kicking myself for sending in that audition tape in the first place, but the Netflix *Mahabharata* no longer feels like the thing I was born to do.

Jane has called a few times to convince me to record the classical kathak set. She thinks it's a huge deal that they've asked, but she doesn't understand how this stuff goes. Their brief asked for something out of the box, but they just want something that caters to the stereotype that Western audiences are comfortable with. That's not who I am.

I turn my attention to the man headed my way with a plate of kababs. He smiles at me as though blinded by the glow of the sun I've swallowed, and that somehow makes me feel like I'm at the edge of a bright cliff instead of at the bottom of a dark well. I'm ready for all that my life can be. Even if it doesn't include bringing my work to a streaming platform near you. I'm ready to find something to do that I don't have to sell my soul for.

The day I woke up in Rex's house, he made me the best omelet I've ever eaten. I feel a bittersweet kick of pain as I imagine Papa grinning his lopsided grin at the irony of being replaced as the best omeleteer (her favorite of his made-up words) of all time.

"You okay?" Rex reaches over and wipes the stupid tear that just slid from my eye.

He doesn't seem to care that Amey's parents' house is bursting with uncles and aunties—each one of whom is surreptitiously focused on our every interaction—and that makes an excited shiver brush down my skin. The other day, after omelets, Rex took the day off, and we drove to his favorite beach near where he grew up in Ventura. It was a chilly gray day, and we walked barefoot on the cold, wet sand as misty rain pelted us and salty air tangled our hair.

It took me an hour of walking before I finally couldn't bear it anymore and took his hand. Mine was cold and crinkled with the rain, his warm and strong. The wet slide did things to the way our palms fit and our fingers intertwined. It made us both suck in our breath.

When the shock of the connection almost made me pull away, he held on. Then he didn't let go for the rest of the day. He'd been waiting for me to hold his hand. The way he treats me makes those words pop in my head over and over again.

I've been waiting.

A voice keeps whispering inside me that this has happened before. That he walked away before.

I can't ask him about his breakup without bringing up why he chose her over me. And I can't handle that yet.

All those years ago, when we flirted on the phone for months, I could have sworn that he'd been this close to asking me out. Then I'd seen him with her. She'd had her arms around his neck, their bodies pressed together.

I'd deleted his number from my phone, eaten the best donuts in the world, binged every one of Hrithik Roshan's movies (because, whoa, could the man dance!), and then I'd put Rex out of my mind. Except, of course, all the times I ran into him because of Amey and the urge to do something really stupid gripped me.

Rex nods his head toward the patio, which is a little more private than here. In a fortuitous twist of fate, Amey has been on call these past two days. We step out onto the terraced stone patio that overlooks the cliffs of Palos Verdes. The bluffs curve around the sapphire bay, where the gleaming Pacific crashes against its confines in great big waves.

The biggest orange tree in Palos Verdes, as my aunt makes sure everyone knows, grows at the center of the patio and scents the air. Rex rubs his thumb over a plump orange, then smells it and smiles. Something squeezes my heart hard.

I'm not twenty-two anymore. We're not those same people, young and shy and desperate to be liked. We're becoming friends now. Friends who throw off sparks the size of Fourth of July fireworks over Disneyland.

Maybe not addressing our past is stupid. Like trying to build a tower without digging a foundation. He picks up a cookie from the plate, breaks off a piece, and slips it into my mouth, and suddenly I want to dig this foundation. I want to pour myself into it like concrete. I want to flow and set into the crevices and corners of all these things I'm feeling.

"I'm a little better than okay," I say, finally answering his question. His smile wobbles on his lips and intensifies in his eyes.

After spending the day at the beach yesterday, he came with me to Tinku and Taj's house for dance practice. He spent most of the evening with my grandmother, helping her fix one of her medical machines while I ran practice. Then he drove me to my apartment, and we ended up talking all night. He finally left at five in the morning and went into the office. I slept half the day, shot a few TikTok dance videos about standing up after being knocked down, and talked to my mother.

I almost told her about Rex, but she was in her preseminar Zen state, and I didn't want to pull her out of it with my excitement. Since Papa, she's really needed her work. Also, a part of me wants to keep Rex to myself a little bit longer. I need to figure out what is happening. I need to believe that it really is.

When I showed up at my uncle and aunt's for practice today, Rex was already here.

"I'm not stalking you, I swear," he said. "Your naani called me. I was helping her with her CPAP yesterday, and I was missing a part. She got the part today and asked me to come back." Apparently, tinkering with medical hardware is one of his hobbies.

"You realize what she's doing, right?" My grandmother is totally playing matchmaker, and I feel like he should be aware of the ambush.

"So, I need to thank her, then?" he said, and I wanted to drop a kiss on his teasing lips. We haven't yet. Kissed, that is.

I really want to.

But there's that whole tower-without-a-foundation thing. Plus, I've known that he's single again for just a few days.

The math of that does not match up with the reality of what these days have felt like.

We finish the cookies, give each other's hands a squeeze like smitten teenagers, and go back inside.

As I spend the evening wrangling my aunt's limbs into the dance steps, Rex fixes my grandmother's excuse machine.

The wrangling has taken a turn for the better, thanks to a breakthrough I had while shooting my videos earlier today.

Cymbals. The tiny brass ones they use during Hindu prayers. I've spent a lot of time these past two weeks wondering how to get my aunts to hear the beat everyone else hears. Then today as I took up the beat with my hands while shooting my routine, it struck me. Clinking the cymbals to emphasize the beats as a cue to move was the answer. It had to work.

As soon as I got here, I borrowed the cymbals from the prayer shelf.

The brass disks are heavy and cool in my hand as I break the choreography down for the aunties and uncles. Some of them are great dancers, fed and raised on Madhuri Dixit and Hrithik Roshan's Bollywood. They all look wildly relieved and impressed with the cymbals idea. Obviously, they too have been perplexed at the disconnection between Tinku's movements and the musical beats.

I walk Tinku Maami through the steps, marking the beat with a clink of the cymbals where the transitions and the movements happen.

Her face gets intently focused, her tongue sticks out from her pursed lips in her effort to concentrate and get it right, and my heart melts. She just wants to dance. Like me. She just wants to lose herself in the music, and she wants people to think she's good at it. Maybe she can't hear the music because she's trying too hard to remember the steps.

The cymbals work where nothing else has. She's still slightly off the beat, and it's going to be a long road to her not waiting for the clinks with her tongue clenched between her teeth, but we've made amazing progress today. I'm glowing with the huge sense of accomplishment from this tiny victory when I find my grandmother to say bye after practice.

She gets right to her agenda and asks me what I thought about Rex's office. "He's going to sell that company for a tidy profit soon," she says. I know there are other Indian grandmothers in LA who would drop in a dead faint if their grandchild dated someone who was not Indian. I guess I should be grateful that my grandmother isn't a bigot. She's just a capitalist. "Isn't the work he does fascinating?"

Naani has always been what Papa called "goal oriented." When I spent time with her as a child, I often got the sense that she was on a stealth mission to gather intel about my parents' marriage. Now I have that sense again, as though she's up to something. Well, she's obviously up to getting rid of my single status, but has she really zeroed in on Rex because of his company?

Of course there's the fact that I've done a terrible job of hiding my crush all these years, and the even more significant fact that he's single again.

"It's a nice office," I allow. "He's also just come out of a broken engagement."

"An engagement is not a marriage. I'm usually not a fan of long engagements, but there is an advantage. If you're with a cheater, a long engagement gives you time to find out." An odd lost look dims her eyes. Then she gets focused again. "Relationships often drag on long after they're broken, anyway. So, he's been out of the relationship for ages longer than we can see. Have you told your mother about him yet?"

"You know Mom's on tour. I'm not sure there's anything to tell yet." As soon as I tell Mom, her hope will spike. I haven't told her about the audition rejection yet, either, because obviously dashing her hopes is my least favorite thing.

As I watch Naani studying me, I realize that I don't want to think about anything more than today. I just want to enjoy feeling happy again.

Naani rolls her eyes with impressive impact. "When will you grow a spine, child?" she says, almost to herself.

Well, I already know she thinks I'm an oddity. I've made my peace with it. My sense of feeling like a black sheep came and went fast. It might have been my shortest phase, but I know that my naani's words were what pushed me into it. Not that I'm upset with her. Whatever her agenda is, I don't doubt that her end goal is to help me.

Recently she's been feeling frailer somehow. Maybe that's what's to blame for her newly acquired meanness. She's not the kind of person who would forgive old age for sapping her energy. I miss the sweet, nurturing Naani she used to be.

"When you do tell your mother about him, don't tell her that he studies stupid people in smart families."

"Naani, that's not what he studies," I say, channeling my mom's calmness. Mom thinks that Naani had to work so hard to be what everyone else wanted in her marriage that since my naana's death, she's making up for all the things she didn't get to say. "Plus, you're trying to set us up. He would hardly be interested if he thought I was stupid." My tone seems to shake her out of wherever she goes off to these days in these bouts of moodiness.

She smiles, the old, kind Naani back. "You have something far more special than being book smart," she says. "But isn't this DNA stuff fascinating?"

Before I can respond, she waddles off toward the wine and samosas, her two favorite things. I do think what Rex does is interesting, but I've already told him I no longer want to participate in his study. That embarrassing night seems like it happened ages ago.

I find Rex waiting for me by the front door. He scans the sea of shoes and sandals and fishes out my flats. "You ready to go?"

"Where are we going?" I ask, fully aware of how excited I sound when he's probably just planning to walk me to my car.

He places my shoes by my feet and takes my hand. "Is it terrible that I don't want to say bye yet?"

It's the very opposite of terrible. I know I'm looking at him like I want to jump into his arms and let him whisk me away to magical lands.

An auntie bustles past, pretending to be looking for something. I try to disengage our hands, but he holds on and tugs me out of the front door with our fingers firmly linked.

"I don't want to say bye yet either," I say as we step out onto the colonnaded front porch where the giant lions keep watch.

He lets out the most beautiful sigh of relief, and my body leans toward him. "A walk? Unless all that dancing has tired you out. We can just grab a drink or coffee."

"Oh God," I say, "you think wedding choreography can tire me out?" I sometimes dance six hours a day.

He looks apologetic. "That's not what I meant. It's just, I watched you working with Amey's mom, and I don't know how you do it."

"Do what? Herd cats?"

"Herd aunties. Which seems definitely scarier." He smiles and touches my cheek.

"Their bark is harsher than their bite. They just want to look and feel beautiful onstage at the sangeet and imagine themselves in a movie. My aunts have been dreaming of these weddings from the moment their children were born. They just want to enjoy it. Just let go. Step out of their lives. That's what dance does, it lets you fly outside the confines of real life." Even when you hear the beat entirely differently inside your head than everyone else.

His eyes intensify, and he leans closer, as though he wants to soak my words in. Soak me in.

Of their own accord, my hands move up to his face and cup his jaw. It's prickly with stubble and cool to the touch. Heat washes over me, melts my limbs. I shove away all the voices that start up in my head and go up on my toes. I'm about to pull him to me when his phone rings.

"Why does your phone hate me?" I say.

"If it's Amey, may I kill him?" he says.

"Promise?" I whisper as he puts it to his ear, and I have to wrap my arms around myself to keep from touching him again.

"That's not possible!" he says with so much force that I'm shaken from my trance.

His gaze slides to me in a panic. "Are you sure?" His thickly arched brows draw together, and the way he's looking at me strums every doubt and fear I've been ignoring.

He takes a step back and turns away from me.

He's going back to her. This was too good to be true.

I'm about to walk away when he reaches out and takes my hand again.

"And the sample was not contaminated?" he says into the phone.

The person at the other end says something he obviously doesn't like.

"Of course I followed protocol. To a T. There must be some mistake . . . fine . . . hold off on the paperwork . . . yes . . . I'll let you know." He disconnects the phone but continues to stare at it.

"Rex?"

He looks up and meets my eyes, and I know something is horribly wrong.

I step back. Thank God I didn't tell my mother. Thank God I didn't kiss him. Around us, the wind rustles through the giant row of blue-green eucalyptus.

"That was my lab," he says carefully, totally unaware of the flight response coiled tightly inside me. "About your blood test from the other night."

A whole new coldness grips me.

"I thought I said I didn't want to be in the study."

He squeezes the bridge of his nose. "The samples had already been sent in before we could withdraw you. I'm so sorry." He looks so worried that every bad scenario associated with a blood test starts to race through my head.

There's this thing my mom talks about: how to root yourself in this moment. To not jump ahead in time or fall back into the past. Jumping forward is anxiety; falling back is depression. Count your fingers and stay here in the now.

I've obviously never been able to follow that advice. Now I force myself to do it. Count my fingers. One by one.

My father just died of pancreatic cancer. A brutally aggressive form. They hadn't been able to stop it, no matter what they tried. It's not as highly heritable as some other types, but I'm still going to be considered high risk for the rest of my life. That hadn't sunk in completely until this moment.

Every part of my body drains of strength. I fold over. Breath gets stuck in my lungs, and just like that, I'm hyperventilating.

He squats next to me and rubs my back. "Hey, I'm sure there's a simple explanation."

He doesn't look like there's a simple explanation for what he's just heard.

"Tell me what it is." I force the words out when my breath eases enough to let me.

We both straighten. He doesn't seem to know how to say it. Which makes the hyperventilating start up again.

"Rex, please!" *Am I going to die?* But I can't say the words. They sound too final. Too much like a prediction.

He continues to rub my back. "Amey and you . . ."

No! This is about Amey? It can't be. *Please.*

"Amey can't be sick." It comes out strangled. Amey is getting married in three months. Grace and he have been together for five years. They're each other's soulmates.

"Mallika." Rex squeezes my shoulders and makes a soothing sound, but I can't stop shaking. "Amey's not sick. No one's sick. Breathe. I'm sorry, I should have clarified that first." But he doesn't say more. He just looks at me with so much concern that it does not help my heartbeat slow.

"Rex!" I say. "You cannot make that face and tell me Amey is okay. Is it me, then? Is something wrong with me?"

"No!" He looks shaken. "No. Well, you're not sick. It's not that."

"Then what's wrong?"

"The blood work." That V that folds between his brows is painfully deep, like he's having to focus hard to get the words out. "It . . . based on the blood work, it's just that . . . with Amey and you . . ." He pauses, and his eyes meet mine with an unholy force. "There's no genetic connection between the two of you. Based on the blood samples you both gave the other night, Amey and you are not related."

CHAPTER FIFTEEN

RANI

1988
Thirty-five years ago . . .

One of the most satisfying things Rani had ever experienced in her life was making Vir Guru write her final essay for her writers' workshop. "Male Authors Writing Female Characters: A Foreigner's Perspective?"

Pure genius, even though she said so herself.

To be fair, he'd done a great job, his opinions so feminine, so naturally fueled by feminist rage, even Rani believed she could have written the paper herself. More honestly, that Vinny had written it for her.

"Please," he begged as she left class. He'd been waiting for her, and he looked desperate. Which, given that he had only seen Vinny that once, was kinda ridiculous. But also sweet. And scary.

Vinny had been far too distracted lately too. She still wouldn't tell Rani why she was so angry with the guy. The ABCD comment was offensive, but it wasn't something their community didn't use regularly. Given that they'd been playing eyeball tennis the entire time they were finishing each other's sentences, Vinny's change of heart had been sudden and inexplicable.

"Sure, but I need one more thing," Rani said, walking away without waiting for him.

Naturally he followed, without so much as a moment's hesitation. "You said the paper was the last thing I had to do."

"Well, this isn't so much something you have to do as something you have to say."

He fell in step next to her, but he let his silence be his response.

"Why is she mad? What did you do?" Rani asked.

His footsteps didn't falter. This was a cold one. He kept his emotions where he could manage them. Rani recognized that only too well. Vinny was the opposite: her bleeding heart sat right there on her sleeve, exposed and ready for trampling. Rani wasn't sure yet if he deserved to get close enough to her friend to break it.

He had been unabashed in his interest. He'd basically groveled. *I've already apologized. What will it take?* he'd said the day after the Diner Incident three weeks ago, after Rani told him to take a hike when he asked for Vinny's number.

Since then he'd washed Rani's car, done a lot of her homework, even helped paint a banner for one of her dance troupe performances.

Nonetheless, he was not getting anywhere near Vinny until Rani knew what he'd done to deserve her wrath. Vinny had told her unequivocally that she wanted nothing to do with him. She wouldn't tell her why, so he was going to have to.

"Maybe if I can talk to Vandy, I can ask her. Then we can both know," he said, jaw barely moving, eyes flat.

Rani scoffed. This time she let her silence tell him exactly what she thought of his lies.

"I didn't do anything to her. Or I didn't mean to."

That stopped Rani in her tracks. She turned to him. They'd reached the campus quad, and the blinding noon sun was making it impossible to look up at his face. "Oh gosh." How had it taken her so long to figure it out? "There was something in that tea, wasn't there? You thought it was for me and you put something in my tea."

It was his turn for stunned silence.

She waited. The last-day-of-finals crowd milled around them.

Finally he spoke. "Listen." For the first time in the three weeks that he'd been begging for Vinny's number, every bit of arrogance and playfulness was gone from his eyes. "I just want to talk to her. I mean her no harm. Just one conversation, and if she isn't interested, you never have to see me again. Neither of you."

"Interested in what exactly?"

He ran his hands through his hair. He had that slightly oily jet-black Indian-man hair that stuck up straight from his scalp because it was too thick to lie flat. "I don't know. I just know that I haven't stopped thinking about her since that day. Maybe it's wanting to finish our conversation about books. I really don't know. It depends on what she wants."

"What do you want?"

"I want her number. I want to talk to her."

Sun or no sun, Rani stared right up at him. He was definitively handsome: intense, thickly lashed dark eyes; square jaw perpetually shadowed with the beginnings of stubble; etched lush mouth. Rani didn't trust men who looked like him. Actually, she didn't trust them no matter how they looked.

"Vinny is not like other people," she said. "She doesn't know how to keep her distance once she befriends you. She doesn't take things lightly. She won't know how to put you in your place if you're an ass to her. Sorry, that's not true. It's not that she won't know, it's that she won't do it, because she won't hurt anyone on principle. The bigger problem is that if she likes you, she won't know how to walk away no matter what."

"If you're trying to convince me to forget about her, you're doing a terrible job of it." Then his eyes said it again. *Please.*

"If you hurt her, I will make sure that you regret it for the rest of your life. I will find a way to destroy you."

The sun moved behind him, and Rani was finally able to study him in the sudden shade he cast.

He didn't flinch or look away. "I know."

Rani flipped her notebook open and wrote Vinny's number down, making sure he couldn't see it. "There's one more thing you should know."

The eagerness in his eyes completely transformed him from broody to bright, and for a moment the terror Rani had been feeling on Vinny's behalf became too large inside her. He held out his hand, eyes on the paper.

When she didn't hand it over, he looked up at her. This part he needed to understand. "Whatever you put in my tea, if you had done that to her, she wouldn't be this mad at you. She got this mad because you tried to hurt me. Don't ever forget what that means."

"I won't."

Rani tore the page out and handed him the number. It was like she'd lit a fire inside him. Veritable sparks exploded from his eyes. He threw his arms around her, totally violating her boundaries. She pushed him away and shoved down the kick of discomfort that being touched always brought.

He raised both hands and stepped away.

"If you hurt her, I know ways to hurt you that you won't ever recover from," she said again.

Instead of mocking her, he smiled. "The mob could learn a thing or two from you two." With that he took off, the number clutched in both hands, as though one hand wasn't enough to contain it.

∿

"So?" Rani asked as Vinny put the phone down. Vinny's face was flaming. Her cheeks always went tomato red when she was bursting with emotion.

She pushed her hair off her face with the back of her hand. The Princess Diana pageboy Rani had made her get suited her; it framed the soft round lines of her face perfectly.

They were twenty-one, and Rani had never seen Vinny talk to a boy on the phone this way, receiver clutched tightly to her cheek like a beloved kitten, eyes glowing like fragile crystals, even more fiery and vulnerable than usual.

"So, let's discuss where we should go shopping for our dresses for the anniversary party."

"Or you could tell me about the phone call with your Romeo," Rani said, throwing herself back on Vinny's circular canopy bed. This bed and Vinny's room were Rani's favorite places in the world. The over-the-top decadence of lying on a round bed never got old.

"There's nothing to tell." Vinny sat there, at the edge of the bed, all stiff with determination. "And he's not my Romeo."

Rani rolled over on her side, a deep sigh escaping her. "You were on the phone for twenty minutes. That's a lot of nothing to tell. Plus, your face says otherwise."

Vinny pressed her hands to her face. "What do you think my face says, then?"

"It says he asked you out." Rani pictured Vir Guru's intensity-laced charm sliding out of the receiver like silken ropes and wrapping around Vinny's already smitten heart.

Vinny's response was to make a face by twisting her lips this way, then that.

"Please tell me you didn't turn him down."

Vinny shrugged, but there was something going on with her face that Rani had never seen there before.

"Why?" Rani asked.

"Because I don't want to go out with him."

"Since when do you lie to your best friend?"

The look Vinny gave her was too sad by half.

"He's already apologized for the tea. It's not like you to hold grudges."

"Why have you let it go so easily? What happened to 'Rani Parekh doesn't do forgiveness'? It's not like you to not hold grudges. Why have you forgiven him so easily?"

The way she said it and the scrutiny that accompanied her words made the flickering light bulb in Rani's brain flash on. Of course! How could she have missed it?

"Vinny, the only reason I'm not upset with him is because he wore me down with his obsession with getting to you. And because I have an A in writers' workshop. Thanks to you. This is about you, not about me."

Vinny didn't answer. She just looked more stubborn and even more tortured. "It's my day to make dinner. Let's go to the kitchen. I don't need another lecture if it's not ready when Mummy gets home." She got up to leave.

Rani grabbed her hand and pulled her back. "I'll help you. We have time before she gets home. Spit it out, Vinny. What's going on?"

"It's not like I've ever gone out with any other guy. Why is this surprising?"

"Because it's not like you to get into conversations with guys over books in diners. Or to mope for three weeks after. You have feelings for this guy. It's obvious from your face right now."

"No, I don't." Her jaw worked. "I can't."

"Why?"

"Because *you* do."

Rani sat up so fast the mattress bounced under them both. "What? No, I don't!"

"Rani?"

"Vinny!"

"Don't lie."

"I'm not! Why would you think that?"

"Because of how you talked about him. Before we met. You never think anyone is handsome. You said he was handsome."

"No, I didn't. I said he was *technically* handsome. And I said it only when you pushed me to."

"Something obviously happened between you two that day."

"The only thing that has happened between us is him getting on my last nerve in his attempts to get to you."

"Before that. Before you thought I was interested." She looked so fiercely determined Rani wanted to hug her. "You did think of him that way. Don't lie. At least a little bit?" God, she really liked this guy, and it was so frickin' adorable.

"Not even a little bit. I swear."

Vinny obviously didn't believe her. People often tended to overlook just how stubborn this girl was.

Rani took a breath and moved next to her. Their legs dangled off the high bed, and Rani thought of all the years they'd spent here like this. "You know I find Indian guys icky, right?" Despite her best effort, she couldn't keep her voice light.

Vinny studied her, her perceptive ears picking up everything in Rani's voice that she hadn't meant to let slip. "You realize how self-loathing that is, right?"

Rani made a face. "I don't loathe myself. I loathe them. So it's them-loathing, not self-loathing."

Vinny blinked. "You loathe Vir?"

Oh dear. "No, Vinny, I do not loathe the man who's making you grill your best friend right now. I really like him *for you*. When I first saw the two of you together, bonding over books like homing lobsters, I had that moment that people are supposed to have—the one where you know you're going to spend the rest of your life with someone. But it was on your behalf. My brain literally went: *Oh my God, I'm stuck with this man for life because my best friend in the whole wide world is going to spend the rest of her life with him."*

"Really?"

"Cross my heart and hope to die."

Vinny continued to look unsure. So stubborn. "But you said he was handsome, and you said he was interesting."

"I didn't."

Vinny narrowed her eyes. "Do I ever forget things people say?"

"It might be a useful skill to pick up. Most things people say deserve to be forgotten. Also, I said he found himself interesting, which means the opposite of what you're taking it as."

"But you were riled up by him. You're never riled up by guys."

"No, Vinny, I was annoyed. He was riled up. Because he thought he had to stand up for what he believes in. Like someone else I know."

Vinny's eyes did that thing, the thing that said: *See! You did like him.* Her face went all determined again, and it covered up all sorts of sadness.

Rani squeezed her temples. Vinny had it bad. But she was going to torture herself out of it if Rani didn't nip this nonsense in the bud.

Because it was nonsense, and Rani needed to put it definitively to rest. Forever.

Great, just great.

Rani took another breath and braced herself. Tightening her body the way she did before a marathon round of kathak chakkars. If she could do fifty spins without stopping, she could do this.

She had to.

Vinny was watching her. Trying to peer all the way inside her. Not that she'd ever see what was really inside Rani, because she was blind to the ugliness inside people. Also Rani was really good at hiding it.

So Rani would just have to spell it out. This one time.

"What you said earlier," Rani said, clearing her throat so the words wouldn't stick. "About the self-loathing? It's not that simple."

That's it. That's all she had to say, and Vinny got really quiet and soft, the way she always did when Rani felt like this. Like monsters were invading her. Like she was a monster herself. A part of Rani wanted to stop. This was idiotic. To go where she never went. Into the ancient past that had nothing to do with her anymore.

The room that had felt bright and sparkly around them a minute ago started to slide into darkness, a net of gray falling over it and sucking away at every bit of comfort.

No. She was safe here. She was safe now. Untouchable. She had been since the first day she stepped into this house.

Vinny didn't push her, didn't touch her. She just sat there, patience emanating from her like the morning mist that bathed them when they walked along the ocean before sunrise. On anyone else, expectation would have taken over; the desperate need to believe that her best friend and she were not coveting the same man would have taken over. On Vinny it was the other part that won out, the part that cared nothing for anyone or anything because she knew she'd opened something up for Rani and the pain it caused Rani was all that mattered to her.

"I'm sorry, Rani," she said so softly Rani barely heard her.

It was enough. It dug the words out of Rani. Sludge from the very edges of the sewer of her past. All she had to do was squeeze it up and out. "The reason I don't date Indian guys, the reason I don't go anywhere near them, is that I can't." Rani tried to relax her jaw as it tightened around the words in a death grip. This was for Vinny. It had nothing to do with Rani.

Vinny didn't say a word, but those filterless eyes filled with everything that was rushing through Rani. She might have no idea what Rani was talking about, but she saw every bit of what it was costing Rani to get it out. Once Rani said the words, they couldn't be unheard. That too, Vinny knew. Still she sat there, wide open. The way she always had.

Cool evening breeze hushed through the open window. The filmy pink drapes fluttered on the canopy. They sat in silence on that gigantic bed.

Rani considered swallowing back the words that fought her so hard that bile inched up her throat with them. But she couldn't push away the hope that had flashed in Vinny's eyes. Hope Vinny would crush so long as she believed there was any chance that Rani was interested in this man who seemed to have found his way past Vinny's shell.

Rani had no interest in Vir. She never would. It was just not something she was capable of.

"I feel physically sick," Rani said, prying those words from her uncooperative jaw. "The thought of intimacy when it mixes with an Indian guy . . . it makes me physically sick."

Realization that had been floating above them in a cloud settled on Vinny's face. Although she had never asked about it, she'd known Rani wasn't normal. It had been obvious when they met. Rani had already had that patina of damaged goods. It was part of her appeal. A darkness that made her interesting to people.

That wasn't what made her interesting to Vinny—Rani did know that—but even Vinny couldn't deny the broken parts inside her. Even though she, with Vinny's help, had done a pretty good job of patching up the most gaping cracks.

Vinny scooted closer until their arms and legs were touching. It was like a pump filling Rani's limp body with air. "When I was little," she went on. "Back in India. Stuff happened." She took a breath. "Ugly stuff. It feels like I'm dying when I think about it. It has to do with that." Muscle memory was a brutal thing, and Rani's throat turned raw, making gagging tears press at her eyes. She clenched her body tight, knowing that letting a single tear fall was not an option. She was never going back there.

Vinny slipped an arm around Rani, squeezed her into herself. Brought her back to this moment. "You didn't need to tell me that just because you think I like a guy."

Rani smiled. "Why didn't you tell me that before I told you?"

Vinny smiled back and wiped her own cheeks with the cuff of her sweatshirt. Rani envied her the comfort of her tears. "Why have you never told me before? Should you talk to someone?"

"I talk to a lot of people." Rani grabbed a tissue from the nightstand and handed it to Vinny.

"I mean someone who can help you."

"Isn't that what I'm doing right now?"

"No. You're trying to help me right now. I meant like a therapist."

"Aren't you thinking about being a therapist?"

"Maybe. But even if I do become one, I could never be your therapist. You can't treat family. It's unethical and illegal too, I think, to treat someone you love."

"Good to know. But I'm fine." She was. Everything was back in its place. "The point of this entire conversation is that when I see a desi man, I never, ever have any feelings of attraction. So, I definitely did not have feelings of attraction toward your boyfriend."

"He's not my boyfriend."

"Not yet. And only because you're too focused on my feelings instead of your own."

Vinny's thumb stroked Rani's shoulder. It was a gesture of such familiarity, it brought Rani fully back into herself.

"Will it help to talk about it with me?" Vinny gave another stubborn, albeit gentle, push.

"Not even a little bit." Rani wanted to forget she'd said those words, forget everything and put it back where it belonged in the lockbox of a past she'd defeated, thank you very much. "I do want to talk about why you're not on that phone yet, calling him back and telling him you want to see him?"

"Rani?"

"Vinny!" She met her friend's eyes, let her see exactly how much she needed to move on.

Vinny sighed. Why was she still not jumping up to pick up that phone? "You want to tell me what else is going on? Is it whatever he put in my tea?"

Vinny started, as though she'd forgotten that happened. "I don't know." Her mouth opened, then closed.

Ah. Now Rani saw it. Her best friend and her inability to do anything without overthinking the life out of it.

"It's just meeting him for a dinner. You're not marrying him," Rani said. "Take one day at a time. It's natural to be afraid when you wait until you're twenty-one to have the hots for someone."

Vinny smiled. "I'm terrified."

"I know. Care to explain why?"

Vinny shrugged and looked down at herself, eyes filled with meaning, as though the question didn't need asking.

Rani narrowed her eyes. There was no way she was dignifying that with a response.

"Come on, Rani, why would someone like him be interested in someone like me?"

"Vinny!" Rani pushed herself off the bed. "Stop it. You're beautiful!"

Vinny rolled her eyes.

"You are! But that's the least important thing about you."

"If you say I'm beautiful on the inside, I'll kill you. That's just something beautiful people say to those who are average."

"But you *are*. You are also beautiful on the inside. That's the part that matters. What's on the outside counts for nothing ten minutes after a person meets you."

Vinny's incredibly beautiful eyes said she heard those words but they didn't register.

Rani wanted to shake her. "Don't you see? The moment you opened your mouth, it was like I stopped existing for this guy. I've never had that happen to me. I would exchange my face for that in an instant. Stop using your inability to see your own beauty as an excuse for being scared. Since when do you hide from what you want instead of going after it?"

Vinny blinked and sat up, finally aware of what an idiot she was being. "Fine," she said.

Rani wasn't done yet. Vinny had to understand this without a shred of a doubt. "Here is the thing that matters, and I want you to really get this into your hard head before you pick up that phone. If you're going to let this guy near you and open up that heart of yours to him, then you'd better make sure you never forget, not even for a moment, how incredibly lucky the bastard is."

CHAPTER SIXTEEN

VANDY

Saturday, 11:30 p.m. . . .

Vir loved to joke that getting Vandy to go out with him was the hardest thing he'd ever done. But he had never had to learn to live without her. He'd never had to deal with the fear of losing Mallika.

He would know what to do. That thought kept running through Vandy's mind.

You were the one who always knew, his voice said. *You chose for us.*

She put Vir's picture back on the nightstand and made her way to the bookshelves that lined one wall of their bedroom. These shelves had been his life, these words constellations he followed in his quest for authenticity. A *Publishers Weekly* reviewer had once called him an "important Indian American voice." Vandy had framed that review for him. An austere black frame with thick white mounting.

It was the only review that hung in their home, next to his beloved bookshelves. Vir had insisted on not having an office. He wrote all over the house. He loved taking his laptop to the beach, and coffee shops, and public parks. *I can't make up different stuff in the same place,* he'd said.

Vandy's eyes skimmed the shelves and sought out the faded book spine that was sandwiched between other faded spines. It pulled her like gravity. *A Bend in the Ganges*. Their first shared love.

The hook he'd so desperately used to get to her. He'd never needed it. Vandy had been a goner the first time those intense eyes slid her way. Even though it had taken him a moment to look past her friend's glow and notice her. A journey no man before him had managed to complete.

Vandy had sworn from the start to not let it matter. What did matter was that once he'd noticed Vandy, the hook had snared him just as hard as it had snared her.

She pulled the book off the shelf. The faded orange leg of the unrecognizable mythological figure loomed over a blue sky gone gray with time.

She turned the page to the epigraph from the *Ramayana* when Lord Rama paused for the last time to survey the land he was being banished from. It had been something Vir often quoted. You never leave your past behind, and yet you must.

The truest words she knew. It had taken her a lifetime to understand them, and she still didn't sometimes.

Saliva gathered in her mouth at the memory of the salt in her tea that first time they'd met in the diner. Not the little hint that had become popular in sweet things these days. He'd put what felt like a heaping spoonful of it in what he believed was Rani's iced tea. It had been Vandy's, of course, and that one sip had felt like an ocean wave taking her under. It had burned down her gullet. Not a small meanness.

He'd never denied it.

Their relationship had started with forgiveness. Why had that never struck Vandy until this moment?

Rani had made him pay. She'd made him write the final essay for her class before she gave him Vandy's number. *If I get an A, I'll think about it,* she'd told him.

She'd made him beg for weeks before she even made that concession.

Rani had gotten an A+. Back then, before Vandy knew his talent, the freshness of her love had soaked up his words, reveled in the feminine rage of them. *Empathy is the heart of character development, not just channeling someone but inhabiting their existence,* he'd told her later. *That essay is what I would have needed to say were I a woman.*

He'd lived for that, for the fullness of understanding life and people, which was such a sharp contrast to putting salt in someone's tea. She'd asked him about it on their first date, a walk on Venice Beach.

I was being immature. My feelings were hurt, and I took it out where it wasn't deserved. And there's no excuse for that, he'd answered honestly. *Seeing the two of you sitting there like you belonged. Like you didn't care about where you came from. Like you were part of the crowd that made me invisible. It made all the things I was already angry about from that argument in class boil up.*

Vandy would find out soon enough that he was always clear about where the faults lay. Where exactly they came from and what they cost. She'd been more focused on how they could be fixed.

So you tried to poison my friend?

Salt is only poisonous if consumed in excessive quantities. I knew she wouldn't drink more than a sip.

If Rani had been the one to drink it, and complained. You could have lost your job.

Is that why you didn't tell my manager, because you thought I'd lose my job?

Is that why you've been chasing me, because you want to know why I didn't, because you want to know what my agenda is?

That's when she'd noticed how he looked at her. With single-minded focus, as though she were the answer to questions he hadn't even asked yet. He'd decided who she was, and he liked it.

I'm hoping it's because you felt what I felt and you couldn't bear to get me in trouble because of it.

Vir and his way with words. From the very beginning his words had been the end of her.

Then it was his actions that had held her tight.

He was right. Vandy had felt what he felt, but that wasn't why she hadn't told his manager about the tea.

The person she wanted to protect him from wasn't his manager. It was Rani. She'd wanted—*needed*—Rani to like him, and Rani had been convinced he was a jerk.

My friend has a sixth sense about people. She's never wrong about them, and she basically thinks you're a scumbag, Vandy had told him.

Exceptions prove a rule, he'd said. *Maybe this is the one time her sixth sense is wrong.*

He'd been right about that too. Those two had become friends soon enough. Until Vandy had ruined that.

As for the rest of the Mehtas, Vandy had needed to force their hand.

What kind of life can he provide? her mother had said. *What do you mean he's a writer? That just means he has no job.*

Vandy had always known she didn't want her mother's life. She would never sacrifice her self-respect for a big house and a doctor's salary.

He loves me. His love is steadfast. That's all she'd said to her mother, because the word she really wanted to say, "faithful," had felt unutterable between them.

Mummy had never asked her what she saw in Vir again. She'd simply changed how she expressed her disappointment. Lying about how well he was doing to her friends in front of him. *Our Vir's last book was a bestseller. Our Vir's book has been optioned for a movie.*

She'd lied about Vandy too, praised her for being domestic. Boasted about how well Vandy cooked and kept house.

Vandy's too busy to cook, Vir had told Mummy's friends at a party they'd thrown when they moved into this house. He'd waited for Vandy to say it first, but when she remained silent, he'd said it himself. *Good thing I love to cook and keep home for my family.*

I do love it, you know, he'd said to Vandy later. *Taking care of our home and our family. I'm proud of it.*

I know, Vandy said.

Then you should also know that your silence makes it seem like you don't. Like you're ashamed.

Vandy wasn't proud of how long it had taken her to acknowledge him as the nurturer, the homemaker. How long it had taken her to see how strong he'd been in the face of the unmanning the world put him through. They thought nothing could be more humiliating than making a man feel less like a man.

Vir had laughed. *Do you think they'll ever figure out what a scam gender roles are?*

How clearly he'd seen the world. How fortunate she'd been to have him.

Just because your father does some things you don't like doesn't mean he's not a good husband or a good man, her mother had said when Vandy had thrown Vir a party on his fortieth birthday and given a speech about all the things that made him a great husband.

Vandy stroked the book in her hand. The thing she remembered being most affected by in the story was the distance life could take you in a matter of moments. One day you were on a beach in a swimsuit, secure in the solidity of the world laid out before you. The next day the world had changed beyond recognition. You had changed beyond recognition. Vir always said that the best stories were the ones where reality shifted in an instant. Everything you believed about yourself fell into question.

She pressed the book to her chest and was about to put it back when something slid from it and fell to the floor. A ghastly jolt of pain radiated from her knee as she leaned over to pick it up.

A Polaroid. The pain in her knee slid into her veins and pumped through her body. It couldn't be. Three sepia-toned faces smiled at her from behind the faded gloss of the photograph.

Rani sandwiched between Vir and her. All three of them had their hands on her swollen belly.

Tahoe, mere months before everything had changed.

Rani had hated having her picture taken. Hated it. Which meant there had been fewer pictures to remove from albums after she left.

Vandy turned the photo over, and there in Vir's perfect penmanship was the inscription "Forever . . ."

Had the picture always been here? Had Vir held on to it and put it there? Had he meant for Vandy to find it?

She dropped into the recliner by the window, one of Vir's favorite writing spots. It had given him a stiff back when he sat here too long with his laptop. But when that's where he wanted to write, that's where he wanted to write.

Vir had left the picture in the book for a reason.

Ignoring the truth won't make it go away. How could Rani's voice still be so clear in her ears?

You know what you need to do. Would Vir's voice always be so clear too?

The answer is closer to home.

She fished her phone out of her pocket. It was time to figure out who'd been in her home. She was going to have to go through the security camera footage. Her fingers hesitated, but she forced herself to pull up the security company's app and started scrolling through the videos.

Footage from the past day was just Vandy walking around the house. Seeing herself on the screen was a shock. Shoulders dragged down, moving with the slowness of a corpse. Slumped into Mika's favorite chair, then Vir's, then Mika's, then Vir's. A translucent ghost with the substance of life gone from her. The exact opposite of the

Sonali Dev

recordings of her onstage at her seminars. A puppet held up by the purpose of others.

There were hours and hours of footage of nothing but the grieving stagnant air in the house that had been Vir's creation. Every painting on the wall, every piece of furniture, every rug and artifact a story he wanted to tell, a setting he wanted to create for their family.

She fast-forwarded through most of it, letting the pain spin through her.

Until everything stopped. In the footage from four days ago, the front door opened, and Mallika let herself in.

She was in shorts and a tank, and she was not alone.

A young man a head taller than her with a mop of curly hair that fell in springs over his forehead followed her in. It had to be Amey's friend, Rex. Vandy wouldn't have been able to place him if not for Tinku and Pinky.

Mallika removed her sandals, and Rex went down on one knee to untie his laces. Then he stood again and slipped off his sneakers, toeing them off as the two gazed at each other. The way their bodies were angled, he might as well have just gone down on his knee to put a ring on her finger.

It wasn't until he stepped closer and cupped Mika's cheek that Vandy realized that Mallika looked nothing like herself. Not because she looked smitten but because her body didn't have its usual buoyancy. Mallika tended to bounce and spin. She'd always been like that, light of step, as though life was making her want to skip.

Now a weight seemed to stoop her shoulders. Rex said something, and Mika smiled reluctantly. At least he could make her smile when she was sad. It was probably the single most important thing in any relationship: the ability to make each other smile when there was pain.

Mallika took his hand and dragged him into the foyer and then up the curving staircase. The cameras covered only the lower floor. Vir had joked that if burglars landed on the roof in helicopters, they would

156

probably also know how to disable cameras. The idea had thrilled her writer husband to no end.

Vandy waited, unable to fast-forward, needing to feel the stillness on the screen, because that sense she'd lived with for twenty-seven years—the one that told her the seeds of your karma always, always germinated—that sense was suddenly alive under her skin. All the way up near the surface, pushing against it, dotting it with goose bumps.

In her hand the faded Polaroid seemed to turn hot.

Time ticked by, so slow that years swept through Vandy, decades. Mallika's dresses at every birthday, her ghagra at every kathak performance. That moment when she'd come back from a trip to India with Vir when she was seven and insisted that she wanted to learn to dance. Vir pretending he didn't notice Vandy's reaction.

How hard Vandy had fought to hide her moment of panic.

Why dance?

Then seeing how good Mallika was. Just naturally. Filled with grace. Ethereal onstage, lilting into movement the moment the music turned on.

Before Vandy could catch her breath, Mallika appeared on the screen again. She raced down the stairs, something clutched to her chest. Rex kept pace with her, then put his arm around her as they got to the bottom. Vandy paused and zoomed in on them before they headed to the door. Tap by tap, enlarging the thing Mallika was clutching. The image got grainier as she got closer.

It wasn't entirely clear what the object in her daughter's hand was, but it wasn't unclear either. Not with the alarm bells clanging inside Vandy.

For a second Mallika seemed to meet her eyes, as though she knew Vandy was watching. She threw a look down at the object in her hand. Vandy had never seen that particular look of determination on her daughter's face, but it was so painfully familiar that it made Vandy's heart crack right down the middle.

CHAPTER SEVENTEEN

MALLIKA

Four days ago . . .

M aybe you were adopted?" Rex asks me.
"I don't think it's that," I say. The shock in my voice is thick. My voice feels changed, like everything I will ever say from now on will come out like this, surprised. "Why would my parents lie about that?" They aren't the kind of people who would differentiate between an adopted child and a biological one, let alone lie about it. Then again, I've always believed they wouldn't lie to me about anything.

He shrugs. Obviously, he has no answer for that.

We're walking around my uncles' neighborhood. Endless stucco walls cascade with hot-pink bougainvillea around gigantic mansions and emphasize our smallness. A steady stream of joggers whizzes past us on the steeply sloping sidewalks. I'm out of breath all the way down to my soul.

"All I know is that my mother lost six pregnancies before I was born." I don't know why I say that. Why I want it to sound like an explanation.

I've never seen a picture of her pregnant.

I've never heard her talk about her pregnancy the way a lot of aunties love to do.

Pinky (*twenty-two hours of back labor and twelve episiotomy stitches!*) and Tinku (*an emergency C-section, which someone who was lucky enough to have a vaginal delivery would never understand!*) revel in the gory details of their labor and delivery. I've heard the stories over and over.

Now I realize that Mom was never present when those conversations happened. No one ever talks about pregnancy and childbirth around my mother.

Is that even true? Or is my mind making it up?

The hollow pain in Mom's eyes at the mention of her pregnancies flashes bright and stark in my memory. I know that's not made up. For some reason I remember things that hurt my parents. I've always known this. I have the most overactive built-in gauge for their pain.

I did ask for details once. I must've been twelve. It was after a sex ed seminar, when Mrs. Clete broke it to us how babies are born. It was horrifying. My friends and I had dealt with the discomfort by making jokes about the teacher's unfortunate name. Who in their right mind thought it was a good idea to show twelve-year-olds childbirth videos?

Mrs. Clete had asked the class if we'd seen pictures of ourselves in our mothers' bellies. Svetlana Bosch had started to cry. We'd learned later that she was adopted. I wonder how she's doing now. I wonder why I hadn't taken the time to ask her why the grainy pictures of ultrasounds that looked like nothing at all had made her cry.

My curiosity for seeing myself as a wispy blob of white clouds in a black sky had been mild at best.

Instead of asking Mom or Papa, I'd gone to my naani. The gauge that told me what would hurt my parents had told me to ask Naani.

Do you think Mom has a picture of me in her uterus? I remember using the word "uterus," because yes, Ms. Clete had also informed us that we were now old enough to use grown-up words for body parts. Penis, vagina, breasts, scrotum, uterus.

Naani had continued to roll out her parathas without pause. Her brows, which were always threaded to the thinnest arches by a beautician who made house calls to take care of her beauty needs, rose enough to let me know that she'd heard me use that grown-up word.

I don't know. They didn't do this big song-and-dance tamasha about these things back then. Why do you ask?

Just curious, I answered. *I've seen Amey's and Aarav's in their baby albums.*

Naani slid a paratha onto my plate and slapped a larger-than-normal dollop of butter on it. Then she fixed me with her sharpest gaze. *Your mom had to be very careful with her hope when you were inside the* uterus. She emphasized the word "uterus," of course. *Your mom and papa had other things on their mind than fuzzy pictures.*

It seemed like a good opportunity for recon, so I'd tried to glean as much information as I could from the situation. *Why did Mama lose so many babies?*

Because some uteruses have a hard time carrying babies. It was something that made your mom very sad.

That had done it. That's how I'd known to never bring it up again. Seeing Mom sad is something I've never been able to bear.

After my grandfather died when I was seventeen, I remember Mom holding my naani and crying as though her heart was broken. Seeing her cry like that had made me so restless I'd needed to do something. Papa had taught me how to make Mom's favorite frittata for breakfast to cheer her up. She'd wrapped her arms around me and held me tight and told me how I was the best thing that ever happened to her.

It had been that easy. Since Papa died, it's like I've lost Mom too. She hasn't cried. Not one tear. And not crying in front of her myself feels like the only way to keep her grief bearable.

Papa always said that the only thing that mattered was the three of us. Our perfect triangular family, stable on every base. If Papa were here,

I'd have gone to him without a second thought and asked why Amey and I are not genetically related.

Things were easy with Papa in a way I can't explain. He was the most chilled-out person. All my friends' fathers, Raj and Taj Maama, my grandfather, they'd been so demanding. About grades, respect, behavior. My cousins still don't drink in front of their parents because they believe it's disrespectful. They had loved to have a drink with Papa. They'd loved to tell him things, to come to him with problems, to involve him in their pranks.

The world came to Mom with problems, but Papa had been the one the family, at least the children in the family, came to. He never judged. He believed in the beauty of life; the complexity of it excited him. To him there was no wrong way to live. He'd once told me that the single most important thing in life was to know what you valued, and once you got that, to never forget you had it.

For the first half of my life I'd called Papa by his name: Vir. He'd never corrected me. I'm pretty sure he loved it. For some reason, it bothered everyone else in the family. When I was thirteen, I heard my naana say to my naani, *What kind of man lets his child call him by his name? That's even worse than letting your wife make more money than you.*

I stopped calling him by his name after that and started calling him Papa.

"Hey." Rex's voice breaks through the thick press of my memories. Apparently I'm crying again.

It feels like what I've just shared with him is too painfully private. Suddenly he feels like a stranger. All the happiness of the past two days feels crushed out of me, like a boa constrictor has squeezed the breath from me.

"I'm fine," I say, and it's such a blatant lie that a laugh accompanies my words.

He wipes the tears from my cheeks. He touches me all the time now. I've been doing it too. His mouth opens and closes. There isn't anything he can say to console me because I'm not even sure why I'm crying.

He manages to find the one thing that won't hurt. "What can I do to help?"

My laugh grows bigger. Why does he have to be so perfect when I feel like the perfection of my life is dissolving into the air around me? The need to turn around and run is back full force. I'm terrified. Too many things lurk at the edges of my vision. Things that feel like they're gnashing their teeth to eat me whole. Like the monsters in my father's stories.

"You're a genetics guy," I say because the technical term for what he does flies out of my head like a metaphor for my grip on everything I believed about my own life. "Can you explain what this means? Could there be an error in the test?"

He keeps his voice flat, not taking any space from my feelings as they saturate the air between us. "Our equipment splices nucleic acid down to point two microns. The absence of genetic connection that we found can be read by machines ten generations behind in technology."

"So what you're saying is that the test cannot be wrong?" I try to smile but fail.

He moves infinitesimally closer to me. "I did have them rerun the test. It's not wrong. I also had them confirm it was you. Your age, sex, race—everything else matches. But we can go back in and run it again with a fresh sample if you want."

I definitely want to do that, but there's more. There's a whole lot more I need to know, and I don't know where to start.

We don't lie in my family. That's the thought that keeps circling my brain.

Without thinking about it, I call my mother. Her voice calms me, then crushes my heart. She sounds exhausted. She's always been the most vital person I know. A force of nature, always peaceful but constantly making things happen. Since Papa's death, however, she's been dragging herself around, trying to appear strong.

Suddenly I'm livid at the world. At everyone who goes on and on about how strong she is, how gracefully she's handled her grief. No one sees that she's depleted all the way to her bones.

Instead of asking her what I want to, I ask how her tour is going. She tells me it's going well. Then she asks me how I am. I tell her the same lie she just told me. And the compass inside me that separates truth from lies spins out of control. I guess we do lie in our family after all. For the first time in my life, I have no idea what to say to her. For the first time in my life, she doesn't pick up on my feelings.

I catch myself in another lie. It's not the first time. These past eleven months, she's had no interest in anything but appearing strong. Her grief is like a mountain sitting atop my own. I tell her I love her and let her go.

It would be impossibly cruel to ask her about the test right now. About why my cousin isn't my biological cousin. Whether they've lied to me all my life. Am I not theirs? Does it even matter? I don't know. I have no answers. Only questions cascading over questions.

The only thing I know with clarity is that if I follow the thread of questions, I'm going to unravel my life. I wait for instinct to kick in. For the voice that tells me to drop it and back away. Because all that matters is that Mom and I have each other.

Rex and I round the sloping curve of my uncles' street, and the panoramic view of the bay shrinks the hills we're standing on, making everything insignificant.

Rex watches me, his focus harsh like the noon sun unfiltered by clouds, but also soft and inescapable like the mint-and-earth smell of eucalyptus that saturates the air around us. He doesn't say anything, doesn't make any assurances, reminding me that there aren't any to be made.

"Maybe it's not as simple as that," he says carefully. "In science we don't accept any theory as fact unless it's been proved."

I give him a look that says: go on.

"All we know right now is that Amey and you are not genetically related."

"Which is not possible if I'm my parents' daughter. Or Amey isn't his parents' son." Amey is a spitting image of his father. It's eerie how similar they look.

There's another long silence.

"Amey is your mother's brother's son, correct?" Rex says finally.

I nod, my eyes hooking into what I see in his.

"If you want to know definitively what this means, we need to test your mother's DNA."

"Like a maternity test?" It sounds strange; an awkward smile escapes me. "In the sense of a paternity test."

He nods.

"How would I do that without her finding out?"

"All we need is some genetic material from her. The most common samples are saliva or hair."

~

It takes precisely twenty minutes for us to make it to the home I grew up in and steal my mother's hairbrush.

I'm shaking as we step out into the sunshine. Manhattan Beach, where my parents live, isn't quite as dramatic as Palos Verdes Estates, but the magic of the ocean is somehow more alive here. The sound of waves, the smell of surf, the sparkle of sand sprinkled into the crevices of everyday life.

I grip the brush like my life depends on it. Thank God my mother isn't a neat freak like Papa was. There's a few strands of her wavy hair stuck in the prongs of her bamboo bristle brush. If this were Papa's hairbrush, there would be no hair to test. The thought is a spike of pain in my heart. How can he be so definitively gone when I still feel him everywhere?

I touch a thick, springy strand that tangles around a bristle and pokes its head up and away. Mom is still here. Mom is all I have. The silver strand catches the sun. Mom has let her hair gray naturally. It's something she's proud of, as though she's broken some construct of the patriarchy by not coloring her hair.

My naani still dyes hers. An auburn brown. Which says everything about why Mom doesn't color hers. I can pick up the phone and ask my naani why her two grandchildren don't share genetic material. I know my naani loves me unequivocally. Maybe even more than she loves my cousins, her other grandchildren. Nonetheless, any conversation with her that involves my parents has always made me feel like a pawn. It started when I picked up on the fact that she and my naana didn't think too highly of Papa.

He didn't think too highly of them either. Mom always seemed to know how to handle their dislike for each other. Then again, Mom isn't like the rest of us lesser mortals. She handles emotions like they're puzzle pieces, ones she knows exactly where to place for them to make sense. She always has an answer. She always knows exactly what any situation needs. *Your mother is magic,* Papa always said.

Except now her magic feels too fragile for my questions.

My stomach churns. I can't call Naani. I know without a doubt that this has to stay between my parents and me. Even having Rex here feels traitorous.

I look over at him. He's driving me back to the lab in his Honda Accord. Something about the fact that he drives a Dad Car makes this terrible moment better.

"My father drove this same car," I say.

He looks away from the road and at me. "I'm sorry. I don't think I ever offered my condolences to you. He was such a great guy."

I sit up. "I didn't realize you knew Papa."

"Amey introduced us when I was thinking about writing my book. He helped me find an agent."

"Your book? I didn't know you'd written a book."

"It's nonfiction. *The Genetic Myth of Excellence*. With the work I've done over the past decade, there's a lot there that busts myths about where stars in any field come from. He really helped me get the structure and the framing for it right. He was brilliant."

"He was," I want to say, but I'm choked by the thought that I'm not sure if he was my father. And the fact that he died without telling me the truth. My entire childhood, my entire life, every conversation, every warm memory feels inaccessible. I can't lose him like this. This is worse than losing him to death. This is like losing his spirit, like losing having ever had him.

Just like that, I'm hyperventilating again.

Rex crosses six lanes of LA traffic and pulls over on the shoulder.

"Mallika," he says, leaning across the center console and rubbing my back. "We don't know anything for sure yet. But we'll figure it out."

That's the problem. Until a few hours ago, I knew for sure who I was. Now I have to figure things out.

I can't seem to say any of that out loud. My breath is pumping from my lungs too fast even as a lump is stuck in my throat.

Rex's hand is gentle on my back, and I try to hitch my thoughts to that.

"My older sister is adopted," he says. "I was a surprise baby after my parents adopted her. I can bet my life that they don't feel any differently about the two of us."

Through the cyclone of thoughts that's flown through my head these past few hours, the idea that my parents don't love me has never entered my head even once. The tightness in my lungs eases, and I stop struggling to breathe.

"It's not about love," I say. "It's about lies. Why would they lie to me about something so big?" That is the issue, I realize. The fact that they've lied can mean only one thing: whatever the truth is, it's so horrible it's unutterable.

That's what I'm most afraid of: the why.

He is right, though. I don't know anything yet. Not finding out is no longer an option. Running from this, letting it be—all the ways I've always dealt with things until this moment are of no use to me.

Now that I'm breathing steadily again, Rex stops rubbing my back and pulls away. I miss him immediately, but I can't get myself to do anything about it. He waits for me to nod to let him know that I'm fine. Then he merges back into traffic to take me to his office.

In less than an hour, I'll know for sure if my whole life has been a lie.

CHAPTER EIGHTEEN

RANI

1989
Thirty-four years ago . . .

I think I might be pregnant." Vandy's voice shook as she made the declaration on the phone.

"I'll be there in five minutes," Rani said before hanging up and rushing over.

Last month, Vinny had been ecstatic at having lost her virginity to the love of her life. Vir and Vinny had been dopey for one another for a year now, and Rani had started to smell the pheromones when they got within ten feet of each other. The fact that they'd waited so long wasn't surprising, given that they'd both decided that the other was the One from the very first time they went out. Since then it had been a matter of "waiting for the right time" because they "weren't in a hurry."

Rani would never know what someone being the One meant or felt like, but it made sense for them. Rani had the exact opposite approach. She had sex with men who wanted to do it and then be on their way. Her only requirement was that whatever interaction she had with a man was on her terms. Her on top always and no other touching.

In high school it was only too easy to find boys who wanted that. As she got older, men seemed to believe that she didn't mean what she said. They thought it was cute to take her on as a challenge. She cut them off instantly. But it was all too much work, and now that she'd proved to herself that she had control over her own body, she'd lost interest.

Vinny and Vir, of course, had overthought this whole "making love" thing to death. When, how, where . . . they were expecting the earth to tremble, and spontaneity had no place in that. In the most vicarious way, Rani had been nervous as hell too. The fact that they shared with Rani every thought that passed through their heads about their relationship was just part of being the best friend and official third wheel.

She waited at the front door, wondering if she should knock or just wait for Vinny to open the door as she usually did because she had to have heard Rani's car.

Usha Auntie flung the door open and presented Rani with narrowed eyes.

"Hi." Rani gave her a small wave.

"Hi." She didn't step aside and let Rani in.

"Everything okay?" Rani asked, trying to keep it nonchalant.

"I don't know, you tell me. It's been months since we've talked."

Not technically true, but true in spirit. "My hours have been brutal. I've still seen you every week, Usha Auntie." Rani's accounting job was kicking her ass, but she couldn't complain because it paid well.

"Yes, but these days I feel like you sneak in and out. You don't stay and talk to your auntie like you used to."

Fine, so it wasn't the job, it was the fact that Rani was the keeper of Vinny and Vir's secret. If that slipped, everything would be over for them.

"Sorry, Auntie. I'm usually here late because of work, and I don't want to wake you. I do miss seeing you."

Finally Usha Auntie softened and stepped aside to let Rani in. "How long have I known you?"

It was a rhetorical question, so Rani just smiled sheepishly in response and tried to think of how to make her escape from the inquisition she knew was coming.

"I can tell from your face that something is going on. It's a boy, isn't it?"

Last week when Vinny, Vir, and Rani were at the mall, Vinny had seen her mother come out of Sears. She had dived behind a Victoria's Secret mannequin, leaving Rani and Vir exposed. Panicking, Rani had run into a changing room. Obviously, she hadn't been fast enough, and Usha Auntie had seen her. Vir had followed suit and run into the changing rooms too.

"What boy?" Rani said, bringing all her acting chops to the fore. When she was seventeen and she'd attended Saroj Khan's dance workshop, Saroj had offered her a permanent spot on her troupe. She'd offered to introduce Rani to some filmmakers and told Rani that she had the potential to be a Bollywood heroine.

The idea of leaving LA was unfathomable. Going back to Mumbai downright impossible. Rani's whole life was in LA. Vinny was in LA. But Saroj was right: Rani could act.

"You know I don't have time for boys." Lying was all about sticking with the truth.

"You're twenty-two. You can't afford not having time for boys. Now is the time to make time so you're taken care of."

"Didn't you teach us that we need to take care of ourselves?"

"Of course you have to take care of yourself. Because you have to have a backup plan. That doesn't mean you can live by yourself. You'll have to have babies. Who will raise them if you go to work?"

That was not a problem Rani would ever have, because she was never having children. Not that she was stupid enough to say that to Vinny's mom.

Where the hell was Vinny? Why wasn't she rescuing Rani?

Oh yes, because she was upstairs freaking out about being pregnant.

"You know we're looking for boys for Vandy. I was thinking we should look for boys for you as well. Do you think Tina is very particular about the match being Gujarati? I was going to call her about it. Naturally I wanted to talk to you first."

This was the real reason Rani had been avoiding Usha Auntie. Vinny's mother had become obsessed with arranging a marriage for Vinny. Rani had not expected to be pulled in as a plus-one to that party!

Vinny should have been able to just tell her parents about Vir so they could stop worrying about her ending up a spinster. But she couldn't. They would never let her marry anyone who wasn't from their caste and community. If by some miracle they compromised on that, they would never be okay with Vinny not marrying a physician. An out-of-work writer was their worst nightmare.

"I know you like to be all footloose and fancy free," Usha Auntie said, wiggling her tweezed eyebrows. "If I loved you less, I wouldn't say anything, but you have to know that there's no point in wasting the best years of your life. The pool of marriageable men reduces as your age goes up."

All Rani wanted was for the pool to disappear entirely, because she was never taking the marital swim. But if she went there, they'd be here a long time. "I'm just not ready, Auntie. I want to work for a while and save up. Get that safety net you're always talking about."

"I was not born yesterday, beta. I saw you the other day. If you were in an unmentionables store with a man, then I can only hope it's someone serious."

Denying it would mean throwing Vinny under the bus. "That was just a friend. From work. I was helping him look for a gift for his girlfriend."

Sonali Dev

Usha Auntie didn't buy the story, but instead of pushing Rani she reached for a book on the console table. "Well, I hope you wouldn't hide something like this from me."

"There's no one in my life, Auntie. I swear."

"I know you kids think I'm being old fashioned, but all I want is for you to settle down before it's too late."

Before Rani could respond, Usha Auntie pulled a photograph from the book she was holding.

Oh dear.

She held up a man's picture. He looked like the weight of the world rested on his shoulders. As though he was afraid to smile lest people take him less seriously than he took himself.

"He's a neurosurgeon at Harvard. Father is a urologist at Stanford. Brother is a cardiologist at Northwestern."

"That's, umm, impressive."

"Right? I told you." She pressed the picture into Rani's hand. "Show it to your friend. She doesn't listen to anything I say anymore. He's in town, and he wants to meet her tomorrow. I've set up dinner at seven. I don't want her to miss this opportunity just because she's going through some American-child rebellion against her mother."

Rani took the picture and ran up the stairs.

When she let herself into Vinny's room, there was no one there. She made her way to the bathroom. The door was slightly ajar.

Vinny was sitting on the edge of the tub, sobbing.

Rani went to her and pulled her into her arms. "Did you take a test?"

Vinny shook her head so vehemently her bushy ponytail did a frantic dance. "I couldn't do it alone." Her gaze went to a box on the vanity.

Rani tore the package open. "How late are you?"

"Two weeks."

"That's not a whole lot." Vinny didn't have the most regular periods anyway.

172

"I threw up this morning. What are we going to do?" she said as though the result was already out.

"Didn't you guys use a condom?"

"We always do. But that day. Um . . . it got . . ." She went red in the face.

"Oh, Vinny." Rani was going to punch Vir. Guys never had to go through this panic. She tossed the photograph Usha Auntie had given her on the vanity and pulled out the instructions from the pregnancy test. "Let's do this." She handed Vinny the piece of plastic that could change their life.

As Vinny got to it, Rani started to tidy up the messy bathroom. No matter how many times she put things in their place, they always ended up in this disarrayed state. It was like Vinny considered putting things back in their place a test set by her mother, and she'd made up her mind not to pass on principle.

"What's this?" Vinny picked up the photograph Rani had forgotten about. Her wet eyes brightened with anger.

"Your would-be husband?" Rani laughed.

Vinny didn't. "Mummy gave that to you, didn't she?" For some reason the memory of Vinny calling her mother *Mommy* flashed in Rani's head.

How the two of them had hero-worshipped Usha Auntie. When had that changed?

How did mothers go from being rocks you relied on to being the rocks you had to climb over to make your own way?

"Isn't it rich?" Vinny said from the pot. Her pink-painted toes stuck out from under the dark-blue denim pooled around her ankles. The strip of plastic sat on the vanity as the timer on Rani's Casio ticked away. "How does Mummy, of all people, think she can dispense advice about marriage?"

"Come on, Vinny. She means well. She wants you to have a good life."

"I don't want her definition of a good life."

After she met Vir, Vinny's relationship with her own dad had all but disintegrated. She barely spoke to him. She could barely meet her mother's eyes. It was like she now had validation to reject the choices her parents had made in their own marriage.

That was Vinny for you. Everything was black or white. Right or wrong. Clear.

But life wasn't that simple. It was in fact an endless expanse of bleeding edges. Having whatever kind of marriage her parents had agreed to have didn't nullify the kind of parents they'd been. Vinny didn't see life that way. She believed that gray areas were excuses for when people chose wrong over right because making the right choice wasn't always easy.

Vinny got up and dropped the picture into the pot.

"Oops." She pulled the flush and watched the neurologist swirl away, along with her mother's dreams.

Suddenly the water stopped spinning and started to rise.

"Shit!" they both said as the waterline rose with alarming speed.

"The neurologist is blocking the opening. Do something!" Vinny said. And just like that they were laughing.

Rani reached into the pot and dislodged the neurologist. With a great big gurgle, the water rushed back into the drain.

Vinny grabbed the soggy picture from Rani's hand, shredded it to bits, and let it drop into the pot again. This time, there was no saving the poor guy. He was swept away into the sewers just as the timer on Rani's wristwatch went off.

The shrill beep startled the laughter from them.

They washed their hands.

"It's going to be okay." Rani squeezed Vinny's arm.

"I know." Vinny's eyes were suddenly clear. "As long as I have Vir and you, everything is always going to be okay." They were both deliberately not looking at the test. "Also, for the record, if I am pregnant, that's going to be okay too." Her eyes were ablaze with fierceness. "If I'm pregnant, I'm going to be the best mother on earth to this baby."

"Yes, you are," Rani said, an odd nervousness vibrating in her chest.

"So, let's look?" Vinny swallowed. "Together?"

"Together."

Hand in hand, they peered at the piece of plastic.

There was a strong red line.

"What does that mean?" Vinny asked.

"I think it means you're not pregnant."

"You *think*?"

Rani dug the instructions out of the garbage, her hands shaking. This time she read them carefully, with the kind of focus a life-and-death situation demanded. "It's negative." *Thank you, God!* "You're not pregnant!"

Suddenly the strength drained from her legs. Her belly churned. She dropped to the floor. She had to breathe. Until this moment she hadn't let herself realize how terrified she'd been.

A baby.

A fucking baby.

A mass of flesh and cells that couldn't protect itself from anything. When there was just too much out there that could hurt it. Destroy it. The ugliest parts of her childhood twisted around her, so fast they turned her like a corkscrew. Hunger and pain and terror.

"Rani?" Vinny sat down next to her. "You're shaking."

Of course she was. They'd just dodged a bullet. And yet it felt lodged in her ribs, ready to explode.

She jumped up and shoved the instructions back in the garbage, her insides trembling so hard she could barely stand. She dumped the used test in too. Then she took out the garbage bag and knotted it up. Then knotted it again, then again, tugging at the plastic ties until they almost snapped. She would take it to the dumpster in her apartment complex, where no one would ever find it.

Sonali Dev

"That was close," Vinny said, not sounding anywhere near as relieved as Rani felt.

Too close.

Too damn close by a mile.

Rani felt blood running down the inside of her leg. Saliva filled her mouth from the bitter bile of hunger. A hand pressed into her mouth, trapping the breath in her lungs. She wanted to scream, but she couldn't because the weight on her chest was crushing her.

"Rani?" Now Vinny sounded scared. Finally. "What's going on?"

"Will you go to the clinic with me tomorrow?" Breathlessness made it hard to speak.

"To get another test just to make sure?"

"Yes, but also because I need to see the doctor too."

"Why?" Vinny's hand was rubbing Rani's back. As though Rani were the one who'd just dodged tragedy.

"You know I never want to have kids. Not ever." She had to say the words. These past few minutes had made it clear how tenuous that choice was. Leaving something like this to chance would be the stupidest thing ever.

No, she was not letting the 1 percent chance of birth control failing be the reason she subjected another child to this world. Not in a million years. There was only one answer. "I want to have my uterus removed."

176

CHAPTER NINETEEN

VANDY

Saturday, midnight . . .

V andy had watched the video of Mallika hugging the hairbrush to her chest so many times that it continued to play behind her lids when she closed her eyes.

Her fingers scrolled to the security footage archives. How had she not thought about this until now? The archives stayed on the server for two years before they were deleted.

She hovered over the folder for June 2022. The month of Vir's death. No, she wasn't ready for that.

She went back to February and opened that folder.

One by one, she made her way through the files. Vir had spent almost all his time those last six months in their kitchen.

Cooking and writing.

The only two things I'm good at, he'd said.

And at loving us, Mika had said.

He had been that. He had been so very good at loving them.

For hours Vandy sat there. Watching him. Imagining him still here, in their kitchen. Breaking eggs and beating them with his fancy hand blender. He'd loved his gadgets, his knives. Chopping vegetables and spreading them on the skillet with its giant glass lid. His vegetable frittatas were her favorite thing in the world.

Perfectly moist, with buttery zucchini and mushroom topped with a golden crust of mozzarella and creamy goat cheese plumping up the center. Garlic and basil tied everything together so the taste lingered in your senses forever.

She let the taste come alive on her tongue, feeling something pleasant when she thought about Vir for the first time since losing him.

On the screen she found herself sitting at the island, watching Vir as he cooked. She'd been his sous-chef. It had been impossibly hard to ignore that these were the last months they had together, but it had also been so easy to forget, to affect what he'd so badly wanted in the time he had left: normalcy.

Living life all the way to the edges. It's what he'd always chased. The experience of being human, of being alive, of feeling. Not by climbing mountains and jumping out of planes, but in everyday things. In family and work. In love.

She thought of the things he'd done for her. So she could be a mother. She thought about the Polaroid she'd found tucked away in their book. That fight twenty-seven years ago, when they'd all made the only possible choice.

In the video the knife moved in Vandy's hands as she sliced with all her focus, trying to meet Vir's exacting chopping standards. He was a beast when it came to prep. Two-thirds of an inch meant two-thirds of an inch. It was a miracle he was even letting her do it. Maybe he'd wanted her to learn her favorite dish. He stepped behind her, wrapping his arms around her, his grip guiding her, showing her exactly how to move the knife, tip down, then pulling front to back.

He had the most beautiful hands.

There was no sound on the video, but she remembered what he'd said.

You know I'm only chance maro-ing.

Chance maro-ing.

Mumbai street jargon that meant being opportunistic in copping a feel when you had the chance to cop one. He'd loved his Mumbai slang.

She watched his body press into hers and wrapped her arms around herself, feeling his touch on her skin. His cancer-ravaged chest pressing into her back, bringing her body to life. His smell, buried under the smell of the chemo drugs, intoxicating her. His lips nuzzling behind her ear. That sound he made. The deepest, growliest sigh. She'd give anything to hear it just one more time.

This is my favorite spot on earth. She remembered the feel of his words falling on the shell of her ear. *Right here in the hollow behind your ear, this is where I want my ashes scattered.*

Despite her best efforts, it had made her cry.

She knew he didn't want that. He wanted to pretend that he would nuzzle his wife's neck for decades to come. That they weren't both soaking up memories.

The tears had refused the confines of his demand and burst from her in a silent gush. Behind her, his body had shaken with sobs too. Just for one moment. Then they both got ahold of themselves and went back to "chance maro-ing" as they chopped zucchini to exactly two-thirds of an inch.

The definitive sense that she would never again be loved in quite the same way squeezed inside her. She'd lost love like this once before. She'd only survived that because of Vir.

Forever . . .

The look of determination on Mallika's face as she clutched the hairbrush came back to her. What did Mallika know?

Had she gone looking for something because Vandy had failed her by losing herself to her own grief? Whatever it was, Vandy was done not being there for her child.

She got off Vir's armchair and let her legs carry her to the kitchen. She took vegetables out of the fridge. Onions, mushroom, and zucchini that her housekeeper stocked in there. She felt Vir's arms around her as she chopped. Touching his knives, his cutting board, his skillet—all of it hurt, but it also stroked the pain, softened it. She fell into the memories, into the smells and sounds, for the first time in almost a year. It brought strength to her arms and let air fill her lungs.

She sautéed the vegetables, beat the eggs, shredded the cheese, and folded everything together. Let it bubble and rise. Gave it time to set and transform.

Finally, when the smell enveloped her so tightly she had to taste it, she removed the lid. Vir had always poked a fork into it and scooped up a piece and fed it into her mouth before slicing it into wedges.

The prongs of her fork sank into the soft resistance. She brought it to her mouth, her first conscious bite of food that she wasn't forcing in because she had to. Her heart raced in that way hearts did when you were awakened from the deepest sleep. In her pocket her phone vibrated with an unholy force.

The fork slipped from her hands. She reached for her phone. God, please let it be Mika!

It was an unrecognized number. Her daughter was missing, so she didn't have the luxury to screen calls.

"Hello." Just as she said the word, it struck her that it was an international number.

There was silence on the line, but she knew someone was there. She felt it. Felt the shock in the silence.

"Hello?" she repeated, then quickly pulled the phone from her ear and checked the number before pushing it back. It was a 98200 number, an Indian cell phone. "Who is this?"

"Hi, Vinny," the voice said finally.

It was Vandy's turn for silence.

It had been twenty-seven years.

It was like she'd heard that voice yesterday. Like she'd heard it every day.

"Who is this?" Vandy had no idea why those were the words she said, but they were the only ones she could make.

A laugh greeted her from the other end. Of course she laughed. "Right. Since we're doing this like a bad movie . . . this is the person who has your daughter. If you want her back, you're going to have to come get her."

CHAPTER TWENTY

MALLIKA

Four days ago . . .

O ne of my mom's most popular memes is "Truth Is the Safest Option." That's obviously a lie.

I've always been in awe of how honest my parents were with me. No questions were ever off the table. No taboos. No conversations we couldn't have. They'd gone on and on about creating a CULTURE OF TRUTH in the family.

Then again, I've always been in awe of everything about my parents. *Perfect.*

The word keeps coming back to me. I've always thought they were perfect. Is that a lie too? I thought their marriage was perfect. I thought everything about our life was perfect. Impossible to replicate. A bar so high, avoiding failure has defined my life.

Rex is watching me as he lets me into the lab. It's almost nine, but there are still a few people working. Apparently, there's a late shift that works with the company's labs in other countries. I watch as Rex hands the hairbrush to someone, explains things I can barely hear through the numb haze that's gripped me.

He explains that they will feed the hair strands into a machine that has the power to wipe away lies and reveal truths. It's going to take a few hours for the analysis to run. It strikes me that this would all have taken me weeks and weeks of waiting if not for Rex.

"Thank you," I say as he takes my hand and leads me to his office. "For?"

"For . . . for being with me right now." I can feel myself at the brink of another deluge of tears, and suddenly I don't want to cry. I don't want to think about this anymore until I know for sure. I'm filled with the sense that this is too important to melt down over without having every single fact. Imagine how foolish I'll feel if it turns out there was some sort of mistake.

"I'm glad," he says. "Not that this is happening. But that I'm here. That I'm the one who's with you."

I think he's trying to say something, but I'm not in a place where I can decipher it.

In my hand my phone vibrates. It's my mother.

"I need to take this," I say, ignoring the way my heart starts to race.

He leaves me alone in his office with the gentlest brush of my cheek.

I let the burst of warmth from the gesture fuel my voice as I answer. "Hi, Mom! How was Miami?"

She says the usual things about how well the organizers did, how generous and receptive the audience was. Then she asks me how my auditions are going.

I'm about to tell her that they didn't want me, but what slips out of me is, "I don't care. It's too much of a reach anyway."

Instead of telling me it isn't and that I can do anything I want, she agrees immediately. "I'm sure there are other shows," she says automatically, and something breaks in my heart.

"Thanks, Mom, for your faith in me." The words are out before I can stop them.

"Of course I have faith in you."

"I thought Vandy Guru never lied." The words pop right out before I can stop them, with far too much force. It feels like the first truth I've spoken in forever, and it crushes my heart.

"It's not a lie." If she's hurt, she doesn't show it. She's fully focused on me now, because she knows something is wrong. "I don't want you to get hurt."

I lean back into Rex's desk. She's talking about the show. I don't care about the show. Auditioning and being rejected seem a million years ago. The idea of her protecting me fills me with rage.

"What if I don't care about getting hurt? What if I'm tired of being treated like I can't handle things?" I'm tired of being treated like I'm fragile. Too delicate for truth.

"Mika," she says. "What's wrong?"

Everything! I want to scream. *Everything's wrong. I don't know who I am. I miss Papa. I miss you.*

I don't say any of that. "Isn't getting hurt part of life? We lost Papa, and that hurt. Does that mean the time we had him wasn't worth it?" The fact that he's gone and that he might not be my father is so huge inside me I can't get a breath in around it.

She gasps as though I've slapped her. "Of course not, beta." Her voice goes quiet. We haven't really talked about Papa. About how much we miss him. Everything I'm feeling is a mess inside me. "I didn't realize how badly you wanted this." Instead of responding to the storm I'm struggling to show her, she goes straight into fixer mode. "Do you want me to call someone at Netflix?"

What? "No! Oh my God, Mom, stop! I'm trying to have a conversation with you. Can you stop being Vandy Guru for one second and be my mom?" Because that's all I want. For her to be my mom. I don't know what I'll do if that stops being true. I want to ask her if my entire life has been a lie. But I can't, not like this, not on the phone, not without knowing for sure.

"I understand how you're feeling."

A bitter laugh escapes me. "No, you don't! How can you understand? This is about who I am. It's my entire existence." *Stop it,* I tell myself. *She doesn't know what you're talking about.* "You always get what you want. You've never wanted anything so much that nothing else matters."

"Mika?" She sounds distraught. "I have. I wanted to be your mom so badly that nothing else mattered." There's suddenly so much pain in her voice I feel tears well in my eyes. "I know what it is to pay too high a price for wanting something."

Suddenly I can't bear it. The pain in her voice, the regret. Has she lied to me my whole life because she feels like she paid too high a price to have me? What does that even mean? It hurts too much to consider. "I'm sorry," I say. "I didn't mean it that way. It's just been a lot."

"I know," she says. "As long as we have each other, everything will be okay. We'll talk when I get home."

I make a sound of affirmation and let her go. But a piece of my heart seems to go with her.

Emotions keep swirling inside me as I stand there like that, playing the conversation in my head over and over until Rex knocks and enters his office.

"Mallika." He says my name, and I let it inject life back into me. I'm Frankenstein's monster, pieces sewn together, with no idea what fuels my beating heart. "Want to grab some dinner while we wait?"

I haven't eaten since I had a bowl of oatmeal this morning, and my stomach lets out the loudest growl now that its hunger is finally acknowledged. I place a hand on my belly, and an embarrassed smile tugs at my lips. "I don't want to go anywhere until . . ." I can't finish that sentence.

"Let's order in." He starts to list the options.

"Chipotle," I say, cutting him off. There's one on the first floor of this building, and I'm craving something uncomplicated and familiar.

"I'll go grab it," he says. "Text me your order." As he starts to leave, I grab his hand.

I don't want him to leave. I don't want to be alone.

I step closer and put my arms around him. I need to be close to someone. I want to be close to him.

He immediately wraps his arms around me and pulls me close. "Mallika," he says into my hair, as though he's figured out what it does to me when he says it. Then he laughs. "God, you smell unbelievable."

It's exactly what I'm thinking as I press my face into his broad chest, which seems to have a heater embedded in it. He smells like relief and comfort. Like deep, harsh wanting. Like escape. A geyser of hot pressure gathers too fast in my body, and just like that I'm reaching up, and his fingers are cupping my face, and we're kissing.

Breathless and ravenous. It's not slow or tentative. It's like an explosion. Everything all at once. All here in this moment. Teeth and tongue and rubbing bodies and sparks as I push into it with my entire being, push into him with a desperate sound. I feel nothing but him. Nothing but myself. He tastes fresh and yielding, the taste of his mouth lush, the texture of his tongue plump and silky. So much arousal grips me I moan from the depths of my being.

He pulls away panting. Or maybe that's me. Our breathing is loud in the room.

"My God," he says and pumps out another breath.

It makes me smile. "Care to elaborate?"

He strokes my face, my hair, my lips. "I don't think I have the words."

"Words are overrated," I whisper, and we're kissing again. I can't stop because this is all I want to feel.

Even though the way this feels can't be real. All of me is alive. Every last inch of me recognizes him. My body is making sure I know it's still here. I'm still here.

I place his hand on my breast, and the sound he makes traps everything I'm feeling. "Mallika," he says, pulling away, but his hand stays where I put it a moment longer, and I want to sink to the floor from the relief of it. "Maybe we should get some food."

He means we need to slow down.

It's a good idea. Food sounds good. A little distance sounds good, but my scrambled brain has forgotten how to take my hands off him.

"I'm not going anywhere without you," he says, and I nod and follow him.

Has Chipotle always been this romantic? Has the food on the walls always been this erotic? We hold hands in the line. Then his hand slips to the small of my back as I make my choices. "Yes, the brown rice, yes, the black beans." Why am I whispering?

Rex's shoulders are shaking with laughter as he places his own order. White rice, pinto beans. Every one of our choices is different. For no reason at all I think about the fact that my parents and I always ordered the exact same thing. We'd place our orders by multiplying the same thing three times over. Simple.

That memory pierces through the distraction I've pulled around myself. But I brush it away. Then our arms are touching as we walk to our table, and I need to focus on walking.

At first Rex sits down across from me. Then, with the most adorable shrug, he gets up and sits down next to me. The feel of his body next to mine works perfectly to keep me rooted in this moment.

When we're done, he asks me what I want to do next. On any other day my answer would be obvious. I try not to think about how different today is and tell him I want to go back to the office and wait for the results.

But my restlessness is an inferno. I want to kiss him again. I want it to take me away. The moment we enter his office, I reach for him. The wanting inside me is an unholy force. Everything I am seems to have been waiting too long, skimming life, hovering at its periphery.

When I push him into the couch and start to pull his shirt from his jeans, a shuddering breath erupts from him. He pulls my hands away. "No," he says. "Not like this."

He's panting. He can't make sentences, and that gives me back the tiniest glimmer of sense. He's right. Not like this. Not when I'm an open wound. Energy drains from me. Tears slip from my eyes.

Wordlessly he pulls me to him. Wordlessly I snuggle into him. Knees pulled close, all of me balled up, contained to keep from bleeding out. In his arms, his breath in my hair, his beautiful voice whispering sweetness into me, I float away into sleep. It's the strangest sensation to feel this safe when I have no idea who I am.

CHAPTER TWENTY-ONE

RANI

1993
Thirty years ago . . .

I can't face Vir," Vinny said when Rani entered the room after they'd performed the D&C. Vinny's eyes were droopy with pain and meds, and Rani wanted to shake her for putting herself through this again.

Rani had picked her up from her apartment and brought her to the hospital four excruciating hours ago. Vinny had cried the entire time, silent tears flowing from her eyes in a deluge, the teardrops not even discernible.

As always, when they saw the doctor, Rani had done all the talking, the answers rolling off her tongue automatically.

How far along are you?

Twelve weeks.

When was your last appointment?

Four days ago. Yes, there was a heartbeat. Yes, all other markers were normal.

Is this your first spontaneous abortion?

No.

It was the fourth.

Spontaneous abortion. How Rani hated that phrase. Even though it also made sense. Every time she heard it, she imagined the body screaming "Abort mission!" because it knew there was no viable way to successfully complete it.

This was infuriating. Why was Vinny choosing to do this to herself? The last time she had found out she was pregnant, it had taken Rani every effort to get excited. How did Vinny forget the pain so easily? How did she manufacture hope as though there was an eternal spring of it inside her? Well, every bit of the pain Vinny had been in after every one of those losses was fresh inside Rani. She hadn't forgotten a single tear.

The first time Vinny found out she was pregnant was two months after she and Vir got married.

It had been an accident, but it had made Usha Auntie and Dharam Uncle forget that they had disowned their only daughter when she ran away with "that gold digger." Oncoming motherhood had legitimized Vinny and Vir's love. No wonder Vinny was so hungry for it.

They had lost that little guy after fifteen weeks. That was a long time to carry someone inside you. Even Rani had fallen a little bit in love with him, mostly because of how in love with him his mother had been. She'd pressed her ear into Vinny's belly to see if she could hear him. She'd sung to him. She would never admit this publicly, but she had even shed a tear—just one, mind you—when he died before being born.

Vinny had been inconsolable. After that it had become a matter of proving a point for her. She'd been obsessed with getting back at whatever power had taken him from her.

Thus far the other side was four–love.

"Can we please go to your place?"

"Of course," Rani said and didn't add that it would be the first place Vir would look. She didn't add that he had a right to be here, holding Vinny's hand and having his own held by her.

The first time it happened, Vir had called Rani in tears. It was 3:00 a.m. Rani had driven them to the hospital because they'd both been too distraught to function. When they'd taken Vinny in to have the remnants of the pregnancy removed from her womb, Rani had gone back to their apartment and cleaned up. Doing something with her hands helped. Using them to dismantle the crib, to gather all the baby stuff that had accumulated stunningly fast. What had they been thinking? That's what kept running through Rani's head. What were people thinking, having children?

She'd taken everything to Vinny's parents' house and hidden it in the attic. Usha Auntie had held Rani tight. Even though Rani had been her perfectly calm self. She wished Vinny was the one getting her mother's hug. Because, man, that woman knew how to hug.

Maybe it's a good idea to wait to have another one until his father can provide for him, Usha Auntie had said.

Instead of a hug, that's what Vinny got.

Vinny's response, as always, was to shut her mother out. To stop speaking to her until she was pregnant again. It had also made Vir quit his job at the bookstore, something he'd taken on while he revised his book, and taken a job at Rani's firm, selling insurance door to door.

Vinny had completed her master's in psychology and was working as a counselor at a private school. The job bored the stuffing out of her. None of the kids ever sought out counseling, because they didn't want issues they were having to go on their high school record, where colleges and future employers might find them.

Which was a bummer because if those kids got a chance to let Vinny help them, the lucky bastards would have much better lives. It might also help Vinny think about something other than wanting to be a mom.

After marriage, Vir and Vinny had moved into the apartment complex Rani grew up in. They now lived in her building, one floor above her. Rani had taken the apartment lease over from her aunt five years ago, when Tina went back to India to live at an ashram in Wardha. Everyone including Vinny had tried to convince Rani to move out after Tina left to get a fresh start. Rani didn't want one. She liked being in a place she knew. Fresh starts were for people interested in leaving behind their current life. Rani liked her life.

Plus, there was rent control. Paying rent from two decades ago wasn't something to sneer at. Not that she wasn't self-sufficient; between her accounting job and teaching dance, she did fine. Rani basically ran Reshma's Kathak Academy now, and Reshma Auntie knew it. She'd asked Rani to buy her out. But Rani liked having money in the bank, and she wasn't about to pay Reshma to retire. She was working hard enough so Reshma had an income now.

No, Rani wasn't a rich woman, but no one owned her. No one ever would. She didn't have dreams anyone could steal from her. She wouldn't break down if someone left her. Except Vinny. But that was never going to happen.

Vinny, on the other hand, would not survive if anything ever happened to Vir. She was barely surviving these babies slipping from her with such disregard for how much they were loved.

Rani helped her sit up and was about to help Vinny get changed when there was a knock on the exam-room door.

"I'm not ready to see him!" Vinny said.

They stared at the door. It was seven in the evening, and Vir had to have gotten home, and not seeing Vinny there, he'd naturally made his way here.

"Tell him I'm not here. Please."

"This is his loss to grieve too, Vinny."

Vinny shook her head violently, bloodshot eyes round with terror.

"You need him too, honey."

"Not right now. Please."

"Fine." Rani went to the door, not sure how she was going to tell him again. Not that he wasn't smart enough to know already.

It wasn't Vir at all. It was Taj, white coated and spectacled, in all his physician glory.

He looked so much like Dharam Uncle that Rani blinked up at him. She saw him all the time, at all the Mehta gatherings. She'd danced at his wedding four months ago. Even so, it was always a shock to see the resemblance. Except the nose. That was all Usha Auntie.

Their eyes met and silently swapped their shared worry over Vinny as he entered the room.

"I'm so sorry, Vandy," he said kindly.

He worked at their OB practice, and obviously he knew everything that had happened.

He squeezed his sister's arm, and Rani had a flash of Raj and him: incorrigible, irreverent, sweaty, teasing Vinny and Rani incessantly. Never could she have imagined they would grow up to be doctors with such perfect bedside manners. Dharam Uncle was exactly like that too, all gentle focus and warmth once he put on his lab coat.

He leaned into Vinny's bed. "How are you feeling?"

Vinny didn't dignify that with an answer.

"Any pain?"

"They gave her some meds before removing the IV," Rani answered.

"Why does this keep happening, Taj?" Vinny asked, eyes filled with so much hope for an answer that even Taj, with all his stoicism, looked like she had kicked him.

"We can never be sure." He swallowed and threw Rani a look. "But if you have four failed pregnancies in three years, it might be time to try something different."

"What does that mean?" Vinny said, voice utterly flat.

"That means all bodies are not the same."

Vinny's jaw tightened. She refused to respond.

"Honey, what I'm saying is that we have to listen to what your body is telling us."

"I want a baby. I'm not going to stop trying."

His pause was long and deliberate. "I think you have to. Not for-ever. But at least for a little while, until we've found out more. Let's do some tests to see what is going on. We should have done that already."

There was the slightest reprimand in that last part. Every time Vinny lost a baby, the doctors told her to rest and wait. She never did.

"Sure," she said, her tears finally drying up, her jaw pushed forward. "When can we run the tests?"

"Why don't we take a breath? Heal from this. Maybe take a little vacation. Vir and you could use the break. Actually let me send you on a trip to Hawaii. I never got to give you a wedding present. But not a honeymoon." He grinned and wiggled his brows at Rani, his attempt at humor painfully awkward. "No sex," he clarified.

Rani tried to smile.

Vinny didn't. "I don't want to go to Hawaii! I want to find out what I have to do to have a baby!"

Taj turned to Rani with a look that said *Can you talk some sense into her, please?* A look the Mehtas had perfected over the years.

Rani hated when they treated her like Vinny's keeper, but someone had to talk sense into Vinny. "You're twenty-seven. What's the hurry?"

"There's no hurry. But you're right, I'm twenty-seven. If it can't happen now, then how will it happen later? Doesn't fertility decline with age?"

That's when Taj said the one thing he should not have said. "Vandy, you have to at least consider the fact that not every woman can carry a baby to term."

And that's how Vinny ended up pulling out all the stops.

CHAPTER TWENTY-TWO

VANDY

Sunday, 5:00 a.m. . . .

"D id you know?" Vandy asked her mother. "Did you know Mallika is with her?" She still couldn't say her name.

"It's not like you to ask questions you already know the answers to." Her mother sounded sleepy but not surprised.

After Rani disconnected the phone, all Vandy had been able to do was sit there in shock, wrapped tight in a cocoon of feelings that she couldn't separate into ancient history and present day. It all came back. All of it at once. The beauty and the ugliness. The deepest comfort and the agony of being torn in half. Knowing definitively that the life she'd built was over and the relief of setting down ten-ton armor.

Finally, when she could move, she'd called her mother.

"Why would you hide something like that from me?"

"When was the last time we were honest with each other? We hide everything." Now? Now Mummy wanted to become the teller of truths.

"Is that what this is? You feel like you lost your daughter, so you want me to know what that feels like too?" She should have felt more rage saying the words, but all her emotions had decided to move outside her and were spinning just out of her reach. Rani's voice wouldn't stop ringing in her ears. Mallika's face as she hugged the hairbrush. Vir telling her it was time to bury bygones.

"I lost two daughters. And you haven't lost any." Mummy's voice was soft, kinder than she'd heard in years. Maybe Vandy was imagining it because it was something she'd craved for most of her adult life, her mother's kindness.

"How can you say I haven't lost her? Why would she be with Rani?" Finally, she said her name aloud, and something seemed to shift in the air around her.

Mummy sighed, and something seemed to shift at her end too. "Don't you miss her?" Vandy knew she didn't mean Mika.

"So, this is your way of forcing us back together? That's cruel, Mummy. This wasn't how I wanted things. She's the one who left."

Twenty-seven years it had taken them to mention this.

Mummy laughed. "Life often ends up not the way you wanted. You've been walking around like a corpse for a year because you've always had a hard time dealing with things not turning out how you wanted."

Vandy gasped.

"You've been angry with me for years because I didn't have the guts to be honest about my life. But before you accuse me of cruelty again, this isn't payback. It's an opportunity to get something you lost back. Life is short, beta, and hindsight is a brutal bitch."

"What am I going to tell Mallika?"

"The truth. Or at least the closest thing to the truth. Which is what I suspect you told the rest of us. Now pack those bags. There's a flight out of LAX in five hours."

With that she was gone.

How casually she'd said those words.

Could it be that easy? Had Mummy always known what Vandy had done? Even the closest thing to the truth was something no one would ever understand. She couldn't expect Mallika to understand it.

No matter what Mallika said, she *was* fragile. Vandy and Vir had wrapped her in cotton to keep her safe. They'd allowed no hardships to touch her to temper her.

Mallika didn't stand a chance against something that had destroyed a connection as unbreakable as Rani and Vandy's. The truth would annihilate her. It had already destroyed too much. Vandy had no idea how Mallika had found out about Rani. But it didn't matter. Mallika wasn't going to bear the brunt of this. Not alone. Not without her mother.

It took Vandy less than half an hour to buy a ticket, pack, and be in a cab headed to the airport. Her mother's words would not stop playing in her head.

You've been angry with me for years because I didn't have the guts to be honest about my life.

Vandy had been fourteen when she first suspected that her father was cheating on her mother. During one of her parents' parties, she'd seen his hands on an auntie's butt as they talked in his den; his thumb had been stroking her. An uncomfortable feeling between Vandy's legs had told her it wasn't just talking. She'd pushed that feeling away, told herself it wasn't possible. That she didn't know about such things.

But it had changed something about the way she saw him. It had stolen her ability to ignore his focus on women who were not his wife. He was famously gregarious and friendly, always the life of the party, and Mummy had fawned over him and catered to his needs so much that Vandy had fought constantly to not see. At seventeen, she'd seen him kissing an auntie through the slit in the guest room door. She'd gone to her mother.

It hadn't been easy. The idea of hurting Mummy had made Vandy want to stay silent. But she'd known it wasn't the right thing to do.

Why are you friends with Rita Auntie? She's not your friend. That's it. That's all she'd gotten out before Mummy cut her off.

Mummy had gone into a rant about Vandy's grades. *Focus on school. Your brothers have never gotten a C. Don't waste your brain cells on things you don't understand.*

It wasn't Mummy's words that had stopped Vandy from bringing it up again. It was what Mummy's words had done to her face. Contorted it with shame and stubbornness but also anger at Vandy for bringing it up.

Vandy had never brought it up again. Turning a blind eye to her father's actions had made her feel physically sick. But she'd done it.

Finally, when she was twenty-three, her battle with herself had ended. Her ability to look the other way was unceremoniously and definitively snatched away from her.

She'd been sneaking into the kitchen for a snack. Graduate school had turned out to be a lot more work than she'd anticipated and far less fun. It had been a few hours since dinner, and all the reading she had to do for her sexual communication class made her ravenous. Vir and she had been indulging in more than their fair share of sexual communication. Vir was—and she blushed as she thought this—insatiable.

Vandy loved that word. Loved it.

What have you done to me? I can't get enough of you. Enough of us. Being with him was the most free she'd ever felt. Every particle in her being out in the open and hooked into life.

Since the terrifying peeing-on-a-stick experience when they'd first started being active in that department a year ago, she and Vir were obsessed with making sure they always, always had condoms on hand. She kept them tucked away in all her purses, at the very back of the glove compartment of her car in an old eyeglasses case. Vir had them in every room in his apartment. Every surface of that apartment had been anointed.

It was a ratty, smelly apartment, but holy hell Vandy was going to miss it when he moved out.

As she made her way to the kitchen, her vagina felt sore. The only sore body part Vandy had ever experienced was her quads, when she did squats once a year when her mother got to her and she decided to "get in shape." This was the opposite. That was disuse of a muscle. This was definitely full and extensive use of a muscle.

Not that Vandy would ever again think of her body as anything but beautiful, not after she'd seen it through Vir's eyes.

I didn't believe in paradise until I found myself in your body. The man had a tongue on him, that was for sure. That thought made her cheeks flame as she made herself a peanut butter and jelly sandwich by the light of the open fridge.

She hadn't turned on the lights because she could hear her parents in the living room, and she couldn't bear another lecture from her mother about eating between meals and dropping a few pounds.

What does it take to count your calories?

If you lost a few pounds, you'd find a husband like that. Insert finger snap here.

Well, Vandy had already found the only husband she wanted. So there, Mummy.

With all the surreptitious care of someone carrying a forbidden snack to her room after an evening of forbidden sex with her forbidden boyfriend, she tiptoed to the stairs. That's when her father's words flew out of the den and pierced her like a poisoned harpoon.

I'm a man. I have needs. His voice was pleading. *It doesn't mean anything. You know it's just sex.*

The sandwich dropped from Vandy's hand and splattered on the carpet.

For an age there was complete silence. Was her mother crying? Was she getting ready to pack her bags?

So you keep saying. If it's just sex, you can get it anywhere. You promised to keep it out of our life. Your partners at the practice are our best friends. Fucking your secretary is not keeping it out of our lives.

They were not supposed to find out. We were being careful.

Dharam! We have adult children! We have their marriages to consider.

I know that! They mean everything to me. Our family means everything to me. I've fired her.

Vandy dropped down on the steps next to the destroyed sandwich. Were her parents negotiating her father sleeping with his assistant and then firing her?

Do you want me to say thank you? Mummy snapped, the first flash of anger in her voice.

No. Of course not. But I'm saying it. Go to Tiffany tomorrow. Get whatever you want. That bracelet Nausheen got that you loved so much.

You better believe I will. But if this happens ever again, if my friends come to me with something like this ever again, diamonds will not be enough.

Never again. I promise. But if I were you, I'd be careful with the threats.

In the end, her mother had been the one to apologize. Quietly. Proving that the woman who had raised Vandy had been a lie, snuffed out and strangled with a chain of Tiffany diamonds.

Plucking the destroyed bread from the carpet, she threw it in the trash. Then she went up to her room and threw up. She never cleaned the mess of peanut butter and jelly on the stairs.

When she came down the next day, the carpet was clean except for the faintest stains, which stayed there until her parents changed the flooring in the house decades later.

Did you spill something on the stairs last night? her mother asked the next morning, studying Vandy as she panfried aloo parathas for her father's breakfast in a pool of sizzling ghee. The kitchen was filled with the aroma of Vandy's childhood: dough and cumin and potatoes frying in ghee.

Vandy didn't hide her disgust. *Good thing you cleaned it up. Now we can all pretend that the mess was never there.*

Her mother had burned her fingers while flipping the hot paratha.

Vandy had walked out of the kitchen as though she didn't notice. She'd made two decisions that day. When she was a mother, she'd raise children in a house not built on lies.

Then she'd gone straight to Vir and told him they were getting married.

Today? he asked, his surprise conversational, as though she'd asked him to go out for Thai food. Not even a trace of fear.

Now, she answered simply.

The week before that, when she got home from college, she'd found that her mother had invited "some friends" over.

There had been a man around her age sitting in her parents' living room between a couple who dressed and acted exactly like Vandy's own parents. The man himself was dressed in a sports jacket with a neck scarf. A neck scarf! What was this, Victorian England?

Thank God Rani was with her.

The neck scarf is kinda hot, Rani said, laughing, as Mummy sent the two of them upstairs to "make themselves presentable."

Rani was a genius, and she'd made Vinny wear bright-red lipstick that made her look like a dollar store version of Marilyn Monroe but without any of the breathy beauty and graceful oomph.

Turns out the attempt at making herself undemure and thus unattractive to the guy wasn't needed. He hadn't been able to take his eyes off Rani even for a minute to look Vandy's way.

Ever since that day, the man's mother had been chasing Mummy down to get Rani to say yes to marrying him.

Since Mummy had handpicked the man for Vandy, it went without saying that she thought Rani had hit the jackpot.

You will never have an offer like this again, she told Rani. *He's an OB from Princeton. A third-generation physician.*

When Mummy wouldn't give up, Rani told her that she was in love with someone else. *The man you saw me with at the mall. You were right after all. I think he might be the one, Usha Auntie.*

Vandy had kicked her under the table as they giggled.

How can you sacrifice a doctor for some man? Mummy said. *Medical degrees are more dependable than men.*

The satisfaction from imagining the heartbreak on her mother's face when she found out Vir was neither from their community nor a physician was delicious.

Vandy stared up at the man she'd just proposed to. He stared back at her with those obsidian eyes that made her believe that love and loyalty existed. And she knew that she'd been born just so she could feel the way she felt when he looked at her.

Rani is meeting us at the courthouse. If we don't get married, Mummy and Daddy are going to parade every eligible Indian physician in America before me.

Or we could tell them we're in love and have an actual wedding. Sometimes Vir's idealism bordered on naivete.

All Vinny could do was laugh. One of her parents' friends' daughters had brought home a man who was not from their community, and they had shipped her off to India overnight and forced her to marry someone there. When Vandy's parents told the story, they didn't tell it as though it were preposterous. They told it with admiration for the parents who had saved their daughter from throwing away her life.

We could tell them, and they'll lock me up in my room, and you'll have to bring the cops over to set me free. Or they might have you arrested for some invented thing and have your visa revoked. They have lawyer friends who can make it happen. Safer to become their son-in-law and then let them figure out how to be okay with it.

So that's how they'd gotten married. Vandy in a red silk dress Rani found for her at the mall on the way to the courthouse, and Vir in the one three-piece navy suit he owned, which made him look like he was interviewing for a job at a bank.

The LA sun burned brightly above them as they went up the ceremonial steps. It had burned even brighter when they left the courthouse as husband and wife. A different sun. A different earth revolving around it.

Vandy stepped out of that courthouse with the deepest faith that she would always have someone shading her from every storm that came their way. She felt like she'd wrapped herself in her oasis, become one with it.

They met Vir's cousin Harish at Venice Beach, where they drank champagne on the deck of the very fancy Le Marina bar that cost them most of their combined paychecks that month. Rani stole Vir's shoes as they walked on the beach and hid them. A wedding custom where the bride's sisters held the groom's shoes to ransom.

Vir paid her a hundred dollars so he wouldn't have to carry Vandy to the car across the parking lot barefoot.

He carried Vandy through the restaurant as everyone hooted and cheered. He carried her up to his walk-up apartment on the third floor, and they consummated their marriage on every surface in their little home.

The next day the news of their marriage was in the *LA Times*. Harish knew the person who did those announcements.

Harish, naturally, had fallen instantly in love with Rani, only to have his heart broken. He'd gone off and lived in France for a few years and married a French woman named Emile. Last year he'd come to see Vir after the diagnosis. They drank an obscure French wine late into the night and reveled in nostalgia. The guys had regaled Vandy with stories of their wild youth in Mumbai, running the streets of Juhu on their hundred-cc Hero Honda motorcycles.

The chicks were crazy for this guy, Harish had declared and then burst into tears. Everyone who came to see Vir knew it might be the last time.

Then Harish had asked Vandy what happened to her hot friend from their wedding day. He'd pretended not to remember Rani's name.

We lost touch.

How many times had Vandy said those words? *We lost touch.*

Every time she said them, it was like plucking shrapnel from her flesh, embedded in her organs, buried in her sinew. Remnants of a friendship that had left no distinction between which parts of her were truly her and which parts were Rani.

All those songs and stories about your heart breaking from losing a romantic love, but no one had ever managed to fit into words what happened when you lost the friend who was your soulmate.

CHAPTER TWENTY-THREE

MALLIKA

Three days ago . . .

When I wake up, I know instantly where I am. I'm lying on the couch in Rex's office with a throw tucked around me. A soft beam of sunrise escapes the blinds and pokes me in the eye.

"Morning," he says. This time he's Edward Cullen–ing it more obviously. There are two cups of coffee on the table.

There's a sheaf of papers in his hand that brings back exactly why I'm feeling so empty right now it's like I'm not actually here.

I slide a glance at the clock on his wall, a flat white plate with all the numbers heaped at the bottom and the hands ticking away. It's past six. I've been out a good eight hours. Which means either my mind is avoiding reality or this man is capable of helping me relax amid the worst emotional turmoil I've ever encountered. Or both.

"Are those the results?" I ask.

Instead of answering, he hands me a cup of coffee.

The look on his face tells me everything I need to know.

Then he says the words. "Your DNA doesn't match your mother's."

The information lands on me word by word.

I. Am. Not. My. Parents'. Daughter.

A confirmation that unravels everything I've ever held as fact.

I should be panicking. I should be hyperventilating like I did in the car. Rex watches me, the report tightly clutched in his hands. He doesn't move to come near me. Last night I needed to escape into him. Today I feel like I'll crumble if touched. I'm grateful for his intuitiveness in knowing that I need space to breathe. Except I'm not breathing.

I suck air, but nothing goes into my lungs. I stand up and start pacing.

I never noticed last night how cluttered his office is. Puzzles and scientific gizmos cover every surface. On his desk a bunch of metallic globes attached to metallic pins constantly dislodge one another and trace a circular path, going around and around endlessly.

"I can think better when I fidget," he says.

I start fidgeting. There are a lot of ball bearings here. Inside tubes and hanging by pendulums and popping out of spring-loaded gadgets. Papa would have loved this room. At least I think he would have.

Doubt slices through me. Will this be my life now? Not knowing anything to be true. Never having known the only father I ever knew.

All the conversations we had fill me at once. Everything Papa ever taught me. He loved to work with his hands. Unlike Mom, who thrives in stillness. He was always trying to kick-start his brain so it could write. He explained it to me once as the story being inside him but refusing to come out unless he cheated it into thinking that he was not thinking about it. He had to trick his creative consciousness with a combination of distraction and self-hypnosis.

Distraction and self-hypnosis are exactly what I need, but despite a room full of toys that is suffused with the essence of the man who turned me into a mass of feelings until a breath ago, I can't dredge up a single emotion.

I'm frozen. Like cryogenic eggs. Seemingly lifeless, but with life inside them. I know the storm inside me isn't gone. I feel sure that it will never be gone. Right now it feels deeply dormant. Everything I am is deeply dormant.

"Hey," Rex says. It's the one word he's had to say to me over and over again, because I've been a mess from the moment he found me sitting with those lions on my uncle's porch. "There might be a simple explanation."

I know the explanation is not simple. It cannot be simple. People like my parents don't lie to their child about her birth for simple reasons.

"I always thought I looked like such a combination of my parents that it made me look like neither of them." I say the words as they pop into my head. Suddenly, I'm terrified of feeling so filterless around him. Suddenly, it feels temporary. Like all reality is fluid, slippery.

He steps close to me and touches the mole over my lip. "That's almost identical to the one he had."

It's strange and disconcerting that he knew my father. I wonder why Papa never told me they were friends when he knew about my monster crush. Everyone knew about my monster crush. I never hid it. I believed I was raised with the privilege of not needing dishonesty to feel valued.

"Obviously the mole is accidental. I'm the exact same height as my mother. Obviously that's not genetic either."

His gaze stays steady on mine. I can tell he's weighing how scientific he should get in this situation. He's gauging my damage. I'm entirely transparent to him. I feel like I'm inside a brightly lit glass house in the dead of darkness. Everyone can see me, but I can't see anyone. Like my entire life with Mom and Papa. They could see everything I didn't know, and I could see nothing they knew.

"Generally speaking, children are rarely ever the exact same height as their same-sex parent. But mole placements can be genetic. Especially if anyone else in his family had the same thing."

"My father's mother had a mole over her lips." I remember how excited my daadi used to be about the fact that I had the family mole. When she was alive, Papa was obsessed with creating a connection between her and me. He'd insisted on taking me to India every few years. But the distance, time, and culture between my daadi and me always seemed too wide a chasm to cross.

It was obvious how much she loved Papa, how very much she missed him. Every single time I talked to her, she cried for the loss of her son. Papa moved to America to go to grad school at the age of twenty-one. He'd lived here for thirty-five years. That was a long time to cry because you didn't like your son's choices and saw them as abandonment.

America stole you from me, I once overheard her say to him. *Why can't you come back home?*

I have a family there, Mai, a life, he'd said with that particular softness his voice only took on for her.

Well, if it was just about the family, then you're the man, Daadi had said. *You could just bring them back. It's America that has dazzled you. It's that country and all its ease you can't give up. It's made you lazy and materialistic.*

I remember wondering if my grandmother's need to believe in her son's "manhood" was the reason she blamed America instead of Mom and me.

Is that true? I had asked when he found me eavesdropping.

I wish truth were that simple, he'd said, because that's how he talked to me even when I was a little girl. The way he would talk to an adult, a smart one at that. *If I didn't have you and Vandy, I might think of going back home. But I also love who I am here, who America allows me to be.*

His honesty always made me feel like I was worthy of trust. Turns out I wasn't.

Mom obviously never thought of India as home. She hasn't been there in my lifetime. She said it made her uncomfortable.

Honestly, it made me a little uncomfortable too, but it also made me feel something deep inside my chest that I couldn't explain.

It's belonging, Papa always said.

It's disconnection, Mom once let slip.

They rarely disagreed.

It wasn't either of those. For me it was the fact that it was too much, all of it. An atomic blast on your senses, and the fact that people on the street stared at you as though you were naked.

Does Mom never go to India because they adopted me from there? Do I have parents in some part of the world wondering how I am?

No! My mind cannot wrap itself around the fact that they would hide my adoption from me. Maybe it's for my own safety? Are my biological parents violent criminals?

I sag against the table, and Rex turns me around and sits me in a chair.

"You said your sister was adopted," I say because I need that distraction-and-self-hypnosis thing to stop imagining grotesque origin stories for myself. "Is that why you chose to do this with your life?" I look around his office.

He's taken aback by the question. "My parents tried to have children for many years, and when the doctors gave up, they applied for adoption and got my sister when she was two years old. One year after getting her, my mother became pregnant with me. Apparently this is not uncommon." He looks sad, and I lean closer to him and take his hand.

"When she was sixteen," he goes on, "Ann was diagnosed with ovarian cancer. They treated her with a gene therapy that was cutting edge at the time. That's when I decided it was what I was going to do with my life. Save lives that way. It's what I meant to do when I went to med school. Then one of my professors was studying mutations, and I became interested in that."

"And your sister?"

"She's fine. As bossy as any older sibling, but perfectly healthy."

The relief in his eyes is a thing of beauty. This is what I've always loved about him. The way he connects with people is so full bodied and true. For the first time a part of me wonders if it's real. How have I never before questioned if the way people appear is actually who they are?

He presses our joined hands to his chest. "What are you going to do?" he says so gently it tugs me away from the spiral of my thoughts. The sincerity in his eyes fills me with guilt. How can I be this person who questions everyone and everything?

"I have absolutely no idea. I suppose I'll ask my mother why they lied to me instead of speculating." As soon as I've said the words, a weight lifts off my shoulders.

His face tells me he likes my answer. Before he can say more there's a knock on the door.

"Come in," Rex says but keeps my hand in his.

A young woman enters the room looking apologetic. She looks young enough to be a teenager, but she has a badge on a lanyard much like the one Rex is wearing.

"Dr. Henderson," she says. "Can I talk to you for a moment?"

"Sure. What's up, Laney?" he says kindly.

"It's about the test we ran on the hair sample last night." Her gaze does a quick slide in my direction. "I was running the samples again to cross-check as you asked and, umm . . . turns out there's a different reading."

I gasp and stand up so fast my chair screeches back. "So there is a match?" My heart is all the way up in my throat. "I knew it!" I say with too much force. I knew it. The test was wrong.

Laney looks from Rex to me.

"Go ahead," Rex says, and she hands him the report.

The entire spectrum of feelings I've ever experienced rushes through me. But relief screams loudest. Thank God. "Thank God." The words escape my lips.

The girl clears her throat, then speaks quickly, as though I've said something awful. "There were two samples on that hairbrush." The quick glance she throws me seems to see my entire life in a flash. "One is from a male, and one is from a female. Both in their fifties."

My hand presses into my mouth. Papa and Mom probably shared that hairbrush. Mom helped dress him and brushed his hair at the very end, when he could no longer do it on his own.

I feel the flow of blood in my limbs slow. A wave of cold washes through me.

Laney clears her throat and hesitates.

Rex puts up a hand to stop her from going on. He's read the results. "I got this. Thank you," he says, and the girl hurries away, shutting the door behind her.

He squeezes his temples, and I know that this is worse than anything that's happened thus far. Everything happening in the room slips behind a curtain again. It's like I'm not here. I don't want to be here.

"Mallika," Rex says, and absurdly I feel sorry for him for being stuck in the middle of this. For being the one to destroy my life. "The female hair sample still doesn't match. But the male one does."

I drop back in the chair.

Say the words, I tell myself. *Ask the question.* "What does that mean?" But I already know. Those words can only mean one thing.

Rex studies the results again, with so much focus I half expect the paper to catch on fire.

"Rex?" I urge because I need him to verbalize what's in his eyes, what's on that piece of paper, what I already know.

"Assuming that the hair samples on that hairbrush belonged to your parents, it appears that . . ." He swallows. "Your father is your biological father . . . but your mother is not your biological mother."

CHAPTER TWENTY-FOUR

RANI

1993
Thirty years ago . . .

Taj had said two things to Vinny the last time she lost a baby. One, to consider the fact that some bodies weren't built to bear children. Two, to run some tests.

No points for guessing which one Vinny had chosen to focus on. Over the next three months, every test was administered and every treatment considered. It was amazing how much time scientists had spent on making sure women could make babies. There seemed to be a procedure for everything. There was even this thing where embryos were conceived inside test tubes, then placed inside the uterus. It all sounded alarmingly sci-fi, and suddenly Vinny was a nerd, inhaling all the research, demanding all the answers.

"The future is now," Dr. Dwayne, Taj's fertility-expert friend, had said. Apparently there were hundreds of little humans conceived outside their parents' bodies running around the world already.

Unfortunately that was useless to Vir and Vinny, because obviously getting pregnant was not Vinny's problem. Carrying the baby to term was.

Not to worry: medical science had been hard at work to make sure no woman went without the experience of creating more people the world did not need. All one needed was the will and a shitload of money.

There was this other thing called cervical cerclage, which involved stitching the cervix shut so the baby would stay put. It sounded horrifyingly painful. It also went with staying in bed for most of the pregnancy to keep the uterus from having early contractions and expelling the baby.

Needless to say, the idea of not moving for close to nine months didn't intimidate Rani's best friend.

"I'll stay in bed for the rest of my life if that's what it takes," she said as they discussed it, and Vir looked like she'd kicked him.

Rani herself was starting to feel like she didn't know what to do with Vinny anymore. Yet neither she nor Vir pointed out what an unhealthy thing to say that was.

Why? Rani wanted to scream, but she knew the answer.

Being a nurturer had always been Vinny's essence, the identity she defined herself by. Taking care of others was the one thing everyone around her agreed she was good at, the beautiful thing about herself she knew and accepted without argument. So, naturally, motherhood was supposed to be the thing she got to pour her soul into, the thing she was born to do, the thing that was her prize for knowing how to care for others, how to put them before herself.

Which was ironic. Because with each failed pregnancy her desperation grew. With the loss of each of the four babies, she'd taken a step deeper into herself and farther away from anyone who tried to separate her from her purpose.

She'd already almost completely shut Usha Auntie out. Marriage and motherhood were supposed to be the two things where she got to show her mother how it was done.

Finally, she'd found the passion her mother had been goading her to find, the cause she'd been waiting to give her life to. Failure was not an option.

All Rani knew was that she wanted it to be over. She wanted Vinny to stop suffering. She'd do anything to have her friend be happy again. Including support her when she let herself be stitched up and immobilized for the better part of a year.

Naturally the honor of having the opening to your uterus sealed did not come without a hefty price tag. Five thousand dollars that Vir and Vinny did not have. All those dilatations, curettages, and evacuations had not come cheap either. Between that and grad school, they were deep in debt already.

The Mehtas had the money, and Raj and Taj paid a lot of Vinny's medical bills without her even knowing, but this new procedure was an up-front cost, and Vinny could not ask her family. Which translated to: she really did not want to. Often in life those two things were indistinguishable from one another.

You know who else had money? Rani Parekh, that's who. What better use of five grand than to give her best friend what she wanted most in the world.

"We will return the money as soon as we have it," Vir promised. "Six months at most." He put away the book he was writing, which had gathered an impressive number of rejections already, and focused on selling postdeath security to people for a premium.

But Vinny and Rani didn't work like that. They didn't keep accounts. They didn't return things; they shared them.

This fifth time, it was taking Vinny longer to conceive. Taj might have been right about her body needing rest. Even Rani felt Vinny's body's exhaustion.

After her poor body failed to give her another pregnancy after six months of trying, the doctors decided to give Vinny shots to release the kraken of hormones to help her rebelling womb along.

Which might be why she was crying right now as they made the drive up to Santa Barbara. It was just Rani and Vinny, because Vir was working away at peddling insurance. Rani was at the wheel, and Vinny was lost somewhere inside that gigantic AAA TripTik map. The venue where the Mystic Mother's Moving Ashram was congregating for community blessings was obviously not meant to be easy to find. Much like nirvana.

Yes, Vinny had decided to try a different approach to this fertility thing. Thanks to Tina Maasi.

"Can you imagine people trying to go places before maps?" Vinny said. "It's just so sad." She dropped giant tears on the map that was taking up 50 percent of the space inside Rani's little Bug. "Everyone must've been lost."

Okay, so that hormone kraken was no joke. Yesterday, seeing a cat walking around their apartment complex had made Vinny sob uncontrollably. *She's lost,* she kept repeating. *What if her family is looking for her? What if a car runs her over?*

They had spent an hour walking around the complex calling "Here, kitty, kitty, kitty . . ." under ferns and behind railings.

They'd finally found a cat with close enough coloring peering down at them from a balcony.

She found her way home! Vinny had broken into relieved sobs.

"I think mapping was invented over three thousand years ago in Babylon," Rani mumbled, because honestly, she was too concerned about their own lost map-carrying asses right now to spare much sympathy for the poor souls who were lost without maps back in the Stone Age.

"Didn't you say there should be a fork in the road soon five miles ago?" Rani asked.

Vinny wrestled the map to a different angle and peered at the tiny print. "I think we might have overshot it."

Rani swerved her trusty Beetle into a U-turn.

Sonali Dev

Some six hours later, after endless more U-turns on roads that scalloped around mountains and valleys, they finally arrived at a mansion nestled on a cliff. The line of parked cars was two miles long, snaking along the final strip of dirt road. The line of humans (sorry, DEVOTEES, the signage reminded them) was even longer and snaked in curlicues all the way around the sprawling property. Women in white cotton saris and men in white cotton kurtas handed out paper glasses of water and tomato-and-cucumber sandwiches in little baggies to weary travelers in white.

Vinny had eaten a Quarter Pounder at McDonald's a few hours ago, and Rani had eaten her usual fries, the only edible vegetarian option at any fast-food place other than Taco Bell. That hormone kraken was a many-splendored beast, and Vinny grabbed two sandwiches, one with each hand, and started to scarf them down.

Rani must've absorbed some of those hormones by osmosis because she followed Vinny's lead and also took two. A great decision, because they were flippin' delicious. So delicious, in fact, that her grumpiness at being there dissipated a little bit.

The white clothes, the lilting spiritual chants piping from concealed speakers, and the angelic smiles on the faces around them created an atmosphere that felt impossible to be angry in. Vinny and Rani were also wearing loose white kurtas over white tights, as they'd been instructed to do in the information packet they had received last week. Tina had been able to find them spots through someone she knew at the parent ashram in India.

It was spiritual networking at its best.

Tina Maasi, naturally, was the one who had put the idea of getting the Mystic Mother's blessings in Vinny's head.

It's the only fertility treatment you need, she'd said when she called Vinny after hearing about the most recent loss. *The Mother heals all. I had an impinged nerve in my hip last year, and one hug from her, and I haven't had a moment of pain. My cousin's daughter went fifteen years*

216

after marriage with an empty womb. She saw hundreds of doctors across India and Europe. She even went to Singapore to have test-tube babies, but nothing. Then the Mother gives her one hug, and boom! She has two sets of twins one year apart.

To Rani four screaming infants sounded like the definition of hell, but Vinny had lit up like a firework at the story.

"Make sure you don't let her hug you too long. If you have four, I'm not helping with them."

"Shut up," Vinny said, grabbing one of Rani's sandwiches after scarfing down her own. "I just want one, but I'll take as many as she'll give me."

"Does Vir know you're planning to have babies with the Mother?"

Vinny splattered a tomato-and-cucumber-laced laugh across Rani's kurta, and Rani started laughing too. They were in the middle of nowhere, dressed all in white and returning benevolent smiles from strangers in the longest line they'd been in since the Madonna concert. How could they not laugh?

Finally it was time for them to be let into the great ashram hall where the Mother would be dispensing healing hugs to her devotees. Thanks to their inability to read maps while crying over their ancestors not having maps, they were all the way at the very back of the line.

"We're out of numbers," one of the white sari-clad volunteers whispered to them. Her regretful face was even gentler than her voice. "I don't think the Mother will be able to hug you today."

Rani wasn't sure if her annoyance was greater or her relief.

She was about to drag Vinny away before Vinny burst into tears again.

"We're not going anywhere!" she said with the kind of force that landed like a bomb in this hushed ambience. "We can still see her, right?"

The volunteer, who had taken a step back and was looking around for reinforcements, nodded. "Of course. The Mystic Mother is for everyone."

"Thank you." Vinny's voice swung across the mood spectrum and landed back on her usual sweetness. "We're so grateful for your help," she whispered, mirroring the rest of the crowd.

The woman looked at Rani for help.

Just ride the wave, babe, Rani communicated with her eyes as she folded her hands in a namaste and hurried behind Vinny into the hall.

It was gigantic, even bigger than the temple hall in LA, and filled with white-clothed devotees sitting cross-legged on the hundreds of white mattresses laid out in neat rows. A white-sheet-covered stage stood at one end, where a band of musicians played Indian instruments and belted out devotional bhajans. The hall full of people sang along, eyes shut, hands joined, swaying to the music in a trance.

Rani turned her completely inappropriate urge to laugh into a cough. But Vinny was otherwise occupied. She was putting all her energy into scouring the room for a spot near the front.

She smiled the most victorious smile, then grabbed Rani's arm and dragged her along (a perfect metaphor for their relationship these days) to the very first row. There was just enough space on one mattress for one person with a child-size butt to squeeze in.

Two very large and very bearded white men, who were completely unaware of the fact that they did not look like anyone else here, occupied most of the mattress. They were singing at the top of their lungs and swaying as though the spirit of something had possessed them.

Vinny settled into the tight spot next to them and then scooted until she was squeezed into one of the men, breaking his trance. He opened his eyes to find her smiling angelically at him. He smiled back and scooted closer to his friend, who in turn also moved, and voilà! There was enough space for one-half of Rani's butt on the mattress next to Vinny.

She obliged, because just standing there while Vinny aggressively grabbed her space from the universe was worse.

The men beamed in the enlightened way of everyone here and, without pausing in their singing, scooted around some more until the entirety of Rani's bum found purchase on the mattress.

Vinny closed her eyes, pressed her palms together, and joined in the singing. Usually Vinny avoided singing and dancing at any cost. The Mehtas were famously tone deaf. Rani had witnessed them dancing at weddings, and she'd wanted to wash her eyes out.

Taj and Raj's wedding had been exquisite torture because they'd found brides who made them look like they had the dancing talent of Javed Jaffrey. Pinky and Tinku were cousins from Delhi who had been competing about everything from the moment they were born. Rani had no doubt they had married the twins only so they could continue to compete for the rest of their lives.

Rani braced herself. Vinny was singing, loudly, as though she'd suddenly forgotten her own inability to sing. Next to her their bearded friends were just as spirited and just as tuneless. It didn't seem to matter to anyone.

Oh, what the hell. Rani had lived with Tina Maasi long enough that she knew the drill. She pressed her palms together and joined in. The intense energy in the room rose up around her. The air was thick with incense and singing voices. It was like nothing Rani had ever experienced. All these people joined together in this moment, giving over to a higher power. Their vulnerability, their faith in their own safety: she tried to analyze it, to resist, but something seeped inside her and filled her lungs.

A live thing wrapped her in its grip. She turned into the sound of her own voice. The peace that gripped her was so deep she gave over to it, vibrated with it, all the fight evaporating from her.

Suddenly her voice turned loud and booming, and she knew someone had put a mic in front of her. She was too lost in the feelings to open her eyes. Her voice, which she knew was beautiful, piped through the speakers across the room and surrounded her. She couldn't stop, couldn't pull back. She went for it, performer that she was. Instead of her body, she danced with her voice and spun with her heart.

When at long last her lids floated open, she found Vinny watching her, tears streaming down her cheeks. Around them the room was filled with smiling people with wet eyes.

Tina Maasi used to cry when Rani sang bhajans as a little girl. It was probably why Rani had avoided it. With dancing she didn't have to deal with people's reactions. She got to get lost inside the dance. With singing they were right there in her face, feeling and feeling, and she remembered being drained by it.

Today she felt the energy coming at her in waves. She closed her eyes again and let it in. She soaked it up and sent it back. Soaked it up and sent it back. Until a hand landed on her shoulder.

Her eyes fluttered open. It wasn't Vinny. A tiny white-haired, round-cheeked woman with a huge white bindi was staring down at her. The Mystic Mother. Small as her stature was, something so bright and tangible emanated from her that without thinking about it, Rani leaned over and touched her feet in a namaskar.

Taking Rani by the shoulders, the Mother pulled her up. "There is Brahmand in your voice," she said. "The entire divine universe rests in your vocal cords." She touched Rani's throat. Her hands were the softest hands Rani had ever felt on her skin. Light and warmth seemed to fill her throat, her chest, her entire body.

"What is it you come here seeking, child?" the Mother said in Hindi.

Rani took Vinny's hand. "My friend wants a baby, and she's having a hard time having one," she responded in Hindi, her eyes glued to Vinny's beloved face.

Something about the Mother's face changed then. "One who asks for another also gets for oneself." She pulled Vinny toward her and wrapped her in a hug. "All will be well," she said. "A friend who loves you like this is rare. No gift is larger than that. Don't forget. Don't ever forget." Her hand pressed into Vinny's belly. Her tiny hand seemed to cover it whole.

The room stilled around them.

Tears streamed from Vinny's eyes. Tears streamed from the Mother's eyes. They were more bottomless than any eyes Rani had ever seen, and Rani tumbled into them headlong.

Vinny and she watched mesmerized as the Mother left them and went back to the stage, but she left behind whatever had filled Rani's chest; it stayed warm and bright inside her.

A loud honking sound startled her. The two bearded men blew their noses into giant hankies and wiped their eyes.

Vinny tugged Rani's hand, and they sat back down, smiles stretching their cheeks. The mic was still in front of her. For the rest of the day, until every one of the hundreds of devotees had been hugged and blessed, Rani sang and sang. Vinny didn't take her hand off her belly, not even on the drive back.

The next week they found out that Vinny was pregnant again.

CHAPTER TWENTY-FIVE

VANDY

Sunday, noon...

O h my God, are you Vandy Guru?" the flight attendant asked as Vandy settled into the golden cubicle designed to skew reality and make you feel like you were not on an airplane.

Vandy forced a smile in lieu of an answer.

She had no idea how she was going to survive the twenty hours before she found out why her greatest fear had come to be.

"I'm a huge fan." The flight attendant's voice pulled her back from the brink of panic. Last time she'd tried to go to India, the panic had been because she didn't want the plane to take off. This time it was the idea of the plane not taking off that made it rise swift and thick. "I own all your books. I've read them multiple times. I read back issues of your column when I need help with life."

God, could she have some help with life, please? "Thank you," Vandy said, trying to be present in the conversation. Trying to find the usual comfort in having helped someone. How she'd clung to it in the years after Rani left. In the months since Vir left.

"My husband proposed to me by writing me a Dear Agony Auntie letter. It was the cheesiest thing ever, but it was also perfect. Sometimes when I struggle with life, I write a Dear Agony Auntie letter to myself, and it helps me figure things out."

"That's beautiful. Thank you," Vandy said, meaning it. "How long have you been married?"

"Six years." The flight attendant held out her hand and showed off her rings. Suddenly her face turned mortified. "I'm so sorry. That was terribly insensitive. I . . . I'm so sorry about Vir. Sorry, I mean your husband. How are you doing?" She looked genuinely heartbroken. Almost as though she'd known Vir.

Vandy was used to this. Her readers always behaved like they knew her and her family personally. Sonja was masterful at using social media to make the world feel like they were close friends of the Gurus. So long as they didn't compromise authenticity, Vandy believed it helped people to see unfiltered, un-touched-up pictures of real life.

Everyone who came to Vandy wanted to be the After. They wanted to be a finished project: a written book, a recorded song. A framed painting. They were so stuck in the despair of the Before that they forgot to focus on the transformation, the doing, the sacrifice. The living.

Social media didn't help. It constantly threw the shiniest pieces of other people's lives at you. The parts carefully curated to include only the After. The runner wearing the medal after the race. The beauty of a sunset without the waking up and showing up to witness it. The ease with which everyone bought into the stories knowing they were only a sliver of the truth, which made them lies, baffled Vandy.

She'd thought sharing her journey of surviving Vir's loss would break that cycle. Turns out what she'd shown was just as much of a lie. Because you had to feel pain, not bury it. Suddenly she felt naked in her grief.

"I'm hanging in there," Vandy said, unable to tell the truth and ask for privacy, but also unable to lie and say she was fine.

She couldn't remember the last time she'd been fine.

Dear Agony Auntie,

My entire life just imploded.

I don't know how to deal with the loss of my husband and now I might have lost my daughter too. But the thing I can't stop thinking about is that I'm going to see my best friend after twenty-seven years. It makes me feel like my entire life was a lie.

Sincerely,
Lost and Afraid

The honesty people put in the letters they sent her, in the questions they asked at seminars—it had always humbled her. But she'd never given thought to quite how much courage it took to acknowledge that you were lost.

To allow advice.

The flight attendant brought her water in a wineglass.

It would have made Mallika roll her eyes. Was there anything more pretentious than serving water in a wineglass?

It would have made Rani roll her eyes.

Vandy touched the cold glass and tried to bring herself back to this moment. "Is there anything I can do to make your journey smoother?" The flight attendant pulled a fluffy white blanket from the overhead bin and shook it open and spread it over Vandy.

An image of doing that for Rani flashed through her entire being. The months before Mallika's birth had shown Vandy that no matter how much she gave, what she was being given would always be more. She'd believed that the one requirement for getting what you wanted was to ask for it, but she hadn't really understood how high the cost could be. She'd never been able to ask for anything after that. Everything she'd gotten since then had been without ever asking for it.

"Thank you," she said, looking around at the empty cabin.

The flight attendant continued to stand there, her eyes filled with questions and anticipation.

Deep exhaustion gripped Vandy. "I'm exhausted," she said. "It's been a long few days. Actually, it's been a long year."

"Of course," the woman said with so much kindness Vandy wanted to hug her. "I don't know how you do it. You're our only guest in first class. I'll make sure you are not disturbed."

With a bow of her head, the woman backed away.

For the first time in years Vandy thought about how absurd her life had become. It wasn't like she'd grown up poor. But Vir and she had been broke for more than half their marriage.

If you marry for all the wrong reasons, you have to live with the consequences. Her mother's voice from long ago rang in her ears.

Vandy had made peace with her mother after Mallika's birth. Mummy was a fantastic naani. After Vandy's father's death, she'd slowly but steadily dropped the beliefs she'd held on to so tightly to justify staying with a husband who never understood the meaning of marriage as anything but being a provider.

Over the years she had accepted all Vandy's choices without question. Even though she'd never felt like she'd had too many choices of her own. But what had really healed their relationship was when Mummy had fallen in love with Vir.

In those last six months, Vir Guru and Usha Mehta had become friends in a heartbreaking act of forgiveness. Mummy had acknowledged that she might have been jealous of the kind of husband Vir was to Vandy. A life partner.

I can understand why you're angry with your father, Vir had said to Vandy. *But I don't understand how you can blame Mummy for choosing to keep a life that had parts she loved and would have lost. Infidelity is never simple, you know that.*

Vandy had been stunned that he'd gone there. But in the last months, he'd wanted to say everything.

All infidelity isn't the same, she'd responded. *I know that too.*

I know. But no matter what the cause for it, the blame never rests on the person cheated on.

He was wrong. In their case, the blame did rest on Vandy. Entirely on her.

Her parents' marriage was nothing like her own. Their situations were as different as could be.

Six years: that's how long the flight attendant said she and her husband had been married. That's how long Vir and Vandy had been married when Mika was born.

The longest years of Vandy's life. How endless and painful each moment had been. How desperately she'd wanted to make time stand still when she tried to hold her babies in. How fast the seconds had spun when her body rose up in protest. Only when the pain came had time stood still and turned into eternity. All she remembered of that time was the restlessness of wanting, the wretched sense of failure and injustice. There had been not one moment of peace.

She touched her belly. Maybe there had been one. When she became pregnant after the Mystic Mother pressed her hands into her womb, Vandy had been absolutely certain that her stitched-up cervix would keep her baby in.

A boy that time.

Vikram. That's what she'd called him in her dreams.

If she named him, maybe he'd stay.

But just like all the others, Vikram hadn't been ready for this world. He didn't like being imprisoned in her womb either. He'd revolted with rage at his mother's hubris in stitching herself up so he'd have no escape.

Losing a baby when you couldn't expel it was like having your insides torn and set on fire. Hot pokers shoved into her pelvis and smashed into her spine. More pain than Vandy had known possible. Even now, just thinking about it, sweat gathered behind her knees and in the creases of her palm. She shoved the thick powder-white blanket aside.

You almost died! Vir's face and Rani's face came alive inches from her own. Alive with the horror she'd caused them, over and over.

I wish I had died. She'd been as reckless with her words back then as she'd been with her wanting. She hadn't yet learned the importance of tempering either word or action with thought.

No more, Taj had said. He'd grabbed Vir by the collar. *You stay away from her.*

Rani had been the one to fight for Vir. Because Vandy hadn't had the strength to move.

What is wrong with you! It's not his fault. Stop acting like a Neanderthal. Rani had always been much more judicious with her words. Except when it came to protecting Vandy.

Except when it came to protecting Vir.

Except when it came to that last fight when she'd left them both.

Pain rolled through Vandy, bringing back the deadness in her heart as she lay there while everyone waited for her to recover, to stand up. To forget. To give up.

The healing hadn't come. The recovery had been slow. Everything had been stagnant. As though her life had stopped being able to drag itself forward.

Why? everyone kept asking her. *Who are you to think everything is in your control?*

There are hundreds of thousands of children who need parents, who need a home, Vir kept saying.

I know, Vandy kept answering, *I know.* But whatever had gripped her was unrelenting.

Her whole life she'd felt like a nobody. She'd never asked for a single thing for herself. She'd felt overwhelmed by everything she did have, things she deserved no more than anyone else. But this she had worked for. She had formed herself to be the kind of person who would be a good mother, a great mother, even.

It was unfair, and she could not let it win. Not the sense of injustice. Not the emptiness, the nothingness. The deep sense of failure.

Loving people was the only thing that made her somebody. This was a love she had to know. Every time she got pregnant, she felt it. She felt like somebody. It filled her up, gave her the kind of purpose nothing else ever did. She couldn't let it go. She couldn't let the babies that died inside her go either. Every time a new life bloomed inside her, she felt like all the ones who came before had another chance.

Even though each loss was like a backhoe driving over her, back and forth and back and forth until there was nothing left of her but flattened flesh.

That last time she'd had no path to inflating life back into herself. Biologically her uterus and her cervix were too damaged to ever try again.

You can never carry a baby again. Her doctor had made her brother say those words to her, or Taj had chosen to be the one who did. He'd cried while saying them. The only time in her life Vandy had seen Taj cry was when he told his sister that the one thing she wanted was a biological impossibility.

The words played in an endless loop in her ears for months after, letting nothing else reach her.

That afternoon she'd been sitting in Rani's apartment, deep inside her own silence. Rani had taken to dragging her out for a walk every day. Resistance was futile. It was always futile when Rani got that look on her face. Her stubbornness etched a deep line into the middle of her forehead. A third eye she used to burn down your resistance when you stood in the way of what she wanted. Exactly like Mika's face on the security camera.

Rani tried to feed Vandy. Dal and rice. Sweeter than they made it in the Mehta household. It was the one thing Vir would not eat. *I like my dal to taste like dal and my kheer to taste like kheer. And never the twain should meet.*

Vandy didn't mind the sweetness in the dal. Usually there was something comforting about it when Rani made it, but right then everything had tasted like bile going back down. It was the only time in Vandy's life that she'd been skin and bones. She didn't remember a time in her life when she hadn't prayed for the weight to drop, when she hadn't been on a diet.

But that first time she found out she was pregnant, the lifelong need to starve herself had disappeared. It had been like being freed from ropes wound too tightly around her. A coming into her body just the way it was.

When she lost Vikram, she was the heaviest she'd ever been. Then six months later, she was lighter than she'd been at twelve, when she was six inches shorter.

You have to eat, Rani kept saying.

She didn't have to do anything.

You think Mummy is finally happy with the way I look? Vandy said, and Rani tried not to reprimand her. In the Before days, Rani would have lectured her about going easy on her mother.

Before Rani could respond, the phone rang. As soon as the person at the other end told her who they were, Rani took the cordless handset into the bedroom.

Paranoia was one of the side effects of having her womb-related failures broadcast to the world. Her brothers called Vir every day to see how she was, her sisters-in-law bought her gifts to cheer her up every time they went shopping, her mother softened and tried to spend time with her. Her father invited Vir to play golf. Vandy was suddenly the pathetic bull's-eye that everyone wanted to dart their charity at. It made her wonder what everyone was discussing behind her back all the time.

Pulling herself off the couch, she dragged herself to Rani's bedroom door. Rani had shut it and was whispering on the phone. Vandy pushed her ear into the door.

"I can come in tomorrow. Yes, it's the copper T. Thank you."

She didn't bother to pull away when Rani opened the door.

"You're having your IUD replaced." It was a statement, but Rani looked heartbroken, which was doubly unfair: the fact that she felt like she had to hide her birth control from her friend *and* that she got to use birth control because she could give birth.

"It's been five years?" Vandy said, the incredulousness in her voice so loud that shame crept through her. It had been five years since she'd talked Rani out of having her tubes tied. Naturally the doctors had refused to give a twenty-one-year-old a hysterectomy. They'd also refused to let her have her tubes tied, no matter how adamant Rani was about never having children. Rani had wanted to take legal action to force the doctors to do it.

It hadn't been easy to convince her to go with the IUD option. Finally Rani had given in only because she hadn't been able to argue with the fact that the end result was exactly the same, but without having surgery that came with risks.

Secretly Vandy had been unable to bear the idea that her own children would not have Rani's children as friends to grow up with. If they had a boy and a girl, maybe they would marry. A childhood friendship morphing adorably into love.

Now here they were.

I'm sorry, Vinny.

Shut up. That stupid apology made rage explode inside Vandy. Lava filling inside her like life rushing into a body taken for dead. *Just shut up. Why are you sorry? Why is everyone sorry? I'm the one who can't do this. How is this anyone else's fault?*

In an instant, Rani was by her side, trying to put her arms around her. Taking over Vandy's role of being physically affectionate, while Vandy felt too dry and parched to touch anyone lest she crumble to dust.

When Vandy didn't melt into her hug, something did crumble inside Rani too, soaking the very depths of her eyes in pain.

I wish there was something we could do. I swear I would do anything. If I could do this for you, I'd do it.

The eeriest silence followed those words. They got stuck in the air like the high-pitched ringing after an explosion. It filled their brains, filled all their empty crevices.

Rani pressed her hand to her mouth and sat back on her bed. Vandy stood there. An age went by. An impossible thing became possible. Slicing through skin, then taking root.

What happened? Vir asked when he came home and saw the two of them still speechless hours later. Sitting there.

Didn't the doctor say I can't carry *a baby?*

He nodded wordlessly, all out of platitudes. It took him a moment to notice that Vandy didn't look sad as she repeated the doctor's declaration.

Vinny, you can't possibly be serious. When she was in distress, Rani, all these years later, still reverted to the accent she'd lost after coming to America sixteen years ago.

Why not? You said you'd do it if you could. What if you can?

You don't know what you're saying, Vir said.

It's not like I'm asking you to sleep with each other. I don't have trouble getting pregnant, remember? That means my eggs and your sperm are working. It's just my uterus that isn't.

When you spent five years talking about nothing but fertility, your vocabulary got absurdly clinical. *Ovulation. Insemination. Impregnation. Embryo.*

Vandy tossed all those words out, every one of them. Desperation and science mingling on her tongue in a brand-new language of hope.

They call it gestational surrogacy. It's just like IVF. Your sperm and my embryo, Vir. Rani would just give her niece or nephew a home where she can live until she's ready for the world. She'd just carry our baby for us.

They'd been helpless against the tidal wave of her excitement.

Their love for her had made them helpless.

Vandy pressed her fingers into her parched eyes. How easy tears used to be for her. Her release, her way to heal. How completely they had dried up now.

Sometimes I don't recognize my wife anymore.

It was a line in one of Vir's books. He seemed to slip pieces of his heart into his stories. It was her favorite thing about his books. She'd dig through the words for clues the way Dolly, his heroine, dug through her world for clues to find the killer. In his earlier books, Dolly Singh had been bumbling and lost, a victim to the machinations of a ruthless world. In recent years Dolly had come into her power. Year upon year, Vandy had watched him create a world for their daughter that felt more fair, more empowered.

The only good thing about knowing he had six months to live was that he'd been able to close up his series and give Dolly a death where she got to save the world. *Singh over My Grave* was his first book to hit a list.

On their very first date he'd told Vandy how he felt when he wrote.

We experience life in parts and pieces. Certain parts of us can only come alive when we're with certain people or doing certain things. Parts of me are alive only when I'm infusing life into my stories.

Turned out she liked to write too, but she used words to unravel problems in the real world, whereas he used them to explore problems by giving them fictional form.

All I want to do is change the world with stories. When he said those words, when they set his dark eyes on fire, that's the moment when Vandy had known she would spend the rest of her life loving him.

He'd loved her back, fulfilled the promise of the love she'd felt that day, given her everything. She'd always known this, acknowledged it. Now it struck her that not only had he given her everything, he'd given her everything on her terms.

After Mallika was born, after Rani left, they had gone from strength to strength, created something huge together. But they'd lost something too. One part of their communication had been shut down like a clump of dead nerves in a working limb. A part of the muscle forever numb, even though the rest of it functioned even more efficiently to make up for the loss.

At the very end, when it had been hard for him to speak around the pain, he'd finally said the words *Call her.*

Okay, Vandy had said without needing to ask who he meant. *You want to see her,* she'd added, not sure how she felt about that, but it didn't matter.

He'd shaken his head, so much pain in his eyes. *Not now. After I'm gone. Call her for you, not for me. Once I'm gone, I'll no longer be in the way of your friendship.*

In the end, Rani had been the one to call. In a matter of hours, they would be face to face again.

CHAPTER TWENTY-SIX

MALLIKA

Three days ago . . .

My uncle startles when he sees me in the waiting room of his practice. I'm trying to convince his receptionist to let me see him without an appointment, so it's really convenient that he saunters out.

Rex, who is standing behind me, steps closer. Yesterday, it would have warmed me. It would have made me hear wedding chants. Now I feel nothing.

He insisted on driving me here. "I don't want to leave you alone right now," he keeps saying.

That too hits like rainwater on the plastic tube I feel encased in. I can't access any part of myself: not my feelings, not my ability to distinguish truth from lies. Nothing. I sure as hell can't access how my body felt yesterday when I climbed him like a tree. He tried to hold my hand in the car on our way here. I tried to push myself to remember the feelings, but I couldn't, so I pulled away. I'm glad he stopped us yesterday because imagine getting something you've waited for after so long and then forgetting what it felt like the next day.

Because I have no memory of myself before today.

My parents lying to me about being adopted now seems like a simple problem. Being a child of a serial killer seems like something I could handle. But being my father's biological daughter and not my mother's? That's a thought I can't even get myself to hold inside my head without wanting to burst with everything it could mean.

"Rex!" If seeing me surprises Taj Maama, then seeing Rex here with me utterly baffles him. "Are you here to see Lydia?"

I've forgotten that his ex works at my uncle's practice.

When Rex looks at me instead of answering, Taj Maama's gaze whips between us, weighing all the possibilities that pop into his head, until one makes panic flash in his eyes. "Is Amey okay?"

"Of course," I say quickly. "I'm not here about Amey. I need to talk to you about something. Can we go to your office?"

"I have a packed day," he says, "and I'm already running late." I can see his brain working to figure out why I might be here.

"Taj Maama, please, this will only take a few minutes." I make the face I've made all my life to get whatever I want from my uncles. It's always been fail safe, and it doesn't fail now.

"Are you pregnant?" he asks. "Do I need to break his legs?" He points his chin in Rex's direction.

"Eww, no!" I say.

"Eww?" Rex says.

"That was for the breaking legs, not . . ." I flail my arms to indicate—what?—the idea of sex with him? "That's totally not eww." Great; my face chooses to feel things again and flushes.

"All righty then," my uncle says. "I'm going to ignore all of that." He circles a finger between Rex and me. "Let's go."

"I'll wait out here," Rex says, and the way he says it makes me feel like I'm going to stay friends with him forever.

He seems to pick that thought from my eyes, and his own darken with something.

Before he can step closer again, I thank him for understanding and follow my uncle into his office.

"So what's going on, Mika?" Taj Maama throws a distracted look at his phone when it buzzes, and it reminds me of how much I loved playing with his pager back when he wore it all the time.

I pull the door to his office shut behind us. "I'll just come out and ask. Do you know who gave birth to me?" Since that report changed my life, I've spent every moment trying to find the right words to ask the question. But when I say it out loud, it sounds absurd.

My uncle's color heightens, as though he's choking on something. "Excuse me?"

"I know I'm not my mother's biological child."

"I'm . . . umm . . ." My uncles have the kind of personalities that are so confident they border on bombastic. I've never seen Taj Maama thrown off his game. He is currently completely thrown off his game. This has got to be worse than I imagined. He recovers with impressive speed. "Did you have a fight with your mother?"

I used to go to my uncles for things my parents didn't want to spoil me with, but I never really fought with my mother in that way my friends fought with their mothers, especially when they were teenagers. Mom is impossible to fight with, always too gentle, too reasonable.

"I know you slept with Garima Auntie before you married Tinku Maami," I say. I don't know where that came from, but his face all but crumbles in panic. At a party a few months ago, my naani had imbibed enough wine to spill her sons' dating histories in the very limited pool of LA desi families from when Mom and my maamas grew up. *Can you imagine Tinku knowing that the woman she's been fawning over for all these years was his first choice?* Age has definitely widened Naani's mean streak to a mean highway.

"Come now!" Taj Maama says, but sweat beads across his forehead. I feel bad for him. I've witnessed Tinku Maami losing her temper at her sons, and it's not for the faint of heart. More importantly, Garima

Auntie is married to Taj Maama's golf buddy, and if Tinku Maami finds out, he'll have to find a new golf group, and that's his worst nightmare. "It's ancient history. Who cares?" He makes a valiant attempt at nonchalance.

"Fine then, I guess Tinku Maami will get a good chuckle out of it."

His laugh is filled with disbelief, but some admiration leaks in there, and it makes me angry that he's impressed that I have the ability for this kind of ruthlessness. "Are you seriously threatening me?" Now he looks scared, and my ruthlessness evaporates.

"I deserve to know why my parents lied to me, Maama!"

"Nobody lied to you." I can't figure out if he actually believes that or if he's lying too. The thing that was the cornerstone of my life, my trust in my family, is gone.

"Tinku Maami always says that you delivered me. Is she lying?"

"She's not. Did someone say something to you?"

"I took a DNA test."

"This has to do with Rex?"

"This has to do with the fact that you've all lied to me all my life." I drop into a chair and press a shaking hand into my forehead. "I don't want to go to Mom. She acts tough, but you know how fragile she's been since Papa."

"Definitely do not go to her with this nonsense."

"Did Papa have an affair?" I just come out and say it. My worst fear. It makes me want to throw up.

"What? No, my God, Vir?" He laughs, and my stomach settles the tiniest bit. "Your papa was obsessed with your mom." His eyes shine with truth. Or I want it to be the truth so badly that's what I see.

"I know I'm his biological daughter." Those words are out before I can stop them. I'm on a slope with skates. "How can it not be an affair? How could Mom forgive him? How could she take me in?"

This time his horror is alive on his face. He starts pacing. "Good God, Mika, you should really let this go. It was not an affair. Trust me."

"Then what was it? How can I let it go when I don't know what I'm letting go of? I've lost Papa once. I cannot lose him again. Not like this."

He groans and turns to me. "It was a surrogacy, okay. You were carried by a surrogate."

What?

It's the absolute last thing I expected him to say. It sounds like something he just pulled out of his hat to derail me. I press a hand to my mouth. "Isn't that where they implant a mother's egg in someone else's uterus? I should still be genetically related to Mom."

"That's gestational surrogacy. There's also traditional surrogacy, where the egg is the surrogate's."

The room starts spinning. My uncle hands me a bottle of water.

So much makes sense now. But so much still doesn't. Why would my parents not tell me?

"Was it someone they knew?" I don't know why I ask that question, but Taj Maama's face drains of color so swiftly that my own blood seems to drain from me. "Who was it?"

"How does that matter?" The way he says it makes my need to know even stronger.

"It doesn't." But if someone carried me for nine months, I should at least know her name. "Why is it such a big deal to give me a name? I love my parents. I love Mom more than anything. I will never do anything to hurt her." At the center of the storm inside me, I zero in on the heart of everything. I love Mom and Dad. I know they love me. This is the only thing that matters, and acknowledging it anchors me back into myself. "I just want to know who it was. Then I'll let it go. I promise."

He plucks a tissue from his desk and dabs his brow. "I really do have to get to my patients."

I cannot let him leave without telling me. I know this in my bones. "Please," I say, and tears rush into my eyes. "I would have asked Papa. He would have told me. You're all I have now. Raj Maama and you." I break down completely. A huge part of being a dancer is being an actor.

Especially in short dramatic bursts. I have my real grief to dig into, the real heartbreak of being lied to. I let it fly.

"Please, sweetheart." He wraps his arms around me. "You do have us. Always."

"Then tell me. Don't make me go to Mom."

His hand goes to the nose that juts out proudly from his face and pinches the substantial bridge.

"I won't tell Mom that you told me. I promise. I'm sorry I threatened you. I won't tell Maami about Garima Auntie either. Whether or not you tell me."

He squeezes my shoulder. "Your mom did an excellent job raising you. You know that?"

That I do know. "Please." I put all my faith in that plea. "Tell me who it was."

"She was your mother's friend. She moved to India after you were born. They haven't talked since then. Her name was Rani Parekh."

The temperature in the room drops. My pulse slows and gets louder. I can hear it pound in my ears. "Thank you," I say, but my lips are trembling.

His phone buzzes. "This is an emergency. I have to go. But call me if you need anything, okay? And remember you promised to let it go if I told you her name."

I could not possibly have heard him right. That can't possibly be true. *Rani Parekh.*

I know that name.

Not only do I know that name, I've met Rani Parekh. I've met her several times, on my trips to India with my father. He always took me to see her.

I grab Taj Maama's arm before he leaves. All I want is to erase what just happened between us, to have him take his words back, because suddenly I don't want to know what they mean about Papa and my parents' marriage.

"Taj Maama, please, please don't tell Mom I was here. Let's not tell anyone that I know."

"I think that's a good idea." He drops a kiss on my head and leaves.

Papa had me meet my biological mother over and over again and never told me that's who she was. I met a lot of his friends and relatives when I went to India with him. I only remember Rani because she was a dancer. That realization makes everything worse.

I know with absolute certainty that Mom has no idea that Papa did that. Had us meet. Taj Maama is right: she can never know that I know. I can't do that to her. I can't have her feel the kind of betrayal I'm feeling.

I don't know how long I stay in my uncle's office, but it feels like an eternity, because when I come out, I'm not who I was when I went in there. The person who steps out is boiling with the kind of rage her body doesn't recognize. I feel like a puppet strung out of shape, like a scrap of paper at the mercy of the wind.

The sight that meets me when I leave the waiting area lands like a spark on kindling and takes up flame. Between one breath and the next, I'm an inferno.

Rex pulls away from a woman I recognize instantly. The woman he almost married. The woman he chose over me five years ago.

He calls my name, but I turn around and start walking in the other direction. They're standing right by the elevators, and a sense that I'm trapped fuels my flames even higher. I find a stairwell and slam into the bar on the door that lets me in. The stagnant concrete smell fills my lungs, and I take the stairs, racing without thought. Flying.

"Mallika!" He's racing after me. "Stop. Wait. What's wrong?"

It's that last question that makes me clutch the railing and come to a grinding halt and spin around. The force of it yanks my arm, but the pain feels good.

He stops before we crash into each other. "What happened?" He tries to touch me, but I stumble back and catch my balance.

"I just saw you with her," I say. "With Linda."

"Lydia?"

How have I forgotten the name of the woman who made me sob into my pillow when I first heard that Rex put a ring on her finger?

Perhaps because she wasn't the one who made me sob.

"It's okay, really. I didn't mean to interrupt. I'll just go. Thank you for . . . for all your help." I start to leave, and he holds my arm. So gentle, I want to shake him.

"What are you talking about? I just ran into her. She works in Dr. Mehta's practice. You know this." His face softens. "What happened in there, sweetheart?"

I pull my arm away. "Don't call me that. You don't have to patronize me."

He takes a step back. "What are you talking about?"

"What am I talking about? Let me see . . . you were just all over the woman you dumped me for five years ago. Please don't make this about the shit going on in my life."

"What?" He looks lost. His expression feels like a reflection of what's happening inside my head. "*You* dumped *me* five years ago. You talked to me for five months and then went out with Rory Spinelli!"

"After I caught you with Lydia!"

"Caught me?"

"I saw you kiss her."

"Are you kidding me right now? It was her birthday. We were friends. I kissed her on her cheek and gave her a hug. I was at that party for you. Because I was going to tell you how I feel. I'd been planning it for weeks. The next thing I know you're telling me Rory Spinelli is your boyfriend. I was so thrown off that I almost failed finals that year. You even told Amey that I had imagined that you liked me."

"Because I didn't want Amey to pity me when you chose someone else."

"Mallika! Why do you think I haven't told Amey we've been together this week? Because he saw how you broke my heart the last

Sonali Dev

time. I was in love with you." His voice breaks. "I . . . I am. I have been since the first time we met at Amey's house over that tandoori turkey."

Everything he says lands on me like lies. "Is that why you spent the past half decade with someone else?"

"I spent the past three years with someone else because you pushed me away. Because Lydia helped me find my feet after you, and I thought I could love her. Then I saw you at Amey's engagement party." When I had called him Sex and made a fool of myself. "And both Lydia and I knew there was no hope." He shrugs. "She'd already been cheating on me. She knew what we had wasn't the real thing long before I admitted it. She still shouldn't have cheated, but the fact that I didn't care means something."

"I . . . I don't know if I can believe you."

"I've never lied to you." He reaches for me again, then changes his mind and pulls away. "But I can't be the one paying for all the lies everyone else has ever told you."

This time I step away. We've moved so far apart, his back is against one wall of the landing, mine against another. The poison darts of his words still manage to break my skin. I open my mouth, but nothing comes out.

He's right that everyone has lied to me. I just never expected him to use that against me.

The silence between us seems unbreakable. Finally he's the one who forces the words out. "Want to know what I've learned about you these past few days?" I really don't, but he tells me anyway. "That you've imagined this perfect life and love for yourself. But you've already decided that it isn't possible to attain, so you run before it falls short. You run from the truth so it doesn't ruin the version of truth you've chosen to believe. I was never going to live up to it. You were already looking for ways to let me go before I did something you could use to prove yourself right. The way you did last time. The way you've given up on that audition for the *Mahabharata*."

242

I straighten. "Okay, thanks for that. This proves that you don't know me at all. I have the right to not compromise."

The most pained laugh huffs out of him. "Working at things even when they aren't exactly how you want them is not compromise, it's life. Reaching for things even when you're afraid they'll disappoint you is courage. You run away because you're afraid things won't be perfect, before you even give them a chance. Before you even know the truth. Just like the thing with your parents. You don't care to know what the truth is. You've already decided to bury everything and pretend like none of this happened, haven't you?"

"I think you've said enough," I say, because he doesn't know anything. I would rather die than subject my mother to what I just found out.

That's when it strikes me that I don't know for a fact what that is. My father kept in touch with my biological mother without telling my mother. And my parents lied to me about my birth. But I don't know why. And that might be the most important part of all this. The why.

He's right about me.

He wipes a tear that leaks from one of his thickly lashed eyes. There's no fight left in him. "You're right. I have said more than I should have. Forget I said any of it." With that he walks past me and leaves me standing there in that unfinished stairwell.

I want to call him back, but I don't know how. For the first time in my life, I realize that I cannot go on if I can't figure out how to reach for what I want.

CHAPTER TWENTY-SEVEN

RANI

1994
Twenty-nine years ago . . .

Birthdays were huge in the Mehta family. Usha Auntie woke her children up in the morning with a hug and the "Happy Birthday" song sung in her lilting Indian way. Then she pulled all of them along as she went through a day filled with food, activities, and celebrations that focused on making not just the birthday person but everyone feel special, as though it were some big national holiday. Raj and Taj loved to cringe and act like it was something they had to put up with, but of course they loved it.

Rani loved it too. Birthdays in the Mehta house were some of her best memories growing up. It was one of the many dabs of spackling the Mehtas had pressed into Rani's cracked heart over the years.

After their seventeenth-birthday trip to Saroj Khan's workshop in New York, Vinny had become less single minded about making Rani's birthdays spectacular. By then Vinny had taken care of all the big things Rani wanted, but some of it also had to do with the fact that Saroj had tried to recruit Rani to join her troupe.

Vinny had thought the offer absurd. Her American mind couldn't grasp the idea of leaving America to live in India. Or maybe she remem bered what Rani had been like when she first got here from India and she couldn't imagine her going back to that. She was right. Even New York had been tough. An old darkness that went with not knowing her surroundings had nudged its way back inside Rani. Without Vinny she wouldn't have lasted a day.

After Saroj's recruiting attempts, Vinny had toned down the grand gestures, but she'd still made every birthday special, despite everything she'd been through these past few years.

It was finally Rani's turn.

The doctor had confirmed Rani's pregnancy one week ago, but she'd wanted to wait a week and make sure. They had fertilized three of Vinny's eggs with Vir's sperm. The entire extraction and insemination process was the wildest thing Rani could ever have imagined. Actually, having the embryo implanted inside her uterus was even wilder.

The first one hadn't taken hold. Which, according to the doctor, was not surprising. It usually took a few attempts. All the hormones they'd been pumping into Rani for the past few months needed to properly nourish the earth, so to speak. Unlike Vinny, Rani hadn't felt any different with the hormones. To be honest, she didn't feel any different with a fetus inside her.

The only thing she felt was a bit nervous about breaking it to Vinny and Vir. They'd been trying hard to act normal and not watch Rani as though she were potted soil with a spring bulb about to poke out of it.

Vir opened the door and let Rani into their apartment. She had a giant Mylar balloon that said "Happy Birthday, Squirt" clutched in one hand and strawberry-shortcake ice cream balanced in the other. Because, of course, strawberry shortcake was Vinny's favorite flavor.

He smiled, but he looked tired. Rani couldn't remember the last time he hadn't looked exhausted. If the cervical stitch had been expen- sive, inserting a test-tube baby into an alien host was basically meant for millionaires. Or could've-been millionaires, because all the money they could invest to turn into millions just went poof every time they did a procedure.

It was a good thing Rani had saved so much money over the years. Even so, after this last bill, Rani was down to nothing too.

Rani found Vinny on the couch and handed her a bowl of ice cream. Vir was making dinner. The apartment was suffused with the smell of sautéing ginger, garlic, and onions. Usha Auntie had invited them all over for dinner, but Vinny had turned down the invitation citing work, her go-to excuse these days.

With a tired smile at the balloon, Vinny pointed at her headphones. She had been transcribing medical notes for extra income this past year. Rani sat down next to her and took a bite of the ice cream Vinny hadn't touched.

The quick glance Vinny slid at the bowl in Rani's hand was heart-breakingly hopeful, but with herculean effort, Vinny said nothing. As a rule, Rani didn't eat between meals. She'd just never learned how to go from starving child to snacker. People often commented on her inability to snack as lucky. Ah well; in a world where your bones showing through your skin was what everyone was aspiring to, she supposed there was some luck in your body never getting the chance to learn how to digest more than the most minimal amounts of food. Rani tried not to throw words like "childhood starvation" at idiots, but it wasn't easy.

Something difficult to decipher might've been happening on the headphones, because Vinny's attention got called away to that. In the time it took Vinny to finish the floppy drive she was transcribing, Rani had made her way through the bowl of ice cream. When Vinny pulled off her headphones, Rani gave her a hug and wished her the happiest birthday. Vinny grinned, and Rani soaked up the flash of old Vinny, her smile as round and full as her cheeks used to be, until the last pregnancy ended. Then she threw a glance at the empty bowl and exchanged a quick look with Vir.

Rani wanted to put them out of their misery, but she had no idea how to do this. She wanted to make this big and meaningful, the way Vinny had always done for her so effortlessly.

Before she could say anything, the clang of the doorbell broke the silence.

"Oh no," Vinny said. "I knew she'd do this." The words had barely left her when Usha Auntie and Dharam Uncle made their entrance, hands filled with flowers and balloons and food that smelled like heaven.

Usha Auntie watched Rani take the empty bowl of ice cream to the sink. The living room, dining area, and kitchen were all one compact space that suddenly felt filled beyond capacity.

"Did Vandy eat ice cream?" Usha Auntie asked in a quiet voice, following Rani into the kitchen.

Vinny never saw it, but her mother's worry was obvious. She had aged a decade since Vinny almost lost her life when she lost a pregnancy with the cervical stitch.

Rani shook her head, and Usha Auntie's eyes got strangely intense. She stepped close and tucked a lock of hair that had freed itself from Rani's ponytail behind her ear. "Oh, beta," she said, her voice a whisper. "Do you know I thank Krishna a hundred times a day that you came into our lives."

Before Rani could find the words to respond around the lump in her throat, the doorbell rang again. In marched Taj and Raj and their very pregnant wives, who looked like they were carrying three babies each.

Soon the noise level in the apartment reached a pitch where no one could hear anyone else. Daler Mehndi belted out "Bolo Ta Ra Ra" at the top of his lungs on the stereo. Scotch and wine and nonalcoholic champagne were poured and downed in copious quantities. Tinku and Pinky had cooked so many appetizers, one would think the entire building was coming to the party.

"Just a little something," Pinky said, removing the plastic wrap from a platter of aloo bondas. "Didn't want Mummy doing all the work."

"Mummy does do too much," Tinku said, ripping wrap from a bowl of dahi bhalla. "I've told her. No more. Let us be the domestic goddesses now."

"I was the one who told her to only make the rice and nothing else," Pinky countered.

"But I was the one who stopped by to help her make it."

Raj and Taj laughed as though their wives were the most adorable of beings.

"I have the best daughters-in-law on earth," Usha Auntie declared, sliding a quick wink at Rani, and fed pieces of food into Pinky's and Tinku's mouths.

Rani took a sip of her nonalcoholic champagne. It didn't make anyone suspicious because she never drank. Another thing people were impressed by. Why anyone thought choosing not to poison herself was remarkable she chose not to dig into.

Vir topped up Dharam Uncle's Black Label before making his way to Vinny and wrapping his arms around her from behind. She looked like she wasn't even here. These days it felt like she left a cardboard cutout of herself in place of her actual self anytime her family gathered, and just disappeared.

It was her birthday. She was the one who should have food fed lovingly into her mouth. She was the one who should have her hair tucked behind her ear and be told how she was a gift from Krishna. She should be laughing and dancing uncoordinatedly to Daler.

"Remember how Vinny used to make me cry at my birthdays?" Rani said just as the song ended and her voice boomed in the tiny space.

Raj and Taj groaned. "The things she used to make us do." They described the pink pajamas with Rani's face to Vir in great detail, even though he'd heard the story a million times already.

"I've never been able to give her a present that she really wanted," Rani said, voice softer than she'd intended this time.

The apartment went silent. How did people always know when something big was coming?

Vinny's eyes filled with so many emotions all at once, Rani's heart squeezed under the weight of all that hope. Vir closed his eyes. Was he saying a prayer?

Rani's gaze hooked into Vinny's as her head gave an affirmative nod. "Until now."

Vir's grip on Vinny tightened. "Rani? What are you saying?"

Rani's eyes stayed locked on Vinny's. "Finally, you get a present you want. Congratulations, Mommy, my niece or nephew has decided to take up residence in my belly until it's time to come out."

Vinny sagged against Vir. For a second they stood there like that, their relief so bright it zipped around the room like a firecracker gone rogue. Then Vinny leaped at Rani, her arms crushing her. They were twelve again and fourteen and sixteen and twenty-one. All their time together, who they were, all of it in that coming together of their limbs. A bright explosion. The darkness of the past five years gone.

Vir pulled Vinny away and drew Rani close and dropped a kiss on her head. A first, but for once Rani didn't care.

"Thank you," they both said.

The rest of the family buzzed with excitement, as noisy as ever. But Vinny, Vir, and Rani were inside their bubble, floating, barely aware of the world spinning around them.

"Don't thank me. I'm charging him or her rent as soon as they're old enough to pay. She or he is also taking care of me when I'm old and cranky, no senior living and all that."

"For any of us!" Vir said.

Vinny just stood there and cried. Finally, Rani had given her a gift that made her cry.

CHAPTER TWENTY-EIGHT

VANDY

Monday, 6:00 p.m. . . .

This was Vandy's first trip to Mumbai. Her family had always flown into New Delhi, and they'd spent two weeks with her father's family there and then one week with her mother's family in Baroda. A pattern they'd never deviated from through Vandy's childhood, except one day trip to the Taj Mahal in Agra when Vandy was fourteen. One of her father's friends and her family had accompanied them. They had three very beautiful, very fashionable girls who'd giggled incessantly behind Vandy's back and touched their noses when they thought she wasn't looking.

What floated up in Vandy's memory now was the fact that her father had spent most of the trip with his friend, talking, making jokes, sitting next to her on the drive, and of course his signature move: the casual hand on the small of her back, and his charming Dr. Mehta smile.

Mummy had spent the day herding the six children, feeding everyone, making sure happy pictures were taken. One of those pictures, the five Mehtas huddled in the shadow of the Taj Mahal, had sat on their mantel until her mother sold the house a few years ago and moved into a retirement community.

Mumbai Airport was nothing like Vandy's memories of India from her childhood. It was like a gigantic mall crossed with a palace. "You were right, Vir," she whispered to herself. "It is beautiful."

After all these years, the air was still familiar, and so very different from America. The moment Vandy stepped off the plane, the thick humidity wrapped around her despite the air-conditioning. Raj and Taj had loved to say rude things about the way it smelled when you first got off the plane, receiving a slap upside the head from Mummy. Vandy had never minded the smell. From the moment she got on the plane at LAX, Vandy had dreaded only one thing: the child beggars on the drive from the airport to her grandparents' home.

Raj and Taj teased her relentlessly about it. Stared at her face and waited for her to cry with a chorus of "wait for it . . . wait for it . . ." Then they high-fived each other when she teared up as soon as she saw the bright eyes in dirt-stained faces staring into the car's window.

Their parents had just looked on, disappointed in her weakness. She'd dealt with their disappointment by keeping her eyes on her hands and not looking out of the car at traffic lights.

Ten years ago, Vir had sought out an organization that worked to get children off the streets, and the Guru Foundation, Vandy's company's charitable trust, had pledged a large part of their endowment to them. It didn't solve the problem, but it did more than just shedding tears had done.

As Vandy walked out of the airport, the heat and humidity tightened around her in an unrelenting hug. She wasn't sure what she'd expected to find, but it wasn't a man in a white chauffeur's uniform standing across the steel railings holding a placard with her name on it.

Vandy couldn't remember the last time someone had used her full name. Rani using it had to be intentional. Or maybe Vandy was over-thinking this.

The driver, Jitender Singh, was a chatty sort of man who was so warm and welcoming when Vandy introduced herself that it was like he'd known her all his life. He took her wheeled carry-on from her and chattered the entire short walk to the car, an S-Class Mercedes with a deep-red interior the color of the soles of the Christian Louboutin shoes her sisters-in-law loved.

Vandy had spent endless years wondering what Rani had done after she left. She'd kept her promise to Rani and never allowed herself to search for her or follow her in any way.

A clean break.

Evidently whatever Rani had done, she'd done well at it, which wasn't a surprise at all.

After asking Vandy about her flight and making sure the temperature in the car was perfect, the music just so, the incline of the seats comfortable, Jitender Singh handed her an ice-cold bottle of water and then left her to her thoughts, which were refusing to stay centered today.

I thought seeing you with your baby would make everything okay, but it hurts too much to be around the three of you.

You don't mean that.

You can't decide how I feel, Vinny! Don't you see. Nothing can ever be the same. You changed everything.

She had. She had changed everything. There had been not one single way to fix it. Although God knows Vandy had tried.

Don't you see. It wasn't just sex. It changed me. Rani had said the words, but they hadn't been necessary. She was different. They all were.

The only thing that hadn't changed was that Rani didn't want Mallika.

You have your daughter. That has to be worth it, right?

There was no answer to that question. At the end of every war, every victor must have to assess the losses and wonder if it was worth it and never know for sure.

The idea of Mallika with Rani was disorienting. Until Mallika was born, Vandy had always held as fact that Rani would be an essential part of Mallika's life. A doting aunt. A fairy godmother who taught her to be badass and beautiful. Family.

Then the idea had become so far fetched, so painful, so complicated, it had become Vandy's worst nightmare.

In less time than Vandy had anticipated, the car pulled to a stop in front of a giant brass gate that slid open. As they passed the gatehouse, a security guard saluted her. Vandy brought her mind to the absurdly chichi surroundings. How was it possible that her anticipation was as great as her terror? For the first time since Vir, she was feeling things. Feeling them large and loud. Her body remembered how holding Rani felt. Their last hug. Their pulling apart. Then suddenly she was seized with an urge to hold Mika. Her body lived to hold her child. She should have held her endlessly, held her every day after they lost Vir. She wanted it so badly now, she found her arms wrapped around herself.

The car drove up the curving palm-lined drive and stopped under a giant porte cochere that belonged to a seven-star hotel rather than an apartment building.

A doorman helped Vandy out of the car. Jitender assured her he'd bring her bag up and saluted her too. She had to make an effort not to salute him back. Vir smiled in her head even as nervous energy shivered through her.

As she entered the lobby with its gigantic chandeliers and a living wall lined with a profusion of ferns, she realized that she'd forgotten to ask which floor she was going to. But an older woman in a silk kurti over pants was waiting for her.

"I'm Ashwini, Rani Ma'am's executive assistant," she said with a smile and folded her hands in a namaste. Her hair was tied back exactly the way Sonja tied hers, but Sonja had never called Vandy "ma'am."

Vandy smiled at Ashwini and ignored the hesitation that made her step falter as she followed her into the elevator.

The elevator stopped on the fourteenth floor and opened into a black marble lobby that led to the only door on that floor. The lacquered wood was covered in copper-glazed ceramic tiles. It took Vandy a moment to realize that the tiles made up a giant Ganesha. A nameplate with swirling gold letters announced that THE DIWANS lived here. Instead of using the doorbell, Ashwini tapped a card on the lock and pushed the door open and invited Vandy into a home that made her feel like she'd stepped inside a resort from the glitziest travel magazine. Spotless white marble, artistic straight-lined furniture, tasteful pops of turquoise and rust. Beyond the airy open spaces were walls of glass that overlooked the ocean.

Still no Rani *Ma'am*, though, and no Mallika either. Voices floated in from one of the rooms, but the voices belonged to neither Rani nor Mika.

Ashwini seemed to read the question in Vandy's eyes. "This way," she said and led Vandy up a dramatic floating staircase and down a dramatic art-filled corridor to a bedroom. "Rani Ma'am wanted to give you a chance to freshen up. She'll be up soon. Please make yourself at home." She showed Vandy the door to the bathroom, asked if she needed anything, and left, shutting the door quietly behind her.

Rani had made sure their first meeting was in private. A totally Rani move. Vandy took her shoes off and went into the bathroom and realized that someone was already living in this room. One look at the toiletries pouch, and her heart did a relieved skip. Mallika!

There was a towel hanging on a hook behind the door, and Mallika's pajamas. Vandy pulled down the pajama top she'd bought Mika last

Christmas and hugged it to her chest, letting her daughter's smell engulf her. A love so intense it almost choked her filled her heart.

A knock sounded on the bedroom door, and Vandy ran to it and threw it open.

"Hi, Vinny."

Vandy's hands squeezed the cotton top she was still holding.

Rani's gaze did a quick dip to it. She shook her head. "Still as sentimental as ever," she said. "Needless to say, your daughter is just fine."

"Where is she?"

"Not even a 'hi, Rani'?"

"Hi, Rani. How are you?"

Rani smiled. "How do I look?" Then, "Your daughter has gone with my niece to have coffee with Hrithik Roshan."

"Excuse me?"

"You know she's obsessed with him, right? My niece is doing a film with him. So they went over to his house."

Vandy started laughing. This was not how she had imagined her first meeting with her estranged best friend to go. Her heart hurt, but it also felt strangely alive.

"It *is* pretty funny, isn't it?" Rani was smiling too. An easy smile. But Vandy couldn't tell if it was real. Rani's real smiles had always been something Vandy had to gauge with her heart. Feel for them rather than see them. "Did you expect to find her tied to a chair in a warehouse like a seventies film?" Yes, the smile was real. One hundred percent real.

"No, but I didn't expect to find her in a 2000s Karan Johar film either."

Rani looked impressed with that reference. Vandy had spent almost twenty years of her life with Rani; didn't she think her love for Bollywood movies had rubbed off? In the most ridiculous habitual response, Vandy felt a rush of pleasure at having impressed her. "You look good," she added.

Rani had always been the most beautiful woman in any room. She was still stunning, but she looked nothing like her old self. There was something entirely different about her.

Carriage? Not more confident exactly, but more comfortable. Everything about her was softer. Rounded. Her hair was thick and shiny as ever, but instead of the cascading layers she'd loved, it was now highlighted and pulled back in a trendy french knot. Her cheeks were full, her jaw just a little less sharp. She was wearing an embroidered linen kurta over flowy pants. Her middle had filled out a little to meet her always large breasts, but with the rest of her not quite as tiny, they seemed to have come into themselves in the new landscape of her body.

She looked powerful and elegant. Vandy's own body felt wiry and vulnerable. Their bodies had switched roles.

"You do too." She was studying Vandy, documenting the changes the way Vandy had just done.

Vandy hadn't thought about how she looked in a long time.

Rani's eyes, dark as onyx, much like Vir's and Mallika's, were softer too somehow. They softened even more. "I'm sorry about Vir."

Vandy swallowed the giant lump that formed in her throat. To her mortification, a drop slid out of her nose, and she sniffed. Rani handed her a tissue from the nightstand. Vandy wanted to ask how Rani knew about Vir. Mallika had probably told her. She wanted to ask how Mallika had found her.

"It happened really fast." That's what came out.

"I know." Her voice was strong and kind. Vandy had missed it so much.

"You do? How?"

Was it possible for the way you were able to read someone you loved to get stuck in time? The face Rani made was so painfully familiar, Vandy's stomach somersaulted with the shock of it.

Rani hesitated before answering. "It doesn't matter. What matters is that I want you to take Mallika back. I can't have her here."

It should have been a relief, and it was, but regret and abandonment came gushing in with it too. The memory of that last fight rose up around them.

I can't be here. I have to go.

For the first time, the steadiness in Rani's gaze faltered. If Vandy's muscle memory hadn't stored up every bit of her ability to decode Rani, Vandy might have missed it, but Rani was scared.

"Then why did you take her in? How did she even find you?"

"I took her in because I knew she couldn't be turned away." Something shifted in Rani's eyes again. "I knew someone once who couldn't be talked off the path she'd decided on. She turned out exactly like you, Vinny."

That made Vandy laugh. How many times had she had to push away the thought of how much Mallika reminded her of Rani?

It did not escape her that Rani hadn't answered the other question. How had Mika found her? And why was Rani scared?

CHAPTER TWENTY-NINE

MALLIKA

Two days ago . . .

I let myself into my apartment and make my way straight to the kitchen, where my father's cell phone sits fully charged in a drawer. I unlock it with my birth date and stare at the picture of Mom and me, where I'm pressing a kiss into her cheek and she's smiling with her eyes squeezed shut. Absolute and utter bliss leaps from that photograph. It takes me a moment to realize that I usually have to stare at Papa's phone for a full minute before I can touch it. Today, I just grabbed it without thought.

I press it to my chest and take it to the daybed that's covered in the clothes I've worn to shoot dance videos. When Rex drove me home two nights ago and stayed and talked all night, he hadn't been bothered by the mess, even though his own apartment looks like the After on a reno show. He'd been curious about each outfit and watched my videos with rapt interest.

The wonder in his fingers as he stroked the fabric, the wonder he has for his own work, the wonder in his eyes when he looked at me: all of it burns in my memory. Now, when it's too late, I realize how obvious it was and how doggedly I refused to acknowledge it.

You run from the truth so it doesn't ruin the version of truth you've chosen to believe.

I miss him so much there's a deep hollow in my chest. There's another sense there as well, one that tells me that he's right, that I've never believed that a man like that might love me. Even if he did, it would never be as great as it is in my head, as great as it was between my parents.

I've tried to recall Papa's face when we met Rani Parekh. I've tried to remember how they behaved with each other. But all I can remember is casual conversation and an uninhibited friendliness he seemed to share with all his friends in India. A loose-limbed ease he automatically seemed to acquire when we were in his hometown.

After Rex walked away from me, I sat in that stairwell for hours trying to figure out how I was going to stand back up. I usually bounce right back and then never think about the thing that knocked me down again. Like I haven't let myself think about the audition since the rejection.

I've never had to work on the ability to get up and bounce away. It's always just been there. In that stairwell, however, I couldn't access it. In the end, something else took possession of my body and made me move. I'd known that I had to find Rani Parekh.

I had to chase the pain down instead of running from it. Because it was inside me.

Papa's phone is heavy in my hand. He gave it to me a week before he died. *I don't need it anymore, but you will.*

For the past eleven months, I've turned it on every few days, when I couldn't bear how much I missed him. I've listened to his voice notes and swiped through his pictures. Papa took endless notes. Every time something caught his fancy, he recorded a note about it. It was like having pieces of him that he left behind like breadcrumbs to help me find my way through my grief. Even more than his books, which are filled with Mom and me, and his family in India, and our family here, and how he feels about all of us and how he wanted the world to be for us.

I click on a note titled "Beauty," and his voice fills the room, deep and gravelly.

I keep trying to write about beauty, and ugliness keeps coming up. Maybe you can't get to beauty without processing the ugliness. Or maybe they're both just here, present, and you can't acknowledge one without acknowledging the other.

He loved saying things like that. Just as much as he loved his absurd dad jokes.

I stare at the phone, and the weight of Rani Parekh is all I can feel inside it.

It's not hard to find her address and number. She is listed in his contacts, clear as day: Rani Parekh Diwan. There's no picture, and I can't quite remember her except for this sense she projected of being a beautiful woman who knows it but doesn't want it to define her. I remember being struck by that sense as a teenager, and now it returns to me in a stark flash. It's how I've always processed the attention I get for my looks.

There's an address in Mumbai listed for her. Papa has made no attempt to hide the fact that he has her contact information. That should put my mind at rest, but it doesn't.

It takes me less than ten minutes to max out my credit card and buy a ticket on my phone, then another few minutes to pack and grab my passport and get to the airport for the flight that leaves in three hours.

I have to know what happened all those years ago. What kind of friend carries a child for someone else? Why someone like my mother lets a friend like that go. Why someone like my father makes sure I meet her every time we're in India. How much does my mother know? I want to know the real truth. Not the version I've chosen to believe.

The only flight I could get is long. Thirty-eight hours, with stops in Europe and then the Middle East and then New Delhi before reaching Mumbai. Dad and I always traveled business class. I'd never given that a thought until I see the seat I'm in. It's the very last row of the five-hundred-capacity jet. There's barely enough space for me to fit my elbows in, but the row is empty. I think about Rex and his big body and how there is no way in hell his long legs would ever fit.

The thought makes pain scrape my insides. I've known what it's like to be with him for only a few days, and my heart feels shredded with rusty shears. I look at my phone. I want to apologize, but his disappointment is a live thing inside me. As long as he's right about me, I can't face him.

There is another call I need to make before I can do anything else. I call my agent. I'm not sure what I want to say to her, but I did tell her I'd get back to her, and I don't want to disappear without keeping my word.

"I'll do it," I say before I can talk myself out of it. "I'll send a new audition tape."

"Really?" She sounds completely surprised.

"I won't go all the way traditional, but I'll tweak the choreography to fit their new brief and still showcase who I am."

"That's fantastic, Mallika. I'll let them know." She sounds ecstatic, and the reflex to run before my hopes are dashed rises in me again. I want to call her and take it back, but I can see my own pattern too clearly now, and I don't.

I have one more call to make. I have to let Mom know where I'm going. My finger hovers over her number, but I can't. I miss her terribly, but I just cannot talk to Mom until I know what happened. I can't text her. I cannot add this to the pain she's already in, not without knowing why Papa kept in touch with the surrogate who carried me without Mom's knowledge.

I can't just disappear either.

There's only one solution I can think of.

Fortunately Naani picks up her phone when I call, because I have precisely a minute to talk to her before I have to turn on airplane mode.

"Mika," she says. "Are you calling to tell me you've made it official with Rex?"

"What? No!"

"Please tell me you didn't break that poor boy's heart again."

So many responses rush into my head, I don't know what to address first.

"Naani, I don't have too much time. I'll fill you in about Rex later. I want you to do me a favor."

"You took the genetics test," she says.

"What?"

"Never mind. What do you need?"

The flight attendant makes an announcement asking us to turn off the service on our phones, and the plane starts to move.

"I have to take a trip. Can you tell Mom I'm safe and I'll be back in a few days?" I think about the panic I know Mom will feel with just that much information. "You know how I said I lost the audition before? I didn't exactly. They've asked for another video, and I have to take some time to think about that. Like artistic introspection. Can you tell her that?"

"Ma'am, I need you to disconnect your call, please." A flight attendant glares at me and stands there waiting for me to do it.

I raise a finger to ask her to give me a minute, but she's not in the mood to indulge me.

"I have to go, Naani. Thank you."

"Have fun in India," Naani says before I let her go.

The flight attendant moves on with an expression that says she knows exactly how to handle difficult passengers.

It isn't until we've broken the fluffy white clouds that I realize what Naani said. I never told her where I'm going.

The sense that everyone in my life knows more about me than I do grips me again. I'm not a puppet. I can't be one anymore. But I have to be the one to cut the strings. I have to stand up on my own.

As soon as we're in the air, I turn on Wi-Fi. I start scouring the internet for Rani Parekh and read everything I can find about her. There's quite a bit there, including information about some films she choreographed dances for back in the nineties.

She's married to some hotshot film distributor, and she's the CFO of their company. There are pieces in *Fortune* and the *Economist* about their power-couple partnership. There are endless interviews with her talking about women in the business side of the film industry. There's a running theme in her interviews: she believes that more women have to be green-lighting and distributing films in order for women to have more meaningful roles and for the female gaze in storytelling to become mainstream.

There is absolutely nothing to be found about her childhood except that she was orphaned at a young age and lived with her aunt in America until she came back to Mumbai at thirty to try her hand at choreography.

After hours of reading, I raise the armrests in my empty row, roll up on my side, and let sleep take me. I dream about being an orphan, about starting my life over in America, about starting my life over in Mumbai. About carrying a baby that's not mine and I can't figure out how it got inside me.

By the time I show up at the address on Papa's phone, after what feels like a lifetime of travel, I feel like I know her, but also like I have absolutely no idea who she is.

The building looks like a fancy hotel with a guard room and high gates. Dad and I always met her at a restaurant or the mall. We never visited her home. Even after all the research I've done on her, when I try to jog my memory about my meetings with her, I come up empty. *Uneventful.* That's the word that keeps running through my brain.

I know Papa, and I know those meetings couldn't have been uneventful by accident, given that she's, you know, my secret biological mother. I've counted, and I met her four times in my life. Other than the first time, when I think she was at the wedding where I fell in love with dancing, I barely remember anything. It's been ten years since our last meeting.

I let the cab go and convince the guard to call Rani Diwan and let her know Vir Guru's daughter is here to see her. I consider saying Vir and Vandy Guru's daughter, but something makes me want to protect Mom.

Which doesn't mean I've stopped wondering why Mom never told me about the surrogacy. She's preached honesty to me all my life.

As I watch the security guard on the phone, looking and sounding respectful even though Rani is not in front of him, the thought that she might refuse to see me nudges at me.

For a moment that possibility gives me relief. I tried. I can leave.

You run from the truth.

The uniformed security guard unlocks the pedestrian gate. Then he takes my duffel bag from me and walks me to the lobby himself.

As I thank him and take the bag back, Rani gets out of the elevator. It's taken her less than two minutes to come down. She looks perfectly put together. It's past eleven at night, and she's obviously just getting back from somewhere fancy. No one just sits at home at this hour in a hand-embroidered silk kurti, a professionally done updo, and perfectly applied makeup.

"I'm Vir Guru's daughter," I repeat.

"I know who you are, Mallika. It's been a while." She has a polished Mumbai accent, clipped and lilting at once.

Her face is a mask. If I weren't a dancer, well versed in abhinaya, I wouldn't know how hard she's trying to not show any emotion.

She throws a look at my duffel bag and probably smells my endless-hours-of-travel sweat. "When did you get to Mumbai?"

I give her the most sheepish and endearing smile I can conjure. "I just got off the plane. I came straight here from the airport."

Finally an emotion flashes in her eyes. Terror. She's terrified by my presence? She puts it away quickly, but no one has ever been afraid of me in my life, and I know it's going to haunt me, that look.

She seems to consider a million things to say. I'm struck by how her expression is exactly like the one Mom gets when she's trying to figure out the best way to handle me when I'm being what she calls quirky. But without the terror.

"Can I help you with something?" That's what she finally settles on.

I've considered a thousand versions of what I'll say to her when I meet her. Until the words leave my mouth, I have no idea which direction I'm going to go.

"My dad said you're very well connected in Bollywood, and I wanted to try my hand at choreography here and was wondering if you'd help."

Her mask is firmly on again, but she lets me see the sadness in her eyes and touches my shoulder. "I'm so sorry about Vir."

I nod, and tears spring in my eyes.

"You must be tired. Why don't you come upstairs?" She leads me into the elevator.

I start babbling about choreography and dance and my kathak training and the work I've done. Then I babble some more about what I know about her career.

I expect her to ask me how I know so much about her. I expect her to ask why I didn't call instead of just showing up.

She doesn't. She takes me into her home with its fancy artsy door and überupscale interior. Someone comes by and takes my bag and hands me a glass of water. Then Rani takes me to a dining table and asks if I'm hungry.

I'm not but I say yes, because I need time to come up with what to do next.

As I eat a grilled cheese sandwich with the most delicious tomato soup I've ever tasted, she asks if I have a place to stay.

"I don't," I tell her.

"Well, you do now. You can have one of the guest rooms. Tomorrow I'll introduce you to my niece, who's working as an assistant director on Hrithik Roshan's next film. She can introduce you to Suman Raqhav, who's working on the choreography for it. How does that sound?"

"Thank you," I say, and it's a testament to my current state that I don't pass out at the possibility of meeting Hrithik Roshan. "That sounds great," I add. Now I just need to figure out how to ask her why she met me for so many years but never acknowledged that she's my biological mother.

CHAPTER THIRTY

RANI

1995
Twenty-eight years ago . . .

As the weeks of the pregnancy went by, Rani kept expecting to get sick or feel excessively hungry, or tired, or something. But she felt almost exactly the way she always did: healthy as a horse. Her breasts were a little larger, which was a bit of a pain, given the whole Rani Parton thing. Vinny and she went out and bought larger, armor-grade bras. Vinny was back to her old self again, every bit of sadness gone from her. She burst with the purpose and positive energy that had always defined her before all this started. It was like the light source inside her had rekindled.

Which was more than Rani could say for herself. She kept wanting to feel something, some sign of a new life inside her. But nothing. Only when Vinny and she went to their biweekly appointments and the doctor pressed the ultrasound probe against her belly and the *zhu-zhuum zhu-zhuum* swishing beat emanated from the machine did Rani believe there was something inside her.

On the outside, for everyone else, she'd turned into one thing and one thing alone. Pregnant.

At twenty-three weeks, there was a little melon sitting behind her belly button when she looked in the mirror. Everyone who saw her wanted to talk about it, to touch it. As for herself, unless she looked in the mirror, she couldn't see it at all.

"Look at how you're glowing!" Pinky and Tinku kept saying. Then followed it up with laments of how terrible they had looked themselves. Which of course they had not. They'd simply looked like they had babies inside them, albeit giant babies.

Fortunately, Amey and Aarav had come out normal sized. With bald pointy heads and humongous noses. They were absurdly adorable three-month-olds now. Born miraculously on the same day. Rani could imagine their mothers trying to outdo each other on each birthday by throwing the most extravagant parties for the rest of their lives.

The first time Rani felt the baby kick, she was sprawled on Vir and Vinny's couch watching *Aladdin* on the VCR. Vinny was cooking dinner. She was nesting something fierce. It was like she'd suddenly turned into Usha Auntie.

Vinny and Vir's apartment was spotlessly clean. Vinny made parathas for breakfast; she packed lunches for all three of them, then made a full dinner of dal, rice, fresh rotis, and two sabzis. She even made fresh yogurt at home. Unlike Rani, Vinny and Vir were not vegetarian, but they now cooked only vegetarian food.

Rani had taken to eating all her meals here. The habit of spending all her time in Vinny's apartment had started a few years ago, when Vinny had either refused to get out of bed because she was pregnant or had been too depressed to get out of bed because she wasn't.

Rani had just been thinking about how Princess Jasmine's life would have been different if she'd had a mother when the creepy villain with the thick mustache who looked old enough to be the princess's father leaned lecherously close. An ugly feeling Rani hadn't felt in a very long time rolled under her skin.

Just then something bumped hard at the inside of Rani's belly. She gasped. Next to her Vir sat up. His suddenly alert eyes went to her hand on her belly.

Another hefty nudge kicked where her hand was. Another gasp escaped Rani.

Vir moved closer to her. "What's wrong?"

His first reaction had been to think something was wrong too.

Why do you think something is wrong? she wanted to ask. Instead what came out was, "I think it's trying to escape."

Her gaze flew to the kitchen, where Vinny was humming Madonna's "Holiday" tunelessly as she cooked. Rani pressed a hand to her mouth, wishing she hadn't said those words.

Vir touched her shoulder gingerly. He was always careful about touching her. "It's okay." He smiled, obviously trying to put her at ease. "He or she most likely does need a little more space now. This is about the time when you're supposed to start feeling the baby moving." He pointed at her belly, a forefinger inches from touching it.

He'd never touched her belly. Vinny touched it constantly. If she was near Rani, it followed that Vinny's hands would be on Rani.

"It's like being attacked by an alien, but from the inside," Rani said without meaning to.

Vir laughed. "I'll bet." His eyes stayed on her bump.

She should ask him if he wanted to feel his child turn her body into a martial arts dojo, but she didn't know how to.

Then another kick landed, and Rani jerked, and it was so overwhelming that she grabbed his hand without thinking about it and pressed it to her belly right as another one landed.

"My God." The words were a whisper as he felt the push.

The weight of their gazes fell on their hands clasped together on her swollen belly, and it turned suddenly gigantic in her vision.

Something tightened in her throat.

"Vandy!" Vir called out, hand still on Rani's belly, voice filled with whatever it was he was feeling.

Vinny was next to them in an instant. Vir let Rani's hand go and pushed Vinny's hand onto where their child had been using his hand as a punching bag until a moment ago.

"She's kicking?" Vinny's eyes were veritable pools of joy. "Did you feel it?" And hope.

Vir nodded and dropped a kiss on Vinny's lips. They stayed like that for a long moment, wet faces pressed together, joined hands pressed into the stillness in Rani's womb.

Nothing happened.

For an hour they sat there like that, nudging and pressing, then being still, but nothing.

"It's okay," Vinny kept saying, huge smile refusing to be wiped away.

Finally they got up and ate dinner as though their hopes hadn't been dashed. All Rani felt like eating today was her favorite meal, rotis and dahi. As she ate, Rani silently begged the baby to move, to give her mother a chance to experience what she so badly wanted.

But nothing.

It was the only time she ever kicked. It was a girl. They found that out when at almost twenty-four weeks she decided to give up on this whole living business and arrived in the world wrapped in slick red silk and utter silence.

Four days after the kicking episode, Rani was at work when the most god-awful pain wrapped around her back. Then water started to leak from her and run down the inside of her legs in a thin stream. She called an ambulance, but it was too late.

The way Vinny cried when she held her daughter was worse than anything Rani had ever experienced. And that was saying something.

Maybe that was it. Maybe all the ugliness inside Rani had been too much for a life that little to bear. It was why Rani had never wanted to bring a child into the world. Her body wasn't a place where innocence could live. She'd forgotten. She'd thought being an incubator would be different, that her friend's goodness would nullify the ugliness she'd buried away.

Vinny collapsed to the floor and sobbed inconsolably until they took her little girl from her arms. Then she disappeared.

For two days, they had no idea where she'd gone. The family's panic and desperation pressed into Rani until she couldn't breathe. She couldn't stop searching, walking around their apartment complex, around all the places Vinny had loved to go, the library, the mall, every beach they'd walked on. Pain arced from her womb without respite, but she couldn't stop walking.

When the cops finally called, Rani prayed for the first time since she'd stopped believing in a higher power. She prayed and she prayed. Then as Vir drove her to the hospital, she prayed some more. She whispered pleas into her clasped hands, promised to sign over her soul. She would do anything, give her own life, take someone else's. All she wanted was to have Vinny back.

Don't take her from me. Please, don't take her from me.

At the hospital they found that Vinny had been in an accident. She'd been walking when a car hit her. She had fractured ribs, a broken arm, and some internal bleeding that they'd fixed in an emergency surgery. When Vir and Rani got there, Vinny wasn't conscious. The doctors didn't have a prognosis yet. Machines beeped and hissed around Vinny's motionless form.

The room spun around Rani, but before she fell to the floor, Vir caught her. She turned in his arms and let her tears spill. He wrapped himself around her, his hurt and terror bumping up against hers. Their pain so tightly connected it rolled into one. Rani pressed her face into his neck. For the first time since she'd left her childhood behind in India, she let a man's smell register in her brain.

The kick of sickness was debilitating, but it also took her out of this moment, away from the unbearable thought of a world without Vinny. His arms tightened around her and kept her from scattering, even as they made her want to struggle and gag.

Rani had been eight when she first felt the weight of a man's body pressing into hers. It was when she'd first known what it felt like to have a hand pressed to your mouth while someone entered your body and tore through your mind. Later she'd learned that having her breath cut off helped her get light headed and escape into oblivion. Now she let Vir's tight grip bring back that panic because the real and present panic was far worse.

"It's going to be okay," he said, his eyes wet, his face wet, his body trembling against hers. "We're not going to let her go."

The weight of men ten times her size crushed her ribs, and she embraced the pain. The ugliness that had killed Vinny's baby. The ugliness that had gone away only after Vinny came into her life. The ugliness that stayed away only when Vinny was near. She'd bear it, go back to the horror of it, if she could only have Vinny back.

"No, we're not," she said. "We're not going to let her go, no matter what."

CHAPTER THIRTY-ONE

VANDY

Now

Vandy watched Rani study her watch. "It's almost time for dinner. Mallika and Ria are almost home. We can catch up after dinner. You can join the family, or if you're too tired, I can have dinner sent up here."

Join the family? Had she had kids after all? Was that why she wanted Vandy to leave with Mallika? Vandy was exhausted, and if not for that "join the family" comment, she would have stayed here in this room until she got to see Mallika and take her home.

Something in Rani's face changed. Of course she would pick up on the fact that Vandy had decided to join them because she'd mentioned family. If she didn't want her there, she shouldn't have asked.

A bell chimed from what looked like an intercom panel by the door.

"Okay, that's dinner," Rani said with the slightest embarrassment tinting her cheeks.

"Was that a dinner bell?"

For a moment Vandy thought Rani would say "Shut up!" in that snarky Rani way. Instead she said, "My mother-in-law and husband have diabetes. They have to eat on a schedule." She headed for the door.

"Can you give me a quick rundown?"

"Of my life over the past twenty-seven years?" There it was, the old Rani snark.

"Of who will be at dinner."

"Sam," she said, sounding like that word meant something. "That's my husband. Sampat Diwan. It was our twenty-third wedding anniversary the day before yesterday. The day Mallika showed up." Her cheeks flushed the slightest bit. "He's a film distributor, and I'm the CFO of our company. We met when I was working as an assistant choreographer for Saroj Khan on his friend's film. He has three sisters who live with us. Ria and Ananya are his oldest sister's daughters. Shlok is his youngest sister's son."

"And you?" Vandy asked as they made their way down the stairs.

"Me what?"

"Do you have any of your own?"

"Any of my what?" They were halfway down the stairs, and the pause was long and loaded. "Kids? Of course not. You know how I feel about that."

"Even now?"

Rani looked incredulous that they were having this conversation. "Why would that change?"

"Do you know why Mallika is here?"

That made Rani turn around. "She told me she's here to meet choreographers in Mumbai. I'm pretty sure she's lying. My guess is she thinks she's found out something about her birth and has questions." How much Vandy had missed this: Rani's clarity, her candor.

"Is that why you called me? So I could answer her questions?"

"I told you why I called you. Because I want you to take her home. I can't have her here." There it was again, the fear. She really wanted

Mallika gone. Again it passed in a flash. "I just need the two of you to leave. Please. We'll have dinner. Then I'll have Jitender drive you to a hotel." She took the stairs again without waiting for an answer.

As they got to the bottom of the stairs, a group of college-age girls ran up to Rani.

"Rani Maami, is it okay for Lara and Pia to eat with us? We have to work on our project all night."

"How are you still not done? You've been working on it all week," Rani answered.

"This professor is a terror. He's literally like impossible to please," one of the girls said.

"Shouldn't your designs please you and not your professor?"

The girls laughed. Especially the tall one, who wrapped her arm around Rani. "That would be true if we were grading our own submissions, Maami-ji."

Everyone started talking at once, and Rani navigated their attention with the ease of someone who did this every day.

Somewhere along the way she threw an introduction over her shoulder. "This is my friend from the US, Vandana Guru."

Everyone said hello in that preoccupied way of young people when they were with their friends. Vandy followed them into the dining room. A hypermodern stone-topped table stretched across the wide-open space. It was laid out with place settings of silver thalis and endless amounts of food in shiny copper bowls. Before Vandy could register the casual splendor and the chatty people gathered around the table, Mallika walked into the room.

She started when she saw Vandy. "Mom! What are you doing here?" Her gaze flew to Rani, who shrugged.

For a moment Mallika just stood there stunned, but then she flew into Vandy's arms, long limbs tangling around her, gathering her scattering pieces back in place, squeezing and squeezing. Her smell was sweaty and sweet, her hair springing free from her messy bun in spikes and sticking to her face and neck. Her beautiful, beautiful child.

You're not angry with me. That was Vandy's first thought.

"I'm so sorry." Those were the first words out of Mallika's mouth, whispered into her ear. "Don't be angry with me, please."

Vandy held her daughter's face in her hands. *Never.* "I'm never angry with you," she whispered back.

It was the truth. She had never been angry with Mallika. Not once in her life. Her daughter was the only person in her life she'd never been angry with.

Tears filled Mallika's eyes. "How did you know I was here?"

"Rani called me."

Mallika looked so guilty Vandy squeezed her in another hug. "Everything is going to be okay. We'll talk after dinner."

Rani, who'd been watching them with one of her stoic masks, pointed to two empty chairs in the middle of the table set for twelve. Mallika and Vandy exchanged a raised brow and sat down.

Two servants came in and picked up the serving bowls and started ladling out food to each person around the table. Then placed the dishes back on the raised stone platform running down the center of the table. Dal, rotis made of various healthy grains, four shaaks, a salad of sprouted beans, and brown rice.

Rani didn't sit down with the rest of them. She took the rotis from one of the servants and walked around the table and served everyone.

"Doesn't this remind you of how it used to be at Naani's house when Naana was alive?" Mika said.

The words shook Vandy. She studied Rani as she walked up and put a roti on Vandy's plate.

"My God, you've turned into my mother."

It was a whisper, meant only for Rani's ears.

Rani straightened without responding. "Everyone, this is Vandana Guru, my childhood friend, and you've all met her daughter, Mallika."

Then she went around the table and made the rest of the introductions. Starting with her mother-in-law, a slight but gorgeous woman with bright-white hair pulled back in a bun and huge solitaires in her ears.

"I hope you're not planning to take your beautiful daughter away from us so soon. She's stolen our hearts in just a day." Her smile was filled with mischief, and she slid it sideways from Mika to her grandson, Shlok.

He pressed a hand to his heart and winked at Mallika, which made her throw back her head and laugh.

The boy was incredibly pretty, and Mika's reaction seemed to thrill him. This entire family was a little too absurdly beautiful. All thick hair, flawless skin, and preternatural bone structure.

"I've decided I'm going to marry your daughter, Auntie. I hope I have your blessings," the boy-man said with a toothy grin. He looked like he was training to be Bollywood's next It Boy.

"Unfortunately she's decided you're more amusing as an annoying little brother," one of his cousins said, and everyone laughed.

"They're right. You are adorable when you're annoying," Mika said.

"But I'm also adorable when I'm not, right?" he said with a wink.

"Maybe I'll get a chance to experience that someday." Mika winked back as though she'd known them her whole life.

More laughter bounced around the table.

"It works better when you let them see your not-annoying side before you propose marriage, beta," the man sitting at the head of the table said with an amused smile.

Rani was standing next to him. She squeezed his shoulder. "And this is Sam." That flush was back in her cheeks.

"The love of her life," Sam said.

"The love of my life," Rani said, and Vandy could tell it was true.

Several "awwws" sounded around the table.

Finally Rani sat down, and everyone started eating.

"This is why none of us are ever getting married," one of the girls said. Vandy had forgotten which one was Ria and which one was Ananya. "Because Maama and Maami are so perfect. It's an impossible act to follow."

Mallika's spoon froze midair. She went a little pale. Vandy rubbed her back, and she smiled again.

"It's why Sam's sisters are divorced," one of Sam's sisters said. "Because our brother is perfect."

"And because our brother was smart enough to find us a bhabhi who's perfect," another sister said.

Rani shook her head as if to brush away the fawning, but her smile was like a floodlight.

She's learned to smile without fear, a voice whispered inside Vandy. When they'd first met, Vandy had never known anyone quite so withheld, so removed from emotions. Watching her cry over the first meal she had in their house had changed Vandy's life. She'd needed to see that over and over again, have Rani reclaim the connection with her own feelings until they brought tears to her eyes. She'd taught Rani to cry but never to smile like this.

"Tell us how Rani Maami was as a child," one of the nieces asked. "She never tells us anything!"

"Just like this," Vandy said, her voice wobbling the slightest bit. "Loyal and strong and generous."

Rani's lip trembled. She quickly dabbed her nose with the napkin on her lap.

Mallika's gaze swept between Vandy and Rani.

"You know her well," Rani's mother-in-law said. "Did you know she convinced Sampat to stop wasting his time on being an actor and to take over his father's company?"

"What she did was save me from becoming a frustrated alcoholic who wasted my life on something I sucked at."

Rani gave him a fierce look. "You didn't suck at it."

Sam laughed. "You're right. I just loved it more than it loved me back." He patted her hand. They touched each other constantly. Rani had hated being touched, except by Vandy. *Vir was the one who changed that.* The thought brought with it such shame, Vandy needed all her strength to push it away.

"Remember what you said to me?" Sam said to Rani. "'Why chase something that's destroying you? Life has so much more to offer than just one thing.'"

Vandy swallowed. "You were a smart man to listen."

"I only listened because I didn't want to lose her, and she was ready to dump my sorry arse." The way he looked at Rani made Vandy's heart squeeze with grief. For all that she'd destroyed, she wished Vir had seen this. She wished he'd known that Rani was okay.

"Knowing what you want in life and what you're willing to sacrifice for it is important," Rani said, slipping Vandy a flat look over her bowl of dahi.

Rani's mother-in-law looked around the opulent room. "It's an ultimatum we're grateful for every single day." The smile she gave Rani was filled with love and respect. "Rani was also the one who knew how to turn around the failing company my husband left behind."

"It was Sam's charm and contacts in the industry," Rani said.

"And your ruthless business acumen," Sam said.

The rest of dinner went by with Mallika and Ria describing every detail of their coffee with Hrithik Roshan, who'd even shot a social media video with Mallika.

Dinner ended with ice cream from a local creamery, which used only cream, sugar, and fresh fruit. It was the best ice cream Vandy had ever eaten. Rani had ordered strawberry along with a bunch of other flavors, like mango, tender coconut, and fig.

"They don't make strawberry shortcake," she said, handing Vandy a bowl.

"Mom, you're eating ice cream? You never eat ice cream," Mallika said as Shlok piled every flavor into her bowl. His cousins teased him for not eating any himself to maintain his figure.

The young people started to talk about the latest Marvel film and moved into the living room. Sam squeezed Rani's hand and said good night to Vandy and helped his mother up to bed. He said he had an early start, but he obviously wanted to give the two old friends some time to catch up.

Vandy found herself on the deep terrace that wrapped around the penthouse that covered two floors of the building. Across Mumbai's jagged Juhu skyline, the Arabian Sea gleamed silver under a full moon, making the night bright with a mix of urban glow and moonlight. The sound of blaring horns and rumbling traffic was absurdly loud even this high up.

Rani leaned into the railing next to Vandy, and they watched the ocean in silence.

A blast of laughter rose from the living room, where Mallika seemed to be having a lovely time with the animated group. Vandy turned around and watched them. "Mallika was right. It does feel like Mummy's house when we were young," she said before she could stop herself.

"I never understood why you thought turning into Usha Auntie was such a bad thing."

Vandy rolled her eyes.

"Really? One choice nullifies everything else she was?"

"You always felt like I was being unfair to her."

"You were. Look at what our lives were because of her. Did you ever consider that she made sacrifices so you could have that life? I wouldn't be standing here today if it weren't for her." Rani stuck a spoon into the half-melted ice cream Vandy had eaten only a bite of. "And for you."

Vandy couldn't tell if there was an accusation threaded in with the gratitude. "You seem to have built a great life."

"Surprising, ha?"

"I'm not in the least bit surprised. Just sad that I missed it."

"Don't, Vinny." Her voice was firm. The old Rani, crystal clear about what she would and would not allow to slip past her defenses. And yet she'd allowed so much love in. Not just here but even before. With Mummy and all the Mehtas. With her and Vir. She'd returned it tenfold.

Then she'd given it all up.

Because Vandy had gone too far and asked for too much. Regret engulfed her.

Vandy had finally gotten what she wanted, and Rani had lost everything.

I'm sorry, Vandy wanted to say. But the words would slam open the dam they'd built so they could go on living.

Don't pity me. I didn't lose everything. I got myself back, Rani had said before she left. *And don't be stupid, Vinny, let's not waste the rest of our lives in regret.*

"You haven't done so badly yourself," Rani said finally as they stood there, their backs leaning into the railing, the wind in their hair, their eyes on all these people who knew nothing of what had brought them to this moment.

"With a name like Vandana Guru, what else could you be but a spiritual leader?" Rani added. "How did we miss that when we were plotting our lives?"

"I'm not a spiritual leader," Vandy said.

"Tell that to your devotees."

A laugh huffed out of Vandy. "That's what Vir called them too."

"I know."

If that wasn't an invitation to tell her something, Vandy didn't know what was.

"Just spit it out, Rani. How do you know so much about Vir? How did Mallika know where to find you?"

281

"If I tell you, will you leave with Mallika tonight?"

Vandy studied Rani. The desperate fear that had always lurked beneath the surface in their childhood, the one thing Rani had worked hard to bury under all sorts of swagger, had almost disappeared as they grew up. Now it flashed like an explosion under the inky blanket of her irises. Rani really didn't want her family to know who Mallika was. She'd obviously never told Sam about her.

"Won't he just love you more if he knew what you did for a friend?" Vandy asked.

"He's never going to find out, okay?" Fear leaked into her voice, into her body as it stiffened and twisted toward Vandy.

"Oh God." Vandy's hands went to her mouth. "Come on, Rani!"

"I don't want to talk about it. Don't do this, Vinny. Please."

"You told him you can't have kids." Rani had said the words over and over again. But it meant something completely different when you said that to the person who wanted to have kids with you. "Why would you lie to him?"

"I didn't lie. I can't. I can't be a mother. Not ever. That was never a lie."

"It *is* a lie, Rani! Why would you turn your marriage into a lie?"

"Does the hypocrisy ever get too much?"

She had missed Rani's candor, so she took that on the chin. "Of course I'm not going to tell Sam anything. When have we ever broken each other's confidences? Mallika and I will leave. At least tell me why she's here. How did she find you?"

"Thank you," Rani said with a little too much relief. "This isn't the first time I'm meeting her," she added finally. She said it quickly, as though she was afraid that she might not be able to.

"What?"

"I'm sorry, Vinny. I wish he had told you himself."

"Vir kept in touch with you?" How was that even possible?

"I don't think he meant to." Rani's voice was soft now. So much of their childhood wrapped up in her tone. "We met by accident, He was visiting India with your daughter. She was seven. We ran into each other at a wedding. Turns out Sam and Vir had common friends. One day, out of the blue, boom! There he was with a little girl all dressed up in a ghagra, with the same fearless smile as you."

"You performed at that wedding." The memories were coming quick and sharp now. After coming home from that trip, Mika hadn't been able to stop talking about the dance at the wedding. "She started dancing after that." Vir had told Vandy she'd really enjoyed the wedding dances and left the rest out.

"Then every time he was in Mumbai with Mallika, we met. I think he wanted me to know her. He couldn't imagine letting me miss out on the wonder he thought she was. It was just an hour. Lunch or coffee. When she was seven, nine, thirteen, and . . ."

"Seventeen," Vandy finished with her.

Rani remembered the ages Mallika was when she'd met her.

"I'm sorry."

"Don't be. I'm . . ." *Oh God, Vir. Why didn't you tell me? How could you do this? Why did you leave me?*

And just like that, there they were, the tears that had eluded Vandy for a year. The flood choked her, took her down body and soul.

Vandy spun back toward the ocean, where no one could see.

Rani wrapped an arm around her, and the mountain Vandy had been carrying on her back, inside her chest, crumbled and collapsed. Her body leaned into Rani, ravenous for the relief from the sorrow of losing her. She'd torn them in half with her own hands. Ripped the fabric of their love so brutally it was irreparable. Except Vir had gotten to repair it. He'd gotten to do it without her. Fresh grief, age-old grief, all of it crushed her at once. Everything. Regret and rage and exhaustion.

The soothing stroke of Rani's hand on her back kept her here, helped her breathe through the pain, kept her standing even as the avalanche flattened her.

"Shh," Rani kept whispering, the way she had done a million times.

She repeated it again now, a million times, as the tears emptied silently from Vandy.

"I think he thought you'd be okay with it," Rani said finally.

"I am. I am okay with it." She'd wanted it so badly. She'd wanted Rani to see Mallika. Once. At least once. She just hadn't known how to make it happen. She'd been too afraid. "I wish . . ." God, why was it so hard to say it. "I wish I had done it myself. I wish I had done things differently."

"No, you don't. We're not doing this. We're not doing regret. You got the exact life you wanted. We both got great lives in the end."

"I never wanted a life without you in it." It felt so good to say it. Even though it made Rani look like she was standing in the path of a tidal wave and she knew she wasn't going to be able to escape it.

It wasn't the first time Vandy had seen that expression on Rani's face. It had been there, just like this, the day Vandy asked her best friend to sleep with her husband.

CHAPTER THIRTY-TWO

MALLIKA

Now

Seeing my mother standing there in Rani Parekh Diwan's home was a shock. But the relief of seeing Mom's eyes light up with that expression she gets when she looks at me, as though I'm the rising sun, was greater. Her eyes have been gauging me all evening to make sure I'm okay. Another thing so familiar it puts something back together inside me. It also makes me glad I never asked Rani for answers. Because suddenly I know without doubt that I want them to come from Mom. This is between her and me, and Papa.

There's something painfully familiar about the way Mom behaves around Rani. I've only ever seen her be like this with Papa and me. Relaxed in a way she never is around anyone else. Not even her own parents or brothers. As though she saves a piece of herself only for us. It's disconcerting to see her like this with a stranger.

Even now, as they stand there on the balcony, they seem to be locked in a bubble where nobody else exists.

Rani's mother-in-law, who reminds me so much of my naani it's eerie, stops me to ask me all about my meeting with Hrithik Roshan.

Sonali Dev

Then she proceeds to fill me in on how her son would have been a star if Hrithik's debut film hadn't released on the same day as Sam's.

By the time I satisfy her with every detail of everything Hrithik said and did, while also agreeing that Sam is actually more handsome, Mom and Rani have moved to the wide terrace skirting the penthouse. They aren't visible from the living room, where everyone is bonding over ice cream and a bunch of other desserts from some fancy bakery in Bandra.

I walk to the other end of the room to catch a glimpse of them through the floor-to-ceiling windows. They are deep in conversation, their bodies tight with tension yet loose with connection.

The terror in Rani's eyes when I first got here still haunts me. She's been incredibly generous, but it's also clear that she doesn't want me here. Like *really* doesn't. She's obviously the one who called Mom and told her to come get me. It's the weirdest thing to know someone birthed you and has absolutely no desire for you.

There are too many things I want to know. Usually, I'd have no idea how to push for any of them, and I'd convince myself that none of it matters because I have too much anyway. But I don't. There's no such thing as having too much. I deserve to know, and I will find out. And no matter how terrible it is, I'll deal with it. I've taken care of myself after Papa. I've taken care of Mom when her grief knocked her out.

This afternoon, when Rani's niece Ria took me to meet Hrithik Roshan, my body kept trying to find an excuse to get out of it. I had a stomachache, a headache. Ria just asked me to chill and said everyone gets nervous before meeting him but then relaxes once they get there.

She was right. The video I got with Hrithik is one of the best things I've ever shot. When I danced as a young girl, I lost myself in it. Then I started to care about what others thought, if they liked it, if I was doing it well. Today when Hrithik asked me to throw steps at him and I did, I forgot everything but being in that moment with him. Later he told me he was struggling with something and my "quirky" classical and hip-hop fusion was exactly what he needed to figure it out.

I am now a person who has spent a half hour of her life dancing her heart out with one of the best dancers in the world. And all because I didn't give in to my flight reflex.

The hurt in Rex's eyes flashes in my head, and my heart gives a god-awful twist. I keep wanting to text him, but I don't know what to say. He hasn't texted me either. Again my instinct is to believe this means he isn't thinking about me.

I stop myself and let myself acknowledge the facts: The way he looked at me that last time like he was leaving his heart behind in my hands. The way he stuck by my side as my world crumbled around me. Of course he's thinking about me. I saw the pain in him as I pulled away. Of course he's hurting just as much as I am.

I just want to grab Mom and go back home. We will, but not yet.

I'm sorry, I text him because that much I can do right now.

When I look up from my phone, I notice that Rani and Mom are huddled together. Rani's arm is wrapped around Mom's shoulders, and Mom is shaking.

Is she crying?

Mom hasn't cried since Papa died. Everyone in the family has talked about how unhealthy that is. Behind Mom's back. No one ever tells her what to do. Papa was the only one who did, but he's gone now.

I run out to the terrace. "Mom?"

She turns to me, and her face is wet, her nose red with the force of her tears.

As soon as she sees me, she tries to wipe her face on her sleeve.

Suddenly, I'm so angry I can't breathe.

Mom hasn't been able to cry for my father, not around me, not around her family. But here she is with this pristine and cold woman letting her see her in this kind of pain.

She doesn't even want you here. She probably had an affair with your husband. Papa brought me to see her without even telling you, without even telling me!

Sonali Dev

I want to say these things so badly I'm shaking with them.

"I'm so sorry," I say instead. "I'm so sorry I forced you to come here." Now I'm crying too. What have I done? Why have I opened these wounds for her?

"Why are you sorry?" she asks. "None of this is your fault." She cups my face. "Why did you? Why did you come here?"

"Vinny, please," Rani says. "Don't do this."

The glance they exchange is so intimate, I don't even know who Mom is anymore.

"Why did you lie to me?" Finally I say the words. They come out so angry Mom gasps.

"I know Rani was the one who carried me. My surrogate." The words are flowing now. "I know you two were friends. Why did you stop being friends? Was it me?" Then I stop because I can't say the other part. The part where I've known her my whole life and Mom doesn't even know it.

Mom wipes her face. "It's a long story."

"You've had twenty-seven years to tell it," I say.

"I know. I should have told you a long time ago." Mom looks at me with so much regret it crushes my ribs. "We were best friends since we were twelve."

Rani presses her hand to her mouth, exactly the way Mom and I do. "I'm sorry. I have to tell her. Please," she says to Rani.

After a moment of stillness, Rani nods.

Mom turns back to me. "Rani carried you in her womb for me. I wanted you so very badly, but I couldn't keep a pregnancy." The pain on her face is almost too much to witness.

Rani takes her hand and leads her to the rattan couch. It's like they're connected by an invisible force field. They sit down, and I sit down across from them. They look at each other, and another silent message passes between them. Then they start talking. They tell me how

288

they met soon after Rani came to stay with her aunt, about how they grew up together, how they never spent a day apart.

They tell me how Mom and Papa met. I've heard the story before, I've known about their elopement, but there was no third person in my version.

Mom tells me how she got pregnant soon after Papa and she were married. Then Rani tells me how Mom spent six years being pregnant and losing all the babies who came before me. The hair on my arms stands on end as they recount each one. Mom's desperation seems to escalate with each loss. Some of the babies have names. Nausea roils in my stomach. They finish each other's sentences. It's like they were one person that entire time.

"I wish I could explain what it was like. But eventually, I think it made me ill. Not just physically but mentally. I lost my ability to see reason. To understand reality. To think about anyone but myself." Mom says those words to Rani. It's an apology, and Rani's eyes, as dark as mine, get unbearably intense before they moisten with tears. That's her only response, but Mom soaks it up.

"Finally, the only way I could see to have a child was for someone else to carry one for me. So we fertilized an embryo, and Rani agreed to carry it for us." Mom looks at Rani with such love. I don't think I've ever seen her look at anyone like that. Not even me.

I want to tell her she's wrong. I want to tell her that her friend isn't who she thinks she is, that I'm not born from Mom's embryo. But I can't find a gap in the pain she's letting pour out of her.

Mom strokes my face and studies me for a long moment. Then she looks at Rani, and something new passes between them. They're giving each other the courage to speak the next part.

"Turns out my uterus wasn't the only problem. My embryos weren't viable either."

"Vinny, please," Rani begs. "Don't."

"She should know," Mom says. "She should know that motherhood has nothing to do with carrying a baby or donating an egg."

"You're my mom. I know that," I say. "Nobody else can ever be my mother."

"Damn straight," Mom says, and for the first time she smiles. "But you came this far searching for answers. So you deserve to know what you came to find out." Rani makes a sound of distress, but Mom ignores it. "Rani carried Vir and my baby for twenty-four weeks and then lost her."

Rani's face has gone white. She no longer looks untouchable. She looks brittle.

For a long time no one says anything more.

Mom holds my hands in both hers as she meets my eyes. "She had to go through that, through losing a child that wasn't even hers. Then while she was still in pain, I begged her to donate an egg." Mom can't seem to stop now. A dam has broken, and her words pour out. "Rani was never able to say no to me. Not her and not Vir. And I had lost all sense of myself, of right and wrong. I didn't care about anything but becoming a mother, something I'd convinced myself I needed to complete me."

I reach out and wipe the tears that slip from her eyes.

"The doctors took one of Rani's eggs and your father's sperm and fertilized it. Then they inserted the embryo into Rani." Mom refuses to look away from me. "What you found out is true. She is your biological mother."

I look at Rani, and she is frozen in place.

It takes a while, but finally her gaze moves from Mom to me. "All I did was give birth to you. I never wanted to be a mother."

Obviously, because she left. "Why did you stop being friends?" Even as I ask, I know the answer. Their friendship couldn't survive my birth. I broke up their friendship.

They look at each other again, and their expressions change again. It's like watching intricate choreography, how they communicate without words. It's unbelievable that they haven't seen each other in twenty-seven years.

This time Rani speaks. She seems to see the inexplicable hurt I'm feeling. "Vinny and Vir were my world, and when you came you completed their world. Your mother was so happy, her happiness seemed to wrap us all in light. Our life should have been complete. We'd always thought it would be when you came. But then something slipped inside me. Somehow I couldn't keep myself in that cloak of light." She keeps her voice cool, but there is such a deluge of emotions in it, I'm swept away.

"I had some terrible things happen to me before I came to America. It messed me up." There is a flatness to her voice when she says it. "Your mother taught me what life could be like. Who I could be. Then conceiving you changed something inside me. It fixed me in ways even she hadn't been able to. But something else got mixed in there. There was pain I couldn't explain. The way I felt made it impossible for things to stay the way they were." She pauses, and Mom takes her hand.

I don't know if she means she developed feelings for me. Did she change her mind about giving me to Mom?

She picks the question from my eyes. "I'm not someone who can ever be a mother. It's the one thing I've always known. You were always Vinny's. I'm sorry."

I know it's going to take a lot of time to make my way through all this. But I look at Mom and I know that I will. I take her free hand and squeeze it.

"But something inside me did change," Rani continues. "It was supposed to be a beautiful time for Vinny and Vir, but the way I felt made it ugly. So I couldn't stay."

"You didn't make it ugly," Mom says. "I put you in an impossible position. I asked for too much. I thought only of myself. I could see you hurting, but I also believed with all my heart, hoped, that we'd be a family again."

"And I knew I would never find my way there. Your family was the three of you, and I had to leave the three of you to it. It was like learning to walk again. I had forgotten how to stand on my own feet since you took my hand. Now your hands were full. Everything bad that had happened to me before I met you had happened because of someone else's actions, someone else's choices. When you came back for me the first day we met, you taught me that I could choose my own actions too, no matter my age. It changed my life. Then I forgot again. So I had to go away and learn again."

They're back inside that bubble, their gazes locked.

"I wish I had come after you," Mom says. "I wish I'd found a way."

"It wouldn't have helped. There was no way out of the corner we painted ourselves into."

I'm the root of all this pain. *Was I worth it?* I want to ask, but neither of them seems aware of my presence. Which is super ironic.

"Did you ever think about me?" I ask. Of all the questions I have, it's the one that comes out.

They both start when they hear my voice.

Rani looks at me with sudden admiration. She knows exactly why I picked that question to ask. "I did," she says. "As Vinny's daughter. As the niece I didn't get to watch grow up." Then her lips quirk in a sad smile. "Maybe I would have thought of you more if Vir hadn't made sure I got to see you."

I press a hand to my mouth, a habit I obviously share with Mom and Rani. "You already know Papa kept in touch with her?" I say to Mom.

She nods. "I wish I'd had the courage to do it myself. I wish I'd told you about Rani and the love you came from. But your father and I made a promise to Rani that we'd never tell you. We owed it to her to keep it."

Now I'm sobbing. Thinking that my mother is not the person I believed she was because she lied has been a brutal weight. She did lie, and she kept the darkest part of her life from me. She's not perfect.

And yet she is. I feel a new freedom in my admiration. I'm no longer trapped by it.

I've been angry with Papa these past few days. Knowing he's my biological father when Mom isn't my biological mother felt like I'd lost him all over again, like maybe I never knew him at all.

Now I understand why he brought me to see Rani. He wasn't betraying Mom. The relief of not having to be angry with my dead father, whom I miss terribly, is overwhelming. They were all just trying to keep the promises they made to each other. I've always had an overwhelming sense of being the product of a larger-than-life love. Now I know I am. Everything else suddenly feels easy to deal with.

CHAPTER THIRTY-THREE

RANI

1995
Twenty-eight years ago . . .

Two days ago, if someone had told Rani that she would sleep with Vir, she would have laughed. Now here they were.

"She shouldn't have asked you for this," Vir said. "*We* shouldn't have asked you for this."

Rani had no idea why she had said yes. But after digging deep into the very heart of her existence, she hadn't been able to dredge up a way to say no. Maybe a piece of her had become invested in Vinny's dream. In her obsession. She knew Vir felt that way too. Swept up in a wanting so strong it felt otherworldly.

Or maybe she couldn't bear that her friend was lost, gone from them, and she'd do anything to get her back.

"It's not fair to you," he said.

"There's no fair or unfair here, Vir!" Rani said. "Vinny needs this."

They were in Rani's apartment. Maybe that was a mistake. But it was the only place that felt right. Rani knew she couldn't do this anywhere else. There was something about this apartment that had allowed her to become who she wanted to be.

She shook out her arms. "Let's just get it over with." She didn't step closer to him.

He didn't either. He stood all the way on the other side of her living room. Tiny as it was, the space was too large and too small for what they needed to accomplish. A distance too far. Miles and miles. But also so close she had to fight for air and breathe through the panic.

"Rani, you okay, sweetheart?" He was one of those people who used endearments easily, but he'd never used one on her. Maybe he'd known not to. He was also one of those people who was so perceptive about other people's feelings that it bordered on intuition. It probably had to do with spending a lifetime with characters in his head, even though he had put away his writing these past few years.

When they first met eight years ago, Rani had felt like he could see things about her she wasn't comfortable with people seeing. He'd seen her discomfort with his perceptiveness too. Given how in love with Vinny he was, he'd had no choice but to navigate Rani. He'd made the effort to let her have her walls. Or maybe it had nothing to do with Vinny and Rani's friendship. He just chose to let people be who they wanted to be.

It was probably why they were standing here today. And her freaking out was not going to help them do what they needed to do.

Last month, they'd tried a turkey baster. After Rani lost their baby, Vinny had become convinced that a traditional surrogacy was the answer, which simply meant they didn't just need Rani's uterus, they needed her egg.

Which also meant it wouldn't be Vinny's baby at all. It was one of those things everyone had thought but no one had been able to say to Vinny. Not with her broken ribs and her stitched-up insides.

At first they'd talked about extracting Rani's egg and fertilizing it with Vir's sperm in a clinic. But they were all already deeply in debt over this. Another ten grand was out of the question.

It was the end of the road.

Then Pinky and Tinku had come up with the story of their cousin who had used a turkey baster.

"That's ridiculous," Vir and Rani had said. But Vinny's eyes had lit up.

The fact that they were in a place where they'd bought a turkey baster, then Vir had filled it with his semen, and then Rani had actually put it inside her and pumped the stupid rubber ball said everything that needed to be said about how this entire thing had crossed all boundaries of sense.

But this was about Vinny, and they'd almost lost her twice, and this needed to be over.

Rani sat down on the couch. "I'm not going to take my clothes off," she said quickly.

"Of course. Whatever you need," Vir said. His voice was kind, and it made her angry that he got to be so in control. That he got to be the one who had to manage her. "I've never seen you nervous," he added.

"Aren't *you* nervous?" she snapped. "Doesn't this feel weird to you?"

"Of course I'm nervous, very nervous. This is unbelievably weird. Even unconscionable." He sat down all the way at the other end of the couch. "Vinny said you wanted to do this."

"It made sense at the time," she said. Because Vinny had made it make sense.

"And it doesn't now?"

She wasn't sure. "Why are you asking me all this? Why did you say yes?"

It was a blur. Vinny having the idea. Them having the conversation. Vir and Rani thinking this was possible somehow.

When Rani had been stuck in the cycle of darkness that was her childhood, she hadn't known that's what it was. She'd believed it was simply life.

After meeting Vinny she'd seen the other side, seen the lightness of love and normalcy. Even though the darkness of these past few years had felt endless, Rani also knew that it had an end.

Her belief that darkness could end came from Vinny, and yet Vinny herself had lost that belief. Rani just had to find a way to end it for her the way Vinny had once ended it for her.

When Vinny woke up after her accident, it felt like they might finally be done with this. Those were even the first words out of Vinny's mouth.

"I want it to be over," she'd said as she opened her eyes and saw Rani and Vir sitting there. "I dreamed that you and Vir were holding each other."

Rani's happiness at seeing Vinny wake up was so great that she'd barely registered her words.

Then a month later, after a slow and silent recovery, after the turkey baster failed to become a father, Vinny had said the words. *The only thing left to try is you and Vir having sex.*

They'd both been surprised by the words. At first Rani thought they were just a release valve. A joke to take away the sting of their final attempt failing.

It hadn't been a joke.

Is using a baster that different from the real thing?

Do you still hate the idea of intimacy with Indian men?

Rani had slept with Vir's cousin after Vinny's wedding, and he was Indian. Sex was sex. Vinny wasn't entirely wrong. It had never been any different with the turkey baster than the men.

If this doesn't work, I'll give up. No more. I promise.

Please just think about it.

It had taken Rani two days to answer.

"I didn't actually say yes," Vir said finally. "But I didn't say no either. You can change your mind, you know."

That would mean going back on her word. Vinny had crushed ribs. She'd almost died, twice.

"Or we close our eyes, hold our noses, and do it." She'd done it with a baster; she could do it with a man.

"Okay," he said.

Which wasn't what Rani had expected him to say.

"Like bitter medicine." He smiled tightly. "The more we think about it, the harder it will become."

"You're right. Do you want to go to the bedroom?"

"That makes sense."

She made her way there, and he followed.

Wearing a sweaterdress had been a fortuitous choice. She hadn't consciously thought about it, except maybe she'd needed something thick and bulky, but if she'd had to remove jeans, she would have been mortified.

She wanted to rub her arms, but she couldn't move. "If this were one of your stories, how would you write this?"

He smiled at his hands. They were avoiding each other's eyes. "This is probably too implausible for fiction."

"Do you miss it?" she asked without thinking about it.

"Yes."

"I'm sorry."

"Most people give me platitudes. Like I'll get back to it when life settles down."

"It will settle down." Vinny had promised. "I wouldn't know how to go on if I had to stop dancing."

Rani had never realized how much she respected the fact that he'd given so much up for Vinny. He'd given up his art to support them.

"I've always respected how you hold on to that. Your art, even though you have to do other things to survive," he said.

She sat down at the edge of the bed. "You have to write again, Vir. You will. It can't be gone." It felt like a lifetime ago that he'd lost his mind because someone misunderstood the voice of a writer.

"Sometimes I think it is gone. It's too painful to hold the stories inside me and not be able to write them. It's easier to cut them off, to bury them where they can't breathe and talk to me." He looked so sad, for the first time in her life Rani had the urge to touch a man, to comfort him.

"We'll make this baby. You and Vinny will have your family. She'll find another purpose, and you know that when she does, there will be no stopping her success. Then you'll go back to the stories you've put away. They'll come to life with all this experience and pain, and no publisher will be able to resist it. And you will be the next big bestseller."

He huffed out a laugh. "Who knew you were such a storyteller yourself."

"Dancing is storytelling. Sometimes when I dance, life's truths become clear to me." She'd been teaching her students "Maiya Yashoda" yesterday, the love song between Krishna and his adoptive mother, and she'd understood, in one fell swoop, why this was so important to Vinny. Why she had to be a mother. And she'd gone to Vinny and said yes. She knew how to do this after all.

"How would you tell this story in dance?" Maybe he did too.

Rani closed her eyes and fell into that thought. "This is the story of a womb," she said, moving her hand in a mudra over her belly. "One shared between two women. The one who carries it in this world must find a way to separate herself from it." Her hands separated, splitting her in half. She stretched up her neck and felt her body, cell by cell, muscle by muscle. It could do things that had nothing to do with her mind.

"How would she know how to do that?" Vir whispered. "How would she know which part of her was shared?"

"She won't. She doesn't feel the need to. She feels like all of her is theirs together."

"But to use the womb she has to find it, separate it."

"Yes. But she's done it before. She's been parts and pieces all her life, with no whole to belong to." Rani opened her eyes, but she was inside it now. Inside the story of her dance.

"What would she need from him?" he said. He'd slipped inside it with her, a hunger for the story darkening his eyes.

"She wants him to tell her that he sees her in parts too. That he knows there are only some parts he can touch." She pulled her legs up on the bed and scooted back.

His eyes asked for permission to do the same, and she nodded and touched the bed beside her.

He moved into the space her hand vacated. "He promises her that he will. He will find a way to touch only the part of her where he is welcome. That he knows how hard this is for her."

They moved until they were lying on their sides, facing each other. Rani let the ice in her heart encase her skin.

"She tells him that she's never had that promise before," Rani said, her fingers touching her lips, then moving from them like voice given form. "Before, she's always had to do it all herself. Sift through the parts. Draw the boundaries. Fight to keep them."

"He asks her to show him her boundaries. To lead the way. To teach him the language she wants him to speak to her body."

And that's how they made their way through it. Two storytellers playing their parts. He took his cues from her words and her eyes. She'd never looked into the eyes of anyone she'd had sex with. But this was a dance.

He unzipped himself, squeezed his eyes shut and readied himself with his own hands. She moved her underwear out of the way. They found the shared womb, from behind the safety of the story that had risen out of nowhere. Even as he entered her, they kept the story going. Stayed in it, until it served its purpose and was gone.

After it was done, she rolled away and moved to get off the bed, the stage. With the dance over, it seemed to catch fire and start to burn. There was a wetness between her legs, and it spun time around her. Rani had never had sex without a condom.

Except when she'd had no say in it.

Before she knew what was happening, her breath started to pump out of her. Violent hefty bursts of it. She rolled into a ball. The blackness taking over so fast she didn't have time to react.

When her eyes opened again, when sound penetrated the blackness, she was on her side and Vir was kneeling on the floor next to the bed, saying her name. Her eyes flew open, and she sat up, knees pulled to her chest. Shame gripped her.

She wanted to apologize, but no words came.

He handed her a glass of water and sat back on his heels.

"Did I hurt you?" There was such remorse, such sadness in his eyes, it was like someone screaming their apology into her face. It felt like screaming herself, from the very pit of her stomach, and wiping everything away but the agony she was releasing into the world.

"Rani?" he repeated when she didn't answer.

"No." It was a miracle she was able to make a sound.

"You sure?"

"Don't you think I know when I'm hurt and when I'm not?" she snapped.

"Why didn't you say something before?"

"Before what?" And it was those words, those words that laid it out, gave what had happened to her form. Acknowledged that no one had bothered to prevent it. The one person who should have and could have stopped it had given up being a person long before then. Had given up being her mother.

It was the finality of that fact that made her laugh. It was an ugly laugh. The ugliest. So ugly, she couldn't believe she was letting it out. For the first time in her life, she was letting it out.

He sat there and let it rain on him, that ugly laugh.

"I have to leave," she said, straightening up.

"Please don't. Not like this." He sounded desperate. Shaken for having shaken her. Vir undone. Not even a bit of his inherent confidence anywhere in sight.

She slumped back down. "I'm fine," she said, but it was such a lie that the ugly laugh was back.

"Don't. Don't say you're fine when you're not."

"Then what should I say?"

"Say everything."

For an endless beat there was silence. She wanted to laugh again. But then all the things she couldn't say started to crawl up inside her. She couldn't pass out again, and she couldn't push them back, so she started to talk. She started with her mother. Then the tenement building. She told him about Virju Maharaj's dance studio and how beautiful her mother had been when she danced, how her beauty had morphed into something else as she drank herself to death.

He'd grown up not far from where she had. Their schools had been blocks from each other. Talking to someone who knew those places, her old places where she'd been shredded down, was somehow easier. Or maybe it was him.

He didn't dwell on the pain tucked into her words. He just kept absorbing them as she dug them up. For every story she told him about herself, he told her one about himself. Being a fatherless child. Entertaining himself with stories when his mother worked and worked. From everything she told him, he found the pieces of survival and picked them up like benedictions.

"Is that why you don't want to get married?" he asked finally. They'd made it to some sort of sacred space where all the unsayable things felt safe to say.

"There's too many reasons. I don't even know where to begin. For one, I don't want to be a mother, and who wants to marry someone like that? Making a family seems to be the only reason to marry."

"That's not true at all. I would marry you just for you. Hypothetically, of course."

She laughed again, her laugh feeling much less ugly inside her. "With all my damage?"

"What damage?" His easy charm was back.

Another laugh slipped from her. "The damage that makes me have blackout panic attacks after sex."

"Does it happen every time?" he asked, that soft curiosity hooking her some more.

She shook her head. "I don't let it come to that."

"What does that mean?"

"I haven't had sex in years. Back in high school and college, I wanted to prove that I was normal, that I had control over my own body. But it wasn't really anything more than part A going into part B."

"The way we just did."

"No. With less connection. Less gentleness. I don't remember the names of anyone I've slept with."

It was the first time something she said broke through his stoicism and he sat up. "You thought that was gentleness and connection?"

It was the most she'd ever known. "Not everyone is you and Vinny."

"You are every bit as deserving of gentleness and connection as us."

He sounded so fierce, so offended on her behalf, something new formed inside her. She leaned over and kissed his cheek. She shouldn't have, because once she had, she couldn't pull away. He turned his face, their foreheads touched. A knife sliced into her heart. They sat there like that as tarry darkness drained from her. Then their lips found each other and fitted together. And it was like meeting a whole new version of herself.

"You deserve everything, Rani," he said, and instead of pulling away, it made her press closer. Because suddenly, out of nowhere, she wanted to. She wanted to deserve everything. She wanted the fierce faith in those words to be true. And she wanted him to show her what that meant.

CHAPTER THIRTY-FOUR

VANDY

Now . . .

Mallika seemed satisfied with the story Vandy and Rani told her. Except one piece of it, every word was true. If a lie caused no harm, how could it be worse than a truth that did?

What possible purpose would it serve to tell Mallika that her mother had asked her father to sleep with her best friend to have her?

Mallika gave Vandy and Rani a hug and left them alone to catch up.

"I guess you aren't going to try and convince me to tell Sam the truth anymore?" Rani said as Mallika disappeared from sight.

"Some truths are best left unspoken," Vandy admitted. She rolled out her shoulders. The weight of secrets could get heavy.

They'd told the Mehtas that they'd taken another chance on an external fertilization and it had worked. The rest of the world knew none of it. The three of them had gone to a cabin in Tahoe for the last trimester, when Rani started showing, and had Mallika there. Everyone outside the family believed that IVF had finally worked for Vandy.

Until Mallika was born, they'd been entirely preoccupied with the pregnancy. The relief and magic of those nervously hopeful nine months had made them believe that they had a chance. Then the truth had emerged from the shadows and made it impossible.

The day Mika turned one month old, Vandy had seen Vir leaning over Rani as she held her. Rani had looked up at him, and such tenderness had shone in their matching onyx eyes that Vandy had felt like a stranger. The three people Vandy would give her life for had been wrapped up in a connection so ethereal that in that moment she'd known exactly what losing them would feel like.

They'd looked up and seen Vandy, and Vir had stepped away from Rani and come to her. But the truth couldn't be unseen after that. It couldn't be left untouched.

She'd asked them what she'd seen, and they'd tried to tell her to let it go. But how did you let go of something that lived in the eyes of those you loved?

She'd pushed for the truth, believing that they'd know how to deal with it once it was out in the open.

Being with Rani that day wasn't only about having Mallika for me, Vir had admitted finally. *I'm not sure how we can navigate that, but I do know that the life I want is with you and Mallika. Who I am, who I want to be, is the person I am when I'm with you.*

When Rani decided to leave, unlike Vandy, he hadn't tried to stop her. *If that's what she wants, we have to let her go. She has the right to live her own life.*

They'd never mentioned Rani again until the very end, when he'd told Vandy to call Rani after he was gone.

I thought seeing you with your baby would make everything okay, but it hurts too much to be around the three of you, Rani had said. *I don't even know who I am anymore.*

You don't mean that.

You can't decide how I feel, Vinny! Don't you see. Nothing can ever be the same. You changed everything.

We'll work it out, Vandy had said. *We're still the same.*

I'm not. It wasn't just sex. It changed me. Vir changed me. I want to live now.

Vandy had asked for the truth, and they'd both handed it to her, and she'd had no idea what to do with it.

A clean break is the only answer. In the end Rani had been the one to fix it. Rani had been the one to leave her life behind.

Vandy had been the one who ruined everything. But all three of them had borne the consequences.

A gust of ocean breeze caught the wetness on Vandy's cheeks. "Do you ever wonder what would have happened if you hadn't left?"

"You know that wasn't possible."

"Did you ever wish I was the one who left?"

Rani laughed. "My God, Vinny! You were Vir's life. How can you not know that?" Her eyes got serious again. "Hearing him talk about you and Mallika was like being with you. You were alive inside him. What was between us wasn't anything like that." She studied Vandy, trying to gauge how much she could take.

"But being with each other changed you both." Vir had fallen into his storytelling with a new focus. Something about the way he participated in his own life, in their life together, had become more present, more pure.

Rani shrugged. "I think it made us better at our own lives, but we never wanted a life with each other." Then her eyes turned intense, everything Vandy and she had ever been to each other brightening her gaze. "But learning to live without you, that was the hard part."

"It's the hardest thing I ever did," Vandy said.

Rani leaned into Vandy, arm to arm, head on her shoulder. It was strange how she still smelled the same. How her smell still calmed Vandy all the way to her toes.

Vandy threw a glance around the marble balcony with its gorgeous ocean view. "I'm glad you got to live the life you wanted."

Rani smiled. "It is a great life. But the great part is what's inside the house, not the house itself." Then she got that look she only got when she mentioned Sam. "You know how you used to say that being with Vir made you believe in the best version of yourself? I didn't know what that meant until I met Sam. I really do love him."

This was a Rani Vandy could never have imagined, comfortable with her own happiness, even reckless with it. And being with Vir was what had shown her how to open herself up to that. The saddest laugh huffed out of Vandy. "I'm glad Vir got to see you happy."

Vandy got up and walked to the railing again. The violence of the breeze had died down with the ebbing tide. The acrid smell of the city hung in the air a little more, but the sweeping scale of what lay before them made it not matter.

Rani came and stood next to her. "I'm sorry. I know this isn't easy for you."

"No, it's not," Vandy said. When she tried to wrap her head around the fact that Vir and Rani had gotten to keep each other when she hadn't, her stomach churned and her body hurt.

When Vandy had sent Vir to Rani's apartment that day, she'd known they were doing it for her. When they'd come out, they'd built something in there she would never have a place in. And yet somehow they'd managed not to destroy her with it.

Vandy filled her lungs, tasting both the freshness of the salty air and the ugliness of the pollution it bore. She closed her eyes and pictured Vir. His frailness at the end, his solidity through the years. The joy on all three of their faces in that Polaroid he'd left behind for her to find. She wouldn't change one single thing about the man he'd been.

"But it isn't easy for you either," she said. She had no idea what Rani and Vir's relationship had been like over the years, but she did know that they'd both lost him.

For the first time tears filled Rani's eyes and spilled over. "Thank you."

For a long time neither of them said another word. They just stood there soaking up the city Vir had loved with all his heart. Even though he'd loved LA just as much.

"I loved your work when you choreographed, by the way," Vandy said finally.

"You watched my films?" Rani looked surprised.

Vandy shrugged.

"If we are doing confessions, I've read every one of your books, and I read the column every week. Even back when it was a blog."

It was Vandy's turn for surprise, and Rani matched her shrug.

"I would never have started the blog if you hadn't spent our youth telling me that I was going to find a way to make a living telling people what to do."

"When you know, you know," Rani said. "Usha Auntie must be thrilled that you found your passion."

They both smiled at their shared memories.

"How is Usha Auntie?"

"Better than ever. She's a whole new person since Daddy died. The quintessential piss and vinegar. But she misses you. Sometimes I get the feeling that she's been plotting for years to find a way to get you back into our lives." Had Mummy let Rani go because she thought she was saving Vandy's marriage? That would make sense because she'd brought Rani up again only after Vir was gone. She'd sacrificed one daughter for another.

Rani's smile was sad. "I miss her too. I miss you all."

Vandy reached over and took her hand. "How do you feel about attending two weddings on the same weekend in LA?"

Rani raised a perfectly threaded brow. "Sounds . . . terrifying?"

Vandy laughed. "Oh, that's putting it mildly. It's Pinky's and Tinku's sons."

"Amey and Aarav? Really? On the same weekend?" Rani started laughing too. "Why am I not surprised?"

"Trust me, no one is surprised. We're all just hoping to get through it alive."

"So you want to drag me right into the eye of the storm?"

"Some things never change. Also, does this mean I don't need to find a hotel tonight?"

"No, Vinny, you don't. I think I might want you to stick around for a bit."

CHAPTER THIRTY-FIVE

MALLIKA

Months later, at the Battle of the Wedding Sangeets . . .

The Hrithik Roshan dance video had gone viral. Of course it had. I now have over a hundred thousand followers on social media. That means those many people see my work.

I also recorded a new audition tape—something classical but *quirky*—and sent it to the producers. I have no idea what is going to happen, but I feel fairly confident that something good will come from it. Something good already has.

My aunts have spent the past months doing exactly what I ask them to, and their dancing has improved to the point where it's almost possible to forget that they are rhythm challenged. Oh, and I made sure they were in each other's dances. It is tradition for the bride's and groom's uncles and aunts to dance at the sangeet. It was nonsensical that they weren't doing it in the first place.

"You're a genius," my naani says. She's looking happier than I have seen her look in a long time. She hasn't left Rani's side since Rani came down two weeks ago for the wedding with Sam, who has replaced my maamas as the world's most indulgent uncle.

He's also possibly the most objectively handsome man in the room. A fact my maamis obviously wholeheartedly agree with. Because they are currently grinding up and down against him on the stage in an impromptu performance of "O Saki Saki."

Sam spins Tinku out and then pulls her back before she spins away and falls off the stage. Then he dips Pinky, while valiantly holding her up as she stumbles back and her legs fly into the air. And he does it all with such smoldering charm that they blush and glow like light bulbs.

Rani looks on with amusement, but despite her best efforts, how smitten she is glows in her eyes. "Some things turned out exactly as we expected them to," she says, and Naani rolls her eyes.

But when Sam throws Naani a wink, she blushes too.

It's official: all the women in the family are in love with him. Even Mom, after he cried when Rani told him the truth about me. I am now officially part of his brood of nieces and nephews.

Naani throws Sam an air kiss and follows Rani as they go off to rescue Mom from a crowd of aunties who are undoubtedly trying to get free advice without springing for one of her seminars or even reading her column, which is as popular as ever. Rani and Mom have taken to going over the Dear Agony Auntie letters over Zoom every week.

The music crescendos, and Tinku and Pinky swing their hips wildly as they dance in circles around Sam. The crowd is going crazy. My heart fills with such joy at seeing them lose themselves that I scream and woot.

Rex wraps his arms around me from behind. "You're a miracle worker," he says. Then, "You think they'll perform at our wedding?"

"That's got to be the world's worst proposal," I say.

"It's not a proposal. It's a feeler," he says.

"Are you testing to see if I'll run away again?"

"Maybe." What I love most about him is how honest he is. After I texted him that I was sorry, he'd just asked me to focus on what I'd gone to Mumbai for. *I'm not going anywhere,* he'd said. *I don't know how to be without you.*

When I got home, he'd asked me why I was apologizing, what it meant.

I'd told him exactly how I felt. All my life I had defined myself as one person. Then I thought I didn't even know who I was. Now I don't want to define myself. I don't want to label what I can and cannot do and be. I just want to do and be.

"Well, I'm not going anywhere," I say. "I don't know how to be without you."

"I love you," he whispers into my ear as my aunts spin around each other and then fall to their knees with their arms thrown out. It is the most frickin' brave and adorable thing I've ever seen anyone do.

"I love you too," I say and go to my aunts as they rush at me, arms flung wide, hair and clothes askew. They fight each other to get to me, and it just makes the moment even more perfect.

Although I'm so over that word.

I've already wasted too much time in the pursuit of something that doesn't exist.

The reason I felt like a black sheep had nothing to do with genetics. It was 100 percent being intimidated by the perfection I perceived in my parents' marriage, my mother's success, and everyone else's lives around me. I was so focused on the perfection around me that I forgot what was actually beautiful in my life.

That is 100 percent on me.

My low self-confidence had nothing to do with what's in those helices in my chromosomes. It has to do with me running from the things I wanted but was afraid I might not get, before even trying. Well, not anymore.

I feel enough now, not because I just found out how hard my parents tried to have me, or what it cost them. But because I am enough. I traveled across the world to find something, and I think that something was me.

312

CHAPTER THIRTY-SIX

RANI

2022
Six months before Vir's death . . .

It had been twenty years since Rani had kissed Vir.

Running into each other at the wedding had been the most beautiful accident.

So, you did decide to get married after all, Vir had said.

I mean, look at Sam, who wouldn't marry him? Rani had said.

But no family? Vir had asked.

Sam is my family, she'd said. She hated that people equated having a family with having children. *But no, no children. I'm only ever having a child with one man.*

She probably shouldn't have said it, because that's what had started everything up again. Sucked them back into that day when their lives had changed.

Vir had followed her wordlessly into the greenroom where she'd dressed for her dance performance. There, in a fevered trance neither of them wanted to control, he'd pressed her into the wall, and she'd kissed him with all the hunger in her heart. They'd fallen into the connection they'd forged at the darkest point in their lives without meaning to.

Pulling away had taken every bit of strength she possessed. Her body had screamed to go back to the moment when it had come back to life. But they'd stopped. This time Rani had known exactly what she could lose.

The day Mallika was conceived, Vir had shown Rani that her body was not an ugly place, that it could feel beautiful things. It was not divorced from her mind. That day she'd experienced her whole self for the first time. He pressed the raw clay she was together, and she let herself be baked into a single being. Wildly enough, it also brought to fruition something Vir had chased all his life. The ability to be fully alive because your purpose became someone else's existence. Creating something out of nothing with just your humanity.

That day resulted in a pregnancy that gave Vir and Vinny Mallika. That day Vir and Rani had promised each other they'd never regret anything or sully it with guilt.

They'd continued to love Vinny as they always had.

The three of them grew even closer over the nine months it took Mallika to arrive into the world. They became one person, a trimurti with one heart and three heads. Rani re-created herself as she created life. Vir went back to writing and created Dolly Singh, a character who let him explore life the way he'd always wanted to. Vinny nurtured them, fueled them with her endless supply of love.

Then the baby came. Vir named her Mallika, which, like Rani, meant "queen."

Vinny wanted them to be one big happy family. But when the connection Vir and Rani had formed that day slipped back out from behind the haze of hope and joy, all three of them knew that wasn't possible. Rani's feelings might have been too bright to hide, but they were not even a little demanding. They wanted nothing outside of themselves, but they did make it impossible for Rani to live a half life after she'd found her whole self. So she'd left everything she'd ever loved behind.

She'd started afresh. They all had. They'd built families that were their greatest gifts.

In that greenroom she'd realized that although Vir's and her connection had been born from sex, it hadn't been about sex at all. Who they were in each other's presence: that was the part she couldn't let go of again.

So they'd gone out to coffee and given each other the gift of a lifelong friendship.

For twenty years after that, they'd continued to meet every time Vir was in India.

They would catch up, spin stories, dig into each other's hearts and pull out pieces they could laugh at and cry over. But they'd chosen to keep it just between them.

Those few hours once every year were for them alone. To be who they were deep inside, beneath their identities as spouse and friend and parent, beneath their love for their art, beneath what everyone else saw them as. Beyond the deep love they'd shared for one woman. This was them outside of every label.

They didn't plan it. They didn't plan for it. When Vir came to Mumbai, he sent Rani a message. I'm here.

They'd spend some time with Mallika if she was with him, and then Rani and Vir would meet alone for dinner, always at the Taj Mahal hotel.

Which was what they were doing right now. Finishing up their meal with the best coffee on earth.

Instead of their favorite table at the restaurant overlooking the bay beyond the Gateway of India, Vir had ordered room service in his hotel suite.

He patted the couch next to him, and Rani moved to sit closer to him. "Thanks for settling for room service," he said.

He was half the size he'd been when they first met. Rani was probably twice hers.

Sam was a spectacular cook. The starving girl inside Rani was finally fed. Sam's need to care for people was what had made Rani fall in love with him. It was also what had kept her in love with him all these years and always would. People who put their need to serve others above everything else had always been her Achilles' heel.

"You can make up for it next time. I'll even order the most expensive thing on the menu to punish you."

Vir laughed, then broke into a cough. He looked tired. He really had lost a lot of weight.

Rani handed him a glass of water. "Are you sure you're okay?"

"That depends on how you define okay," he said, then leaned over and dropped a kiss on her cheek.

This was unusual, but there was such gentleness in the press of his lips, such sweetness that she pressed into him before pulling away.

"What was that about?" she asked. "Are you breaking up with me?"

He laughed again. "God, I'm going to miss you," he said for the first time in his life.

She straightened up. His mother had died seven years ago. He hadn't been back since the funeral.

"Vir?" She squeezed his arm.

He gave an exhausted groan that was laced with something else.

"Are you in pain?"

"All the damn time."

Her hand went to her mouth.

He pointed to her. "All three of you do that."

Rani didn't need to ask him who he meant.

"It's end stage. It's everywhere."

"Vir, no!"

"Please. Don't."

"You should have told me. Should you have flown?" Her hand pressed harder to her mouth. He'd traveled all the way back just to see her. "Oh God, Vinny. Does she know?"

He shook his head. He hadn't told them yet. Vinny was going to be destroyed.

A tear slipped from his eye. She pulled him close, and they sat there like that forever.

"How am I going to tell them?" he said finally.

"Sam's cousin is the best oncologist in India. We're going to go see him tomorrow."

"No, we're not. I'm going to kiss you one last time. Then we're going to spend the night talking, the way we did that day. Then we're both going to go home and make the best of the rest of our lives."

So, that's exactly what they did.

"Can I ask you something?" he said when it was time to say good-bye. "Why did you pull away that day in the greenroom?"

"Because I wanted to keep you. Because I couldn't lose you again," Rani said. If they'd given in to the wanting, they would have had to give up their chance at staying in each other's lives. They would have tainted the most beautiful thing she'd ever experienced. "And I would have lost Sam too. And also Vinny." Which was a strange thing to say because she'd already lost Vinny.

His exhausted eyes brightened. "Will you take care of her when I'm gone?" he said.

She wanted to tell him he wasn't going anywhere, but they had never lied to each other. Pain squeezed in her chest even as hope bubbled in her heart at the thought of seeing Vinny again.

Vir smiled and touched her cheek. "And let her take care of you too."

She had to laugh at that. "You know that's impossible. Too many lies stand in our way."

"Maybe it's time to see the lies for what they were: acts of love," he said. "And no one is better at love than Vandy and you."

In that he was not wrong. She pressed his hand into her cheek. "I promise to try," she said, letting herself admit the truth for the first time in twenty-seven years. She wanted nothing more than to have Vinny back in her life, even though she couldn't imagine how it would ever happen.

ACKNOWLEDGMENTS

The seed for this story came to me years ago, when a friend was struggling with infertility and I wondered how far I would go to help her. That is the heart of this story for me: How far do we go for love and for what we want? And it would never have made it from that simple, universal question to a novel without the help of more people than I could ever name. But I'm going to attempt it all the same.

First, my editor Alicia Clancy, who is tireless in her pursuit of helping me reveal the story I want to tell. It is a rare gift to have an editor who nurtures your work with this much love and passion. So, thank you. Thank you also to the entire team at Amazon Publishing, who multiply that love manifold in bringing my books into the hands of readers. Ashley Vanicek, Sara Shaw, Chrissy Penido, Erika Moriarty: you're absolute gems! And my brilliant agent, Alexandra Machinist, for helping me keep it together through it all.

The best, yet hardest, part of writing is in bringing the entire sweeping thing together one detail at a time. I'm blessed to have a writing sisterhood who hold my hand every step of the way. Barbara O'Neal, Virginia Kantra, Jamie Beck, Liz Talley, Priscilla Oliveras, Sally Kilpatrick, Tracy Brogan, Robin Kuss, Clara Kensie, CJ Warrant, Melonie Johnson: you make it possible, and you make it fun! Alisha Rai, Nisha Sharma, Mona Shroff, Annika Sharma, Suliekha Snyder, Farah Heron, Sona Charaipotra, and the entire badass band of South

Asian writers, this journey is infinitely richer and more meaningful because of you. Thank you!

This book would definitely not be the same without the professional expertise of Dr. Deepali Kothary, MD, and Manjiri Sathe, and the generosity of Namrata Desai, Subodh Thatte, and Deep Sathe in being my LA tour guides, or without Gaelyn Almeida, who puts up with my obsessive brainstorming every day.

Thank you as always to my family, Annika, Mihir, Manoj, Mamma, Papa, and Simba. I know I've gotten progressively weirder with time, but you've gotten progressively more indulgent. You are my entire world. And finally, thanks to you, my readers. It is because of you that I wake up excited every morning brimming with stories. I wish I had the words to tell you how very grateful I am. Thank you. And again, thank you.

BOOK CLUB QUESTIONS

1. Do you believe that lies can actually be a love language?
2. Are there conditions under which infidelity can be explained? Emotional infidelity versus physical infidelity—discuss with respect to the choices Rani and Vir make.
3. Why do you think it is so important for Vandy to be a mother? Does she go too far? Is there such a thing as going too far when it comes to what you want?
4. There is some relativity between what happens in Vandy's marriage and her mother's. How do you think the two marriages do or don't differ?
5. DNA tests are becoming increasingly common. Do you believe they complicate relationships or simplify them?
6. The destruction of something important to Vandy, Vir, and Rani propels them to have lives that they love. Do you believe tragedy can help you find your best self?

ABOUT THE AUTHOR

Photo © 2018 Ishita Singh Photography

USA Today bestselling author Sonali Dev writes Bollywood-style stories that explore universal issues. Her novels have been named Best Books of the Year by *Library Journal*, NPR, the *Washington Post*, Buzzfeed, and Kirkus Reviews. She has won numerous accolades, including the American Library Association's award for best in genre, the *Romantic Times* Reviewers' Choice Award, and multiple RT Seals of Excellence; has been a RITA finalist; and has been listed for the Dublin Literary Award. Shelf Awareness calls her "not only one of the best but one of the bravest romance novelists working today." She lives in Chicagoland with her husband, two visiting adult children, and the world's most perfect dog.

Find more at https://sonalidev.com.